ORIE'S STORY

A Virginia Tobacco Plantation Princess Faces The Civil War and Reconstruction

A Novel

Gail Tansill Lambert

ISBN: 154285301X
ISBN 13: 9781542853019

PREFACE

*O*rie's Story is based on the life of Orianna Russell Moon and was inspired by a memoir written by her son William Luther Andrews on the seventy-fifth anniversary of Lee's surrender at Appomattox. His memoir was titled *A True Romance of the Civil War* and was completed in July 1936, the month and year of his death at age seventy-one. The memoir captures the memories and tales of a family as told by a son about his beloved mother as well as the Southern gentleman's views of the Civil War.

Luther Andrews' memoir was passed on to this author by Charlotte Digges Thomas Churchill, presently of Atlanta, Georgia. Her mother was a granddaughter of Isaac Moon Andrews, son of Drs. Orie Moon and John Andrews. Charlotte is the great-grand-niece of her namesake "Lottie" Moon, the renowned Baptist missionary to China in the nineteenth and early twentieth centuries.

William Luther Andrews was born at Viewmont Plantation in Albemarle County, Virginia, the second son of six which survived infancy. This twenty-first-century retelling of the tale uses a literary style as was common in the 1930s, such as an abundant use of capital letters for dramatic emphasis.

PROLOGUE

Orianna Moon Andrews, MD, was living in a rough board dwelling of two rooms, built of planks cut from trees on a small tract of woodland in Tennessee, near the Alabama border. The year was 1871, and on a summer evening around dusk, a group of angry men hollered across the Tennessee River to the ferryman to come take them across the river. Orie was alone with her two young sons. Dr. John Andrews was out on a call to assist with an impending birth at a home that was a considerable distance away.

Around eleven o'clock at night, the fourteen-year-old son of the Tennessee River ferryman from Mangum's Landing let loose a loud halloo, the signal that Dr. Andrews was needed. Orie moved with accustomed haste from her bed and went out to receive the caller. Her sons, James and Luther, both wide awake from the urgent shout outside, scrambled out of bed. The boys rushed to their mother's side at the open front door and listened to the messenger try to catch his breath as he sat on the back of a horse lathered in sweat, its flanks heaving from exertion.

"My daddy says to run to the woods and hide because the KKK riders are coming after you. My daddy will try to hold them until you can get away."

James yelled back, "Why are they after us?"

"Hush, son, and both of you get back in bed. Get under the covers. Stay out of sight. Now go!"

Orie was calm as a box turtle on a dirt road, but both boys knew better than to talk back to their mother. They got under the thin covers of the bed they shared and listened to her ask the very same question.

"For what reason do we have of entertaining the Hooded Band?"

"Ma'am, they say y'all are Yankees come down South to stir up the colored folk against the white families."

James and Luther looked at each other in astonishment. What Yankees? Their family was from Virginia, from Viewmont plantation near the James River. Their mother and father had been Confederate doctors. Luther felt his heart beating loudly against his nightshirt and shivered in the humid warmth. Everybody was afraid of the Ku Klux Klan. Hidden beneath their dirty hoods, they stopped for nothing once they got on those horses and thundered through the woods in the pitch black of night. The boys strained to hear their mother's words. Her voice sounded tired. And angry.

"Tell your daddy to tell them my doors are not locked, but I am armed, and the first person who enters my house will be carried away." Orie's voice was clear and strong.

"Yes, ma'am," said the boy, and the two brothers could hear him cluck to his tired horse and begin the sixteen-mile journey back to his father's ferry, on a path that should not bring him face-to-face with the night riders.

The boys heard the desk drawer open on the other side of the wall and the sound of bullets filling the chambers in the cylinder.

"I wish Father was here," Luther whispered.

"Scaredy-cat. Mama took out her pistol on Turkish bandits on a boat crossing to Asia, and she'll do the same to the KKK in Tennessee."

But had she ever killed anybody? Luther didn't think so. He fell into a restless sleep, dreaming about pine pitch torches flying through the night sky into their rough board cabin, while men yelled and horses brayed and reared up.

Orie stayed up all night facing the door, pistol in hand. She was not afraid, but she did not wish to be asleep and surprised when they came. Things were bad enough in the South without night riders making trouble.

After daylight, John Andrews, exhausted, rode up to the cabin. Orie met him before he reached the door, gun still in her cramping hand.

"Trouble?" he asked.

"They never came," she replied and told him what had happened the night before.

Refusing even a cup of coffee or a cold biscuit, John Andrews immediately rode his horse to Mangum's Landing.

"They was eight of them," said the ferryman. "I told them you people was from Virginia and been Confederate doctors and the missus was a missionary woman and had herself a outside place with benches in the trees to preach the gospel to the colored folk yonder. They left, but looking ugly and acting mad that their party had been called off."

John thanked the ferryman and headed back home. The war was over, but the fighting had not stopped. The poverty-stricken South was a place of fear and want, and John saw the uneasiness of the backwoods whites and the open threats to frightened Negroes. Safety and peace were in short supply in the South.

While waiting for John to return, Orie thought about the decision to leave Virginia for John's home in Alabama, where the war had not left the town in ruins. But the war had also left its mark here, where bankrupt families flush with worthless Confederate currency were too poor to pay for doctoring or much of anything else they needed. Defeat had already lasted longer than the War.

CHAPTER 1

THE SOUTH

The Civil War was essentially over two months to the day after the birth of the "red head," William Luther Andrews. On that day, General Robert E. Lee surrendered to General Ulysses S. Grant at Appomattox Courthouse with a Confederate force of 28,000 starving, ragtag soldiers, surrounded on the north, west, and south by Union forces of 120,000 well-fed and well-equipped troops. On that day, Union soldiers suffered the loss of 260 men; the Confederate army lost 440.

Viewmont, near Scottsville on the upper reaches of the James River, took the news with unutterable sadness. All that they had suffered was just the beginning. The people were impoverished and families had lost fathers, husbands, sons, and brothers. The future looked terrifying.

Only Robert E. Lee was able to comfort and encourage the people for whom he had fought and lost a war—and lost their independence along with it. The former general, who'd commanded an army in battles that resulted in thousands of Southern deaths, became president of Washington College in Lexington, Virginia. In that capacity, he taught the rising generation of Southern youth "to be loyal to their re-united country…"

Following Lee's words, another generation of Southern Boys fought alongside Yankees in France for Democracy during the Great War, under the leadership of a Southern-born president, Woodrow Wilson. Indeed, Lee's example of reconciliation was a complete renunciation of the hatred produced by war since the beginning of time. The wars between Greece and Troy went back at least to 1000 BC, when the Greeks invaded and destroyed Troy in what became Turkey. Fear and loathing have no expiration date. Robert E. Lee taught us otherwise.

The demagoguery of ambitious politicians in both the North and the South added fuel to the fires of sectional prejudice. The South's right to peacefully withdraw from the voluntary connection it had with other states was pitched against the North's desire to keep the South's wealth and power in the Union. Both sides had passion and righteousness for their causes, backed by discussions and arguments both written and spoken. Ultimately, it was not reasoned leadership but the larger military forces and greater population of the industrialized North that gave the North the victory.

In Confederate General P. G. T. Beauregard's postwar report titled "The First Battle of Bull Run," he strongly held the conviction that the war "was in no sense a civil war, but a war between two countries—for conquest on one side, for self-preservation on the other." In any event, the war was never a civil war in which the South fought to overthrow the US government and take over the nation.

Slavery, too, was part of the conversation. When Lincoln called up his first draft 75,000 of troops, the purpose was to march into the Seceding States and force them back into the Union. When Northern voices called for the abolition of slavery, Lincoln declared the purpose of the troop call up to be to save the Union.

Slave-owning plantation masters were well aware of the unsustainability of slave labor, from both an economic and moral point of view. At Montpelier in Virginia, the home of President James and Dolly Madison, Madison made the written observation that in order to pay the bills and keep slave families together, with 50 percent of his workforce under the age of five, he was forced to sell off his best land, piece by piece. Southern planters were also in communication with England through trade and family connections. They could see the progression of antislavery acts in Parliament leading up to the Slavery Abolition Act of 1833, which included provinces throughout the British Empire, with some exceptions in the Far East that were eliminated by 1843. This act provided compensation for slave owners who would be losing their property; former slaves over the age of six were redesignated as apprentices, with servitude to be abolished in two stages.

Founding Fathers Jefferson and Madison were openly troubled by slavery in America, but at the same time decided that the economics of the time made the sudden abandonment of slavery unsafe and unworkable. Part of a letter by Thomas Jefferson to Edward Rutledge, a slaveholder, the youngest signer of the Declaration of Independence and a member of the South Carolina House of Representatives in 1787, reads: "I congratulate you, my dear friend, on the law of your state for suspending the importation of slaves, and for the glory you have justly acquired by endeavoring to prevent it forever. This abomination must have an end, and there is a superior bench reserved in heaven for those who hasten it." Certainly the days of slavery were numbered.

Be that as it may, the South was not allowed to withdraw from the Union, and military force was sent to back up the orders. The new government, the Confederate States of America, was headed by Jefferson Davis, who called for men to defend the new republic with a policy of "defense, not aggression." Men from the South signed up for the Confederate Army to repel the expected invaders. While aristocratic families from the North, like the Roosevelts, did not fight in the Civil War, white men from Southern families of all classes did so in great numbers in proportion to their small population. The Confederate medical department was especially well supplied with volunteer doctors, according to Samuel H.

Stout, MD, late medical director of hospitals of the Department and Army of Tennessee, who said that the Southern states were "well-supplied with educated and chivalrously honorable surgeons and physicians."

The South, moreover, was not without friends in the North, especially in New York City and Maryland, where pro-Southern riots broke out in protest against the Federal Government's war on the South. There was reason to believe that the lust for war and violence was only in a minority of Northerners.

Among the Southerners who answered the call for help to defend their new nation were Robert and William Andrews of Florence, Alabama. The two young men enlisted in the Fourth Alabama Infantry in the Third Brigade under Brigadier General Barnard E. Bee of South Carolina. Bee was born in Charleston to prominent parents whose roots stretched back to the American Revolution and was himself a West Point graduate and an officer in the US Army before resigning his commission. His older brother Hamilton Bee was also a Confederate general, and their father had been a leader in the Texas Revolution. This was a military family of highest distinction.

For Billie and Robert Andrews, the march to Virginia, which was mostly by train, started in May 1861 in Dalton, Georgia, and by July was moving from Winchester, Virginia, to Manassas Junction. The hundreds of young soldiers were full of fighting spirit and camaraderie as they sang Dixie with their strong male voices; they were fit, determined to be victorious, and idolized in their gray uniforms. Wherever the train stopped for wood and water, there would be a bevy of girls to greet them with flowers, cakes, and fruit.

But ominous was the lack of ammunition wagons for the guns and only a few country carts drawn by poor-looking horses and very few field pieces. "Courage and cotton" summed up these Boys in the Fourth Alabama Infantry.

Dr. John Andrews could see in his mind's eye his younger brothers, Billie and Robert, marching northward to protect Virginia, where their ancestors had fought for independence from the British. Could he remain in Memphis, far from the fight, when Virginia was about to suffer an armed invasion? He could not. He hastily arranged his affairs with his two uncles, with whom he had lived since finishing medical college in Nashville the year before. He journeyed by himself on horseback and by train, arriving at Manassas Junction mere days before the Battle of First Manassas.

Dr. John enlisted in his brothers' regiment and found himself on the battlefield holding a key position on the Confederate line. Never to be forgotten was hearing the voice of Brigadier General Barnard Bee utter the famous words: "There stands Jackson like a Stone Wall. Rally behind the Virginians!" The nickname "Stonewall" stuck. Then too, Dr. John was witness to the terrifying sound of the Rebel Yell heard first in battle at Manassas when "Stonewall" Jackson gave the order "to wait until fifty yards from the enemy and yell like Furies when you charge!"

But it was the horrifying sounds of war that pervaded Dr. John's very soul—the thundering cannon fire from field artillery, fife and drum commands, officers shouting orders, soldiers firing rifle-muskets, the screams of the fallen, and the sound of minié balls smashing into flesh and bones, horses, hills, and trees. The sulfuric smell of gunpowder loomed over all.

Only a few minutes after General Bee had dubbed Jackson 'Stonewall,' the Fourth Alabama was charged by greatly superior numbers. Bee steadied his untried troops, who died rather than yield their exposed position, the taking of which would have cut the Southern forces in half and caused a rout at the very outset of battle.

Bee was mortally wounded in the charge. Among the first of the Fourth Alabama soldiers to fall was nineteen-year-old Billie Andrews, torn through by grapeshot from Federal artillery. Dr.

John, fighting alongside, caught him as he fell and removed him to the rear of the battle line near some thickets. Billie lived long enough to send his love to his family back home and give John his watch and revolver. With tears streaming down his face, John turned back to his post of duty, just in time for a charge that put the enemy to flight.

A countercharge followed. Some three hundred yards from where Billie fell, a fellow soldier was hit. A rush of blood followed from an artery in his thigh cut by a minié bullet. Dr. John went to his aid and stopped the bleeding by ligating the artery using instruments from his pocket case. The ferocious countercharge continued, forcing Dr. John to leave his wounded soldier. While pausing to collect his instruments, he was ordered to halt in an insulting way, which so angered Dr. John that he picked up the fallen friend's loaded musket and shot the soldier coming at him through the heart. He quickly threw down the gun, picked up his instruments, and fled, shots coming at him from the charging enemy. Upon reaching the safety of his Company, he was examined for wounds. No injury was discovered other than bullet holes in his clothes.

Later in the afternoon, Dr. John endured a second great shock when twenty-one-year-old Robert fell by his side, his hand smashed by a minié bullet from a Yankee musket. John and a comrade-in-arms carried Robert to the relative safety of the sheltered side of the brick-built Henry house, soon after Stonewall Jackson retook the hill from Union forces. Later that day, the protected area was turned into a tented field hospital, where a commanding officer came to see the wounded and immediately commissioned Dr. John as a surgeon for the wounded men of the Fourth Alabama. The largest and bloodiest battle in American history up to that point had commenced.

CHAPTER 2
THE BATTLE OF MANASSAS

On July 21, 1861, the farmhouse on Henry Hill became a target for Union cannons. Because shots being fired in a battle nearby were hitting too close to the house, Mrs. Judith Carter Henry, an eighty-five-year-old invalid widow, was taken to the spring house for safety by her son, daughter, and a hired colored girl. In their absence, Confederate snipers took up positions in the house. In the meantime, the spring house appeared no safer than the farmhouse, and the widow begged to be returned to her own bed.

It was after she was back in bed and the Confederate snipers had left that Artillery Captain James Ricketts turned his cannons on the house and fired. An artillery shell crashed through Mrs. Henry's bedroom wall and threw her out of her shattered bed. The shell took off one of her feet and caused massive internal injuries. She died later that day.

Her daughter, Ellen, had taken refuge in the fireplace chimney and lived, but lost her hearing in the cannon blasts. Mrs. Henry was counted as the first civilian casualty of the Civil War. Later that day, Dr. John Andrews was shaken by news of her death. *In a civilized world, a woman would not be torn apart in her own bed by countryman turned against countryman.*

In the understaffed tented field hospital set beside the ruins of the Henry house, Dr. John ignored eye-stinging sweat that rolled down his face as he tended to his brother Robert and to the deluge of broken Boys of the Fourth Alabama. He demanded morphine for soldiers with torn midsections gaping open. The word was out that the Yankees had plenty, but Southerners had to bite the bullet. Robert, though pallid and not fully responsive, was conscious and not screaming, so John hurried to the beds of soldiers in more immediate peril. Quinine, sulfa, tourniquets, and bandages were in good supply and Dr. John was already seeing candidates for amputations that would have to be performed soon.

Even though the shade of the tent blocked out the sweltering heat of the direct summer sun, the interior of the tent was airless, with the stench of gore, oven-hot heat, and flies. As more wounded Boys were carried inside, talk of the battle outside became crazed and confused.

One soldier with a badly broken and bleeding foot said, "Everybody's gettin' shot. Ain't nobody gonna get through this." The soldier was groaning and writhing in pain, having been brought in with the help of another soldier with his arm around the badly limping man.

Dr. John went to him and wiped tears from his frightened face with a cloth wrung out in cool water before he probed the foot for a bullet or shrapnel. The sound of men in pain and shaking with fright gradually became an added layer to the horror of war as he worked to bring those Boys a measure of comfort and assurance. With some, he touched their foreheads and prayed for them, watching their breathing ease and stop. The details of the battle raging around them were lost on Dr. John and the others in the field hospital as they battled against pain, loss of limb, and death. Later he would read newspaper accounts, listen to stories of individual soldiers, and read snatches of General Beauregard's "Report of the Battle of First Bull Run":

"About mid-afternoon the Federals were in such firm command of the battle that Gen. Beauregard, in desperation, gave orders to the other commanders to 'go forward in a common charge' which he led, with his reserves, of the entire line of battle. He led it with 'such dash' that the 'whole plateau was swept clear of the enemy...'"

It should be added that Beauregard's "dash" was greatly aided by the flow of reinforcements from General Johnston's Army of the Shenandoah. This was achieved by the general's near-miraculous ability to slip his army past Union troops in the Great Valley to the station at Piedmont, where the Manassas Gap Railroad ferried them, one brigade at a time, through the night and into the next day to Manassas Junction. The artillery and cavalry marched overland and were in place long before the last of Johnston's army arrived.

At the end of the day that saw momentum swing to favor the Confederate Army, Beauregard reported that the enemy's whole line "irretrievably broke," and the enemy fled across the stream called Bull Run in "every available direction." Victory belonged to the Confederate States of America.

The price paid that day on both sides was severe, but worse for the Confederate Army, which had fewer total possible replacements. Lost in the battle to the South were Brigadier General Bee, Colonel Francis Bartow, Colonel Fisher, who fell at the head of his troops, and Colonel Egbert Jones. Also severely wounded was General Kirby Smith. The number of Confederate soldiers killed was estimated to be 1,982 and wounded 1,582. Federal forces lost similar numbers. The Federal retreat from the battle turned into a rout after soldiers came upon the road to Washington jammed with the carriages of Congressmen and picnickers who had driven out to see the expected victory over the rebels from a hillside.

The Union Army's expectation of defeating the massed Confederate Army that day, thus opening the road to Richmond, the Confederate capital, and make a quick end to the war, proved shockingly wrong. Just as surprised were the Confederates, who, having won the battle, thought the war was over.

The damage done to the South by the Civil War was harsh and long-lasting. An exception was the City of Lynchburg, Virginia. In January 1861, Lynchburg voted to stay in the Union, but in April the citizens repealed that decision. Coinciding with the repeal was Lincoln's Proclamation on April 15 calling for members of the Virginia militia to be sent against the seceding Southern States. The option was no longer simply to stay in the Union or leave, but to fight against the Southern States or join them.

With three railroads and a canal system in place at the beginning of the war, Lynchburg functioned as a transportation and communication hub for the Confederacy and was therefore a Union target. In 1864, Union General David Hunt and his forces arrived. Confederate General Jubal Early saved the city from the brunt of the battle by running empty train cars repeatedly through the area, as if reinforcements were rushing in. Hunt bought the ruse and retreated west.

Saved from destruction, Lynchburg became the world's leading tobacco market in 1886 and steel manufacturing boomed, giving the city the nickname "Pittsburgh of the South." In the 1930s, when Luther Andrews called the Civil War a "Folly and a Crime," he was speaking for two generations of Southerners who were bereft of breadwinners, property, and life savings along with never-to-be-realized husbands, children, poets, and inventors.

CHAPTER 3
TWO CONFEDERATE DOCTORS

The tent-shaded field hospital on Henry Hill in Manassas was spared cannon fire and minié bullets after the rout of the Union forces back to Washington, but the victors were not cheering. Facilities for the wounded and dying were severely lacking, leaving the wounded in pain and in deteriorating hope of recovery. The ones able to be moved were carried to the Washington and Richmond Railway and taken to the small town of Culpepper, thirty miles south. Residents of private homes took in the wounded soldiers with prayers and tender care, but the number of wounded outstripped the supply of homes in that very small town. The next step was to move the soldiers able to withstand yet another move to homes and makeshift hospital wards in Charlottesville, some sixty miles farther south, as well as to Orange, another small town but closer than Charlottesville.

For Dr. John's younger brother Robert, the ordeal of the crowded train and chaos in Culpeper left him in a fearful state of delirium. The train was crowded and slow, taking from twenty-four to thirty-six hours to go from Manassas Junction to Charlottesville. There were no provisions for food, water, or medical care, although Dr. John was with his brother and did the best he could for him and the soldiers in their train car. Dr. John had readily agreed to have his brother removed to Charlottesville, where the University of Virginia's classrooms, lecture halls, and medical school facilities as well as public buildings and private homes were being turned into a military hospital, named Charlottesville General. But conditions prior to their arrival had been so poor, Robert was barely clinging to life.

Arrangements were made for the wounded brother to be cared for at the home of Mr. Godwin, a distant relative of the family, with Dr. John as Physician and Surgeon-in-Charge. Also under his care would be as many other soldiers as possible at the University, where the makeshift hospital wards were being overwhelmed by the large number of casualties coming in from the Battle of Manassas.

In Charlottesville, Dr. John borrowed a horse and rode back and forth from the hospital wards to Mr. Godwin's house to check on Robert. The hope was that his condition would turn for the better in this much more favorable situation of peaceful, comfortable, and hygienic surroundings as well as proper medical attention.

In Charlottesville, however, Robert suffered further decline, with unrelenting fever, abdominal pain, diarrhea, and intestinal bleeding. Robert's smashed hand was not the main source of his health crisis, it was the dreaded typhoid fever. Dr. John had seen too many young men die in the past days to be ignorant of how close to death Robert was. The nursing efforts of young Florence Godwin, daughter of the household, were no more than a finger in the dike against the wash of toxic bacteria that were wreaking havoc in Robert's body.

In an agony of fear for the life of his younger brother, Dr. John requested help from Dr. Charles Alston, supervising doctor on the ward. After examining the suffering soldier, Dr. Alston concurred with Dr. John. "Typhoid fever. He needs surgery to stop the bleeding. I'm sorry. You know this is a difficult situation." Dr. Alston looked at Dr. John with sympathy.

Dr. John spoke his piece. "I want a third opinion, and from the best surgeon obtainable. I do not think I could face returning home to Alabama without either of my two beloved younger brothers." As soon as Dr. Alston left the room, Dr. John collapsed in a chair, overwhelmed by feelings of fear and dread. "God help me" were the only words he could utter.

The next day, when Dr. John returned to the Godwin house, Dr. Alston was already there with a young woman of arresting beauty, with chestnut hair and blue eyes that revealed a world of sympathy, kindness, and intelligence. She was petite and beautiful, in a simple navy blue dress, with only a gold watch for jewelry.

The astonished young doctor was startled by Dr. Alston saying, "Dr. Andrews, meet Dr. Moon."

The visitor was the third physician. The woman proceeded to examine the patient with a calm demeanor and practiced manner that inspired in Dr. John immediate trust in her as a physician. The three doctors began their consultation immediately after Dr. Moon had finished her examination. Dr. Alston again advised surgery to stop the intestinal bleeding. Dr. Moon argued that without anesthesia, the added injury to his body would only hasten the delirious boy's end. The two other doctors concurred and packed the boy's chest with ice in hopes of reducing his fever and changing the odds to the better for surviving an operation the next day.

Early the next morning, Miss Florence Godwin reported that her patient's condition had improved in the earlier part of the night, but in the early morning hours he relapsed and remained in about the same condition as on the preceding day.

All agreed that surgery was the only alternative, although Dr. Moon concluded from her experience and training that the boy would not survive surgery, but in any case would not survive without surgery. With such a mind-set, she deferred to the greater experience of Dr. Alston and ably assisted in the surgery. The infected tissue was removed and the bleeding staunched. There was nothing left to do but pray and await signs of returning vitality.

After the operation Dr. John gave in to his fear with heaving shoulders and quiet sobs. Dr. Moon placed her hand on his shoulder and whispered her sympathy for his sorrow. Dr. John looked up and saw tears in the eyes of this heretofore dispassionate surgeon. In gratitude, he reached for the gentle hand on his shoulder and held it.

Dr. John stayed by Robert's bedside, and the boy lived through the day and night. When his two colleagues returned the next morning, Dr. John reported on his condition. "He's slipping away… He'll be the second offering from his Father's family to the cause of a cruel, unnecessary War…"

The end came the second day after the operation, with the three physicians standing together by Robert's bedside. Dr. Alston's arm was about the grieving brother's shoulder, while with one hand Dr. Moon held his shaking hand and the other held Robert's on the bed before her. When the boy's life was gone, Dr. Moon drew a sheet over the pale face and closed the unseeing eyes. She and Dr. Alston led Dr. John to a chair, and then Dr. Moon returned to the bed and, took a long look at the face she would never see again.

As Dr. Alston and Dr. Moon walked together to their wards after reporting the death, Dr. Alston made the remark that the death of Dr. Andrews's brother was "an unusually sad case."

"Why do you say that? All of the deaths have been tragic, and at least Dr. Andrews was with Robert until the end. His brother did not die alone and uncomforted."

"That family's sacrifice has not ended yet. His nineteen-year-old brother, Billie, died on the first day of battle and on that hot day was buried in a common grave on the battlefield while Dr. Andrews was tending to Robert and dozens more soldiers. Now his other brother, Robert, will suffer the same fate; he will fill a grave far from his home and people in Alabama."

"Why must this be so?" she asked with bewilderment.

Dr. Alston said, "The Confederacy can only concentrate its transportation facilities on War purposes, and it would be impossible to procure funds from Florence in time to ship the remains home or even provide a decent burial in Charlottesville."

Dr. Moon, who had never in her life suffered a lack of funds and had never parted with such an amount of money without first consulting her family, went directly to Dr. Andrews and offered an immediate loan to cover the cost of transporting Robert's remains and a train ticket for himself to accompany his brother. Dr. John accepted the offer with gratitude and took an immediate leave of absence to make the arrangements for the journey back home.

In Florence, people from the city and surrounding county came out in large numbers to honor the Methodist-Episcopal Reverend Andrews's young sons, who had died defending their Southland, and many were the regrets that the remains of William might not rest beside those of Robert. The funeral for Robert was the first in Florence of many thousands of funerals to come in the South, and fortunate were those towns with remains to bury as the fighting continued in places generally far from the young soldiers' homes. The lamentable deaths were never accepted as anything but the supreme sacrifice of the flower of Southern manhood for the Southland worth dying for.

Before he left Florence, Dr. John paid a visit to the Forks of Cypress cotton plantation outside Florence, the large antebellum home of Sarah Moore-McCullough Jackson, widow of James Jackson Sr. Her husband had come to America as an enterprising Irish émigré who settled in Nashville as a merchant. He married Mrs. Sarah McCollough, a widow, while in Tennessee, and acquired property and friends before he and his family came to Florence. The congenial and energetic Jackson became part of the landed gentry, a planter and eventually president of the Alabama Senate.

Mrs. Jackson welcomed the bereaved Andrews and offered condolences for the loss of his two brothers. "I grieve for any of our Boys in Florence who are lost to us because of this terrible War."

John Andrews took her frail hand with both of his and thanked her for her sympathy. "I come with news of your son. James was wounded at Manassas the same day my brother Billie was killed in battle. My brothers and I and your son were soldiers of the Fourth Alabama Infantry. Because I was a medical doctor and treating Robert and other wounded soldiers at the field hospital, I was commissioned as a medical surgeon by an attending officer. Your son was one of the wounded and I recognized his name and hometown. Most of the wounded were taken to Charlottesville General Hospital by train from Manassas. I accompanied Robert and had the care of many of the wounded, including James, until after Robert died, and I was able to come home with his body for burial."

"I've been informed of his status as 'wounded in battle.' Can you tell me more?"

"I can tell you he was alive before I took leave. I will seek him out as soon as I return to the hospital ward."

Mrs. Jackson sent him off with God's blessings.

Through the day of Robert's death and far into the night, Dr. Moon, even as she tended to her wounded Boys, could not escape the death scene in her mind with the young doctor and the terrible loss of his two younger brothers from the battle. Her sympathy for Dr. John Andrews overshadowed even her exhaustion and concern for her still-living broken Boys in the Gray and Blue. Sympathy consumed her.

CHAPTER 4

ANNA MARIA BARCLAY MOON

O rie, calm and effective on the outside, was numb beneath the surface. Unwilling to depart from a soldier's bedside at crucial moments, she went too long without sleep, and when she did close her eyes, the nightmare of the cries of suffering pulled her back awake. Without time to eat or the appetite for it, she fainted in a corridor. She was rushed to a bed. Dr. Alston was summoned and he hurried to her side, fearing typhoid fever above all, a more potent dealer of death to the young soldiers than musket and cannon fire and capable of spreading to the medical staff as well as the wounded Boys.

Dr. Alston examined his colleague with skilled hands, eyes, and ears. "Thank God, no signs of infection." He reported to his staff that Dr. Moon, however, was in a serious state of physical and emotional exhaustion. "I am very much concerned about Dr. Moon. Recovery requires removal from the conditions that precipitated the breakdown as well as the danger from contagious infections. And pray that she recovers in time to return to the ward and apply her skills where they are desperately needed."

The men murmured in agreement, caught each other's eyes, and agreed, *She's a woman. This is man's work.*

Dr. Alston ordered a messenger to be sent to her family immediately. Her home at Viewmont was but ten miles from Charlottesville, but it was slow going over rural, mountainous dirt roads. The message was received late that day by Dr. Moon's mother, Anna Maria Barclay Moon, who wrote a return note to assure the doctor that she was prepared to leave at dawn the next day to bring her daughter home. She signed it with a flourish.

Early in the morning, Anna Maria gave Uncle Jacob instructions for the day and asked him to tell the old driver, Uncle Ned, to prepare the horse and carriage. Mammy Jinny was to have the bedroom ready for the invalid, and Anna Maria had already told her four younger daughters that they were to drop everything and assist her when she and their sister Orie arrived.

Off they went, the horse clipping off the distance on the rural route to Charlottesville. Anna Maria prayed fervently for the Good Lord to spare Orie, and Uncle Ned urged on the high-stepping horse to keep climbing from James River level up and over Carter's Mountain into the valley.

At the University of Virginia hospital wards, a military orderly took Mrs. Moon to Dr. Moon's bedside. The pale young woman looked so altered in spirit, her mother was shocked. "Orie, dear! I'm here to take you home. Uncle Ned is in the carriage waiting to take you back to Viewmont. Orie! Do you hear me?" *Where was her strong little woman?* Anna Maria reached down to touch her cheek, but Orie brushed away her hand and moaned, "He's gone, another one gone. Death stalks us."

"Orie, it's Mama," she whispered softly.

Orie opened her sad, uncomprehending eyes. "I'm so terribly sorry. Your son died during the night," she intoned, and tears streamed onto her pillow.

Anna Maria blotted her daughter's tears with a lace handkerchief and saw the depth of Orie's suffering. Eight years now a widow, Anna Maria was suddenly seized by a familiar pang of grief for the loss of her husband, who had so doted on Orie. Surely if Edward were here, he could help Orie escape from the horror she was experiencing. The solemn and demanding child loved only her father, or so it had seemed to the beautiful and gracious Anna Maria Barclay Moon, who it might properly be said was accustomed to being first in the hearts of everyone.

Upon word of Mrs. Moon's arrival, Dr. Alston made his way to Dr. Moon's bedside and noted his colleague's lack of response to the presence of her mother as well as the mother's grim visage.

"Mrs. Moon, I'm Dr. Charles Alston, supervisor of the ward's medical staff. I am personally grateful for your speed in arriving. I am very concerned that she not linger here in danger of serious infections that have afflicted so many of our patients. Dr. Moon is quite ill herself from utter and complete exhaustion of mind, body, and spirit. She has also endured the terrible grieving of the soldiers' families. She must have peace and be apart from the War until her strength returns."

Anna Maria listened to the doctor's words with attention and felt both alarmed and indispensable; her daughter would recover and it was up to her to bring this about, not only for the sake of her family, but for the sake of the South in time of War.

"My dear Dr. Alston, I will do all that is humanly possible for my daughter and trust in the Lord to bring her safely through this. I am grateful to you, of course, and I thank you for sending word so quickly. How long—"

Dr. Alston interrupted. "No one can say in cases like this. Dr. Moon has been heroic in her duties here, forgoing everything for the sake of her patients. All the doctors and staff are in her debt for burdens she carried for all of us, but in the end, she's a frail mortal and took on too much. Dr. Moon is one of the most intelligent, talented, and hard-working doctors I've ever had the pleasure to work with. She is beloved by her patients and respected by her colleagues, who have watched her pour out her strength for these unfortunate Boys."

Anna Maria offered her hand to the young doctor and thanked him for graciousness in a time of agony. He took her hand, kissed it lightly, and looked into her brimming eyes. He straightened up and walked briskly away, with Anna Maria's eyes on him until he disappeared into the busy corridor. For her, the hours of War were harsh beyond endurance, but sympathy for each other can overcome the most bitter fears and sadness. Anna Maria turned her attention to her daughter.

The same young orderly who had greeted them, barely a teenager, and Uncle Ned helped Miss Orie lie comfortably in the carriage, resting in the arms of her mother. The elderly servant spoke softly to the horse, encouraging her to move gently rather than with the speed required earlier when coming to fetch the young miss. Orie's eyes were blinking in confusion and she moved with some restlessness. Anna Maria kissed her daughter's eyes shut and stroked her forehead, thanking the Lord for His bountiful mercy.

Orie's four sisters at Viewmont rallied around her, each one outdoing the other in attentiveness. By the third morning at Viewmont, Orie's blue eyes were no longer blank, but glazed with sorrow. Anna Maria, a still-young and lonely widow, let loose her pent-up affections and spent hours each day by her daughter's bedside, not allowing her to awaken alone to remember her dead and dying young soldiers.

Lottie, short for Charlotte and six years younger than Orie, read to her sister from books of travel adventures that would put Orie to sleep almost as fast as Colie's books about romance in big cities. Colie was an affectionate nickname for Sarah Coleman, named after her grandmother and matriarch of Viewmont. All the children had nicknames. Sweet Mary was called Mollie and Edmonia, renamed after her father Edward died when she was two years old, was called Eddie.

They all vied for Orie's attention. Mollie thought fairy tales would cheer her up, and Eddie made paper dolls for her. Orie's younger brother, Isaac, would visit when his work outside on the farm was finished for the day, and Mammy Jinny would slip in from the kitchen from time to time with soup, fresh spring water, and beaten biscuits in milk with honey.

As Orie grew stronger and slept less, Lottie sought her out for desperately desired serious talk. The younger sister had established a reputation at the Virginia Female Seminary at Botetourt Springs for her intellectual interests as well as being a fun-loving student leader. In her second year, the school's name was changed to Hollins Institute, and the *Religious Herald* claimed it to be "the equal, if not superior" to any school for women in America. Her graduation essay, titled "Women's Rights," brought attention to the young woman from Viewmont Plantation. After graduating Albemarle Female Institute, a school reputed to be equal in academic depth to the University of Virginia for men, Dr. John Broadus, pastor of Charlottesville Baptist Church and a founder of the Albemarle Female Institute, as well as chaplain of the university, called her "the most educated woman in the South."

The younger sister pulled up a chair and sat beside Orie in her bed. "Orie, I want to travel to China and convert the women and children to Christianity. Unless the women are converted, the children will never be, and Chinese men won't permit foreign men to speak with their wives or sisters." Lottie desperately wanted her revered older sister's approval for her plan.

"Ah, yes!" Orie agreed, recalling her time spent in a Bedouin sheik's harem tent just after finishing medical college. "Uncle James had a medical degree, but the sheik never let him into his harem or let the sick ones come out and be touched or seen by an adult male, no matter how holy a man and skilled a doctor he was. But I was allowed to come into the harem and treat his wives and children. It was easy, when I learned to speak conversational Arabic, and they knew what 'Wash your hands and face' meant and

I said it all the time. Indeed, it did cut down on ophthalmia, that dread disease that causes blindness. It's said there are more blind people in Syria than in any other country of like size. But even so, for those people, water was almost too precious for anything but drinking. It was a pity."

Lottie thought about another pity, the fact that she was wasting her life at Viewmont when God was calling her to China.

Orie wasn't finished. "I still dream at night about my two years in the Holy Land. I had never felt so needed and cherished as I was by Uncle James and his family and the Bedouins under my medical care."

"Oh, Orie, I wish I could have gone with you, but Mama told me I had to finish school. I think she wouldn't let me go because she had lost Papa and we were all afraid you would never come home. But nothing stops you. You traveled all that way to join Uncle James, and you doctored the women and children of the desert Bedouins. You are a remarkable woman, Orie."

"Lottie, dear, remember that I had a medical degree and I was able to be a great help to our uncle. Be patient and you will be a great missionary someday." She was sitting up in her four-poster bed and speaking with some of her old authority, with Matilda the Maltese cat watching the activity from her perch atop pillows next to Orie.

"Orie, I have a Master of Arts degree from Albemarle Female Institute and I speak five languages and I've finally accepted the Lord and was baptized in the Baptist church almost three years ago. I know Mama needs help here at Viewmont, and with the War going on, there's nothing for me right now anyway, but I am long-ing to go into the foreign mission field."

"Lottie, dear, that's impossible right now."

"I'm thinking ahead, when the War is over." She lowered her voice. "Maybe God intends for us to go to China together. You would be the medical missionary, and I'll tell the Chinese women and children about our Lord, Jesus Christ. You've done this before in the Holy Land." Lottie's eyes were pleading.

Orie was taken aback by her younger sister's seriousness. "Lottie, I'm already spoken for as far into the future as I can possibly see. I am a surgeon in the Confederate States Army." She looked at Lottie face-to-face and wondered how her brilliant sister could have anything on her mind other than the War.

Lottie stared at her sister in shock. "You would go back to the hospital ward, Orie? Haven't you done enough? If you go back, you'll die. You can't do that."

Orie lay back down on her large four-poster bed, cradling a small white eyelet-decorated pillow, recalling the anguish she had caused her mother when she refused to back down from her desire to travel to Jerusalem. Her mother's arguments were valid and numerous: that she was still ill from the exhaustion of medical college and moreover, it was madness to believe she could safely travel alone to the barbarous wilds of the Holy Land, ruled by the despotic Mussulmen of the Ottoman Empire.

Her mother had argued with her, pleaded with her, and prayed for her to stay, but to no avail. Her mother's tears had vexed Orie, not persuaded her. In the end, Orie could not leave Viewmont fast enough. She went to Jerusalem to be with her uncle and his family and to be his medical assistant. Her beautiful and famed mother did not have the chance of an unarmed Yankee on a Southern battlefield to stop her.

Lottie understood her sister's silence as a no. Orie would not go to China with her and she would return to the military hospital as soon as she was able. Lottie's disappointment was impossible to quell, but her words covered it over.

"I'm sorry I brought this up, Orie. You are still ill and you are under Mama's rules of Bed Rest. Please forgive me and don't tell Mama I talked to you about this."

Orie took Lottie's hand and squeezed it. She hadn't meant to cut Lottie off so abruptly. Her thoughts jumped back to her girlhood, when she cared only for her father, feeling she had nothing in common with her sisters or her mother or her two brothers.

But that changed when she returned from the Holy Land. Lottie had hung on her every word as Orie spoke to groups in Albemarle County about her travels, and now that Orie was a baptized Christian, the two young women found common ground at the heart of their souls in addition to a mutual regard for higher education for women and women's rights.

Finally, now, shame was catching up with her. How cruel she had been, thinking only of herself and her books. Even before her father died, she only wanted to go away to school and leave them all at Viewmont. She was accepted at Troy Female Seminary after two years of preparing herself and had graduated with honors. Inspired by speakers invited to the school to speak to the students about various fields for women to enter, Orie applied to the Female Medical College of Pennsylvania in Philadelphia and put aside forever the expectation of a traditional home-centered; life for a Southern woman for herself. The Female Medical College in Philadelphia was the first school in the world to train women in medicine and offer them an MD degree. It was founded by Quakers who opposed slavery and championed women's rights. The standard two year course of study was intense with practical experience gained by opening a free clinic for women and children.

Orie began medical school in 1853 after her father's death that same year and graduated in 1857. This experience put her together with women from across the country who believed as she did about the great value of women MDs in medicine, in particular for patients who were women and children. She had studied late into the nights and took great care with her patients in the free clinic. She had written her thesis on the connection between cardiac and pulmonary diseases. After graduation the exhausted new doctor was put to bed at home at Viewmont, largely because Anna Maria had been terrified that Orie had inherited her father's weak heart. The invitation to join her Uncle James in the Holy Land as his medical assistant had proven irresistible to Orie, who left her sickbed and left Viewmont.

But Lottie need never know how truly indifferent and selfish she had been. Now she was a grown woman who had seen War and Death and terrible wounds and scalding grief. She would recover and return to a life of service. And Lottie would go on her merry way, just as she had always done, the tiny and pretty sister with the most personality and friends and always a success at whatever she tried her hand at. From now on they would be friends as well as sisters.

Her mind raced. *Charlottesville.* Back to early July, when Uncle Ned had driven her mother, brother Ike, and herself to Charlottesville. "Come to the bank with me, Orie," Anna Maria had said. "I'll be talking to the bank president about converting our assets into Confederate bonds and currency."

As Orie had sat in a chair next to her mother, she found herself face-to-face with a poster calling on Southerners to take up arms for the war, and particularly called for doctors and nurses. Filled with zeal, Orie had asked the bank president where she should go to offer her services as a medical doctor.

While Anna Maria had sat there speechless at Orie's sudden pronouncement, the gentleman showed Orie to the recruitment building. Orie signed up, waited impatiently for her assignment, and attempted to speed up the process with a letter to General John H. Cocke:

Viewmont
July 19, 1861

My most respected Friend,

Owing, I suppose, to our regular postal arrangements, your kind communication of Tuesday has just been received.

I have not as yet entered into service; neither shall I, without consulting you, if you will allow me that high privilege! I have been willing and even anxious to be engaged in ministering to the wants of the sick, but after you so kindly proposed to take the matter in hand, I thought it would be better to wait and learn the result; and in the meantime assiduously to review my medical studies, hoping thereby to be better qualified for a medical attendant. …

I would prefer to be in a Surgical Hospital where I would assist in the operations.

Please say to the authorities, that I will give the services of myself and a servant gratuitously, if they are willing to incur our expenses for dwelling and board. I will go anywhere or do anything if they see fit to assign me, if it is to follow the army and seek the wounded on the field of battle.

Yours with the highest regard
And Christian esteem,
Orie R. Moon

This letter was soon followed by one from Lottie telling General Cocke that Orie had entered into a temporary arrangement with the medical faculty at the university but would make no permanent arrangement until she had heard further from him and would prefer to be assigned "nearer the scene of action."

Orie pondered the weight of time. *That was in July, barely weeks ago.*

Dr. John Andrews returned to the hospital wards in Charlottesville from his home in Alabama after burying his brother to quickly learn that Dr. Moon had fallen ill and was recovering at Viewmont. Furthermore, he was needed to take over the ward assigned to Dr. Moon, which had simply been added to Dr. Alston's duties.

As John went about examining patients in the former Dr. Moon's ward, he sought out James Jackson, the son of the widow Mrs. Jackson Sr., who lived at the Forks of Cypress cotton plantation. John did not want to take the time to visit the soldier shot through the lungs at Manassas, but had told the widow he would do so. Dreading the visage of yet another death-gripped Alabamian, John silently approached the bed on the roster assigned to James Jackson Jr.

The soldier was sitting up in bed and reading a book; it took several seconds for him to look up and see John awaiting his attention. "Hello," he said pleasantly.

John smiled at the soldier, barely able to contain his relief. "You are Private James Jackson from Lauderdale County, are you not?" The son did not much resemble the father he had seen in the oil portraits hanging on the walls at the Forks of Cypress, a handsome man with a fresh, healthy, ruddy complexion. There had also been portraits of the large and portly man posing with handsome horses, and his widow explained that he was a "patron of the turf," having imported a large number of thoroughbred horses into the South from Ireland.

"Yes sir, can I help you?" Jackson's voice was low and lyrical.

"You've done that already." John went on to explain his connection with Florence and the visit to the Forks of Cypress. The two men shook hands, and before John took his leave, he said, "I ask God's blessing on you and your mother daily. I pray now that we will meet again in better times."

Back at Dr. Moon's former ward, John heard over and over about the "wonderful woman" who had served them so well. To be sure, Dr. Moon had never been far from his mind since the day he met her at his dying brother's bedside, and even while accompanying his brother's body home for burial and while sharing his grief with his family over the deaths of his brothers, his mind was never far from thoughts of Dr. Orie Moon.

When things were calm, Dr. John asked for leave to check on Dr. Moon as his out-of-ward patient and to repay the loan she had given him. He hired a horse and left the war-choked city of Charlottesville and climbed Carter's Mountain, passing by Jefferson's Monticello as well as James Monroe's Ash Lawn–Highland and Blenheim Farm, originally the property of Robert "King" Carter's grandson Edward Carter. Beyond Redlands, the mansion built for the family of Robert Carter III, was Carter's Bridge at the Hardware River, which marked a corner of Viewmont.

On Scottsville Road, within fifteen hundred acres of property, stood Viewmont, perhaps the oldest Great House in Albemarle County, dating back to circa 1730. The large frame house with massive twin chimneys on either side stood at the summit of a long earthen driveway with graceful trees lining both sides. Dr. John could not help but picture the beautiful doctor therein and felt a pang of excitement flash across his body.

CHAPTER 5
AT VIEWMONT

As Dr. John rode his horse up the long driveway to the entrance, Uncle Ned came out to greet him and open the gate. He introduced himself as a doctor from Charlottesville General Hospital there to see Dr. Moon. Uncle Ned took the doctor's horse to the stable for water and rest and pointed the way to the privy and the well house where the doctor could refresh himself. The old man remembered the frantic trip to the hospital to fetch Miss Doctor Orie.

Uncle Ned and Dr. John went about their business, and soon Uncle Jacob was at the door to usher him in, calling Mammy Jinny to see to the guest. She invited him to sit in the long hallway furnished with small ornate tables and chairs and plush wood-framed sofas. Dr. John chose a finely polished bench to sit on, along with his doctor's bag, to avoid soiling fine fabric with horse sweat and saddle smell. Mammy Jinny went upstairs to find her mistress, murmuring all the way up.

Dr. John gazed about the hallway, admiring the poplar trim and plaster walls. The floors were smooth heart-of-pine planks. It was a grand hall with high ceilings and a candle chandelier. Dr. John learned later from Dr. Moon's brother that the bricks for the twin chimneys were made on site by slaves and the house was constructed of timber cut from the property and whip-sawed right there.

Anna Maria met Mammy Jinny, having excused herself from Orie's bedroom, and drew her aside. "We heard a rider arrive, Mammy Jinny. Who's the visitor?"

"He say he be a doctor from the Wards in Charlottesville. He come to doctor Miss Orie. But I never seen one so young before. A real doctor is old and this one ain't a bit old. He be waitin' in the entry hall. He say his name be Dr. Andrews."

"I'll let Miss Orie know he's here. You can give him some fresh well water and something to eat. I'll send for him when Miss Orie's ready." She expected to see Dr. Alston at some point. Anna Maria rather liked young Dr. Alston.

Anna Maria went back into Orie's room and held her hand. "A doctor from the hospital is here to see you. I'll stay with you if you wish me to."

"Is it Dr. Alston?"

"No, dear, it's a Dr. John Andrews."

"Ah, well. Is he coming up right now? If he is, I shall have to make myself more presentable." *Dr. John Andrews. Mercy!* Her heart began to pound.

"Nonsense, Orie. He's not here to pay a social call. He may not stay long at all, if the Wards are as busy as they were when Uncle Ned and I came to fetch you." Anna Maria wondered at the reaction of her most sensible daughter.

"Of course, Mama, and I am tired. But could you hand me the cologne on my dresser? I'd like to feel a bit freshened." Orie's mind was spinning like a whirling dervish in the desert.

"The lavender or the rosewater, dear?" Anna Maria asked from the dressing room.

"I don't know, what do you think?" Orie asked with a tremor in her voice.

Dear merciful heavens, thought Anna Maria. What ails the girl? Ten minutes ago she was almost her old self bossing around sweet Mollie.

She returned to her daughter's bedside with the rosewater and looked closely at her. "Are you feverish? Your skin looks flushed." She felt Orie's forehead and found it damp.

"I'm hot, Mama. It's hot upstairs under the covers." She looked impatient and annoyed.

Anna Maria smiled and relaxed. "I'll go downstairs and introduce myself and send him up. Do you need anything?"

"No, Mama, I do not." *Just please go.* As her feelings formed words in her mind, Orie instantly felt the heat of shame as she recognized her own ingratitude for all the hours and hours her mother had spent with her the past weeks.

"Fine, I'll be out of your way." Anna Maria waltzed downstairs, eager to see this young man who had perhaps caught her daughter's eye.

Mammy Jinny had brought Dr. John fresh water from the well and cold cornbread. Upon seeing Mrs. Moon descend the wide stairs, he stood and introduced himself.

Anna Maria, like any mother with five daughters, took in all that she heard and saw with no discernible appearance of doing so. She was thinking that he *was* young, possibly younger than Orie, but very presentable, and after a chat about his ride from Charlottesville, decided he was well spoken while not overly polished, a trait she did not appreciate in a man. And thankfully she found him neither arrogant nor silly. She kept him company until his cup was empty and plate clean.

"Do you need to freshen up before seeing your patient, Dr. Andrews?" *He looks clean, but he's coming from a hospital, after all.*

"Thank you, but your man Ned showed me the well house when I arrived."

"Then you are all set. Take the stairs. My daughter is in the bedroom on the right. She still tires quickly and needs a nap in the

31

morning and afternoon and early to bed at night, but she's eating now and sleeps better at night than just a week ago." She watched him take in the information with full attention.

"That's all good news, Mrs. Moon. If you'll excuse me, I'll attend to her now." He wiped his mouth with a handkerchief, picked up his leather doctor's bag, and climbed the stairs.

Hmm, thought Anna Maria. Life can turn on a copper penny. Could it be that Orie has taken a fancy to a mere mortal man? The day was becoming interesting.

Dr. John knocked lightly at the solid wood bedroom door. "It's Dr. John Andrews. May I come in, Dr. Moon?"

Orie took a deep breath to steady her voice. "Yes, of course, Dr. Andrews. Please."

Dr. John opened the door and, leaving it ajar, came to her bedside and took her hand in his. "My dear Dr. Moon, when I was told you were ill and recovering at Viewmont, my mind would not rest until I could see you for myself. I also thank you for your kindness to my brother when he was so ill and for your generosity to me. You will never know how much it meant to my father to have his son brought back home and for me to help with the burying. Here is the money I owe you. I will put it on the table beside you with greatest thanks."

Orie gazed back at the face she had not stopped seeing in her mind since the day his brother died. "I was glad to help. I could not bear the thought of your second brother buried without honor far from his home." She paused. "And please call me Dr. Orie. We are colleagues, after all…and friends who share a great deal of sorrow."

Still holding her hand, Dr. John responded, "If you will call me Dr. John, I will call you Dr. Orie." Orie smiled, liking the touch of his warm, much larger hand.

Orie found the young man's masculine presence energizing and appealing. He smelled of horse sweat and the outdoors, and his voice brought back memories of her beloved father.

Dr. John questioned her about her health, noting the strength of her voice, the color of her skin, and the tone of her muscles. He took her pulse and listened to her heart. *She lives.* He didn't think he could bear another death.

Too soon, Anna Maria came upstairs to confer with her daughter's doctor, and then a flood of feminine activity swirled around him as Lottie, Colie, Mollie, and Eddie came in to visit their sister and meet the handsome young doctor.

When Anna Maria was satisfied the girls were minding their manners in spite of their giggles and efforts to gain the attention of the visitor, she left the room with the door wide open and went downstairs.

Mammy Jinny, fanning herself, complained about the August heat. "But at least it be quiet downstairs," she said, glancing upstairs with a knowing look.

"I'll have to rescue the doctor soon. I don't think he's accustomed to the company of a roomful of young girls. But I'll say the young man is a pleasant change for the girls, and I think even Orie is enjoying his company." She waited for Mammy Jinny's response, which was not long in coming.

"Ma'am, Miss Orie, she be a doctor, too, and will catch that young man in a shortcoming and be tired of him afore we can disbelieve it."

Anna Maria sighed. "You're probably right. She's set in her ways and she's twenty-seven, not seventeen. I declare that young man is younger than Orie, and what man would put up with that bossiness of hers? And she doesn't want anything but her books and her doctoring."

Mammy Jinny shook her head. "She be the first daughter of the most beautiful plantation lady in Virginny and I tell her to mind what you do, but she pays me no never mind."

"I expect God has different plans for Orie," said Anna Maria.

CHAPTER 6

ORIE AND JOHN

Although it was only mid-August, it was after seven o'clock when Anna Maria used the excuse of shorter days in asking Dr. John to spend the night and avoid the risks of riding in the dark back to Charlottesville. Orie's sisters, who had pleaded for the visitor to stay for supper, now begged him to stay the night.

"Ike will see that you have everything you need," said Anna Maria, unwilling to let the occasion come to an end. Isaac, the Moon family's sole surviving son, shared the overseeing of Viewmont plantation with his mother. Isaac, called Ike, and his wife, Margaret, had met Dr. John at the supper table, and Ike agreed to take the slightly younger doctor under his wing and welcome another man into the mostly female society for the evening.

Ike's older brother, Tom, a medical doctor, had died five years ago while on his way out West with his wife and baby. They never got there. Cholera broke out on their riverboat near Fort Leavenworth, Kansas, and after sending his wife and baby to safety, Dr. Tom ministered to the cholera victims. Tragically, he contracted the disease, died, and was buried near Fort Leavenworth. Possibly he might never have returned to Viewmont. After marrying a woman with family in Dardanelle, Arkansas, he chose to move there before attempting to go to California. His widow, with baby Thomas II, returned to Virginia and lived at Viewmont for a year before she remarried and moved away. The itchy-footed first born's decision to leave Viewmont turned out to be permanent.

Dr. John accepted the invitation. "The hospital Wards are not so crowded now from the battle at Manassas Junction, and Dr. Alston told me to take my time coming back. He's concerned about Dr. Orie and wants her back and well."

Far from home and still feeling the acute loss of his two brothers, Dr. John rested in the glow of this lively family. His time with Dr. Orie had been very brief, but he would see her again tomorrow. His visit, plus the excitement of the girls, had tired her, so she was served supper early on a tray brought up by Mammy Jinny. Meanwhile, Dr. John had a chance to be charmed by Mrs. Moon, Dr. Orie's four younger sisters, and the congenial Ike and his wife, whom everyone called Mag. Dr. John enjoyed the table conversation, talking about his home in Florence and his brief medical practice in Memphis, avoiding subjects regarding the dead and dying soldiers and Dr. Orie's collapse. He went to sleep that night thinking about seeing Dr. Orie in the morning. He couldn't remember when he last looked forward to the next day's dawning.

At breakfast, Dr. John joined Mrs. Moon and Orie's four sisters at the dining room table, laden with food prepared in the kitchen building outside by the servant Martha and three helpers. There were eggs, tomatoes, streaked pork, berries, cream, melons, cornbread, preserves, coffee, and buttermilk. Ike lingered over a cup of coffee and asked Dr. John how he had fared during the night.

"I slept well, thank you, and will be seeing Dr. Orie when she is bathed and dressed this morning. She was tired last evening, and I hope to see some improvement this morning."

Ike nodded. "Indeed. I'll see you at dinner time. It's going to be hot and I may take the afternoon off if it thunderstorms."

The sound of Ike's heavy shoes followed him out the front door; he avoided the dining room door, busy with servants bustling to and fro from the kitchen building. Ike crossed the porch, sailed down the steps, and moments later was on his horse heading for the fields near Carter's Bridge.

Mrs. Moon invited John to visit the library in the study while waiting for the housemaid, Cornelia, to call him upstairs. Meanwhile, she would be about her business checking with the servants and the girls with their lessons.

Dr. John was used to home libraries. His father had a small one with books mainly on religion and the Methodist-Episcopal Church. His two Horton uncles in Memphis, his mother's brothers, had a more varied library, but he had never seen a private library as extensive as the one at Viewmont. He leafed through Macaulay's *History of England* and wished he had a lifetime to absorb the knowledge stored in that room. Art, architecture, agriculture, Greek and Roman classics—was there nothing left out? He was like a fisherman when the shad were running.

Soon, however, he was called by Cornelia and made his way up the stairs with a heart like a lion's, eager to see Dr. Orie and coax a smile from her that would bring the summer sunshine into the room. He knocked lightly at the bedroom door and called out his name. The response was different from that of yesterday. She sounded as eager to see him as he her.

"Do come in, Dr. John!"

He hesitated only slightly and saw that her smile was more radiant than the sun itself coming through the window, its drapes open. She was sitting up in her four-poster bed wearing a nightgown covered by a soft lacy bed jacket. Her dark chestnut hair flowed about her shoulders and the sweet scent of lilies created a scene far removed from the sickroom of yesterday.

"You look lovely, Dr. Orie. I mean…you look well, very well. Your color is good. Yes, good." Dr. John groaned inwardly. *She's ravishing. I can't take my eyes off her. How can I possibly touch her?*

Orie held out a small, perfect hand and Dr. John grasped it with both of his hands, resisting the urge to bring her hand to his lips, smiling at her instead.

"I hope you slept well, Dr. John. The doctor's life is filled with strife. I know that well, and just as I have rested, it's good that you also are absent from the Wards while the need is not so great. My mother and brother are most willing to offer you some brief sanctuary after the terrible loss of your brothers and the frantic workload in the Wards."

"Why, that is most kind of your family, most thoughtful, most generous. Of course, my first duty is to see that your recovery is complete." He disengaged his hands and picked up his stethoscope. He listened to the sounds of her heart while his own heart was pounding so, he feared the whole world could hear it.

He checked her reflexes after helping her sit with her feet hanging down the side of the bed. "Excellent," he murmured. "Do you feel like standing?"

"With your help," Orie answered softly.

He helped her up easily and they walked about as he held her close. She, in turn, leaned into his side, depending on his strength to allow her to shift her weight from one foot to the other without fear of dizziness and collapse.

"That's good. I couldn't ask for a better patient. Dr. Alston will be pleased."

"Will you tarry a while at Viewmont, Dr. John?" Orie's demand was cloaked in a question, with the understanding that she wanted him by her side for as long as possible.

"Yes, I can stay a while as I see improvement, and then I will return as often as necessary until I think you are completely out of danger." Dr. John's relative social inexperience with the female sex, other than his mother, deceased now half a decade, and his little sister, Elizabeth, was smoothed over, to his great relief, by his medical training.

Orie smiled. "Thank you. Of course you realize that it is for the good of our Soldiers that I ask you to tarry, so that I may return to the work of healing the sick and wounded Boys." Orie listened to herself talk. Did she sound as silly as Colie and Mollie did around young men they were flirting with?

"I understand. And it's not only my duty but my extreme pleasure that I am allowed to be your doctor."

With dignity intact and the immediate future assured, both breathed a bit easier. Orie said that Cornelia would bring her dinner on a serving tray, and afterward she would rest while the heat of the day was upon them. "Will you return to me after my rest?"

"Even sooner if you desire it so," he answered. They both blushed.

Orie prepared to do some medical reading while the morning daylight was strong and not too hot. Dr. John hoped to spend time in the study before noontime dinner and quietly left the room, closing the door behind him. He went down the stairs and nodded to Cornelia, saying that Miss Orie was alone in her bedroom. Dr. John was relieved to see the study was empty except for books and furnishings. Where to begin? There were complete histories, poetic works, fiction, scientific travel, French conversation, volumes on Virginia law, and medical books.

Dr. John picked up the book he had leafed through earlier, Macauley's *History of England,* and looked for the County of Rutland in the East Midlands. That was where his ancestor had emigrated from in 1654. He had disembarked at the wharf in Annapolis, Maryland; *his* great-grandson Robert Lial Andrews was born in Philadelphia, the largest English-speaking city in the world outside of London at that time. He graduated College of Philadelphia in 1768 and traveled to London to be ordained into the Church of

England in 1772, returning to America to serve as Rector of the Episcopal Church at Yorktown.

Dr. John's father, the Reverend Robert Lial Andrews, was a Methodist-Episcopal minister who was born in Williamson County, Tennessee, perhaps much like the rural County of Rutland in England. His people were not wealthy planters living like royalty on large tracts of land, but they were good people. He knew that as well as he knew the sun rose in the east and set in the west.

CHAPTER 7

LIFE AT VIEWMONT

The dinner bell clanged outside at noon and all work ceased. Field hands, drivers, and the overseer came in from the fields and found shade under the trees or gathered at wooden tables and benches. Kitchen girls came out with platters and baskets of food, while men lined up at the well with tin cups for cool water from a bucket hauled up by a rope. Throughout the house, the occupants made their way to the large dining room.

Dr. John waited for Ike to come in from the fields, which he did with head and hands damp from a dousing of well water. He escorted Dr. John into the dining room to a chair beside him. In the brighter light of midday, Dr. John took in the massive size of the chimney as well as the elaborate plaster and woodwork decorations on the walls and ceiling. The wallpaper scene looked as if it were adorning a dining room in France or England. The floor was oak and the woodwork walnut, he surmised, judging by the dark color and grain. His physician's eye took in such details as if surveying human anatomy.

The conversation was light and lively, thanks to the four sisters and their mother. The food was more abundant and varied than at supper the previous night and even at breakfast that morning. With a young man's appetite, Dr. John helped himself to large servings of everything, including peach pies, fried chicken, ham, cornbread and biscuits, corn, okra, beans, cucumbers, and peppers. Pitchers of apple cider were refilled twice. All the while, Orie's sisters sought his attention with questions about the fashions and goings-on in Alabama and Memphis.

After dinner, Dr. John and Ike retreated to the quiet of the study and Ike offered the visitor a pipe and tobacco. Dr. John enjoyed the rare indulgence, lighting up with pleasure.

Ike talked about tobacco fields, work animals, and field hands. "Things are decent right now, but the tobacco market in London is understandably shaky," he said. "Now that the War has actually begun in America after decades of hostile talk between the planters in the South and industrialists in the North, the buyers don't know what to do. 'watch and wait' is what we are hearing."

"The cotton plantation planters in Alabama are worried too," said John. "I heard endless discussions over what was ahead when I was home in Florence."

"We are all in turmoil, if the truth be told. A Northern blockade of goods to and from England against the South is a real threat. Will the War be over in a matter of months? No one knows, but everyone speculates," said Ike.

Dr. John found the conversation engaging. Accustomed to lengthy discussions devoted to medicine or religion, he was finding it not at all difficult to go beyond those narrow parameters of thought. Would his devoted-to-the-church father approve of conversations focused on markets and finance? Maybe. Anything seemed possible.

Ike invited him outside to walk about and see the kitchen garden and outbuildings. On the other side of the hill were about thirty-five cabins for the slaves and their families. The estate grounds were like a rural town with a smithy, smokehouse, packing house, spring house, barns, and tool sheds. The kitchen garden was a series of rectangles with internal pathways of grass or tan bark. There were composted hills of squash, melons, and beans and perennial vegetables carefully covered with aged manure. The garden rows were well-watered and weeded.

"Who is the master or mistress of this garden?" Dr. John asked, thinking there was no end to the riches of Viewmont.

"My mother is the mistress of it as we speak, but the real master was her brother, my uncle James Barclay, who is not yet back from preaching to the Jews and ministering to the Arabs in the Holy Land. He lived at Jefferson's Monticello for several years as the owner, but found that being master of Monticello did not give him the time he needed for his church and missionary work. He lived there only four years. But in that time, 1832 to 1836, Uncle James restored the original terrace gardens and gained a great deal of respect for the art and science of horticulture. You may not know that Jefferson had an extravagant love for the earth's flora. He even wrote, 'No occupation is so delightful to me as the culture of the earth and no culture comparable to that of the garden.' The year I was born was Uncle James's last year at Monticello, but my mother says she and her family were frequent guests there. Everyone desired a tour of the garden and grounds to see the results of the seeds and plants Mr. Jefferson had brought from France and Italy. My uncle insisted that Anna Maria and Edward at Viewmont have grounds that might someday rival Jefferson's at Monticello."

Dr. John could barely refrain from showing his humble origins as the son of a minister in Alabama, his mouth open and staring at Ike as if he had never been invited over the threshold of the house of a former president of the United States.

"I passed by Jefferson's mansion on my way here from Charlottesville. I understand it's quite a remarkable place," said Dr. John, making an effort to keep up his end of the conversation.

"Indeed it is," said Ike. "Complete strangers and the oldest of friends expected to loiter there at will and even eat from the larder, so that Uncle James had no time for even his drugstore business. Then too, his great experiment with planting the mulberry trees for silkworm production had not been successful. His mother felt that he was wasting the family's money repairing Monticello; he decided she was right and sold it to Uriah P. Levy, a US naval officer. Levy put much of his own money into further repairs and restoring the mansion but is usually away on duty or in New York on business. Levy's mother presided over Monticello until she died and is buried there. An overseer now lives there. They say Levy is not well and is seldom in residence."

"My father is a Methodist-Episcopal minister. What church is your uncle a member of?" asked Dr. John.

Ike laughed. "All of them." Then he backtracked when he saw John's earnestly puzzled face. "I mean, his mother is a Baptist and then he married a Presbyterian and joined her church. Just to show you her religious zeal, she gave all of her jewelry to fund Presbyterian missions. But then the Presbyterian-turned-Baptist Alexander Campbell gained converts and there were great Campbellite revivals in Charlottesville and Scottsville."

"I am not familiar with Campbellite revivals," said Dr. John.

"The church is limited to this area at the present, you see. Uncle James and Aunt Julia became Campbellite disciples, and Uncle James gave his time preaching in disciples' churches and working to found a missionary-sending body."

"That's a subject dear to my father, but he decided early on that Alabama and Tennessee are mission fields too."

"Agreed, sir. Christ himself said to spread the Gospel everywhere, but Uncle James wouldn't rest until he could bring the Gospel to the Holy Land itself. In 1849 Uncle James offered himself to the newly formed American Christian Missionary Society and left the following year for the Holy Land with Julia and their two sons and one younger daughter. He was for many years the first and only missionary for the Disciples of Christ Church. He provided funding for the venture through his own financial support as well as family money."

Dr. John's head was spinning. In his family, the choice of a church had already been set before he was born. How his family's denomination changed from Church of England to Episcopalian to Methodist-Episcopal, he supposed, had to do with the Revolutionary War, plus time and place, as Philadelphia and Yorktown were worlds apart from rural Tennessee and Alabama, but none of that had anything to do with him.

As Dr. John wondered why he was being treated like a visiting head of state, Ike, two years older and far more well traveled, was only doing what he had been told to do by both his mother and his wife -- to treat with kindness and attention, because Orie seemed smitten by him. "Let Orie tire of him and send him away. We don't want to be blamed if he dodges her charms," his mother had said. Later, Mag said the same thing.

The two young men walked over to the fruit orchard, which, like the one at Monticello, also had peach, apple, cherry, and pecan trees. Ike looked heavenward and said, "The sky has cleared up, so I had best ride on over to the tobacco fields in the distance yonder and see if there are any problems. I have to be the first to know if there is blight or sloppy hoeing or damage of some kind. The tobacco will soon have to be harvested and hung up to dry. It's a busy time for us, and the signs are good for a decent harvest. I just hope the battles stay away from us, at least until the harvest is in and the hogsheads are packed and on the bateaux down the James bound for Richmond, then on to London. So many things can go wrong even without a war." Ike shrugged his shoulders and visibly succumbed to worry, looking older than his twenty-five years.

Dr. John nodded in sympathy, but thought himself very much inferior to Ike, who was contending with complex burdens that untold numbers of persons depended upon him to carry out successfully. Dr. John reckoned that the scope of matters at Viewmont was beyond his capacity to even fully imagine. In contrast to his small world in the classrooms of the medical college in Nashville or the hospital ward today, or even his boyhood at his father's knee in a small parsonage, Viewmont was connected to the worlds of international markets, large cities, and the thousand cares of over-seeing a slave workforce and keeping up with the myriad tasks of a prominent family.

Seeing the downcast look on the face of his charge, Ike assured him that Viewmont was not all about work. He would take John fishing for shad and small-mouth bass in the Hardware River or the James and go riding on the property in the cool of the evening. "Viewmont has the best hard cider in Virginia," Ike claimed. Dr. John thanked him for his time and his kindness.

They walked back to the stables and lingered in the shade of an ancient oak as they slaked their thirst with dippers of cool water. Then Ike was on his horse and trotting across a field. The heat and humidity caused a haze to obscure the mountains in the distance, and the field crops appeared to simmer in the sun. Hawks flew overhead, circling and shouting their cries. The sound of cicadas waxed and waned in the growing heat. It was a land of milk and honey, but he need not tarry there, as the sickroom was *his* workroom.

Dr. John retreated into the cool darkness of the house, where Dr. Orie was resting upstairs. Cornelia, hearing his riding boots tread the floor in the hall, greeted him and asked him to "please pay Miss Doctor Orie a visit in her room."

He slowly took the stairs, wondering how in the world he had managed to be in this princely house hobnobbing with the family of a Virginia tobacco planter in the neighborhood of Jefferson's Monticello. Were they simply grateful for his service as a doctor to the soldiers who had won a great victory for the Confederacy? Was he making too much of what was maybe simple civility to a doctor from Alabama bereft of two younger brothers? He must hold back his too-tense admiration for Dr. Orie.

He knocked tentatively at the bedroom door. "Dr. Orie?"

Orianna, puzzled by the sound of the slowly approaching footsteps up the stairs and the timid voice, answered without hesitation, "Yes, please come in!"

Dr. John assumed his professional bedside manner and spoke with authority. "How are you this afternoon, Dr. Orie? Did you enjoy your dinner? Did you rest well afterward?" His smile showed a distant but not unpleasant interest in his patient, and his eyes never rested on hers.

Orie was acutely aware of his demeanor, so different from when they parted late that very morning. She answered his questions obediently, all the while searching for a reason for this open departure from his former attitude of—she said it squarely to herself—passionate love interest.

"What have you been doing these past several hours? Has Mama been entertaining you, perhaps?" She could feel his discomfort. Had her mother upset him?

He looked puzzled. "Oh, she's busy, although most helpful and gracious."

Orie was not satisfied with his answer. It was clear she sensed something was wrong. "Did Ike show you about the grounds and perhaps take you fishing?" Someone was responsible for Dr. John's sad face, and she was going to find out who straightaway. Ike was a likely source, being unhappy himself. He had not yet reconciled himself to his older brother's death and felt that taking his place as the elder brother was unfortunate, if not catastrophic.

"Yes, Ike has been treating me like a brother, and after dinner we spent time smoking pipes in the study and then walked out to see the garden and orchard. It's everything I ever imagined a Virginia tobacco plantation would be. But it's overwhelming, the responsibilities of managing such an estate. I don't envy Ike at all, I fear for him, especially with the War in Virginia. He can't just slip away like I can, literally behind a stand of thickets on a hill and then on a train to Charlottesville."

Orie sighed. "Ike can make singing birds seek sanctuary as if in a storm. I'm afraid he lives under a dark cloud that can envelop those near him. He can't help it, and doesn't mean to."

Dr. John finally looked into Dr. Orie's eyes. "I thought Ike was letting me know that Viewmont was a world apart from me and to discourage me from thinking I was anybody more than a country doctor in the Southern army."

"Oh, my dear, dear friend. Nothing could be further from the truth. You and I have shared our lives in such a way that life will never again be as it was. Ike was sixteen years old when our father died unexpectedly, but Tom was twenty-one, and we all thought he would return in due time with his family and practice medicine here and be the master of Viewmont. It was his duty, after all, as the firstborn and oldest son." She kept her eyes on Dr. John and saw that she had his complete attention.

"Ike had his law degree from the University of Virginia and had passed the bar exam and expected to live on as a gentleman farmer and rural lawyer. But when Tom died five years ago, all that changed. Ike never wanted the responsibilities he shoulders now and sees no relief from them." Orie paused, remembering the shock of her father's death and then word from Tom's wife two years later that he was dead.

"I dare say that *is* a large burden for a young man who expected his father to be the master of Viewmont for many years to come, and even then Tom would have come home and assumed leadership with eagerness and young ideas." Dr. John shared a great deal of sympathy for Ike, but was almost giddy with relief that Dr. Orie and he were, indeed, very close friends with a bond he intended to never see broken.

"What happened to your father, if I may ask?"

"His heart was weak and he took to his bed in the autumn before he died in January. He thought he was going to die, even saying his farewells to us, to Tom and me especially, because he begged us to be baptized before he died, but neither of us would do it. Then he rallied and even went on a business trip. He was on a steamboat on the Mississippi between Memphis and New

Orleans when the boat caught fire. My father struggled to carry a very heavy suitcase from the boat and died of a heart attack on the riverbank. He was forty-eight years old."

"My dear friend, I'm so sorry." Dr. John sat on the bedside and kissed her cheek, holding her hands. Tears slipped from her eyes. Dr. John kissed her tears and the tears overflowed. He reached for his handkerchief and dried her face as tenderly as if she were a small child.

"Please forgive me," said Orie. "I never cried when he died and I loved him so. But I was angry with him for leaving me. His death was the worst thing that ever happened to me."

Dr. John kissed her again on the cheek and when her lips sought his, he responded with growing passion. "I love you, Orie Moon," he said quietly.

"And I you, John." She looked up and kissed him again.

At the end of the week, Dr. John left Viewmont and rode back to the wards in Charlottesville. He reported to Dr. Alston that Dr. Moon was recovering nicely, that after a month of bedrest she needed now to begin sitting up more and taking short walks in the house. Time was needed to rebuild her strength. He would keep making visits to Viewmont, but would honor his commitment to the Boys in the ward and let Dr. Moon know how they were faring. Dr. Alston was satisfied with Dr. John's report; Dr. Moon's former ward became officially Dr. John Andrews's ward.

Orie took John's advice by shortening the number of hours lying down in bed each day from the day before. She took turns leaning on her sisters as she walked from room to room and once or twice a day would go up and down the stairs. She took at least one meal in the dining room with the others. But always the face of her beloved John stayed in her mind's eye. It was for him that she wanted to be well and strong.

Her family took notice. They encouraged her and praised her for her efforts. She gained strength with added weight and was able to sleep through the night without waking up and crying out for cool water or a cool cloth over her eyes. Colie and Mollie teased her lightly about her "gentleman friend" and Orie just smiled. Lottie gave up confiding in Orie about her determination to go to China's mission field together one day. Orie called upon her mother for advice on how best to keep her face and hands smooth and soft and her hair fragrant and shining. Matilda the Maltese cat spent most of the day and night in Orie's room, purring incessantly as if sharing her mistress's contentment.

"She be in love with that doctor friend," Mammy Jinny warned.

Anna Maria smiled and nodded as she rejoiced in her heart. God had spared Orie's life in that hospital ward against the ugliness of typhoid fever and an exhaustion that no woman could bear, and now there would perhaps be a son-in-law to shore up the family. If only Edward were alive! He would be happy for his daughter and their joy would be complete.

CHAPTER 8

ROCKY ROAD

Dr. John returned to Viewmont early and often to check on the well-being of his out-of-ward patient. The people at Viewmont became familiar to him and he to them. When separated from Orie, Dr. John experienced pangs of longing for her that would not go away until they were together. When Uncle Ned heard him coming up the long drive to the house, he took his horse to cool down with hardly a word needed between them. Uncle Ned recognized lovesickness when he saw it and chuckled, and Mammy Jinny confirmed the talk inside the Main House.

After a month of bed rest, Orie was impatient to be with John everywhere and all the time. She counted the hours as wasted until she heard the horse trotting up the drive and a shouted greeting to Uncle Ned, then the greeting at the door from Uncle Jacob, followed by the sound of his brisk footsteps up the stairs to her room. She would throw open the door, invite him in, and embrace him as if to never let him go. He would shut the door, pick her up in his arms, set her down on the bed, and kiss her nose, eyes, and lips.

"It's tiresome here without you, John. Can we take a walk outside? It's not hot today."

"Yes, my love. It's good for you to be outside. We'll walk until you feel tired and then we'll rest. I'll tell Cornelia and your mother where we're going."

Orie wore a gauzy full-length cotton shift with a matching light shawl for comfort in the heat. She slipped into soft kid-leather shoes and put on a sun hat, picked up a Japanese fan, and pinched her cheeks for roses to bloom on them. She joined John downstairs, already equipped with a stout cotton quilt to rest upon, both of them deaf to Anna Maria's warnings against over exertion and too much sun.

"I'm her doctor," he reminded her. Anna Maria laughed and waved them good-bye.

John put his arm around Orie and held her as close as possible as she ambled, delighting in the sky overhead and grass beneath her feet. They walked beside the drive toward Scottsville Road. In a private shady spot, John spread out the quilt and helped her down to a sitting position. He arranged to sit with his back to her, acting as a back rest.

"There, how do you feel?"

"I feel like I would rather lie in your lap, but we are outside with who knows how many eyes upon us, so I am happy to rest with at least our backs together, dear John."

He turned around and kissed the back of her neck until she shivered with pleasure and cried for him to stop. "I will if you tell me the story of Viewmont, which I do not know," he said.

Orie gazed at the tree-lined drive up the slope to the house. "Viewmont is old, and so especially loved because it has been here all along, as far back as people can remember. Joshua Fry built it. We believe it was the first Great House in Albemarle County."

"I don't recognize the name," said John. "Was he a Virginian?"

"No, he was born in England and educated at Oxford, but he was not the firstborn and so would not inherit his family's estate. He came to Tidewater Virginia and married a wealthy widow and

51

they had five children together. He was also made a professor of mathematics and natural science at William and Mary College. Because of his position, he came to be introduced to the fine families in Virginia. People liked him."

"Why so?" John asked. He didn't know what he expected her to say. He knew he was picking a quarrel.

"I suppose because he was well educated, young and adventuresome, and dependable," Orie answered. "He became a member of the House of Burgesses, was a surveyor to the crown, and served on a commission appointed to determine the Virginia and North Carolina line. He did a lot of exploration up the James River and patented lands in what is now Albemarle County. He built a home and moved his family from Goochland to Albemarle County early on, perhaps near 1737."

"That was Viewmont?"

"Yes, and his neighbor at Shadwell on the Rivanna River and closest friend was Peter Jefferson, father of Thomas. Fry and Jefferson were the two highest magistrates in the county. The self-educated elder Jefferson was Fry's intellectual equal, with the *Book of Common Prayer* alongside volumes by Pope, Swift, Addison, and Shakespeare, but Fry was the higher ranking magistrate."

"I see," John said in a low tone.

Orie could feel his shoulder muscles slacken against hers. She turned toward him and asked softly, "What is it, dearest? What's wrong?"

"I grew up in a Methodist-Episcopal parsonage in Alabama. My father is a Methodist-Episcopal minister and a kind and devout Christian. My mother died five years ago and life has been hard, but good nevertheless. I will never say an unkind word about my family, but the life you live, the travels, the tutors, the education you've received, appear to me to be close to royalty. I love you with all my heart, Orie, but I fear I am not a suitable husband for you. I would never be my own man, and I don't think I could live like that. My father never envied anyone. I'm afraid I could not pass that test."

Looking him straight in the eye, Orie said, "Very well, then. I will never beg a man to marry me. If you are so repelled by the way my family lives and welcomes you with affection and care, I cannot undo what has so twisted your mind that you can turn away from me."

John was stunned. He had not imagined for a minute that she would accept what he had to say and not even say she loved him in spite of their different stations in life. What kind of a woman was she? How could he have ever thought she would marry him? Had she been merely sick and bored and he amused her? He had seen Uncle Ned smile to himself after taking his horse this very day. Were they all laughing at him?

With pinched lips he helped Orie up, offered his hand, and they slowly walked up the slope to the Main House. Neither spoke. Inside, as soon as he saw Cornelia, he called her and passed Orie's care to the maid. Furious with himself for thinking he was the equal of these people, he said his farewells and took his leave as quickly as Uncle Jacob came to open the door and bid farewell.

On the long ride back to Charlottesville, he concentrated on what was real, such as the pace of the horse, the rough terrain, and the miles to go. All other thoughts he blocked out.

Back at the hospital ward the next day, he set his mind on his work and was glad of the necessity to do so. To keep busy, he visited the university library and sought out historical books of early Virginia and Albemarle County. He perused sketches of Viewmont and statistics showing the number of slaves and tonnage of tobacco yields in various years. He learned that Joshua Fry was commander-in-chief of all Virginia troops in the French and Indian War and George Washington was his second in command. They were marching on an expedition against the French in Ohio when Fry died from injuries after a fall from his horse near Cumberland,

Maryland. The year was 1754. Fry was buried with honor. Carved in a nearby tree were words by George Washington: "Under this oak lies the body of the good, the just, and the noble Fry."

George Washington was second in command to Joshua Fry of all Virginia troops in the French and Indian War? John read the same passage twice more. When he believed Orie was exaggerating the greatness of her family, he found that she had understated their worth. Why? Was she covering up her extreme wealth and heritage so that he wouldn't feel inferior?

Obsessed, he read on and discovered that Virginia Governor Edmund Randolph bought the mansion from Fry's heirs and used it as a retreat from 1786 to 1798. And that Captain John Harris, the richest man in already fabled Albemarle County, took it over as his primary property in 1803. From Viewmont, Captain "Jack" Harris "ruled three thousand acres of prime Virginia real estate spread over ten different plantations. His domain reached to New Orleans, Memphis and Kentucky, where he traded tobacco and cotton. It is said that he owned 800 slaves, but only 160 were counted in Albemarle County in 1830.

John went on to learn that Captain Jack buried his first and childless wife, Frances, on the property in 1816. Later he married a lovely young widow, Sarah Coleman Turner Barclay, of the wealthy Philadelphia Quaker Barclays, financiers of the American Revolution. Her youngest child was Anna Maria Barclay, who married the captain's nephew Edward Harris Moon.

John paused. *Anna Maria and the deceased Edward are Orie's parents.*

John groaned anew. Orie's beautiful and wealthy mother, Anna Maria, had been married by arrangement. The same would happen to Orie, and he, John Summerfield Andrews, would not be the designated suitor. It was clear to anyone with brains and breeding that he had been mad to think of himself as a suitable husband for Orianna Russell Moon. A mad fool.

At Viewmont, Orie was equally yoked in misery. When John handed her to Cornelia as if she were a five-year-old being returned to her nanny, Orie ignored both the maid and John and went upstairs by herself at a pace that belied her still-fragile small body. She shut her door with a slam and threw herself on the bed. Her sobs and muffled screams were terrible to hear. The whole household stopped to listen. Anna Maria came hurriedly to the foot of the stairs and was soon joined by Cornelia and her other four daughters.

"What happened?" asked Eddie. "Did somebody die?"

Anna Maria embraced her youngest child and kissed her forehead. "No, darling, but it must seem that way to Orie. I think she and Dr. John had a lovers' quarrel. It may not be serious at all." At which point they all looked upstairs with eyes that did not match the hope held in their mother's words.

Colie spoke with forced bravado. "Mama, I'm sure you had lots of lovers' quarrels before you married Father, but Orie never lost her heart to anyone before."

Mollie chimed in, "Her love for John was like a story written by Sir Walter Scott. It was too good and pure to be true."

Lottie was silent, looking grieved for Orie.

"Ladies, stop the drama and go about your business. I'll give Orie some time to cry this out and then talk to her."

"Yes, Mama," they said, and scattered away.

"Miz Moon, do you want me to stand a'side her door and let you know when Miss Dr. Orie be done carr'in on?" Cornelia asked.

"No, thank you. I'll knock on the door when I think it's time, but thank you, Cornelia."

"Yas'um, Miz Moon. I's sorry she be so broken-hearted, I surely am."

Anna Maria looked at Cornelia, who was probably about the same age as Orie, and was grateful for her sympathy for her young mistress.

Meanwhile, upstairs Orie's thoughts were dark and swirling. She pictured her Boys back at the ward and how devastated she had been seeing their suffering and deaths. They were lucky. They died for a cause and will be beloved by their fellow Southerners for all of eternity. There will be monuments for them and their descendants will praise them. Mine is the greater sorrow and tragedy, she thought. Just a foolish woman broken by false charm in the throes of War. I'm not the first woman to be so misled, nor the last one, I'm sure. My life is a bitter cup to sip from. If only I had been the least bit wary of the disarming stranger from Alabama. My father might have seen the woes ahead and saved me, perhaps, if he were still living. As it is, I'm utterly undone and can see no reason to have any hope of happiness from now on.

Anna Maria stayed away, hoping for some sign of a break in the grieving, but by bedtime she knew she had to walk down the hall with her candlestick and make that knock on Orie's door. There was no answer and the door was locked. "Orie! Open the door. You are scaring everyone in the house. Let me in this minute."

Orie sat up. It was completely dark outside. She had been asleep for hours. Then it hit her: John was gone and her heart was broken. She slowly moved from her bed and opened the door. Her beautiful mother looked careworn. Anna Maria looked at Orie standing there, still in her gauzy white cotton sheath, so small and sad. She put down her lantern and reached out and hugged her daughter, forgetting everything she had planned to say.

"Gracious, it's dark in here. Let's light a candle." She lit the candle on Orie's bedside table and another on the chest of drawers. "There! That's so much better!" she exclaimed, as if the darkness in the room had been the source of the problem all along. "Can I bring you something to eat? Fresh water in your pitcher?"

Orie took stock of her symptoms. He mouth was so dry her tongue cleaved to the roof of her mouth, and her head ached. Her right hand had fallen asleep under her arm and tingled uncomfortably. "Yes, but it's late, Mama, and you look tired. I can take care of myself."

"You get on your bedclothes and I'll come back with a bowl of peaches left over from supper and a biscuit and fresh water. Do that for me, darling, and I'll be back."

Anna Maria closed the bedroom door and was met by Mollie in the hallway with a lit candlestick in the dark. "Is she all right? Can I help you, Mama?"

"Dear Mollie, yes, you can help me carry back food and drink for your sister. She looks cried out right now. I'll listen to her side of the story tonight and maybe she'll wake up in the morning in a better frame of mind."

Together they ventured downstairs and outside to unlock the kitchen building, needing both candlesticks to find their way around. The whole household was asleep except for the two of them and Orie upstairs. They filled a tray with leftover supper and a pitcher of water, then closed the kitchen and went back to the Main House and up the stairs to Orie's bedroom. Mollie helped her mother set the supper tray on a table and left the room, following the light of her candlestick.

"Thank you, Mollie," Orie called out, and Anna Maria smiled at her in approval.

Orie had changed into her nightclothes, and she drank the water and ate the peaches, bacon, and biscuits with a show of some appetite. Anna Maria relaxed in a small rocker and hoped her experience with courtship would be helpful to her inexperienced daughter.

When she finished eating, Orie wiped her mouth with her napkin and broke the silence. "John has left me."

"Oh, my darling, I'm so sorry."

"Why are you sorry, Mama? Did you like him?"

Anna Maria paused. "Why, yes, I did. But what did he do? Maybe I don't like him anymore."

"He won't marry me. He says he's not a suitable husband for a Viewmont bride. But I don't believe that. He doesn't love me, and he never did. And if he means what he says, I would never marry a man who won't accept a person because she lives in a Great House and comes from a 'royal' family, as he puts it."

"He *won't* marry you because you are from a *fine* family? Whatever is he thinking?" Anna Maria's perplexed expression mirrored her inner confusion.

"He thinks you all will hold him in low esteem because his family is of humble origins and cannot measure up in any sense of the word to the Moons and Barclays and Jeffersons and on and on."

"Orie, I'm shocked. He's a physician who volunteered his services to the Confederacy, coming all the way from Alabama. He was a practicing physician in Memphis. Why would we not think highly of him?"

"It's pride, Mama. He's a prideful man and that's a sin. And all the worse because he boasts that his father is a minister and perfect in his humility. He must be a humble man, because his son has taken all the pride with none whatsoever left over."

Anna Maria smiled. "I am very tired and I must get to bed. Let's sleep on this tonight and talk again in the morning."

"Very well, Mama. Maybe tonight I will have no dreams at all. That's my hope."

Anna Maria embraced her daughter and kissed her forehead. She snuffed out both candles and closed the door.

CHAPTER 9

LOVE ALTERS LIFE

Anna Maria stopped Uncle Jacob after he was finished setting the day's schedule for Mammy Jinny and her servants. "Uncle Jacob, may I have a moment with you, please?"

"Yas'm, Miz Moon." He took in the harried appearance of the Ole Miss and waited for her to speak.

"I am concerned about Miss Orie. She's not eating, not sleeping, and not recovering." She paused and looked at his sad eyes.

"No ma'am, Miss Orie, she ain't fit a'tall."

"Tell Uncle Ned I will need to be driven to the hospital wards in Charlottesville this morning, and tell Martha we will need lunch on the trip. And pack water and apple cider. And a quilt in the carriage."

"Yas'm." So much sorrow, he thought. Broken hearts sometimes don't never mend. Mammy Jinny has her ways, but I loves her. Miss Orie sho' 'nough loved that young doctor, and now his sorry face done gone. I don't know what Miz Moon can do about it, but it ain't over until she say so.

By early afternoon, Anna Maria was at Charlottesville General Hospital, asking for Dr. Alston. When he was told Mrs. Moon was there and waiting for him, he headed immediately to the reception area, looking forward to the pleasure of seeing the lovely mother of his convalescing colleague. He saw her before she recognized him and was taken aback by the finger-drumming, anxious look of the still-beautiful woman.

He approached her quietly. "Good day to you, Mrs. Moon. I am Dr. Alston. It's a pleasure to see you again. What can I do for you?"

"Oh, Dr. Alston. I am so relieved to see you. May we speak in private?"

"Of course, dear lady. We can speak just down the hall in a meeting room. Please follow me." He briskly led the way down the corridor and opened the door to a small room, a former classroom. He took a chair for Mrs. Moon and one for himself, facing her.

Anna Maria swept her voluminous skirt aside and sat at the edge of her chair, all but trembling in her anxiety. She addressed him directly. "I am in great distress over my daughter. She is not at all well and declining as we speak."

"What! I am at a loss here. My last report from Dr. Andrews was that she was well and recovering her strength by the day. However, that was a month ago. If you please, tell me what has happened to her condition." *How could things go so wrong? Was Dr. John negligent after all that Dr. Orie had done for him? Impossible.*

"Since Dr. Andrews was last at Viewmont at the end of August, Orie has stopped eating, stays in bed, and roams the house at all hours of the night. She's lost all the weight she regained since coming home from the hospital and then some." Anna Maria paused.

"Why is this so? Did she overdo and relapse?"

"So…you don't know. Orie and Dr. Andrews were in love—at least Orie was in love with him. He abruptly broke off the relationship. Since that day, my daughter has been despondent. I realized yesterday she is not getting over her broken heart. She is dying, Dr. Alston."

"Surely not! She is a woman with extraordinary determination and skills. She has much to live for." He knew he was denying what Dr. Moon's own mother was telling him, but he kept seeing the radiant young woman in the halls as she attended the young soldiers.

"She is all that, but fragile nonetheless. She took to her bed with exhaustion after medical school, but rallied after a decision to assist her uncle in the Holy Land. She was fearless dealing with despotic sheiks and bandits. Now she is brave and uncomplaining but headed straight for death's door."

"So you attribute her disastrous decline to the breakup of her relationship with Dr. Andrews?"

"She admitted as much when she said Dr. John does not love her and will not marry her."

"He *said* those things?"

"Well, not in so many words, of course. The young man is a gentleman and the son of a minister, but he said he could not provide a life for her anywhere near Viewmont standards and is therefore not an appropriate husband for her. My daughter believes he never loved her and is using this excuse to be rid of her."

Dr. Alston shook his head with concern. "I will speak with him. I have worked with him since he took over Dr. Orie's Ward and know him to be hard-working and honest. There may be some misunderstanding, and maybe I can help. We need Dr. Orie back on staff. I will see him today and come to Viewmont as soon as tomorrow, at least to examine your daughter and make some medical decisions."

Anna Maria rose from her chair and held out her gloved hand to the doctor. "I am deeply in your debt, Dr. Alston, and feel a glimmer of hope where there was none."

He took her hand and pressed it lightly. "I thank you for coming to me. I will do all that I can and promise that I will tread carefully."

"Thank you, doctor."

Anna Maria went back to Viewmont with her heart less burdened. It was a start. Her prayers were being answered.

Dr. Alston sighed. What could he say to John Andrews, his col-league? Perhaps the initial attraction and sense of gratitude to Dr. Orie had worn off and he was trying to back away and doing it badly. Only slightly older than Dr. John, he was nevertheless in a senior position with degrees from Hampden-Sydney College, stud-ies at the University of Virginia, and a medical degree from New York University, plus longer medical practice. He understood the perverseness of the human heart, especially as found in someone only recently away from the supervision of his father and medical school regimen and far from home. Add to the mix the sudden bereavement of his two brothers, and it was little wonder that he should succumb to the charms and kindness of Dr. Orie. But that in no way meant he should *marry* the woman, no matter what he might have said in passion. He would tread very lightly.

Dr. Alston sought out Dr. John and asked him to stop by his ward before leaving the hospital. Dr. John agreed, but not without some hesitation. A second glance revealed sadness that was not ap-parent a month ago.

At the end of his shift, Dr. John went straight to Dr. Alston's ward and followed him to a small unoccupied room. They each took a chair, and Dr. Alston asked him about his out-of-ward pa-tient, Dr. Orie.

"She's well, and recovering her strength by the day." His voice was flat and his eyes downcast.

"I'm sorry to differ with you, but her mother was here to see me early this afternoon with disturbing news of an ominous decline in her health."

Dr. John suddenly looked alarmed. "What do you mean by that? Explain yourself, sir."

"She's showing signs of disintegration, brought on, according to her mother, by your absence. Apparently there had been an un-derstanding between you two, and since you announced the end of this relationship, her efforts to recover have been abandoned. Mrs. Moon is now fearful for her daughter's life."

Dr. John covered his face with his hands and groaned.

"So it's true you forsook her?"

He looked up and cried out, "I wanted to protect her, not harm her!"

"From what? From a doctor's care and friendship? You are cruel, sir."

"No, I loved her and wanted to marry her, but after seeing her at Viewmont, I knew I could not provide such a life for her. I'm not a fit husband for Mrs. Moon's daughter." His face was a picture of agony.

"I see. I will go to Viewmont tomorrow and see for myself the state of her health. Good evening to you, sir." Dr. Alston rose from his chair, left the room, and shut the door with vigor.

In the doctor's barracks that night, Dr. John prayed with an anguish he had not felt since the death of Robert. "Forgive me, Lord. Please help me undo the harm I have caused Orie."

In his sleep he suffered the torment of a nightmare in which he was unable to save the innocent life of a faithful princess. She was chased by swordsmen, thrown into a muddy ditch, laughed at by bystanders, and dragged behind a royal carriage. All the while, a voice from heaven thundered at him to *protect her, save her, love her.*

He awoke drained of strength and with remorse so relentless that it blotted out all hope for the day at hand and all the days to follow.

CHAPTER 10

PITY THE LOVERS

D r. Alston arrived at Viewmont on his horse the morning after he discussed Dr. Orie with John Andrews. Uncle Jacob greeted him at the door and ushered him into the entry hall before alerting Mammy Jinny.

"Miz Moon will be comin' right down, Dr. Alston, sir. She be waitin' for you. Miss Dr. Orie be a big worry for her."

Anna Maria's entrance down the staircase was almost immediate. "Come, sit with me before we go upstairs," she said, leading the doctor to the front sitting room with the large fireplace. Uncle Jacob returned with a silver service, which he placed on a side table decorated with a large vase of fresh flowers from the garden outside. There were steaming pots of coffee and tea with cream and sugar nearby. Anna Maria poured coffee for the doctor and tea for herself. She placed thin ginger cookies on a plate along with salted cucumbers.

"How was your travel here?" she asked with smile. *Be gracious— don't weep and wail like a demented soul.*

"As the morning is fine, I was glad to be outside and away from the Ward for a change. And the countryside is remarkably beautiful." He sipped his coffee and smiled at her. This was a pleasant departure from his usual busy and oftentimes grim rounds of seeing his patients, his stomach churning as he left them.

"As the mother of a doctor, I can well appreciate the need for a change of scenery from the hospital and the chance to be outside in God's glory. Nevertheless, I am also mindful of the state of my daughter's health and will admit to you that she is uppermost in my mind and your coming here today means more to me than I can ever express to you."

"As a colleague of Dr. Orie's and a fierce admirer, I will say openly that I will do whatever I can to help her."

"Thank you, sir." Anna Maria looked down at her folded hands and spoke softly. "Orie defies defining. As a girl growing up, she paid no heed to the fun and frolics available to her in this household. She loved her books and her father, who doted on her far beyond his other six children. She loved him only, but even for him, she refused to become a Christian, which broke his heart. It was not until after Edward died and she graduated from medical school and joined her uncle and his family in the Holy Land that she asked for baptism there. Actually, at the Pool of Siloam."

Dr. Alston smiled. "Oh yes, the healing waters for the medical college graduate."

"Yes, she has taken her brother Tom's place as the physician in the family. And since her baptism, she has served as a Christian medical missionary in her heart. During the years after her father's death, she endured the danger of traveling abroad alone and the complexities of, say, dealing with an amorous sheik without losing her life or taste for adventure. She joined the Medical Corps when the War broke out, and with a great-hearted dedication to the cause, she did her absolute best to treat and save or at least comfort those Boys on both sides of the battle who were in her care."

"I saw that myself," said Dr. Alston.

"But now she is defeated. I can only pray that the good Lord will put back in John's heart the feelings for Orie that were so patently clear to all when his visits here were almost as assured as the sun rising in the morning."

"Mrs. Moon, as I'm sure you remember, I was the last one to examine your daughter, and I released her into your care when her physical exhaustion was such that death could have overtaken her at that time. The punishing hours and emotional toll of the suffering and deaths of her patients had foreseeable consequences, but she overcame all of that, according to Dr. John and from what you have said. I'm really quite anxious to see her myself."

Anna Maria called in Uncle Jacob and asked him to fetch Cornelia to accompany Dr. Alston up the stairs to Orie's bedroom. She walked outside in the bright sunshine of the late September day, up the slope to Edward's grave, and prayed beside him for the health and happiness of their daughter, closing with *Please, God, spare Orie this heartbreak.*

Anna Maria walked away thinking new thoughts. She had liked John Andrews. Orie was the opposite of silly and frivolous, and she would not have loved an unworthy man. She could have married any man in Virginia, because no family would have turned down such a match. But she chose John Andrews, and even in the face of abandonment, she had not renounced her love for him.

When Dr. Alston came back downstairs, Uncle Jacob sent Cornelia to fetch Anna Maria, and she came quickly. They returned to the front sitting room, and Mammy Jinny soon appeared with a tray of ham sandwiches and a pitcher of cider chilled in the springhouse.

Anna Maria could not read the doctor's thoughts and gave up trying. "Well, sir, what do you think?"

"I agree that you acted properly when you came to the hospital yesterday to confer with me. She is grieving her love's rejection to the point of death. After the physical breakdown in August, this woman simply cannot sustain another such episode, albeit a breakdown this time driven by her emotions. I, too, fear for her life."

"What, then, shall we do?" Anna Maria, although vindicated by her call to the hospital for help, felt even more afraid now that the doctor agreed with her. She felt panic rise in her chest.

"I spoke with Dr. John last night. I confess I don't know the man. I had never met him before we met in the Wards, I don't know his family, and I'm not familiar with Shelby Medical College in Nashville. Dr. John gave me the impression that he had Dr. Orie's best interests at heart, but that may not be the truth. The Godwins in Charlottesville, who took in Dr. John's mortally wounded younger brother, were distant relatives and did not know him personally. Also, Dr. John enlisted two days before the battle in his brothers' regiment, the Fourth Alabama Infantry, and had not been called in Memphis when he was a practicing physician. He was not appointed a medical officer until his commanding officer at the field hospital at Manassas appointed him because of the immediate and dire need of doctors, and he was already treating the wounded with his personal set of surgical tools. He was clearly a trained physician. I wonder why he enlisted as a regular soldier."

Anna Maria's panic subsided. "You have a cynical outlook for such a young man," she observed.

"Also, I know for a fact that he borrowed a rather large sum of money offered by Dr. Orie when he needed to accompany his brother's body home to Alabama for burial."

"Mercy, that sounds like a Christian use of money to me. But Orie never shared that story with me or her brother, which is not like her."

"War turns right and wrong upside down, I'm afraid," said Dr. Alston. "In wartime, the rules order men to kill. Lying, stealing, and destroying enemy property can win praises and medals. Men believed to be honorable can take advantage of the chaos of war and do things they would never do in peacetime. In short, emotions are high and judgment often faulty in the midst of war."

"What, then, should we do in this fallen world?" *Was he just so young he could no longer see the good in mankind? Or was she getting old and too naive to believe the real horrors of the world?*

"There are things in her favor, such as the fact that she has not succumbed to disease in her weakened condition. But we must treat the despondency, and surgery has no answer for that." Dr. Alston gave Anna Maria time to reflect on this reality.

"I must tell you that the whole household has tried everything we know to help Orie overcome her heartbreak, but instead we've seen her accept the loss of John's love with a deathly calm, and nothing detracts her from this determination."

"This is not unheard of, unfortunately. What I will do is report her condition as I saw it today to Dr. John. I will have to make a judgment as to whether he should be involved at all after that, but the risk is worth taking, I do believe."

"Then go and do what you think best. And I wish you Godspeed, sir." She offered her hand, and he took it with great solemnity.

He rode back up Carter's Mountain and down into Charlottesville with his mind roiling. Much depended on Dr. John's reaction to the news of the very real crisis the man himself had brought about. He therefore must read the man's mind and not be fooled by possible false appearances and lying words. Orie's wealth could be the object of Dr. John's efforts to gain control of the fragile woman's emotions. The thought of such evil made the very skin on the back of his neck blaze red hot with anger.

CHAPTER 11
DECISION

It was dusk and chilly when Dr. Alston arrived back in Charlottesville. He walked into the hospital and asked an orderly if Dr. Andrews was still there.

"Yes sir, Dr. Alston. He told me this morning to send you to him as soon you came to the hospital today. He's waiting to see you."

"Thank you for the message. I'm on my way right now." He hurried toward Dr. John's ward, thankful that he didn't have to go out looking for him after a very long day. He found him at the bedside of a bandaged soldier, taking his pulse.

When Dr. John looked up, Dr. Alston pointed to the conference room they shared the day before and motioned for him to meet there. Dr. John nodded in agreement. Dr. Alston found two chairs at a table and tried to gather his thoughts while he waited.

Dr. John joined him within minutes. "How is she?" he asked.

"Despondent. Morbid despondency."

"I'm sorry. And I'm afraid I don't know what to do. My father would have me pray and read the Good Book, and I've done that, but I cannot do what I must do."

"Which is?"

"Ask for a transfer and leave her." He saw the expression on Dr. Alston's face and added, "Because I love her."

69

"The hell you say. You are talking utter nonsense. There is a woman, a splendid woman, who is at the moment dying for the love of you, and you turn your back on her. And you say you love her. That is not love, it's the vilest kind of hatred." Dr. Alston's sardonic tone threw Dr. John into a dismayed appeal.

"I cannot marry her. She'd be throwing away all chance of happiness. At first my love for her was like the taste of nectar and ambrosia, and the more I feasted of it, the more satisfying—nay, blissful—her company became, and there was no surfeit. On the contrary, I could never have enough of seeing her, hearing her, and, yes, tasting her kisses. Such bliss as that does not last, but this did. My higher self finally set me to rights, forcing me to face reality. I am a simple country minister's son who has been trained to doctor the sick and injured. The plantation house, the servants, the slaves in the tobacco fields—these are foreign to me. The wide, flower-strewn path we were on would soon narrow into a bitter, rocky, thorny trail that ends at the top of a cliff. I cannot let that happen. Yet each hour apart from her sears me with anguish that only grows worse."

"What would Dr. Orie say if you told her these things?"

"I already told her I was not fit to be her husband."

"And what did she say?"

"That she would not marry a man such as that."

"Do you suppose she meant she would not marry a man who did not want to be her husband?"

"All that is beside the point. I am not willing to marry a woman unless I believe I could give her a good life and make her happy."

"It seems to me you are leaving Dr. Orie out of this discussion. You have left her for over a month now. Is she happy? Even with all her family there and the servants and mansion and food and all that money can buy. Is she happy?"

"No, I hear that she is not," said Dr. John.

"And what is missing from her life? You alone. Think, man. She left that life to minister to the Arabs in the Holy Land and again to serve the wounded and sick soldiers in the Confederate hospital. Why would she not do the same to live with the only man she has apparently ever loved? Why do you think so little of her that she would of necessity cling to the old life at Viewmont? Do you love the woman herself or only the one surrounded by the wealth and pleasures of Viewmont? Can you separate her from Viewmont as she herself has done?"

"But I'm the man, the oldest son. It's my responsibility to look ahead and make decisions that are best for everyone, not just my wishes and wants."

Dr. Alston rested his head in his hands while Dr. John looked on. "I am really tired and I have patients who need me right now in this hospital. I will see them before I go to bed. Tomorrow, tell me what you will do about Dr. Orie. Either you or I must ride out to Viewmont and tell Mrs. Moon and Dr. Orie what you decide to do. Will you ask for an assignment elsewhere or will you return to Dr. Orie in friendship? Friendship that may or may not result in marriage. Goodnight to you, sir."

Dr. John watched him walk away and close the door with the click of a latch. The dilemma has to end, he thought, agreeing with Dr. Alston. He had to make the decision he had so far been unable to make. For better or worse, he had to decide.

CHAPTER 12

PRAYERS

Dr. John went to bed wishing it were all over. The attempt to relate Bible verses to his situation with Orie set his head spinning. He thought about what his mother would say to him if she were alive. Mary Drucilla Horton had married the Reverend Andrews at the age of eighteen, and she died at thirty-five. She was the mother of five, and when she died her youngest was four years old and her oldest fifteen. John remembered her as gentle and kind, always busy with her children and church work, happy being the wife of a minister. What would she have told him other than to pray and study the Bible? And to be kind and have courage, because God would show him the way.

John lived in Nashville while attending medical college a few years after his mother died, and after graduation he lived with her two businessman brothers in Memphis during his first year as a practicing physician. No one in his family had ever set foot on a Virginia tobacco plantation.

His mild-mannered father would say the same thing as his mother, but his father had never faced a situation like this, daring to propose marriage to a woman completely above and beyond his economic and social class. What would nineteen-year-old William say to him, or twenty-one-year-old Robert if they were still alive?

John had no one to talk to about this decision.

Yes he did. *Orie.*

John slept all night long for the first time since away from Viewmont trying so hard not to think about Orie Russell Moon.

When he awoke at daybreak, he asked Dr. Alston to oversee his ward and rode a horse up the familiar road over Carter's Mountain and down to Viewmont on the Hardware River. When he approached the long driveway to Viewmont's entrance, he dug his heels against the horse's side and began to gallop up the driveway. Uncle Ned heard him coming and ran out of the stable to see who was coming at a gallop to the Main House. When he saw that it was Dr. John, he waved his hat and yelled, "Hallo!"

Dr. John waved back and slowed down as he reached the open entrance gate, and Uncle Ned waited for him to arrive at the top of the driveway, then helped him down and took the horse. "I done missed you, Dr. John. I expeck the others have too." His smile was broad.

John shook his hand and thanked him for the welcome, feeling more than bit like the undeserving Prodigal Son. Uncle Jacob came to the door and ushered him in, smiling too, but maintaining his dignity as he led him into the front parlor. Uncle Jacob called for Cornelia, who startled him by appearing immediately from behind the hall door. "Go fetch the Ole Miss," he whispered to her. She practically took flight running up the stairs.

The young man who had grown up in parsonages deep in rural Alabama thought to himself, *I'm home.*

Then they all heard it. A scream from upstairs. From Orie's bedroom. For five uncomfortable minutes they waited. Finally, Anna Maria came down the stairs with her customary poise and grace. John had remained seated all the while, feeling that he had lost the right to dash up those stairs and be by Orie's side. Others who had been faithful to her were there instead of him.

Anna Maria greeted John with tentative warmth, clasping his hand with both of hers. "Orie is awake now and wishes to see you.

She has not been at all well, but you're the doctor and can use your own judgment." She smiled wanly at her small joke, and John took some courage from it.

He walked upstairs as if in a dream where time moves in slow motion. He knocked on the door. "Orie?" he whispered.

"Come in, John." She was sitting up in her four-poster bed, propped up by pillows and wearing a creamy silk bed jacket over her gown. Matilda the cat stared at John as if he were an intruder.

He approached her in a restrained rush. "I'm so sorry, Orie. I was wrong to leave the way I did. I was so afraid I would bring harm to you, knowing I could not offer you much beyond a roof over your head and all of my love."

"It's all right, John. I've had time to think and I take it to heart that you love me. Maybe we shall never marry, but I've lived away from Viewmont and have not missed the splendor, and I have been away from you, and I have missed you. I can't say any more than that."

"You don't need to, Orie. My mother always told me that God would show me the way, and I am back here with you. My fears for you were hurtful, and I beg your forgiveness. I lacked courage in myself and faith in you."

"John, the scream that you heard? It came from me. When Cornelia burst into the room to tell me that you were downstairs, the scream came unbidden. Whether from fright or joy, I cannot say. What I could not live with was to never see you again. And now that has not happened. That's all I asked. But I can go no further. I'm tired."

"All right, Orie, my…may I say it? Orie, my love?"

"Yes, but you must go now. I am tired." She closed her eyes.

John backed away with his eyes on her as if he feared never seeing her again. He shut the door gently and slowly made his way down the stairs and into the sitting room, where Anna Maria was waiting.

"She's tired," he said.

"Yes, we know," she said. "It will take time, John. She may... never trust you, you must know that."

"And I must learn to trust myself as well. I love her more than my own life, but fear for our future robbed me of courage. I am ashamed."

"Go now, John, but come back soon. Pray for courage."

He nodded and took his leave.

Anna Maria sat down, alone and exhausted. Love is a glorious burden, she thought. Her marriage to Edward had been arranged by her loving and shrewd childless stepfather, Captain Jack Harris. In his will he left Viewmont to her, his openly favorite stepchild, born at Viewmont after the death of her father, so she never knew a father other than the captain. He left his business to his intelligent and capable nephew Edward Harris Moon. The ploy worked. Edward asked for Anna Maria's hand in marriage and she accepted. Together they enjoyed a grand home as well as prosperous business interests. She liked and respected Edward and soon came to love him. Even now, eight long years after his death, Anna Maria grieved the loss of Edward in her life and all that he had meant to Viewmont and the community at large. Meanwhile, she and her son Ike strived to maintain Viewmont. There was War in the land and she knew not what lay ahead.

God seemed to have different plans for Orie—and for all of them.

CHAPTER 13

PATIENCE

As much time as he could get off, John Andrews took it to ride out to Viewmont and visit Orie. The frequency of his visits matched that in August, but there were differences. Orie was frailer, and walks with John resembled nothing so much as two old people holding each other up as they struggled to traverse a field under a bright October sky. There was no evidence of innocent new love replete with teasing words, soft touches, and spontaneous kisses landing on an upturned face.

No, Orie and John were careful with each other. Tender love was clear, but also a hesitation to touch or speak. Contentment not to be apart was enough.

Color was returning to Orie's face, and added weight filled in the hollows of her now less gaunt face. John marked every new sign of Orie's returning strength and took to timing and measuring their walks to the well house, the stable, the barn, the blacksmith's forge, and the apple orchard with the watch Billie had given him on the Manassas battlefield before he died. Orie, not forgetting her training as a medical scientist, did the same with the gold watch her father had given her. As the breezes blew warm and then chilly, John and Anna Maria fussed over the proper apparel for

76

Orie, both of them anxious that she avoid pneumonia, a common cause of death in patients weak from illness of any kind.

John's greatest ally was Anna Maria, who saw in him her daughter's choice, although Orie was far from well and would possibly never be able to return John's feelings in a way other than her present passive acceptance of his presence. Anna Maria wept for them while she prayed in the privacy of her bedroom at night.

Ike was nearby in the fields or at the dinner table, but always occupied by his own worries and work load. For the most part, the four sisters steered clear of Orie as well as Orie with John. Anna Maria overheard Eddie whisper to Mollie that she never wanted to fall in love. Orie's inconsolable weeks in bed left her youngest sister with a very dark impression of the throes of heartbreak. Colie, from a distance, saw Orie's anguish as highest drama, and took note of *true* romance's compelling power.

Only Anna Maria sympathized with Orie and grieved with her over her loss and wounded spirit. An affair of the heart was the coin of the realm for an "Ole Miss" like Anna Maria, who ruled Viewmont with quintessential Barclay grace and charm, and had an inherent beauty whether she was young or old, sick or well, happy or unhappy. There were cousins, sisters, nieces, and nephews with stories of love lost and sometimes gained. Anna Maria was always the first to know and the last to forget when it came to romances and matchmaking. She looked forward to five weddings at Viewmont and five sons-in-law to watch grow into their prime and, with her daughters, fill the house with children. Anna Maria ached to see her tribe increase. She and Edward had done their part. Now she was a bystander with a quiver full of arrows she fully intended to use.

The arrows, happily, were the well-worn ones she had always favored: the patience of love, the reliance of God in their lives, and the restorative power of physical well-being. With October's chill came heartier appetites, and Anna Maria was able to tempt her daughter with Martha's savory soups and stews made with venison, turkey, pork, and chicken. Fruit pies, puddings, and cakes were there for the taking, and corn, beans, squash, and greens were piled on her plate. Longer walks contributed to a zest for mealtime and deeper sleep at night.

When Orie became restless with boredom when John was away, Anna Maria asked Ike to start sending sick and injured slaves for Orie to treat, as well as neighboring women and family members, as she had done before signing up for duty at the sprawling Confederate Charlottesville General Hospital. The hospital had grown to a capacity of five hundred beds, and she had been one of between fifteen and fifty doctors coping with the trainloads of sick and wounded soldiers after the Battle of Manassas. While she was on duty there, her world shrank to what could be accomplished from one hour to the next.

Orie's patients at Viewmont came to her with burns, broken bones, lacerations, fevers, and diarrhea, along with women's complaints and children's diseases. With October's colder nights and days of rainy chill, respiratory illnesses became common, and Orie's academic interest in cardiac and pulmonary diseases helped her with diagnosis and treatment. Soon people were asking for her every day, and the invalid's robe was cast off in favor of her unadorned full-length dark cotton print dresses.

John's visits, no longer conducted at Orie's bedside, were instead robust walkabouts as they shared news about John's sick and wounded soldiers at the ward and Orie's patients, their treatments and resolutions. They were again becoming colleagues as well as companions.

"Forty percent of the Boys still in the Wards are there due to gunshot wounds, and amputations go on every day and night," John said.

"Dearest, that is too sad to contemplate," Orie replied.

"But the fine thing is that artificial limbs made by G. W. Wells in Charlottesville are considered more handsome than ones from France. Isn't that a wonderful thing?"

"Indeed it is, John. It's surprising, too. Uncle James and his family and I resided in Paris for several months on our way home from the Holy Land, and we found their art as well as their crafts to be of the finest quality. In fact, the Parisians were tiresome in their conceit over the Americans about every little thing. So I do find pleasure in that story."

John noted that their conversations were becoming quite lively, with few subjects off-limits to Orie. Pleasure and even laughter had found them again; they had become friends who enjoyed each other's company beyond all else. It was Orie who finally touched his lips with her fingers and let herself be drawn into his arms with a new passion that broke through her self-imposed barrier to their former joy.

The question of their love for each other was never raised thereafter.

CHAPTER 14

IKE MEETS THE ANDREWS AND HORTONS

Time was pressing. Orie returned to Charlottesville General Hospital in late October. She was welcomed back by her colleague Dr. Alston and officially by Dr. John Lawrence Cabell, professor of anatomy and surgery at the University of Virginia, called upon to manage the facility. Orie was named Superintendent of Nurses.

The position pleased her to the extent that she was an efficient and knowledgeable supervisor, but her relations with the mostly male corps of nurses were often fractious. She lived for the daily contact with John, and her hours were much more regular than those of an attending physician. When their time off coincided, John would hire a carriage and go home with her to Viewmont.

Soon, both were ordered to report to Richmond for work in the Confederate hospitals where the war-wounded count was rising by the day. John argued his case for marriage right away, and Orie said yes before he finished his proposal. They laughed in their joy and embraced. "No more separations," they vowed. "We will live together and die together."

Upon hearing the news, Anna Maria was in joyful tears and immediately began planning for the "right-away wedding" to take place on November 28 at Viewmont. First she called Ike into the study.

"What is it, Mama? Is something wrong?"

"No, son, something is right. Please sit down and hear me out. We must step quickly, because there is much to be done"

Ike, worn out from the long hours and worries of the tobacco harvest, wanted only to rest from his labors. "What do I have to do?"

"First things first, dear. Orie and John are getting married. On November twenty-eighth. Here at Viewmont."

"That is good news, and Mag and I will help out." Ike's face beamed and he relaxed in his chair. *Parties ahead and the women will handle it.*

"Of course you and Mag will be a great part of the wedding. But son, we must contact John's family and invite them to the wedding and have their permission to go forward with the wedding plans. After all, John is the oldest son and we must let his family know their plans."

"Mama, is a trip necessary? Why not just send a telegram?" Ike frowned at his mother.

"That's not the way we do things at Viewmont, Ike. Things have to be done properly or there may be regrets down the road."

"Mama, there's a war going on and Reverend Andrews has already lost two sons in battle, and Orie and John have been reassigned to a Confederate hospital in Richmond. Things can't always be done 'properly.'"

"Isaac, this must be done. I want you to take the train from Charlottesville to Florence, Alabama, and meet with John's father and with his brother James and sister, Elizabeth. The boy is a young man, but his sister is still a girl. Then go to Memphis and meet John's mother's brothers. John's side of the family must at least be introduced to you, because you are Orie's brother and the only male member of her immediate family. They will become part of our family on November twenty-eighth. Nothing is more important right now than to help Orie and John start married life in the good graces of both families."

"All right, Mama. I'll go and meet our newest relations." Ike kissed his mother on the cheek and left her writing notes to herself on what had to be done in the coming too few days. It occurred to him that he would be better off away from Viewmont than in the eye of the hurricane he could see coming. He would pack today and ask Uncle Ned to drive him to the train station tomorrow. Mag could come with him in the carriage to the train station for company, and they could let Shep come along for the ride, too. When Edward's Shep had died not long after Edward passed away, Anna Maria found a small sheepdog on a nearby farm and brought it home to Ike. He called the pup "Sheppy," but now the small, short-haired, black, tan, and white sheepdog was called Shep and Ike was his master. The field hands in their gossip told each other that "Mista Isaac had no chir'en on account 'a his heart was onliest big enough for Shep and Miz Mag." Ike and his Shep were inseparable.

Ike waved good-bye to Mag and Uncle Ned and Shep from the train and settled in. The Virginia Midland Railroad ride to Florence was a long one, and Ike was concerned about a possible Union raid against the train. Otherwise, Ike rather enjoyed watching the changing scenery outside as the train rumbled south, and it was a rest after the months of work overseeing the tobacco fields. He would, however, rather have rested at home in front of the fireplace with Mag sewing nearby and Shep at his feet.

When Ike arrived in Florence, he hired a driver to take him to an inn and sent a message to the Reverend Andrews telling of his arrival. This was done, and soon he was at the Methodist-Episcopal parsonage knocking at the door.

The housekeeper opened the door and invited "Mister Isaac Moon" into the parlor, where Reverend Andrews was absorbed in reading a newsletter of sorts. He stood up, shook hands with the visitor, and welcomed him to his home and to Florence. "I have received telegrams from both my son and his future mother-in-law and I am most pleased to have this opportunity to meet the brother of my son's intended wife. Please sit down, sir."

Ike did so and, looking around, commented on the gracious atmosphere of the town and the warm welcome of his host.

"I'm sorry my wife, Winnifred, is not here to meet you. She's at a church conference in Birmingham leading our delegation from Florence. I shall join them after services on Sunday."

The housekeeper returned with cups of hot tea and shortbread cookies, then disappeared into the back of the large house.

"How is my son getting along, Mr. Moon, and what kind of reports are you hearing about the battles in Virginia and elsewhere?" Reverend Andrews asked.

"Please call me Isaac, sir."

"Certainly, if you wish, Mr. Moon," the reverend said.

Ike expressed sorrow over the deaths of Billie and Robert, and the minister thanked him and his family for making it possible for John to accompany Robert's body home for burial.

Both men were practiced in the art of conversation and talk flowed freely, especially for Reverend Andrews, who had questions about the Moons. Ike brought up his uncle James Barclay's travels to the Holy Land as a medical missionary for the Disciples of Christ Church with his wife, two sons, and younger daughter. Ike made a point of telling the reverend that Orie had been baptized by her uncle in the Pool of Siloam after joining them.

Upon hearing these things, the older man's face glowed with interest and his regard for Ike increased visibly. He himself had never been to the Holy Land, or to a foreign land as a missionary, but regarded where he had been placed in life, namely northern Alabama, as a rich mission field.

"Very true, I'm sure," Ike replied, respectful of the man's experiences in the far-distant-from-Virginia Deep South.

"But of course, the Andrews family came from the Midlands, England, to Philadelphia, a city renowned for commerce, the arts, and scholars My great-grandfather went to college in Philadelphia and traveled to London to be ordained into the Church of England. As an ordained priest, he became rector of the Episcopal Church in Yorktown and was a professor of natural philosophy and mathematics at the College of William and Mary."

Ike straightened up in his chair, thinking such details would be important to his mother. "Sir, it warms my heart to know that your family has roots in Virginia and that you are part of the brave settlers who opened up this country for commerce and settlement."

"As well as to spread the gospel, Mr. Moon."

"Yes, of course, Reverend, sir." He would not report things he *didn't* say to his mother.

"My great-grandfather also served as chaplain to the troops of George Washington's Continental Army. His son John Andrews was a soldier of note in the Continental Army. I am named after the chaplain and my son John after the soldier. They were magnificent patriots. Indeed, I was proud of my own three sons for enlisting in the Confederate Army and marching against those who would dare invade our ancestral land and bring such destruction."

Ike was swayed, thinking this family was worthy in every way possible to be linked with the Moons. "Without the aid of Virginia's former sons, I fear we would have lost the battle at Manassas and already be in the hands of our enemies, and we thank you." His thoughts touched again on his older sister. Much as he had always looked up to Orie, he was grateful to her now for her choice of a husband from this family. He was also humbled by the wisdom of his mother, the product of a finishing school for girls in Richmond, for insisting that he meet John's people. She had been correct, as always.

He was later introduced to Elizabeth, who was doing her schoolwork and said she would rather visit with Mr. Moon than continue endless pages of arithmetic. Ike, used to the antics of his four younger sisters, welcomed into his life his newest little sister the minute she turned her eyes on him. She was a pretty girl with freckles, ginger-colored hair, and gray-green eyes.

"I've already lost big two brothers, you know," she said. "Something tells me you are going to be a jolly new brother."

"That is exactly as it should be, and a man cannot have enough little sisters, especially one as pretty and smart as you," said Ike, to her delight.

"How many sisters do you have?" she asked.

"I have one older sister, Orie, who is marrying your brother, and then I have four younger sisters, all older than you except for Eddie, who is ten." By the time he left the house, he felt that he really did have a new little sister and was pleased by the fact.

Ike went back to the inn in a much better frame of mind, looking forward to seeing the child Elizabeth again and spending some time with James, John's youngest brother. The next morning he slept late, and drank his coffee and ate his eggs, grits, and bacon at the inn. Afterward, he set out walking, for as a country gentleman, he liked nothing more than to walk the sidewalks of a town and look into store windows. He entered a shop selling ladies' wear and toiletries and bought a dark plaid woolen cape and matching warm bonnet for Mag, picturing her rosy cheeks and big eyes looking out from under her new bonnet. For Mag and his mother and sisters, he added cut-glass crystal bottles of gardenia-scented perfume and ordered the items to be shipped by train to Charlottesville. It occurred to him that Federal troops might stop the train and confiscate the goods inside, but the thought was not serious and dropped from his mind.

He supped that evening with Reverend Andrews, Elizabeth, and James. Elizabeth, shy at first, let James talk about the patriotism of the Alabama boys quitting Florence Wesleyan University by the droves as they signed up for the Confederate States Army. The faculty members, too, were resigning their positions and joining the CSA. The college was closing and would house CSA soldiers instead of students in the dormitories.

"How many students did the college have before the War broke out?" Ike asked.

James did not know, and Reverend Andrews spoke up. "Florence Wesleyan started out as LaGrange College, founded by the Methodist-Episcopal Church in 1830 across the Tennessee River on LaGrange Mountain, but was relocated, to a major extent, to Florence and renamed in 1855. It started out with a hundred and sixty students. The small original college became a military academy. Entrance requirements for Florence Wesleyan University were high."

"If you don't mind, I would like to know what they are. I am managing Viewmont's tobacco plantation with the help of my mother, but I've always wanted to be a teacher."

"The admissions requirements lean heavily on the classical model of education."

"Very good." Ike nodded.

"The requirements start with 'an acquaintance with English grammar, arithmetic, geography, and Latin and Greek grammar in addition to the ability to translate substantial parts of Caesar's *Gallic Wars*, Virgil's *Aeneid*, Jacob's or Felton's *Greek Reader*, and at least one of Xenophon's *Anabasis*.'"

"That's a high bar to qualify for admittance, indeed," said Ike.

"And rightly so," said the Reverend. "LaGrange-Wesleyan alumni have become state governors, military generals, members of the Protestant clergy, and teachers. Teaching, as you should know, is the first profession, because all other professions require teachers first," he added with a smile.

Ike agreed, smiling back.

Reverend Andrews continued. "I am proud of my great-grandfather, who was both an ordained clergyman and a professor at William and Mary, but as a Methodist-Episcopal minister, my administrative duties and my parish take all my time. I enjoyed ties with Florence Wesleyan and spoke there at times, but I am not on the faculty, alas. And you, sir, did you attend college?"

"Yes sir, I have a law degree from the University of Virginia and have passed the bar, but I am busy with the tobacco crop and I help with teaching at home. My sisters have all been tutored by me as well as by our parents and the tutors my father brought to Viewmont over the years. Orie, your son's fiancée, grew up with a bookish nature and spent a year at Troy Female Seminary in New York before medical school in Philadelphia."

"I see," said Reverend Andrews, mentally discomfited by the idea that John's wife would be so unlike his mother, a woman who loved her home and family above all else. He hoped John understood the immensity of such a choice for his life partner. He knew she was a doctor, but thought of her more as a glorified nurse from a planter's family in time of War rather than as an educated surgeon. Details about Orie from John had been largely absent and the engagement happened almost overnight, or so it had seemed to John's father.

"Papa, I would like to go away to school like Miss Orie did, but not up North," said Elizabeth, thinking out loud.

James laughed. "Why would you want to go away to school? You hate schoolwork."

"Because I want to live in a big house with lots of girls, who would be like sisters to me." James stopped laughing. He was as kind-hearted as a big brother could be, but he didn't often think about how lonely it was for Elizabeth since their mother died. Their stepmother was a "fine woman," as they say, but with her stepchildren she was distant, and she was often away attending to church duties as the wife of a minister. With an always busy father immersed in his studies and church responsibilities and three older brothers with their own lives and friends, Elizabeth usually had only the somber housekeeper to keep her company and look after her. "Mama Winnifred" was not the warm, happy woman their mother had been.

Ike broke the silence. "You must come to Viewmont to visit when this War is finished, Elizabeth. You will learn to love Orie and Lottie, Colie, Mollie, and Eddie. They will be your sisters."

"Can I, Papa? I like their names. I think they must all be pretty and I would like to be their sister. Will they like me, Ike?"

"Elizabeth, you must call him Mr. Moon," said her papa.

"Nay, sir, I told her last night that I will soon be her new big brother and to call me Ike, which is what my mother and sisters call me at home. And yes, they will like you very much, Elizabeth," said Ike, turning toward the girl.

"If you wish, sir," said the Reverend. "But only in the family, not out in public, Elizabeth."

"Yes, Papa," said Elizabeth, secretly thrilled that the visitor had taken up for her.

At the end of the evening, the small family wished him Godspeed on his visit with the Horton brothers in Memphis and a safe journey back to Viewmont. Before Ike left, Reverend Andrews led him into the study and pressed upon him a tin box containing Confederate currency and gold coins. "This is for my son as a wedding gift. Please see that it gets to him yourself."

Next was Memphis and the illustrious Horton brothers. Ike had been to Memphis with his father on business trips, and although he didn't see himself as cut out for business, he liked seeing the Mississippi River and steamboats and having visits with Uncle J.N. Moon, his father's brother and business partner.

He found lodging after the Memphis & Charleston Railroad ride across Alabama and Tennessee and sent a message from the hotel to the Horton brothers, announcing his arrival. The two gentlemen invited Ike to their house for dinner in the evening after their day's work, which left him with time to seek out J.N. Moon, his uncle.

His uncle, thinner and with gray hair, welcomed Ike warmly into his office near the Mississippi River waterfront. "You're looking fine, boy, and I know your father would be proud of you. How is your mother? And your sisters? And Viewmont?" Finally he asked what the occasion was that found him in Memphis.

Ike reported the news about Orie's upcoming wedding, and his uncle had one question.

"Is he a good man?"

"We think so, yes, and without a doubt he loves Orie."

J.N. seemed satisfied, and he filled his pipe with tobacco. His office windows overlooked the river, and Ike took the pause to watch the busy waterfront with barges and steamboats arriving amid shouts and sounds he could hear through the closed windows.

His aromatic pipe lit, J.N. talked about how he missed his brother Edward and lamented the loss of Edward's business acumen and connections. "There was nobody to match your father's influence in the cotton market. I heard tell you have a law degree from the University of Virginia. Are you going to use it in the pursuit of your father's business interests?"

"No sir, J.N. I'm tied down seeing to the tobacco crops at Viewmont and mighty worried about the War coming on. It would take an army to protect Viewmont, and Virginia doesn't have enough soldiers and cannons to protect Richmond, I'm afraid."

"I greatly fear you are correct, Isaac, and Memphis is going to get hit hard soon. We are a Confederate stronghold right now, but the Union Army, sure as I'm sitting here, is going to come down the Mississippi and take Memphis by storm as well as Vicksburg and New Orleans, and cut off supplies to the Confederate states."

Ike had hoped to hear better things from people far from Virginia, but businessmen had to know the lay of the land or lose out, and businessmen knew all about supply lines. So did Ike, when it came to tobacco getting to London and revenue making its way back to Virginia.

Ike hired a carriage to go shopping on Beale Street, but when he got there, he felt the need of Mag's fashion advice as to what he should have, so he hesitated. But when he saw a heavy woolen cloak in a plaid similar to the one on the cape and bonnet he had gotten for Mag, he made the purchase for himself and ordered it to be shipped to Charlottesville. They would make a handsome pair in their carriage going to wedding events as well as upcoming Thanksgiving and Christmas parties. He and Mag could surely come to Memphis in the spring to do further shopping.

That evening at the Horton's, the talk was of War, rumors of War, and again War. Ike thought about the Beale Street haberdasheries and how he probably should have made more purchases while Memphis was protected by the Confederate Army. Who knew what springtime would bring?

Otherwise, the Hortons were pleased at the news of the upcoming wedding of their nephew, although still saddened by the deaths of Billie and Robert at Manassas. The only good thing was that Mary Horton Andrews had died before the two boys were taken from her. That was small consolation, though, for the two Horton brothers, who had lost their sister and two bright young nephews within the space of six years. Worse, the War had barely begun. May the Lord have mercy on them all.

And so the occasion, meant to be a happy one as two families began getting to know each other, was also an occasion to explain the perils each was facing. Now the single-minded Ike, having thrown the full force of his strength and concentration into overseeing the cultivation, harvesting, and shipping of the hogsheads of tobacco down the James River and Kanawha Canal to Richmond, understood that Virginia was not the Union Army's only target. But by the grace of the Good Lord, he had succeeded in what he had to do. This time he had gotten the tobacco to Richmond.

In Memphis, however, no one could be distracted from the talk of Union blockades on the Atlantic and Gulf of Mexico and

Union armies appearing in steamboats down the Mississippi. The South's trade could be strangled and leave the merchants and planters destitute. No matter that one Southern boy defending his homeland was worth three or four Union soldiers marching for pay, the South was no match when it came to industrial power, financial strength, and numbers of men available to enlist and train.

No one from the Horton or Andrews families would be going to Viewmont for the wedding. November 28 was too soon to make plans, and the men were fearful of Federal attacks on trains before winter set in. They knew what was coming.

They all sent their best wishes to the engaged couple, along with prayers for their safety as they relocated to Confederate hospitals in Richmond, and prayers for a happy life together. In addition to the tin box of Confederate currency and gold coins from Reverend Andrews in Florence, Ike was asked to bear similar gifts to John from the Horton brothers as well as from J. N. Moon.

Ike was touched by their generous gifts in this time of economic uncertainty, but when he packed the wedding gifts in his suitcase, he began to worry. He feared the worst from the enemy, from sabotaged trains to belongings being confiscated from the "rebel population." Oh, how he missed Mag and Shep and Viewmont.

Departing from Memphis and viewing himself as a walking bank vault, he hunched over in the damp chill of November and never let his suitcase out of his sight, suspicious of any man who landed even a casual eye on his person or suitcase. Afraid to doze off, he did anyway, awakened with a start when the train's rhythm was altered in some fashion. He gradually succumbed to weariness and slept in ever longer segments of time. Briefly, he forgot about the tins of currency and gold coins in his suitcase and breathed easily, thinking about such things as the desire for a cup of hot coffee and a plate of potatoes and pork. Then he remembered, and his head ached from worry, and he fell back asleep with nightmares of running from Union soldiers intent on despoiling him of his future brother-in-law's wedding funds.

Time passed. Nothing untoward happened. The train chugged along, drawing ever closer to his Charlottesville stop. He listened to the conversations of men speaking about the prices of grain and cotton and the illnesses of relatives and troubles with machinery and work animals. The sounds of travel droned on.

By the time Ike stepped off the train in Charlottesville, his spirits were soothed and his confidence was back. Uncle Ned, Mag, and Shep were there to greet him. He had wedding gifts for John and pleasant stories of their new family additions as well as the visit with Uncle J. N. Moon. He was home. Everything would be all right.

CHAPTER 15

THE UPCOMING WEDDING

The wedding overtook the War as the most talked about topic in the halls of Albemarle County for a few heady weeks. The Barclays, Moons, and Diggeses heard the news, inwardly digested the news, and suddenly found time to visit Viewmont. Who was Dr. John Summerfield Andrews? Would this marriage advance or detract from the prestige of their fair Virginia family? Most of all, everyone wanted to meet the man who had won Orie's heart.

In the meantime, Orie was occupied with her work at Charlottesville General Hospital, and at home Anna Maria was making a thousand decisions without any apparent interest in such details on Orie's part. Anna Maria was also taking action on any number of things that could have ground the silky-smooth wedding march to a halt.

Lottie and Mag helped entertain the stream of cousins, aunts, uncles, nieces, and nephews who wanted to meet the fortunate suitor and observe the bride-to-be, while Anna Maria made plans for food and entertainment, with Martha in charge of the kitchen. Uncle Jacob reigned over the house. Uppermost in Anna Maria's mind was a trousseau for Orie. Rebecca, the daughter of Uncle Jacob and Mammy Jinny, was a seamstress, but there just wasn't time to accomplish all that was needed.

"I would have liked a spring wedding in early June," Anna Maria said to Mag, "with time to introduce John to the family and parties for Orie to enjoy before taking on the burdens of a household."

"Truly, War or no War, Orie would not want a wedding any different from what you are planning, and the War conveniently covers up her inclination to simply work until the day she marries her love. You are holding the family together, and nothing is more important." Mag later told Ike that Anna Maria was a "masterful mistress of Viewmont."

"Thank you, dear heart, I couldn't do without you," Anna Maria said, giving Mag a kiss on the cheek. "And Ike has become John's best man and champion since his trip to visit John's family. I had no idea of the prominence of John's family here in Virginia at the time of the Revolution, and our relatives have come to regard John with great esteem. John's family connections to the Episcopal Church, the College of William and Mary, and George Washington's Continental Army have been met with interest in the family. None of us had any idea."

Ike joined his wife and mother and sister in the sitting room after several guests had departed, his face still shining from excited conversations with the men.

"As a Mason myself, the knowledge that Dr. Andrews's great-great-grandfather was the first Deputy Grand Master of Virginia Masons certainly makes it easy for me to welcome him into the family as my brother. For the military-minded, the fact that John's namesake was an officer in General Washington's Army makes him a hero to all of us, and even more so to know that such a man is fighting with us for independence yet again, this time against a hostile president and an invading army."

Lottie spoke. "Let's not forget that Orie is a heroine in her own right, joining the War in the hospital Wards after returning from a journey to the Holy Land, where she was baptized and ministered to ailing Arabs. Orie spoke to throngs of ladies intent on hearing her tell about her travels to the Holy Land. Everyone knew she was very well educated and intelligent, but no one expected such displays of courage. On the ship across the ocean, the captain of the ship took an interest in her, saying it was too dangerous for a young lady such as herself to dare travel unescorted, and was she not afraid? Without a word, she took out her revolver and shot a gull flying past, which fell dead on the deck with a single firing of the weapon. 'Afraid of what?' she asked. We are told the captain said, 'Afraid of nothing under the heavens, on land, or on the sea.'"

"It was like a lecture circuit with practically every lady in southern Albemarle County wanting to be in the presence of Miss Dr. Orie from Viewmont," Mag added.

"I was not invited to hear her speak," Ike reminded Mag.

"Of course not. The ladies like to keep their own company when it suits them, and I've told you everything she told us."

"I never heard of any real danger she was in. It was all about things that could have happened."

Mag's eyes narrowed. "Orie's peril was real when she hired two boatmen in Constantinople to row her across the Bosporus to the continent of Asia. By her own account, they stopped rowing about midway across and demanded to be paid a second time or they would return her to Constantinople. Their demeanor was surly and threatening, and they were clearly taking advantage of the young American woman traveling by herself. Oh, Orie was angry at this treatment. Instead of wailing for mercy and emptying her purse, she took out her revolver and ordered them to 'go on to the Asian shore.' The two boatmen rowed as if the American Navy was chasing them all the way to the shore and fled before she could call the authorities. Oh, the ladies of Albemarle adore Orie."

As his wife, mother, and sister glared at him, Ike admitted he had heard that story but had forgotten it because there were so many stories. He also remembered that having a wife and responsibilities at Viewmont kept him from accompanying his older sister on her adventure to Jerusalem and saw no reason to bring up the old argument that he should have gone.

They did agree that there was no one like Orie.

Ike held up his right hand in a mock toast. "It's a mating of eagles!"

Anna Maria looked at his empty glass tumbler. "That's quite enough, Ike. How much cider have you had this afternoon?"

"I'm only half jesting," he said, and took his leave from the sitting room.

With customary family humbleness somewhat restored, Anna Maria went to check on the guest list numbers and Mag and Lottie went back to sewing for the bride's trousseau.

Rebecca, a skilled seamstress, was working on Orie's wedding-day travelling dress, a plaid silk taffeta with yards and yards of the luscious fabric for the skirt alone and snowy lace for the collar and cuffs. Rebecca fretted while working under the pressure of time, but it was a welcome break from the butternut gray of trousers and jackets for the Confederate soldiers, who were facing wintertime with a great lack of warm uniforms. All the women at Viewmont, including the women in the fields, were engaged in making bandages and warm uniforms for the soldiers, but several of the housemaids, led by Cornelia, volunteered to work on Orie's trousseau. They received yards of soft thin cotton to make undergarments and set to work embroidering roses and tulips to "prettify" them for Miss Dr. Orie.

Cornelia's sewing group worked together after supper in the dining room by candlelight in the early November darkness, and Martha brought them hot cider and gingerbread. Cornelia, carried away by thoughts of Orie's broken heart and now joy, of the soldiers marching off to do battle becoming increasingly ragged, cold, and hungry, started humming "Swing Low, Sweet Chariot" while she worked. Others picked up the humming, and soon they were all singing quietly.

Mammy Jinny joined them after her duties for the day were done. Anna Maria looked in on them, attracted by the singing and candlelight, and when she saw that they were sewing petticoats and pantalets for Orie's trousseau, tears ran down her cheeks. Difficult as Orie could be, there was a simple goodness and courage about her that was impossible to overlook. Later that night the women returned to their cabins, carrying lanterns and whispering hushed good nights, trying not to awaken sleeping babies and children.

The next day, the wife of a field hand came up to the Main House with a crocheted shawl and hat, rich in colors, for Mammy Jinny to give to Miss Dr. Orie. "Tell her my husband, Sylvester, is healed up good from where the hatchet done split open his leg and we thank her for doctoring him and we wish Miss Dr. Orie a happy life with her doctor husband."

Mammy Jinny took the gifts and admired her work. "Miss Dr. Orie will look mighty fine in what you done made her. Come back tomorry. I'll see you get wool to make a shawl and hat for yo'sef."

"I'll do that, Mammy Jinny. I sho will." She walked back to her cabin behind the Main House, thinking she could crochet a shawl and hat in time for Viewmont's winter festivities and shortened work days. She thought about Miss Orie and her walks with Dr. John down the cabin rows to speak with the slaves about who was ailin' and who was busted up. She was sure no other tobacco plantation had their own doctor in the family for the slaves too. But the War was taking the two doctors to Richmond, and the slaves would suffer from the lack of care by and by, she reckoned. The rumors she was hearing had her scared silly, and she didn't know what to think. Would the Yankee soldiers carry the slaves off to the North and make them work in big, dirty factories or kill all the white folks and burn their big houses? Or would they set them free? And then where would they go and how could they eat? She didn't like the War. She was afraid of the killing and burning and stealing. She didn't want the War to come to Viewmont.

Eddie, who loved to sew, was cross-stitching dogwood petals on a pair of pillowcases and also continuing to knit mittens and caps for the soldiers and pray for the nameless young men as she knitted. Mollie found Eddie thus occupied long after her bedtime. "You should be in bed, dearest. The candle's too short to be working so late, and you need your sleep."

"Please don't send me to bed, Mollie. I worry about the poor soldiers and the cold weather coming."

"You're an angel, Eddie," she said sweetly.

"No, I'm not."

"Why do you say that?" she teased.

"I don't know. Maybe Papa will be pleased if I help the soldiers."

"Darling, you are an angel, and yes, Papa is pleased with you. I'm certain of it. You were renamed Edmonia because he loved you so. Mama wanted another son for Papa, but he said you were the baby he was waiting for."

Mollie continued to regard with concern her younger sister looking so sad. "Come to bed now, and tomorrow we can sew together for Orie and I'll tell you stories about Papa. He and Mama were the grandest couple in all Albermarle County."

Eddie smiled. "And I was their baby girl."

"The family was complete when you were born. You were the seventh child, the luckiest number in Christianity, because it represents the Holy Trinity plus the four corners of the earth. God watches over us all."

"Even Mammy Jinny?"

"Darling, you know Mammy Jinny is just crotchety and old. She thinks all the womenfolk spoil you and we'll be sorry. She loves you but wants to see that you have some discipline, too."

"Everybody is my mother and I have no papa," Eddie observed.

"Oh, get on to bed, Eddie. I am tired and you are cranky and sad. We all need sleep." Mollie led her to her bed and tucked her in with a kiss on the forehead.

Mollie sighed. Orie would be married soon and leaving Viewmont. The War was continuing and getting worse, and Eddie was weepy and fatherless. Mammy Jinny was wrong. They were not spoiling Eddie, they were afraid for her. All of them grew up with a father's love and strong hand, but not Eddie, who suffered like none of the rest of her brothers and sisters. Mollie would do anything for her little sister, but she could not bring back her papa from the dead.

CHAPTER 16

THE BRIDE-TO-BE

Without Orie at hand to tell her mother all the things she would or would not do for her wedding, Anna Maria indulged herself without limits. This was her first daughter, in love with a fine man for the first time in her life, and she was twenty-seven years old. The Civil War had begun and the near future looked grim. Why not therefore make it a day at Viewmont that would never be forgotten for its brilliance, gaiety, and still-splendid abundance?

Anna Maria found a seamstress of highest reputation for wedding finery in Richmond who was willing, on such short notice, to design and sew a bridal gown of white silk satin for Orie. Since the bride-to-be was not available for fittings, Anna Maria borrowed Orie's measurements from Rebecca for the seamstress in Richmond to use. From the florist, she ordered fresh orange blossoms to be worn as a bridal headdress, as well as to decorate the house. Pearls from the jeweler to match the white satin gown and white satin slippers adorned with pearls completed the ensemble. Anna Maria was beside herself with pleasure in anticipating the upcoming wedding.

Her trip to and from Richmond had been by train from Charlottesville, although Anna Maria favored the packet ships from Scottsville down the James River and the Kanawha Canal over the noisy and smoky wood-fueled railroad steam engine. But winter weather was making its appearance and river travel in the cold was a hardship. On the way back, the wailing train whistle lulled the happily tired mother of the bride to sleep, dreaming of Orie's wedding day and happily ever after. The subsequent days and nights took their toll on Anna Maria. She snapped at Mollie, fell asleep listening to Ike report on the farm's day, and sent Uncle Ned on an errand when Uncle Jacob needed him.

Two days before the wedding, Orie returned home on leave from the hospital ward for her wedding. John would stay in Charlottesville and come for the dinner and festivities the night before. He would wear his dress military uniform for both events. Orie's mind was swirling with thoughts of her soldiers back at the ward, some of whom were being transferred to Richmond. And she missed John.

Anna Maria, on the other hand, could hardly wait to sit down with Orie and go over all the wedding details, planned and ready for fruition.

"My darling daughter, we are all in a delightful dither over the wedding, and you look as beautiful as a bride could possibly look. I want you to see all the preparations and try on some things Rebecca has made for you. Your trousseau is packed in lavender and shows the handwork and love for you from Viewmont."

"Mama, I am too tired to think, and I want to go upstairs and lie down. Would it be all right if I looked at the things tomorrow?"

Anna Maria's expectant smile disappeared momentarily, but she recovered with practiced poise. "Yes, of course, darling girl. I'll bring up some hot tea and biscuits and let you rest. Tomorrow will be a very full day." Anna Maria swallowed her disappointment, but understood that patience is a virtue above all others at times like this. It would be better that the young woman be well rested before taking on the demanding role of bride. Still, she shook her head. If only Orie, for once, would pretend to be gracious and charming to her mother.

Tomorrow they would decorate the household with fragrant orange blossoms throughout and begin to receive guests who would be staying over the night before the morning wedding. Anna Maria was sorry her brother James Barclay, his wife, Julia, and their children would not be there for the wedding. They were lingering in Europe on their way home from the Holy Land. She understood that James was protecting his family from the War in Virginia, but she missed him terribly. Weddings were the best as well as the worst for stirring emotions that could lie dormant during the course of everyday obligations and tasks. Edward would not be presiding over the wedding in his frock coat and commanding manner, so she wanted her older brother beside her all the more. Tears fell. *Nobody cared how she felt.*

The next morning, Orie was up early as usual. After momentary disorientation, she realized she was at Viewmont, not Charlottesville General. Her wedding was tomorrow. She took a deep breath. Her life had not begun on the day she was accepted at Troy Female Seminary, but would begin on the morrow, when she became the wife of John Andrews. She would become one flesh with him into eternity. That was what bliss was.

She dressed quickly to make her rounds, not to see soldiers waiting for the touch of her hand and a smile of encouragement, but to visit the slaves in cabin row to see if any needed medical assistance before the wedding and before the move to Richmond. Word got out to the slaves that Miss Dr. Orie was coming after she left the Main House in her heavy gray cloak. Hastily assembled, they waited for her in the early morning chill, gathered close to their cooking fires. She greeted each one with affection and concern, and they responded with thanks for her care, and one held up a baby now well who had been sick. Wedding wishes were shouted out as she made her way back to the house for coffee and ham, eggs, and apples.

When she returned to the Main House, Martha was handing out trays of hot food to be carried to the dining room by her helper girls. Orie sat beside Colie, who gave her a hug.

"I think I understand why people cry at weddings," said Colie. "I'm so happy for you that I tear up for no reason, and then I'm sad because you're going away and everything will be different." She daintily daubed her tears, keeping the moisture away from her gray silk dress.

"Dearest Colie, you are being sentimental, and I want my little sister with the bright eyes and big smile back." Orie looked at her sister in wonder. How could it be that Colie was a young woman now and the days of their girlhood were behind them? And thankfully so, for she had not been a child who thrived on the social calendar that befitted Viewmont and her prominent parents. She realized, however, that she would miss her three lively younger sisters and their giggles and pranks. Poor Eddie, though, was not a part of the sweet fun. She had been a fretful baby, and then she was a small girl when her sisters were busy with their studies and parties. She had been her father's pet, but he died before Eddie was old enough to remember him.

Orie would leave a large and loving family and her place in it was secure, even though she would never achieve the role her mother played, a role she never wanted. She was an MD and would soon be the wife of Dr. John Andrews. She never knew she could be so happy.

Anna Maria, who had eaten breakfast before daybreak, latched onto Orie at the breakfast table. "Orie, dear, I'll be in your bedroom with your wedding dress to try on as soon as you finish your coffee. If anything is amiss, Rebecca can fix it. That's first on our list. Then James's in-laws from Staunton will stay here, and Mag's family will be here for the family gathering this evening. Tom's widow and son and her new husband will stay the night—" Anna Maria came to a stop, seeing by the expression on Orie's face that she no longer had her daughter's attention. She bent down and touched Orie's smooth cheek. "Enjoy your coffee. I didn't mean to rush you. I'll see you upstairs when you are quite ready."

Anna Maria gracefully departed, stepping into the hall before ascending the stairs, thinking she needed to get Uncle Jacob started with hanging the orange blossoms. Too soon and they would wilt, too late and Uncle Jacob would have to maneuver his helpers around the guests. That wouldn't do at all.

After breakfast, Orie retreated to her bedroom, forgetting that her mother was there waiting for her. Anna Maria had placed the gleaming white silk satin dress on the sofa, and on the table beside it were the wedding slippers, white silk stockings, and headdress.

"What's this?" Orie raised her voice to her mother.

Anna Maria's smile faded quickly. "What do you mean, 'What's this?' It's your wedding dress, of course."

"Mama, I have a wedding dress. Rebecca measured me and fitted me and sewed every stitch by herself. It's her gift to me."

"Darling, that's your Best Day dress and it's for after the wedding, when you and John depart to your home in Richmond. You are Young Marrieds now, and you'll have visitors welcoming you into Richmond society and your friends and neighbors coming to visit you. It's a special time in your life that you will always look back on with the greatest pleasure. Maybe next summer the dreadful War will be over and you and John can go on a honeymoon."

Orie's nostrils flared as she struggled to quell her impatience. "Mama, there is a War going on right now. It may end badly. I can hardly think beyond the next day."

"Oh, my darling, you are overwrought. I'll bring you some laudanum and let you rest. You'll feel better about the wedding dress later. A photographer will be here to take pictures to be treasured by all of us for years and years."

Orie gazed steadily at her mother with a silent plea to cease speaking and leave.

Anna Maria gazed at the wedding dress. She wanted so badly to tell her oldest daughter that the white silk satin dress was of a quite modest design, similar to the dress worn by Queen Victoria when she wed Prince Albert in 1840, that her head was pounding. Also, the Queen wore a much more regal veil and orange-blossom headdress. On the other hand, their event was the epitome of a simple American wedding. Instead of the service taking place at the Royal Chapel of St. James's Palace, Orie's wedding would be at Viewmont. Rather than a wedding breakfast at Buckingham Palace, Orie's would be at Viewmont. Anna Maria had no apology for Orie regarding this simple, quintessential American wedding. Oh, but her head was in a vise of nervous exhaustion.

Orie, in a similar effort to restrain her tongue, took herself back in time to her year at Troy Female Seminary, the most highly regarded school for young women in the nation in terms of intellectual challenge. Upon her application, which her father favored and her mother did not, she thought she would not wish to continue living if she were turned down.

She was accepted. She thanked her father profusely for the opportunity and warmed up to her mother for dropping her outspoken misgivings over the matter.

Mammy Jinny, however, never gave her stamp of approval. "Miss Orie, you be sorry when you go so far north and there be shaggy wolves attacking the young ladies. I seen pichers of women up North and they be all stern-like and mean. You gon' miss yo' mama with her pretty ways and yo' sweet sisters."

After that, Orie avoided Mammy Jinny but dared not be rude to her, as such behavior would have merited a slap across the face by her mother. He papa would have punished her...somehow. She couldn't even imagine her father's shocked disappointment.

When the time had come to leave home for school, her father and Cornelia accompanied her on the train ride north, arriving at the substantial Romanesque building in prosperous Troy, almost within sound of cold currents in the upper Hudson River. Edward had introduced himself and his daughter to Emma Willard, founder of the institute and then taken his leave with Cornelia. Orie had thought then that her Life had Begun.

At the school, Orie had watched. The students had divided themselves into groups of which she was not a part. There were circles of girls from New York City, Boston, and Philadelphia. They already knew each other. There were girls from small towns in other states who knew no one else and so formed friendships among themselves. Orie alone seemed to belong to no clique. Some things never change. She had always preferred books to the company of others while growing up. While Orie did not attempt to socialize, as her mother would have done, others knew her as "the girl from the South." The staff and teachers had been unsmiling and strict, the studies difficult, and she was poor in math. She couldn't find her way around the city of Troy. The speech of the townspeople was almost incomprehensible to her and the Hudson River nothing like her James at home, flowing past tobacco fields and dense woods along the tree-lined riverbank.

Speakers had come to the school, acclaimed in their different fields. A women's education authority from England came to document the school's methods, suggesting that Troy Female Seminary was the best in the world for women's education. Suffragettes came and spoke about women's rights. Medical doctors spoke on the topic of female doctors, especially needed for advanced medical care of women and children.

Ellen, a student from a small town in Wisconsin, had sat beside Orie at lunch one day and asked her if she missed her home. No, she had said, she did not.

"I miss my mother and papa," the girl had said, "but they want me to stay here. Especially Mother. She wants me to have Opportunities."

"My father is pleased, but Mama wanted me to go to her school in Richmond and said she practically told them when I was born to expect Orianna Moon."

"Why didn't you want to go there?"

"The school is there to prepare girls to be like my mother, who is gracious and charming and runs the plantation and the lives of everyone in the family."

"My mother does that and she graduated from a Normal school, where she earned a certificate to be a teacher."

"My mother learned to do needlework, paint, decorate, play musical instruments, converse in French, and take lessons in religion, literature, and practical math and science. She performed in recitals and acted in plays. She and the other girls entertained and met young men from Virginia schools." Orie knew exactly what she was missing.

"I like to paint and sew and decorate. I might be called clever in such a school. Here, the lectures are tiresome."

"I find them exhilarating," Orie had said. "I can hardly sleep, my mind is so stimulated."

Ellen had looked at Orie closely. "You really are an Emma Willard girl. Lots of us are not. "

An "Emma Willard girl." Orie had smiled. Throughout the day she would spy a mirror and wave at the Emma Willard girl she saw in the reflection.

With nothing to say that would not infuriate her daughter, Anna Maria left the room, and Orie took to her bed where she continued to remember, with Matilda beside her purring, happy to have her mistress back in her own bedroom.

The festive evening proved to be a stark contrast to Orie's boarding school memories. The evening passed like the stars in the Milky Way glittering and moving about in the enchanting darkness. After a wash in flower-scented water and French-milled soap from Paris, Orie was helped into her layers of clothing by Cornelia. Against her skin were the softest white cotton pantalets and chemise, followed by petticoats, corset, and corset cover. The dress for the evening was of emerald-green silk shantung, and she wore emerald earrings, necklace, and bracelet. A headpiece of ribbons and evergreens set off her blue eyes and creamy skin.

Flickering candles eternally cast shadows of romance over all things, and when John arrived in his military uniform, Orie swooned into his arms to the delight of every family member present. The dinner was served in the Great Hall with toasts of champagne begun by John Digges Moon, Edward's older brother, who lived at nearby Mt. Ayr and was the husband of Anna Maria's sister Mary. Ike followed with a grand toast, as did a number of the gathered gentlemen, followed by a blessing given by the minister at the Scottsville Baptist Church. Uncle Jacob supervised the serving of dinner by Mammy Jinny and Martha's helpers. Orie remembered afterward the aroma of hot seafood, meats, vegetables, and sauces, the sound of silverware on china, and the soft praises for the various dishes by the elaborately dressed guests. Cake with the sweetest frosting was the dessert.

After dinner, the ladies retired to freshen up before bed, while the gentlemen moved to the study for cigars and bourbon and brandy, items that Ike made sure were available, although he was a Baptist and did not drink alcohol. John walked Orie to the staircase, where she blew a sweet kiss as she ascended the stairs in her rustling silk shantung evening dress.

This was Orie's last night as a maiden, alone in her large four-poster bed under woolen blankets, embroidered quilts, and soft sheets. Her dreams would reflect the flickering lights of the candelabra, sconces, and fireplaces as well as the sight of John smiling down at her in his splendid gray uniform throughout the evening. Heaven and earth had come together for Orie, the Moon sister who did not believe in Romance.

CHAPTER 17
THE WEDDING

The Wedding morning dawned cold and cloudy on November 28, 1861. Lottie woke Orie up and recited a calendar verse for weddings: "If you wed in bleak November, only joys will come, remember." Lottie gave her a kiss and urged her to wake up "to greet this glorious day."

Orie shivered from the chill in the room and excitement, while Lottie brought out a warm day gown to wear before dressing for the Wedding. Downstairs, all was in a state of excitement as guests and family gathered in the dining room for a prewedding breakfast in anticipation of a formal breakfast and grand reception after the ceremony.

In daylight, the orange blossoms arranged in festoons above the two fireplace mantels and the door frames were much more evident than the night before, and the perfume of the blossoms quickened in the fresh morning air. Even Eddie, already in her best party dress, was all smiles at the decorations and played the little hostess well. Lottie, Colie, and Mollie were like the Three Graces, the mythical daughters of Zeus and Eurynome, with their constant attending to the modern-day Aphrodite, their sister Orie. Young, beautiful, and modest, they were the personification of gracefulness.

Although Uncle Jacob dominated the scene in his distinctive frock coat, seeing to the needs of everyone and then finding someone to carry out the task, it was Anna Maria the matriarch who was giving the orders, looking radiant in her pleasure at the elegance of the decorations and well-garbed wedding guests. John was there, but Ike and his friends kept him busy away from Orie, and there was an atmosphere of laughter and excitement before the exchange of vows.

As soon as Anna Maria could catch Orie's attention, she directed the girl upstairs to her bedroom, with Cornelia in close attendance.

"Tempus fugit! Let's get started before time gets away from us. Cornelia and I will help you with your dress and fix your hair and help you with your jewelry." Anna Maria draped the shimmering white gown over her left arm and invited Orie to feel the creamy smoothness of the silk satin.

Orie, away from the cascades of candlelight in the darkness of last night's dinner party and John's impossibly handsome presence, faced her mother and spoke resolutely.

"No, Mama, I am wearing Rebecca's day dress for the wedding and the reception and the travel to Richmond. I cannot and will not dress twice more this day. It is senseless to do so, and I have neither the energy nor the patience to spend the time it will take."

Orie and Cornelia both looked straight at Anna Maria. In a flash of truth, she understood that this was a quarrel she would lose. She could weep later, but at this moment she held her head high and replied, "As you wish. This day is for you and John and you will have your say."

Orie embraced her mother and kissed her cheeks. "Thank you, Mama. You've made this the happiest day of my life."

Anna Maria scooped up the white wedding dress and left the room, saying, "You don't need me to help you put on the day dress. Cornelia will help you."

"Yas'um," said Cornelia, and she began to lay out the striped plaid silk taffeta dress with long sleeves and white lace collar and cuffs. "I watched Rebecca work on dis here dress, and ever'body thinks it's as purdy as Joseph's Coat of Many Colors. I surely do."

"Bless your heart, Cornelia." Orie's own heart felt full to overflowing. She quickly asked for a handkerchief and dabbed her eyes. I'm as sentimental as Colie, she thought, surprised at herself. *People do cry at weddings.*

Anna Maria, with the splendid wedding gown cradled in her arms, went to her bedroom, spread it out on her velvet love seat, and gazed at it. The tears ran down her cheeks unchecked. If only I could have just *seen* her in that dress, I would be happy. Not happy, but happier than I am. I must stop weeping and repair my blotchy face. I'm utterly undone. She left her room and went to the stairs, looking down until she caught a glimpse of Mammy Jinny. "Come up!" she mouthed, gesturing.

Mammy Jinny, old as she was, sashayed up the stairs and followed Ole Miss into her bedroom. Mammy Jinny saw the forlorn wedding dress on the love seat and shook her head in disapproval.

"Please bring me up a cup of strong hot tea, and I am going to rest just a bit. Can you let me know when the preacher begins to look around for me and checks his pocket watch? Just tell Ike to hold him off and I'll be right there."

"Yas'm, I surely will. Ain't nobody gon' disturb you while you drink yo' tea and rest yo'sef."

"Thank you, Mammy Jinny. It's just a sinking spell. I'll be fine after some quiet."

Her weeping was finished. She looked at the wedding dress and meditated. Lottie can wear it. And Colie and Mollie and Eddie. They *will* wear it. And I will take apart the orange blossom headdress and share it among the girls to wear in their hair as Orie's attendants. Anna Maria smiled at her own cleverness.

The midmorning wedding service was conducted by the Reverend A. J. Doll, a local Baptist pastor blessed with a strong voice who had begun to preach regularly to a large number of Negroes on his two-acre hillside on Hardware Road. The Scottsville Baptist Church's most recent pastor had been the Reverend R. B. Boatwright, who had quit the church to volunteer for the Confederate Army several months earlier and was elected to serve as chaplain in the Forty-Sixth Virginia Regiment. His congregation had wished him Godspeed and said they would miss him and pray for him.

The Scottsville Baptist Church, founded by Anna Maria and her husband in 1842, had no official pastor in November 1861. No Baptist preacher in the area, however, would have turned down a request from Mrs. Moon, thanks to her years of hosting itinerant Baptist preachers at Viewmont in return for Sunday services prior to the building of the church at Scottsville.

The wedding service for Orie and John was simple and direct in its message. Reverend Doll read from several books in the New Testament written by Paul about marriage and the similarity of the joining in marriage of one man and one woman as set out in the Book of Genesis to the marriage of Christ and his Bride, the Church. How two people were joined by God into "one flesh" with the command by God in Genesis to "go forth and multiply." There was to be love and reverence, each for the other, and as Eve had been taken from Adam's rib, the woman was not her husband's superior or inferior, but his equal, his companion and helpmeet; and as the woman had come from under the man's arm, the husband was to always protect his wife. The husband was to love his wife as he loved himself, because as one flesh, his wife was part of himself. Reverend Doll emphasized "one woman," because there was a sect that believed a man could have more than one wife. He made it clear that Orie was to be John's *only* wife till death shall part them.

Reverend Doll's sermon made a good impression on the family and friends at Viewmont, counting the conjugal couple first. The

Reverend handed the wedding ring to John, who slipped it on the ring finger of his beloved.

CSA Captain of Cavalry Orianna Russell Moon, MD, was now also Mrs. John Summerfield Andrews, MD; together they were the Drs. Orie and John Andrews. The congratulatory clamor was boisterous and sustained. "Hear, hear!" was among the shouts of joy heard through the closed windows by the servants and field hands, who stood together outside echoing the shouts.

The wedding was all that Anna Maria had hoped for, and so the wedding breakfast and reception started on a high note. Captain Jack Harris's famous gold service was brought out to good effect, and the sumptuous breakfast reception in the Great Hall and dining room began with a steady stream of food-laden trays coming through the dining room door from the kitchen outside. Ornate crystal punch bowls of iced fruit juices vied with eggnog to quaff the thirst, while the marvelous smells of creamed turkey and steamed oysters set mouths to watering. Fires roared in the twin fireplaces, one in the sitting room on one side of the house and one in the dining room on the other side. Martha's dark rich wedding cake was spiked with brandy and sweet dried fruit, so that the new couple could rightly look forward to fruitful years of wedlock and a houseful of children.

After setting out food for the white folks, Uncle Ned helped pass around platters of ham biscuits and johnnycakes, hot hard cider, and small servings of wedding fruit cake to the jovial folk outside. They moved down to their rows of cabins and played music on mandolins and danced round the fires in a festive mood to match the wedding inside.

Wedding toasts were given, praising the couple and the two families and the Southland from Virginia to Alabama. The first toast was again given by John Digges Moon, the older brother of Edward, the deceased father of the bride.

Anna Maria's brother James's father-in-law from Staunton made an eloquent toast to the Moon family and then read a telegram from James: "Although I deeply regret the physical absence of myself and my family at the wedding of my most cherished niece, Orianna, I count it as a triumph for Christ that she was granted the safety of our Lord to arrive in the Holy Land and ask for baptism by my hand at the Pool of Siloam and afterward to bring healing and the presence of the peace of the Lord to the Muslim tribe of the Bedouins. May the Lord's blessings be upon Orie and John forever more."

There were tears in the eyes of many guests. Embroidered handkerchiefs were at the ready.

Orie spent time with each of her sisters, while the older set was bent on giving her advice about married life that could save her from heartbreak and hardship. Orie's forbearance that day was believed to have been due to the prayerful pleadings to the Lord by her sisters to replace her short temper with a silent tongue.

As gentlemen are wont to do, they sought each other out in the study and the Great Hall and commenced to smoke their pipes, imbibe, and discuss the latest issues. The War was off-limits for conversation on this happy nuptial day, but Ike Moon skirted the issue, telling about the late Andrew Stevenson, who had lived on Carter's Mountain at Blenheim Farm and had been a Congressman from Virginia, Speaker of the House, rector of the University of Virginia, and Ambassador to the Court of St. James. It was three years after Parliament passed the Anti-Slavery Act of 1833 that Stevenson had been sent to London. Sections of public opinion expressed resentment over the choice of a slave owner as a minister to the UK. Worse, Daniel O'Connor, an Irish statesman and emancipator of the Irish Catholics in Ireland, was reported to have denounced Stevenson in public as a slave breeder. Stevenson was so outraged at the charge that he challenged the man to a duel.

Many who were present had heard the story and knew the man under discussion.

"Indeed, a duel, by God!" one man exclaimed.

"Hear me out," said Ike. "Very fortunately, Mr. O'Connor backed down, suggesting that he had been misquoted, but Stevenson was so wroth, he would have taken up his sword then and there, apparently feeling responsible for the honor of every planter in Virginia."

The gentlemen stamped their feet and canes in agreement.

Ike continued. "And you all know Stevenson's Blenheim Farm on Carter Mountain." John Digges Moon spoke up with a raspy voice. "Are you saying that Stevenson had anything to do with Carter's freeing of 450 slaves, the largest such manumission to date?"

"No sir, but that's the same Carter family up in Westmoreland County that freed those 450 of his slaves in 1791. After the Virginia Legislature legalized the manumission of slaves in 1782, Virginia's free black population grew to perhaps 30,000 by 1810."

The gentlemen laughed with the glee of a full belly and the weight of Ike's little-known facts.

"Ike, you're a schoolteacher at heart and we admire your lectures," one man said. "Go tell that to Lincoln and let him see how we take care of our own problems. The Union Army makes the Revolutionary War look like a costume drama, while fighting the North is like staring down endless hordes from Satan's hell. "

"We want no part of it, but we'll fight to the end for the South," said another.

"Hear, hear!" they all said in unison.

When Anna Maria stepped out from the parlor to see what was afoot, the men's tobacco pipes suddenly needed attention while they changed the nature of the discussion. John Digges Moon winked at his sister-in-law. She gave him a rueful smile and rejoined the ladies, leaving the gentlemen to wander off in search of more bourbon, wedding cake, and roasted oysters. Talk of the War was too much on their minds to politely avoid the topic.

John wished his family were there with him. He missed Billie and Robert with all his being. How could he be so happy and so sad at the same time? Orie clung to him, leaning against his ribs below his protecting arm, and was besotted with love for her husband and the whole earth below the heavens.

The photographer had the newly married couple pose for pictures. Orie stood beside John with her right hand on John's left shoulder, brilliant in her "Coat of Many Colors," looking at the camera with a calm and confident face. Her waist was stylishly no larger than the span of a thin hand, while no headdress adorned her hair, shiny golden brown and parted in the middle, with high-fashion sausage curls from ear length to her shoulders. John wore the long gray wool coat of a Confederate major of cavalry, decorated with gold buttons down the front and gold braid on the sleeves. His trousers were dark and under his coat was a snowy white shirt, flat bow tie, and vest with white dots on a dark field. He looked at the camera, his handsome face tinged with the merest hint of trepidation.

CHAPTER 18

RICHMOND

If it can be said at all during wartime that a couple can create a social splash when arriving at a capital city, Orie and John did just that in Richmond. Orie's family connections opened doors to them of the most highly connected people in Richmond. John's great-grandfather was his entry into the heady world of the Masons, owing to the fact that the Reverend Robert Lial Andrews was the first deputy Grand Master of Virginia Masons. John's brother-in-law, Isaac Moon, was also an active and worthy Mason.

Orie and John attended several open houses when they first arrived, and Orie dutifully wrote home to her mother about the social events. What she did not write was that the distinguished townhouses were overheated and airless, the Victorian furnishings splendid to the point of suffocation, the food indigestibly heavy and sweet, and conversation about the War either idle chatter or foolhardy boastfulness.

John, on the other hand, was an enthusiastic Mason and took pleasure in meeting fellow Masons. Orie did not fully understand or appreciate the Masons, because they were, after all, a secret society, and John had been a Mason before he was a married man. This was not a problem that bothered Orie.

She may not have understood or appreciated the Masonic world, but she knew that George Washington had been a Mason, along with many prominent men in the early days of the American Republic. A story she heard later came from the Civil War, during the burning of Atlanta by General Sherman and his troops. The Cheshire family lived on Cheshire Bridge Road east of Atlanta, when Union troops came and prepared to set fire to the estate. But upon inspection of the property, information was passed to the commanding officer that the property owner was a Mason. The order to burn the property was immediately rescinded, so the Cheshire home survived the burning of Atlanta. Masons believed "tis folly, for sure, not to be a Mason!"

The society Orie favored was that of her Boys at the Chimborazo Hospital, the "hospital on the hill," which started out as extensive wooden barracks for volunteer soldiers from throughout the Confederate South. They had come to Richmond for organization and drills, but within a few weeks they moved on to the front lines in Northern Virginia, leaving behind one hundred nearly new wooden buildings on Chimborazo Hill. The Surgeon-General of the Confederate States of America, Dr. Samuel P. Moore, commandeered the buildings for his department, and the hospital was established in October 1861. It became known as one of the largest, best-organized, and most sophisticated hospitals in the Confederacy.

Because Chimborazo Hospital was where soldiers were brought after emergency treatment at field hospitals, it was, for many of them, a convalescent hospital where sick or wounded men came to recover and stay for a period of time. The average number of patients was around 3000 with a peak patient load approaching 4000, a figure never imagined before the firing of shots against Fort Sumter in Charleston Harbor. John's duties became routine, working from early morning till late in the evening and then home with Orie to their apartment in Richmond to rest and be together.

Orie tended to suffer and grieve along with her Boys, although professional training did not allow her anguish to show through. Soldiers with infected wounds received her constant attention, as did many with dire cases of typhoid fever. "It's a strange way to live," she told John. "When I come home, I am breathless to be in your arms and think of nothing but the joy of our love, but my thoughts keep running to the hospital, to those broken Boys in their suffering. I am filled over the brim with my work and you."

John's feelings were not as dramatic. "I am satisfied to be here and not be constantly reminded of my brother Robert and his sad death in Charlottesville and Billie's death on the battlefield. Also there's morphine here and chloroform and even women to come and read and tend to the Boys. The main worry is fuel. According to the quartermaster department, by December fifth, we had already run through four cords of wood. One cord is a stack of wood eight feet long, four feet wide, and four feet high. We cannot use less wood, and winter is just beginning. But I'm not worried. Virginia alone has plenty of timber, and it just takes time to get organized. Best of all, you are here. I am happy, Orie."

Mr. and Mrs. Pittman of the Barclay family in Richmond had hired out the daughter of two of their most trusted slaves to clean and cook for the couple, and so Orie was relieved of housekeeping duties, for which she was thankful. The girl's name was Ruth, and she was careful and gentle in all of her actions, but Orie missed Cornelia's quiet, homely, and comforting presence. Ruth was quiet, but in an unnatural way, as Orie sensed that she was hiding her thoughts. Was she planning to flee from the apartment where she was now alone much of the day? That part would be easy enough, but how would she escape the city and seek freedom in the North? Orie sighed. For all her travels and experiences, she preferred country people and was probably too suspicious of the hardworking but citified Ruth.

"How old are you, Ruth?" Orie asked when she noticed the girl's uneasiness when John was in the room. Had she been warned about white men taking advantage of servant girls?

"Fifteen, ma'am."

"That makes you near in age to my sister Mollie."

"Yas'm," she answered, not meeting Orie's eyes.

Orie tried to picture Mollie cooking breakfast and supper and cleaning house for two strangers. "You do a nice job, Ruth. Did your mother teach you the household arts?"

"Yas'm, she sho'ly did." She smiled at Orie for the first time, and Orie smiled back, remembering smiles from the Bedouin women and girls after they got to know and trust "El Hakim" for the healing care she brought them in the Holy Land.

Her colleagues at the hospital were not so different from her doctor brother Tom when he was alive, but some of the soldiers were unlike any boys she had known. The soldier from New York who had lost his leg when the wound festered spoke with such a heavy Irish brogue she couldn't honestly understand him. He sometimes cried out loud and was probably cursing her and others around him. She thought he would shove her to the floor and run away if only he could walk. How alone and full of hate he was when all they wanted to do was help him, even though he was a Union soldier and Lord only knows how many Southern boys he had wounded and perhaps killed.

Another scene from the ward flashed through her mind: a Southern boy from the Georgia mountains cried only when he thought nobody was hearing him. Orie shook her head, flouncing her curls about her shoulders, with tears in her eyes and left the small dining room, while Ruth went back to clearing and washing the dishes, being careful to not break the delicate china.

John, refreshed by the smallest respite from the hospital wards, had already left the apartment for a meeting with other surgeons to discuss plans for hospital chaplains. Orie and John both prayed over the soldiers in their care but felt that the love of God needed to surround the Boys from all possible aspects: from the women volunteers, as well as the army nurses and Christian slaves hired out to the Army for whatever needed to be done. Local pastors must help. Jesus saves us all.

John came back with the information that 97 percent of Confederate chaplains in the field were Protestant preachers, and many joined the Army as common soldiers to share their burden. Some had been quickly commissioned as chaplains, holding revival meetings and prayer meetings, exhorting the weak and the strong to serve the Lord with all their heart, soul, and mind. The Army had been formed hastily without official chaplains, but as the organization progressed, the Confederate Army soon boasted a strong corps of chaplains dedicated to preaching the gospel and baptizing the converted.

With 3,000 soldiers at any one time at Chimborazo Hospital, the surgeons asked for the help of Richmond churches to send volunteer chaplains to the wards. This was done to great effect by local pastors, many of them pastoring more than one church as they stood in for younger pastors who were on the battlefield, but not wanting to lose a single soul for Christ through negligence. For the Jewish soldiers, there were rabbis in Richmond who made their way to the wards to make sure their Boys were comforted by the Word of God, and there were Catholic priests for the many Union Boys in their care. In the case of an unconscious sick or wounded Boy, any pastor could be called to pray over him before he passed away.

"When the War is over," said John, "no matter what the outcome, there will be a great need for medicine and mission work in our war-torn Southland."

Orie marveled at John's ability to look forward, beyond the trials and horrors of the day-to-day. She fed on his strength and made an effort to blot out the news that in November the Union Navy had captured Port Royal in South Carolina, thereby cutting off that port's trade with Britain and giving the Navy a convenient base from which to cut off other Southern ports. The strangulation of the South from US and international trade had begun.

She worried about her Uncle James and his family still in Europe. She thought of the daily passenger packet ships and freight traffic plying the James River and Kanawha Canal with tobacco, timber, and wheat from Virginia bound for England, while other ships brought tea, coffee, sugar, medicinal needs, and everything else they did not produce locally. Where would the revenue to fund the Army come from if not from trade with London? How long would their precious supply of morphine last at Chimborazo? She shuddered, reliving the suffering at Charlottesville General, where there was no chloroform for surgery or morphine for catastrophic wounds. "Please, no, Lord," she prayed.

Only John's sheltering arms gave Orie rest from her mind's racing with real and imagined woes ahead of them. The warmth and tenderness of John's caresses stoked a fire within her that burned away her fright.

CHAPTER 19

CIVIL WAR WINTER

By mid-December, the hundred and twenty wooden barracks that made up Chimborazo Hospital were operating like a small city, spread out on the top of a steep ridgeline east of the Richmond city limits and above the Confederate Navy Yard on the James. The cold wind blew as doctors made their rounds and the support staff of nurses, launderers, evangelical colporteurs bearing Bibles and religious tracts, stewards, matrons, pastors, and volunteers were forever coming and going. Slamming doors and the sound of heavy muddy boots on wooden floors were the order of the ordinary day. The frigid draftiness of the barracks did somewhat relieve the foul odor of sickness in the wards, with the unfortunate result that action against one made the other worse.

So the winter of 1861–62 differed greatly for Orie and John from the summer of '61. Instead of badly wounded soldiers suddenly swamping the unprepared facilities in Charlottesville, there was now a steady stream of wretchedly sick boys coming from the winter encampments, for winter weather changed the modus operandi on the battlefield. Military offenses were almost impossible to mount on muddy, impassable roads, but the defenders could not sneak away to check on homes and families, or the enemy would take note and their troops would gladly advance without a struggle. So the Southern Boys were staying put, constructing and living in small log cabins or tents spaced close together, but, alas, without clean water, disposal of waste, or adequate fresh food. Exposure to rain, sleet, and cold further compromised a soldier's ability to resist disease.

As a result, John was seeing diseases he had only read about in medical textbooks. Cases of smallpox, yellow fever, scurvy, and malaria sent him to more experienced doctors and the small medical library for help. Seventeen- and eighteen-year-old boys from rural areas were getting sick from first-time exposure to large groups of people and coming down with chicken pox, whooping cough, measles, mumps, and scarlet fever. John was seeing death and morbidity on a scale he had never before imagined. Each death touched a part of him that still mourned for his younger brothers killed at Manassas.

Orie, because of her experience in Jerusalem with the scourge of ophthalmia, was constantly warning the nurses to wash their hands. The nurses, many of them disabled soldiers, were unaccustomed to taking orders from a female medical doctor, and some undermined her orders. The situation was better than at a field hospital, though, where a soldier infected with typhoid fever would be treated and then sent back to his lice-infected straw mattress.

Which is worse, thought Orie, as she checked the new arrivals on a snow-spitting morning in December, a painful death inflicted by a minié bullet to the chest of a soldier in battle, or the slow death of a soldier hollowed out by dysentery and the swift passage of blood and mucus from the body? Transmitted by ever-present body lice, dysentery caused soldiers to suffer severe diarrhea, high fever, excruciating headache, rash, and delirium. Orie counted their deaths as heroic as those resulting from mortal battlefield wounds, but medals for valor were given out by military officers, not the Medical Corps. She wept especially for those boys.

John asked a new doctor from Charlottesville General if he had any knowledge of Private James Jackson from Lauderdale County with a lung wound suffered at Manassas. The news regarding the Alabama soldier was surprisingly good. The short balding surgeon with a gray goatee from Prince Edward County told him that James had recovered completely.

"Where is he now? I'll write to his mother and let her know I am watching out for my fellow Alabamian."

The older man looked closely at John. "That's very kind of you. Even if she's heard from her son herself, it always pleases a mother to know that her Boy is not without friends from home. My wife and I have two sons in the army and any sort of good news about them is a priceless treasure. Long spells of hearing nothing upsets my wife terribly."

John agreed. "The wound James suffered at Manassas could well have taken his life. And you may not know that although he was the son of the late James Jackson Sr., president of the Alabama Senate, James was a planter, not a military man, and he joined the Alabama Fourth right away in April on his own as a private. Others in his position might have insisted on entering as an officer, but he did not. I will always hold him in high esteem for that."

"Indeed. After he recovered at Charlottesville General, he returned to Alabama and helped organize the Twenty-Seventh Regiment, Alabama Infantry at Fort Heimen, Tennessee. Early this month he was promoted to Lieutenant Colonel."

John beamed. "I think that fort is being built on the Tennessee River near Florence, my hometown. May God shine a light on James and keep him and his mother under His protection."

"Amen!" replied the doctor.

As December wore on, sick soldiers continued to arrive, and many beds were still filled with soldiers either dying slowly or relapsing before full recovery. At a meeting of surgeons, the doctors were asked to stay on through Christmas. John brought up the subject with Orie that evening at their apartment.

"The assistant surgeons will be asked tomorrow if they will stay on duty through Christmas. We need to think about our plans, darling. Is your heart set on Christmas at Viewmont?"

Orie put on a pensive face and joined John in the overstuffed chair he favored, and he placed his arms around her. "Truly, darling, I feel safer in Richmond and have dreaded the packing and train ride home with all the commotion. The sick boys are staying here, and I would rather stay here too. I'd like to spend our first Christmas together, just the two of us."

"Dearest Orie. We truly are one flesh. What you want is my wish also. Tomorrow I will sign on to continue duty through Christmas."

"I will do likewise and consider this Christmas to be a gift to our Lord Jesus Christ in thanks for our marriage." She lifted up the palm of his hand and kissed it as he bent toward her and brushed her ear with his lips.

"Tomorrow is another day," John whispered, "but let's give thanks for the long, dark nights of December ahead of us."

CHAPTER 20
THE NEW YEAR, 1862

New Year's Day 1862 in Richmond dawned cold and sunny with gusty winds sweeping fallen leaves across streets. Accompanying the young Doctors Andrews to the reception at the home of President Davis were Orie's distant cousin James Digges and his wife, Mary. Orie was fond of them and pleased to be taken to the much-anticipated reception in their fine one-horse carriage with room for four passengers and a driver.

"The breeze today would be called a lazy wind in Ireland," remarked the older woman, cozy under her fur carriage blanket.

Orie squeezed her husband's hand under their heavy wool blanket. "Why do you call it lazy? I call it very brisk and almost as cold as the wind across the Hudson in Troy," she said in a teasing tone.

James chuckled in anticipation of his wife's well-practiced wit.

"It's too lazy to go around you and so it cuts right through you," Mary said.

John and Orie laughed and the mood was bright. The Diggeses' jollity was well known and appreciated. Orie, long content to be a quiet and serious girl from a rural plantation, found that she liked the verve of city life—the constant activity on the streets and sidewalks of Richmond, people from all walks of life, and stores with goods in them to take home. She noted the strength and independence of women, now that so many husbands, fathers, and brothers were away at the War.

On this New Year's Day reception for the citizens of Richmond at the White House of the Confederacy, Mr. Davis had been President of the Confederacy for less than a year. He was inaugurated on February 19, 1861, at the First Confederate Capital in Montgomery, Alabama. The Capital was moved to Richmond when the new nation was at full strength after Virginia, Tennessee, Arkansas, and North Carolina joined forces with the original seven states.

President Davis, his wife, and their three young children moved into the Confederacy's executive mansion in August 1861, after living in the new Spotswood Hotel since May. The President's wife was the former Varina Howell of Natchez, Mississippi. Their children were small—Margaret was six years old, Jefferson Davis Jr. four, and Joseph two. The youngest was William, born in December.

James and Mary ushered their two guests toward the receiving line to meet President Davis and the First Lady. While waiting, Mary speculated about the First Family, whispering in Orie's ear, "I don't expect we'll see the dear children. Mrs. Davis gave birth to a third son less than a month ago and that's why she's seated in a chair next to the President." To John, she said that Mr. Davis was not well and listed his maladies from memory: recurring bouts of malaria, facial neuralgia, cataracts in his left eye, unhealed wounds from the Mexican War, and insomnia.

"The poor man," said John with some alarm.

"Yes," said Mary, "but he's a Southerner and will prevail come what may. You know he was a West Point man and a hero in the Mexican War, don't you? He rather expected to be appointed a General in the Confederate Army, but the lot of them unanimously tapped him for President."

"I like the fact that he was named by his father, who fought in the Revolutionary War for Thomas Jefferson. In fact, Mr. Davis grew up to become a Jeffersonian Democrat dedicated to the principle of states' rights under the Constitution. Alabamians are great admirers of Jefferson Davis," John added.

James said, "Virginians respect him as well. Mr. Davis is an educated man and self-taught well beyond his formal schooling. They say he's a student of classical history and literature as well as a constitutional scholar. I've heard him talk on how the Romans used the slave system to teach the captured warriors and their women and children to speak the language and learn a trade and Roman customs before they became freedmen. For example, the father of the great Roman poet Horace was a former slave who bought his own freedom and paid for his son's education, which brought him into the highest circles of Roman society."

"Slavery is much on people's minds. Do the Northern abolitionists understand how many freedmen there are already in Virginia, I wonder?" John mused aloud.

"I think the abolitionists are more interested in punishing Southerners than freeing slaves," James said darkly.

As they moved closer to the receiving line, John and Orie listened to the President's gracious welcome of each visitor to the White House of the Confederacy, followed by an introduction to his wife, Varina.

At last it was their turn. James introduced his wife and then Orie and John, saying, "Mr. President, I'd like to present to you my cousin Dr. Orianna Russell Moon Andrews and her husband, Dr. John Andrews, Confederate States of America Army Medical Corps." Turning to Orie and John he said, "Drs. Orianna and John Andrews, this is our President, Mr. Jefferson Davis."

Although dressed in the obligatory presidential civilian frock coat, Mr. Davis bore himself with the erect posture of the former military officer that he was. "I welcome you both and I give you my personal thanks for your service to our soldiers. It could be a long War, but the independence of our beloved Southland is what we are all striving for. May God bless you both."

John noted the president's apparent blindness in the left eye and the thin, careworn face. His figure was slight but strong, and taller than average. He looked to John to be in his midfifties. The President then turned to his wife and introduced the two young doctors to her. Varina greeted them with interest but did not begin a conversation, with so many people in line yet to greet.

Orie wished she had her mother's knack of taking in a person's whole being at once without seeming to stare, but did the best she could. Varina was beautiful and considerably younger than her husband; her complexion was a darker shade of olive than Orie expected of the daughter of a Natchez, Mississippi, cotton plantation owner, and her accent was not syrupy-sweet Southern. Orie liked her.

James and Mary guided them to a table, where they waited to be served punch from a large crystal bowl by a young lady with consummate Southern charm and grace.

"I am most pleased with Mr. Davis's grand New Year's Day reception, aren't you too, James?" Mary asked.

"Indeed I am, and very proud to be with our young doctors today. It's also important to keep up the morale of the people, and President Davis shows his sagacity by spending this first day of the new year with the people of Richmond and setting the tone of hope and strength for the months to come." Nods of agreement were freely given.

Dainty sandwiches and squares of cake arrayed on large platters as well as sugar mint candies and bowls of nuts tempted John, who fixed a plate for Mary first and then Orie. James declined, saying, "I'm saving my appetite for something more to my liking later on."

"Oh, but everything is delicious!" Mary said. After months of political indecision and the abrupt start of the War, she felt safe and proud on this festive day.

Orie agreed readily. In her heart she was proud of the Commonwealth of Virginia. Rather than bend to the power of men willing to subvert the Constitution to impose their rule on the South, they were forming a new nation that would be bound to the Constitution, as was intended by the Founders of the United States of America.

"Do let's move on," said Mary. "We must leave time to greet the Governor of Virginia at the Capitol building."

"It's just two blocks north of here and may not be so crowded," said James. "I'll signal our driver and have him take us there." He donned his hat, outer coat, and gloves.

A crowd had already gathered at the Capitol on a hill overlooking the James River as they arrived. "Don't let's rush, although I know I's cold, but I want you to gaze upon Thomas Jefferson's magnificent Greek temple to the gods of justice," James said in his finest oratorical voice, while keeping his eye on Mary Digges. Before she could correct him, James said, "Yes, I know it's modeled after an ancient Roman temple Jefferson admired in Southern France, but it looks Greek to me and its classic simplicity of proportions speaks to the universal desire of mankind for purity of justice." James stopped speaking while the three looked upon the first public building in the New World constructed in the Monumental Classical style, built in 1788. "Now let's go inside and get warm," James said, leading the way inside while John held the door open for the ladies.

The Governor was standing in a receiving line with his family, while dressed-up Richmonders sampled the punch and waited in line to wish Governor John Letcher a happy new year. The marble interior of the great building buzzed with the hum of voices, and the crisp clack of military dress shoes marching in precision echoed under the dome of the rotunda. Candles were lit, as the afternoon sun was beginning to dip outside, and the air was chilled by the wind of winter. The historic importance of the day was lost on very few and the unuttered thought was: Will the Confederate Capitol still be standing a year from today?

As they waited in yet another line that day, Orie explained to John that Governor Letcher from Lexington was a friend of her family's at Viewmont and married to a Staunton woman whose family had ties to her Uncle James Barclay's wife, Julia.

"Your brother made a student of me last summer regarding Albemarle County and points west and the James River and Kanawha Canal. I understand the ties between the towns of the Shenandoah Valley and the river and canal that carry wheat to Richmond and bring back goods from the East. Ike is happy that John Letcher is Governor," John said, grinning at Orie. "Ike can't stand to leave an Alabamian in ignorance of the glories of all of Virginia."

"He's a Virginia homebody," Orie said, "and all those books of Father's feed his love for our homeland. It's fortunate that you are an able and willing student."

When introduced to Orie, Governor Letcher immediately recognized both the names Moon and Viewmont. "I count your family and Viewmont Farm among the best that Albemarle County has to offer to the rest of Virginia," he said. "It's also a great honor to meet two young physicians who have the care of our soldiers in time of war. I will keep you both in my prayers and thank God for you." The Governor was a middle-class family man with the look of a doting parent. John and Orie were instantly at ease with him and with his wife, the former Susan Holt of Staunton.

After they were through the receiving line, friends of James came over to greet him and speak their minds. "I never imagined the Yankees would invade Virginia with thousands of troops and artillery pieces, be thoroughly routed by our brave Boys, and still be waging war," said one man.

"It's all the fault of those damned abolitionists," said another.

"Exactly so. They want us to free all the slaves without compensation and then what would happen?" The gentleman looked around for answers.

"I'll tell you, sir. The planters would go bankrupt and the slaves would riot and starve. That's what the Yankees want to see, by

George, and we won't let it happen." The man's face was turning red with passion.

A woman with her gloved hand holding her husband's arm said with indignation, "They hate us, and they have always hated us. I would think that they would be glad to see us leave and say good riddance!"

The gentlemen agreed with short nods in the affirmative, but several looked uncomfortable with a woman speaking out. Mary Digges took the lead as James's wife and invited the women to have some punch and cake. The men exchanged looks as the ladies strode across the marble floor to slake their thirst with orange fruit punch.

"I'm sorry I spoke up in such a harsh tone," said Martha Sullivan, lately from Savannah. "But I'm angry and frightened. Why don't they just let us go? Even though we Southerners fought for independence from England and built the country as Founding Fathers and should be treated with the greatest of respect, they...they hate us and are doing everything in their power to destroy us."

"It's true what you're saying, but we must stand firm and they will tire of the War and go back home," said Mary. "Virginia was not a secessionist state a year ago, but look at us now. Lincoln's tyranny caused this war."

Another woman changed the subject. "What do you think about the President's wife? You know, her father's people are Northerners and she went to an academy for young ladies in Philadelphia. I also hear that she preferred living in Washington those fifteen years Mr. Davis was a Congressman than on a cotton plantation in Natchez. Where is her allegiance, I wonder?"

A rather short and stout lady bedecked with heirloom jewelry confessed, "I feel pity for her. She was eighteen when she married Mr. Davis, a thirty-six-year-old widower who lost his first wife to malaria after three months of marriage. He never got over her death, of course, but after eight years of mourning spent studying constitutional law and classical literature as a recluse, he lost his head over the pretty young woman he met at his older brother's housewarming party at his new mansion on a cotton plantation. Her father did nothing but lose money given to him by her mother's people. But what can you expect from a Northerner, even if way back there was a Governor on his side of the family?"

Sidestepping the snideness against Varina's less-than-financially-successful father, Mary told them that Varina had lost her firstborn at age two. "Nobody knew what killed the baby. Some unknown disease, and that's worst of all. How can you protect a child from something like that? Varina has had her share of sorrow. Let's not make things worse for her."

"You are correct, of course, Mary. Speculating on her allegiance is unkind and a waste of time. I do apologize for my words."

"Believe me, dear, we are all upset. Think no more of it," said Mary.

When they joined the men, James was ready to go and they took the carriage to the Spotswood Hotel on Main Street, a new five-story brick structure with an ornate iron façade, where Richmonders went to dine on occasions such as New Year's Day. The ornate marble lobby was crowded and noisy with good cheer, especially at the bar, but James was given a table in the dining room near the splendid crystal chandelier, which pleased Mary and his two young guests.

"Did the gentlemen solve the problems of the War?" Mary asked lightheartedly when they were settled in their chairs.

"Actually, a gentleman I did not know from Norfolk had some interesting views on the matter. He thinks President Lincoln is acting out of fear that the separated South will join forces with the British and go to war against what's left of the United States," John said.

"Am I correct, John, in saying that?" James asked.

"Indeed you are, sir, and furthermore, he backed up his words with some pertinent history. In the War of 1812, the United States sent a raiding party across the St. Lawrence to test the defenses of Canada. The idea was to annex Canada and then have possession of the whole of North America, and we would never be threatened by the British again."

"But that never happened," Orie pointed out.

"No, it didn't, for two reasons," John said. "One, the Canadians fought back and they made it clear they did not want to be made part of the United States. Second, the British built a warship so powerful that it could destroy any ship in the US Navy as well as blow to bits any town on the American side of the St. Lawrence they pleased. And another such ship was already on the drawing board. That was the end of such dreams. Now, a war against the South and Britain together is Lincoln's nightmare."

When the food came, served on signature Spotswood china and fine crystal, the conversation turned to the praises of Southern ham, sweet potatoes, corn pudding, greens, and oysters. Yeast rolls, cornbread, and biscuits were hot from the oven, and the two men chose one of each, while Mary asked for a yeast roll and Orie took a high, light biscuit.

"Mercy, this is all so good, I can hardly stop eating," said Mary, and soon the conversation turned to happy new years of times past. When the band played "Auld Lang Syne," everyone in the candlelit dining room fell silent and listened, many with tear-stained faces, John among them. Less than six months ago, John had lost his two younger brothers, and the grief had stayed with him.

When they were back home in their apartment, Orie and John talked about the long day, although they were tired and aware that they would be leaving their warm bed early in the morning for hospital rounds.

"This is a New Year's Day I will never forget, John," Orie said. "Being away from the hospital for a day and being with people who were enjoying themselves has made me feel like I am more a part of the whole new nation and the excitement of it all."

"The world is watching us, Orie. All over the South, hearts are hopeful and happy. Mine is doubly so. Our love was forged in war and our marriage celebrates the same year of its beginning as the Southern Confederacy. May God bless both."

Arm in arm, they left the parlor for their warm bed, each with their own thoughts reflected in the heart of the other.

CHAPTER 21

THE ARAB'S BLESSING

The last days in January saw a thaw. The temperature was up in the high forties, the sun was shining, and the wind was resting, worn out from constant blowing. Orie arose, felt that the hard edge of the cold had softened, then sat back down on the bed, suddenly nauseous. Then dizzy. She lay down. She lifted her head. Too much. She lay back down.

John was dressed and looked in at her. "Orie, dear, it's time to get up."

"John, I'm nauseous and dizzy. I need to rest here awhile."

He came over quickly and felt her forehead for fever. "No fever. Anything else? Stomach pain? Sore throat?"

"No, dearest, and I feel fine as long as I don't move. "

"Can I bring you something to eat? Some bacon and coffee?"

She jumped off the bed and threw up in the china washing bowl, then lay back in bed, trembling. John took a washcloth, poured some water from the pitcher on it, and laid it on her forehead. He took a chair and watched her relax and become drowsy.

"You have to stay in bed today. I'll tell them at the hospital you're not well. I think you are all right, but you may have something contagious and we need to keep you away from the soldiers. I'll tell Ruth and she can keep an eye on you." He left with the china washing bowl and pitcher.

He had his breakfast in the dining room and gave instructions to Ruth. "Dr. Orie has a sick stomach this morning, but she'll need some tea and toast later on."

"Yas sir, Dr. Andrews. I'll look in on her and take care a' her all day. Don't you worry none." She was glad it was Dr. Mrs. Andrews and not Dr. Mr. Andrews she'd be looking in on all day. She hadn't thought about being a nursemaid to the couple.

Ruth cleaned up from breakfast and helped herself to some coffee and a biscuit until she heard the sounds of the Dr. Missus moving around. She looked in the bedroom, and Orie was dressed for work and combing her hair.

"Good morning, Ruth. I'm sure Dr. John told you I was sick today, but I'm feeling much better. I'll have a very light breakfast, some tea and toast, and I'll have a hired driver come get me."

"Yas'um. You have something to eat and then we'll see how you feel. Do you want it in the bedroom or in the dining room?"

"The dining room, please." She was mystified. She felt fine, but still a bit trembly. This was not like exhaustion.

Orie went to the hospital and felt better than usual in the warmer air of the day's thaw. She passed word to John that she was at work and would go home with him in the evening as usual.

Orie felt fine at the hospital, until she came to the bedside of a boy in abject wretchedness, suffering from dysentery. Her heart went out to him, but then she breathed in the smell of acute diarrhea and immediately had to leave his bedside and be sick outside the wooden structure. Feeling better, she went back inside and then was too busy to even think about herself again. That night, she told John about her day,

"Thankfully, there's no fever and no other symptoms. I think something you ate yesterday didn't agree with you," he said. He spoke blandly, but in his mind he was searching for a disease that started off with intermittent nausea and dizziness. Nothing came to mind.

The next day was the same, except that she felt worse and stayed home all day. On the third day, Ruth said to her, "Maybe you gon' have a baby. I seen women sick like this a'fore and thas what it turned out to be."

Orie laughed. "I'm looking for diseases I may have caught from the soldiers, and this is not one of them. You may be right, Ruth. I'll consult with Dr. John when he comes home tonight."

The couple sat down to supper, Ruth serving them a hot dinner of cornbread, beans, pork, and cabbage, and a rice pudding for dessert. Orie felt better in the evenings, but still had little appetite and a queasiness that was never far from her. After supper, they sat together in the parlor.

"John, dearest, I may have news for you, for us. I think I may be pregnant."

When she told him her period had been due two weeks ago, he began to add it all up.

"Orie, darling, I think you are right. I was so concerned about you. I couldn't see what was in front of my eyes. I'm just so happy you are not sick, that you are all right."

There was much to discuss that night. The battlefield continued to be quiet, and the patients were coming in steadily with illnesses rather than battle wounds. The thaw in the weather seemed to point to a time to leave Richmond.

"You'll have to give up your commission, Orie," John said.

"I've been thinking the same thing," Orie replied. "Lots of doctors above me in rank will be happy to see me go, as well as those army nurses below me in rank. Some refuse to accept me as a medical doctor and call me 'nurse.' It's humiliating. I love my work and I am a real doctor. "

"Well, the South is that way, I'm afraid."

"No, not just the South, darling. No man would come to the Women's Female Medical College of Pennsylvania in Philadelphia, the City of Medicine, for treatment even though it was free. All we could do to practice our skills was open a clinic for destitute women and children, and they flocked to us."

"Nevertheless, we must get you back to Viewmont. I'll ask for a furlough long enough to make the journey with you and then come back here. It's for the best. I don't know of any other way."

"I'm happy, John, but I don't want to be apart from you."

"If there was any other way…" John choked up. Being apart from Orie was terrible, but the main thing now was to keep her safe. Viewmont was the answer.

John made the arrangements, and Orie resigned her commission as a captain and assistant surgeon, CSA. John, with Ruth's help, packed Orie's clothes and belongings in a great trunk and hired a driver to take them to the train depot.

The belching wood smoke, shrieking whistle, and screaming brakes made the ride an agony for Orie. She was nauseous the whole time and could do nothing to relieve her misery. She was embarrassed now, having made light of the complaints of pregnant women before experiencing the suffering herself.

By the time John got her to Viewmont, she was more nauseous than ever, having been afraid to eat while on the train and now too sick to want anything at all. John, too, was drained of energy.

Anna Maria took them in like a commander rearranging troops. "John, Martha will fix you up with what she has in the kitchen, and I will get Orie to bed and get some tea to stay down. Uncle Jacob will see that a cot is brought into Orie's room for you to sleep on."

Lottie was there to help, as well as Colie and Mollie. Eddie had been feverish and coughing, so she would be kept away. Ike was away for drills with the Forty-Ninth Regiment of the Virginia Militia. All things were done in good order, and soon enough, Orie was asleep upstairs and John had eaten his fill and was beginning to think everything would be all right.

In the parlor, John told Anna Maria about the work they had been doing in the hospital and the apartment in Richmond and how happy Orie and he were. And now they were happy and excited about the baby.

"Orie looks so wretched, John," Anna Maria said. "I was not sick like this with any of mine."

"I've spoken to two other doctors who have delivered babies, and they were of little help. As a rule, they see the mother at childbirth, not in the beginning like this, unless the mother is sick and at risk of losing the baby. Orie shows no signs of anything dangerous. No pain, no fever, no bleeding, but this has been a long and hard day, granted."

"I trust you, John, and truth to tell, she got into bed happily and dozed right off to sleep after taking tea with milk and toast."

In the morning, John was off to Richmond and Orie blinked back tears to see him leave, but was secure in the wonder that she was carrying his baby and he would be back. In the meantime, she would make herself useful doctoring her family and former patients. The nausea would end. Best of all, she was as safe as possible from the contagious diseases she had been exposed to that could put an end to this life she was carrying. Already her attachment to this new little being was uppermost in her mind. She must take all care to be healthy so that the baby would have a good chance at life. John's baby. Her baby. Her prayers took on added urgency. May the Lord keep them both safe for the baby.

She remembered the blessing given to her on the occasion of her farewell at the Bedouins' encampment outside Jerusalem. The oldest Bedouin sheik, white-haired and long-bearded, stood over "El Hakim" (the Doctor), raised his eyes and extended his hands and said: "May your children be as many as the stars of the sky and sands of the sea and may you never have a daughter."

At the time she did not approve of the exclusion of female babies, but since she did not believe in unchristian prayers, she thanked him for the Arab blessing and thought no more about it. Now she thought she would like a male child in the image of his father. What greater gift to her beloved John? But, whether male or female, the baby would be their gift from a loving God.

After considering his new circumstances while on the train to Richmond, John decided to visit the Moore townhouse there, where Ruth's family lived. Ruth's father, the butler, answered the door and recognized Dr. John Andrews as the man whose wife had hired Ruth. The master and mistress were both at home on that Sunday afternoon and asked Uncle James to send him in.

John introduced himself and took a chair near the roaring fire in the fireplace. "First of all, I want to thank you both for finding the apartment for Orie and myself and lending out Ruth for hire to help us during the day."

"Is there a problem, sir?" Robert Moore asked impatiently, ignoring his wife's frown at his impolite haste.

"Oh, never, sir! But circumstances have changed. My wife is pregnant and I have taken her back to Viewmont. She resigned her commission and will not be returning to Richmond."

Robert was all smiles and hearty congratulations. "That's wonderful news, and exactly right to take her home and await the birth in a safe place."

Sarah, too, was pleased with the news. "Anna Maria will be a grandmother!"

"And so regarding your changed circumstances, and they are, indeed, changed, what can we do for you?" Robert asked.

"I have no further need of our apartment or for Ruth's services," John said. "I have made arrangements for a bed in the doctors' barracks and will eat my meals at the commissary with the other doctors and officers."

Sarah said, "Mercy! Much as Ruth enjoyed her work, she told her mother she was lonely there and wished for more company, that the two of you were gone all day long every day. The new government is advertising for slave owners to hire out their folk to hospitals especially, and Ruth wanted to do that. As for the apartment, the rents have tripled in price since you arrived in November, and the owner will be glad to have it vacant and be able to rent it out at a higher price. So this is a fortunate change in several ways."

"Will you have a cigar, sir, and a glass of bourbon and stay awhile?" Robert looked pleased as punch.

John smiled. "Thank you, sir, but I have much to do and must be back on duty at the hospital early in the morning."

"As you wish, sir." Robert appeared ready to celebrate everyone's good fortune as soon as John was out the door.

Sarah wished him well, and Robert walked him to the door, noting that John had a driver in a carriage waiting for him. "Please let us know if there is anything we can do for you. Sometimes it takes an old Richmonder to get things done around here, especially now. By George, the city has never seen the likes of such crowds here, all itching to be a part of the new Confederate government."

They shook hands, and John was on his way. He had the driver go by the apartment and wait until he packed his clothes into a couple of suitcases and then let him off at the Chimborazo Hospital in front of the doctors' barracks. Three young men were on their way out for Sunday supper and invited John to come along. He quickly realized how hungry he was, too busy all day to stop and find a place to eat. His companions that evening were all surgeons and all Southerners. The evening was spent in clever banter and witty conversation.

"Two battles so far. Score: Yanks zero, Rebels two!" The loudest one shouted as they walked down the street. The four young men were greeted by a group singing "Dixie," and laughter was everywhere. They ducked into a tavern, and there was more singing and shouting. This was a new side to the war that John had

143

not been a part of. He drank hot coffee, ordered two servings of fried fish and potatoes, and missed his brothers, but longed for Orie even more.

That night in the barracks, John said his silent prayers, asking for protection of Orie and the child she was carrying. Sleep came quickly.

CHAPTER 22
VIEWMONT, WINTER 1862

"Orie, letter for you!" Colie called out as she came running up the stairs.

Orie sat up in bed and heard her mother say in a loud whisper, "Hush, girl! Orie's resting."

Colie came rushing in nevertheless, waving the letter before handing it to her sister. "It's from John. I knew you would want it right away."

"It's the first one since the package of them came a week ago. I'll open it up and see when he mailed it," Orie said. Sitting on the side of the bed, Orie used her letter opener so as to not tear anything and looked at the date, with Colie hovering beside her.

"It's February twenty-second. It took a week to get here." Orie held the letter to her chest and turned away from Colie for privacy to read it.

"I'll leave you in peace, Orie. John has written almost every day since he returned to Richmond." She sighed. "I hope I find a husband like John someday." Colie wandered out of the room dreamily.

With Colie gone, Orie kissed the words on the paper and looked for signs of John's presence, such as a smudge he might have made with a finger.

February 22, 1862
Chimborazo Hospital, Richmond

My Precious Orie,

Your sweet letter of February 17 arrived today. I will wear it in my breast pocket until the next one arrives. It is a comfort to have something you have touched next to my heart. I have been very busy but I stay well and miss you with every breath I take. I want so much to take you in my arms and hold you and soon there will be signs of our baby. How I long to be with you.

I have rather sad news. You remember, of course, James Jackson from Florence, who was wounded at Manassas, recovered, and helped organize the Twenty-Seventh Regiment, Infantry, Alabama. He's a lieutenant colonel and was captured by the Federals at the Battle of Fort Donelson on the Cumberland River. I don't think he was wounded. Please pray for his quick release.

You say you are feeling better except for nausea in the morning still. Do whatever Martha and Mammy Jinny tell you to do, my darling. As long as you are able to keep down some food at dinner and supper, you will regain your strength. Be patient!

Are things still quiet at Viewmont? How I wish I were there! I'm relieved that although Ike is often away on militia drills, he's assigned to Albemarle County and not far away.

My love to you and the baby-in-waiting and thanks to your mother and brother for the sanctuary you have in Viewmont.

A thousand kisses for my sweetest love,
As ever, your devoted and loving husband,
J. S. Andrews, MD

After the midday dinner, Orie asked Ike to see her in the parlor and tell her about the Battle of Fort Donelson, where John's friend from Florence had been captured.

"Orie, since he mentioned the battle, I'll assume your condition permits news that may be disturbing to you," Ike said. "Fort Donelson was a major defeat for us, but not something we cannot overcome."

"How many soldiers were captured?" Orie had on her I-want-answers look.

"The figures are on everyone's tongues because they are so hard to believe. Our General Simon Buckner asked for surrender terms from his old friend General Ulysses S. Grant. 'Nothing short of unconditional surrender' was his answer. As far as we know, this was the War's first demand for an unconditional surrender and Buckner was appalled. Looking at the situation, he decided he had no choice. He turned over some 15,000 men, 20,000 rifles, 48 pieces of artillery, 17 heavy guns, 3,000 horses, and large commissary stores."

"Go on," said Orie, her face pale and grim. "How many killed and what was the objective?" She was thinking about her classmates at Troy Female Seminary and the Women's Medical School in Philadelphia. Did they know what was happening in the South? Did they approve of this bloody invasion? Could nobody stop the fratricidal outrage?

"Those figures are well known also," said Ike. "The South lost 1,500 to 3,500 men, while the North had 500 men killed and 2,000 wounded, but those numbers don't seem to bother the architects of the War. Three thousand Confederates escaped, but the South was forced to give up much Southern territory in Kentucky and Tennessee. The Federals had taken Fort Henry on the Tennessee River ten days earlier, so now they control the Tennessee and Cumberland Rivers along with the railroads in the area. Losing Nashville, the first capital city in the Confederacy to be lost, is a serious blow to Confederate morale, and Nashville will become a huge supply depot for the Union Army."

Ike did not tell Orie about the warning from the Hortons in Memphis in the fall that Union forces would cut the South off from everything they needed to survive and strangle them. It was happening. No quarter had been given. "Old army friends" were no longer friends or the honorable gentlemen the South thought they were dealing with.

Nashville in Union hands—how ghastly, Orie thought. "Does Mama know all this?"

"She knows we lost a serious battle, but it's far from here and we are still safe."

"That's enough for her to know."

"I agree," said Ike.

"Although I gave up my commission and am no longer a Confederate Army captain, I am still part of the Army in my heart and I am grieving for those soldiers," said Orie.

"A problem we have to contend with here is what to tell Peter and the field workers. There are rumors, and some are worse than the truth. But we'll deal with that when the time comes," said Ike.

Orie joined her sisters in the parlor doing their needlework and sewing. Anna Maria arrived after conferring with Martha about food supplies and began working through a pile of mending. "It's getting harder to make purchases, so wear your clothes lightly," she said, and smiled as they looked at her with mouths open.

"Mama, we are never rough on our clothes," Mollie complained.

"I'm teasing you, darling. I know very well you girls are all careful with your everyday dresses as well as your go-to-party and Sunday dresses. It's just that it's a bit gloomy here at Viewmont at times, and I want you to know that your work is necessary and we have each other for company and food enough. We even have a new baby to look forward to, God willing, in the fall."

Ever-efficient Orie checked to see who was working on what. The list was impressive: baby clothes and bandages, blankets, and trousers and hospital gowns for the soldiers.

"Well done!" she exclaimed, after examining the quality of the work they had done. She took a seat and a tear slid down her cheek.

"Are you quite all right, dear?" Anna Maria asked in the suddenly hushed room.

"Yes, quite," Orie said, brushing away the tear. "Forgive me. I miss John and I love my family and my struggling new country." She was glad for the work to do with her hands. She alone had piled up coats and gowns and bandages for the soldiers until there was a stack higher than a horse ready to be hauled into Charlottesville.

Lottie caught the spirit. Her fingers flew with needle and thread and she began to hum. Then they all hummed and then sang:

Oh, I wish I was in the land of cotton,
Old times there are not forgotten,
Look away! Look away! Look away, Dixie Land!

After the laughter subsided, Orie told them that back in July at Charlottesville General Hospital, soldiers had told her that Federal troops had marched into battle at Manassas singing "Dixie." At the end of the day, they fled in defeat. Since then, only Confederate troops sang "Dixie," but they sang made-up lines ending with the words "We'll die for old Virginia."

Eddie heard them singing and came out from the study. She lingered at the doorway. "May I come join you?"

Anna Maria put her work aside, got Eddie settled in a chair with good light by a window, and gave her cloth to roll into bandages. Her big sisters welcomed her into their august midst.

Lottie, still enjoying the fun, put to the tune of "Dixie" the words "We are the Moon sisters, Hooray! Hooray! On Viewmont's land I'll take my stand, to sew and stitch for Dixie! Away, away, away down South in Dixie!"

Anna Maria smiled at her girls and hoped that all of them would be content to stay at home until the War was over.

Orie smiled back. It *was* a sweet life. But she knew it would not last.

CHAPTER 23
EARLY SUMMER 1862

The war effort continued at Viewmont as the large gray cloud of fear hovered overhead and deepened. Anna Maria, her six children, and the slaves all bent to the task of providing food and clothing for the sorely oppressed Southern troops.

All had their jobs. Anna Maria and Ike were in charge of the farm and household. Tobacco, the golden leaves of prosperity, had to be planted, watered, and cultivated, then harvested, cured, and packed for shipping. It was a long process and fraught with the possibility of failure at every turn.

Orie had to be careful and remain in good health until she delivered the baby in the fall. With the warmth of early summer, Orie felt strong and took long walks after making her rounds to check on the field hands and women under her care. She was content to wait for her baby to come and for her husband to return.

Lottie put all her energy into her family and the War effort. Colie, Mollie, and Eddie studied their lessons, sewed and packed food for the soldiers, and prayed. They were busy and happy with the warm weather and lengthy days.

Anna Maria, lingering over her weekday "Confederate coffee," asked Ike when it would be over.

"When it's over, Mama."

"Next month it will be a year since the Battle of Manassas. Didn't we think it would be over in a few months, especially since the Confederate Army routed the Federals?"

"We hoped, so, Mama. We surely did," said Ike.

"I'm getting tired, son. The constant worry about everything and not knowing what the Yankees will do next cannot go on much longer."

"I know it, Mama. But we are luckier than most, and what would folks do without us?"

"That worries me too, Ike. If the Yankees raided Viewmont, it would be like taking over a town; they could get everything they needed except guns and ammunition."

Under his breath, Ike muttered, "They have all the guns and ammunition they need to destroy us ten times over."

Orie joined her brother. "I have a letter from John that disturbs me. There was a naval battle on the Mississippi at Memphis early this month and it seems that our forces withdrew without clearing away Yankees. John is very concerned about Memphis, because that's where his two uncles live."

"Yes, I know, because I visited them in November to invite them to your wedding. They truly feared the rumor that Lincoln was going to blockade all the rivers and ports surrounding the South and lay siege to the whole Confederacy. It seemed impossible last fall, but our ports are falling. Back in April the fortress at Island Number Ten, which protects the Mississippi River as it winds south toward the Confederacy, surrendered after battling Union gunboats since February. In May, New Orleans fell. From last fall to this spring, Union and Confederate navies dueled in the waters of the Gulf of Mexico. New Orleans was our largest city and had one of the few shipyards available to us."

"How did that happen?" Orie asked, wondering how she could have been so tired and preoccupied that she had not understood the gravity of the events John touched on in his letters, always putting his concern on her health and the safety of Viewmont.

Ike shot back, "They have been relentless with all the troops, artillery, food, and equipment they could possibly need. Even more, they have ships that are faster and better than ours. But ten Union soldiers are not worth one of ours."

Orie thought back to her days at medical school in Philadelphia. The city was busy day and night with traffic on the streets and people on the walkways. The Delaware River traffic was continuous, with no end to the barges and steamboats carrying both passengers and cargo. She looked around at the quiet woods and fields of Viewmont. They were two different worlds. Why did anyone have to oppress and prey on weaker ones? Was that the law of nature? But this was a Christian nation. America was supposed to be different.

"All those battles were far away. What about the James?" Orie asked.

"Plenty of action on the James," said Ike. "Back in March at Hampton Roads, our ironclad CSS *Virginia* knocked Union blockaders out of the water. The news in Richmond brought out cheering crowds celebrating the end of the blockade and nearly the end of the war. The next day, the North's ironclad, the USS *Monitor,* came to do battle, and the two ironclads pounded each other all day long to a stalemate, with both ships damaged. Two months later, the Union Navy returned."

"Oh, Ike, they are like wolves—they keep attacking. The battles are like Hercules fighting the Lernaean Hydra, a huge serpent with nine heads. As soon as Hercules cut off one head, two more grew. But Hercules was a myth and the Federal forces are not," said Orie.

Ike pondered her analogy, then got back to the news. "The Yankees forced the destruction of the repaired CSS *Virginia* in the shallow waters and attacked the only defense left on the James, Fort Darling at Drewry's Bluff. They attacked with three ironclads and two wooden gunboats against the fort while General McClellan's infantry marched on Richmond along the line of the York River. What saved us was a group of our boys who salvaged the guns from the CSS *Virginia* to fire from Fort Darling, and they drove the Yankee squadron away."

"How far was this from Richmond?" Orie asked, hoping it was closer to Hampton Roads. After hesitating briefly, Ike answered, "Seven miles."

Her face showing shock, Orie said nothing, thinking of John in Richmond, *seven* miles away from the Union Navy.

"Orie, you receive letters from John almost daily. Why have you not followed the battles?"

"He *mentioned* the battles but did not imply that we were in any danger, and most of the letters contained not one line about the war. But now when I hear about the battles one after another, I am seeing a completely different picture."

Ike began to explain how the South started out with no military force at all, while the North had large and experienced Army, Navy, and Marines. There was some catching up to do. He decided not to bring that up.

"Do you want to hear about Memphis? Our Boys were courageous above any in history, but we lost Memphis."

"Yes, Ike, I need to know."

"Our Boys assembled a fourteen-boat 'River Defense Fleet' made up of merchant steamers manned by civilian crews and armored with bales of cotton."

"Oh dear heavens," Orie cried. "I hope they were battling Union rowboats."

Ike ignored her whimsical wishing. "Eight of our boats faced down a Union fleet of five ironclads and two rams at Memphis. The vessels rammed into each other and fired pistols at point-blank range. Seven of the eight Confederate boats could not continue the battle, while only one Union ram was sidelined. The daredevil heroism of our Boys is the talk of the world." Ike could not help boasting a bit, basking in the reflection of the Southern soldiers' heroism.

Orie thought otherwise, seeing maimed and twisted bodies, faces and limbs scalded by steam, and devastated families.

Ike continued, "Cotton and courage is not enough to win naval battles, but the Yankees will never defeat us on land. Many more of us will die, but we will successfully defend our Southern soil. We will prevail."

"I pray you are right, dear brother," said Orie, as she walked away toward the servants' cabins carrying her medical bag. Lottie was already there, preaching the gospel and praying with them.

CHAPTER 24
BETTER TIMES, WORSE TIMES

Maybe Ike is right, Orie thought. Our Boys are doing better fighting on land, which requires great courage, not just the best equipment. She was hearing tales about Confederate Colonel John Hunt Morgan over in Kentucky. The Federal forces were all over Central Kentucky the summer Orie was at Viewmont waiting for her child to be born.

Union forces had taken Cynthiana and threatened Lexington and Paris in Kentucky. Confederate forces led by Colonel Morgan were ordered to Lexington, leaving Paris entirely undefended. In a surprise move, Morgan and his raiders moved toward Paris and were greeted with cheers and welcomes. That night his scouts informed him that the Yankee forces were coming to attack him. He moved out, only to encounter them on their mission. Keeping calm, Morgan outmaneuvered them and continued to Richmond, Kentucky, where he enjoyed a grand welcome by the inhabitants. Recruits joined up and were given mounts and armed.

According to Ike, Morgan's plan to stay a few days to rest, dine, and recruit more mounted soldiers was cut short by news that a large Union cavalry force was on its way. Preferring to live to fight another day, Morgan and his Raiders pushed on to Crab Orchard, where he found about 120 wagons and $1 million worth of Federal stores and equipment. Unable to take the supplies over the broken ground to Confederate camps, he gave orders to the Boys to destroy the Union cache. They did with great fervor. Next was Somerset, a Federal depot, where they destroyed another $1 million worth of stores and recaptured a thousand stand of arms that had been taken from Confederate forces at the disaster at Fishing Creek. All told, in twenty days, Colonel Morgan increased his force of 870 to 1,200, caught and released over 1,200, confiscated seven thousand stand of arms, and destroyed $7.5 million dollars' worth of stores, arms, and subsistence. His loss was ninety men. He was also forced to destroy stores that the South desperately needed but could not take, due to the presence of armed Union soldiers who could appear out of nowhere into a town, a stand of woods, or a dirt road.

Back in Tennessee, Colonel Morgan captured Gallatin, a town twenty-five miles north of Nashville on the Cumberland River, and secured the telegraph office to counter any and all Union messages coming in. The captured Yankee telegraph operator, now a prisoner, joined in the party celebrating the day's events at the home of a "Secesh Lady" and "passed the evening with song and dance" and the retelling of the heroes' adventure. Danger, death, and destruction beset them relentlessly, but when fortune rewarded their efforts, Southerners responded.

The stories encouraged all the good people at Viewmont. Truly, the courageous Confederate Boys were venerated beyond all measure throughout the South, and they believed the sacred soil of the South and the courage of the Southern Boys would put an end to the vast multipronged Yankee invasion.

Otherwise, food throughout the South was becoming more and more scarce, but Viewmont was still able to set a decent table and the field hands and servants were not doing without, thanks always to Anna Maria and Ike, who would find or make a way to keep Viewmont supplied. Always there was music and dancing at the village of cabins and singing and readings and entertainment inside the Main House. Life was to be lived, not wasted in worry.

September 17, 1862, was a sad day when Generals Lee, Jackson, and Longstreet took on Federal forces at Antietam on the western Maryland side of the Potomac. In all, 23,000 soldiers were killed, wounded, or missing in the single deadliest day of fighting in American history. Union forces numbered 75,500 while the South had 38,000. President Davis announced that the fight had been brought to the enemy, "who pursues us with a relentless and apparently aimless hostility."

Antietam battlefield, with its hilly topography, was ideal for artillery warfare and both sides had come prepared, although many Confederate guns were obsolete by Civil War standards, and Union guns were more accurate with a longer range. The battle was called "a great tumbling together of all heaven and earth." Reinforcements brought in by General A. P. Hill late in the day saved the Confederate Army. With such great casualties on both sides, the next day was spent burying the dead and caring for the wounded. That night General Lee crossed the Potomac with his broken but not defeated Army, heading back to the South. After that battle, Lincoln issued his Emancipation Proclamation, freeing the slaves in the South, where he had no authority, but not in the North, giving the war the dual purpose of preserving the Union and freeing the Southern slaves.

Orie was shaken by the news and Ike, too, was shocked at the outcome of a battle he had believed would mark the beginning of the end for the Federal forces. It was after Antietam that Orie learned of the defeat of Confederate troops at Shiloh in Hardin County, Tennessee, back in April. It started out well: Generals Albert S. Johnston and P. G. T. Beauregard launched an attack on General Ulysses Grant's army camped on the west bank of the Tennessee River. General Johnston was killed in the otherwise successful attack. General Beauregard decided to rest his tired troops that night, during which time Grant's army received major reinforcements. The next morning a Federal counterattack completely reversed the Confederate gains from the day before. Confederate forces retreated from the area, ending their hopes of blocking the Union advance into Northern Mississippi.

The Battle of Shiloh was the bloodiest battle in American history up to that time, with an estimated 23,750 casualties out of 66,812 Yankees and 44,699 Confederates. The constant battles were draining the numbers of the undermanned and ill-equipped Southern forces.

Ike told his foreman, Peter, about Lincoln's Emancipation Proclamation, wanting the field hands and others to hear it from Peter and himself rather than through the grapevine.

"Yas sir, Massa, we done heard about them Yankees freeing the slaves, but we think they gon' haul us off and put us to work Lord knows where. We better off here in the tobacco fields," Peter answered.

"That's what I think, too, Peter, and we need everyone in the field working hard to get this tobacco harvested and cured and packed away in hogsheads for shipping downstream to Richmond. That won't happen if the field hands slip away with empty promises of freedom by the Yankees."

"No sir, you is right, and I'll try to keep them right where they is at."

"Thank you, Peter," Ike said, and got back on his horse, with Shep along for company. He felt a little less worried.

While occupied with tasks that freed her mind, such as sewing and rolling bandages, Orie dreamed of her child and what kind of a future he or she would have. She also thought back to the year she spent at Troy Female Seminary, studying in the land of the Yankees.

The school on the upper Hudson River was a serious-minded place and Orie approved of that, because she was herself an unusually serious-minded young woman, especially coming from the South, the land of sunshine and ease.

At first the other girls left the Southern tobacco princess alone, until Lucy from Ohio discovered that quiet Orie had opinions very much like those of the rest of them. Lucy's friends sought out Orie out of curiosity, and then the girls from New York, Boston, and Philadelphia began to pay attention to her.

"Orie, where do you attend church? I don't see you at the First Presbyterian Church next door and Harriett says you don't go to the Episcopal Church either," asked Helen from Boston one rainy afternoon in the school library.

"I don't attend church because I'm not a Christian," Orie replied.

"Well, then, what are you?" Helen was mystified.

"I'm an agnostic, of course," said Orie. "Mama and Papa are persistently and annoyingly religious, and I am not. There's nothing more to it than that."

"I thought all Southerners were religious," Helen insisted.

"Most of them are, but I am not. I am interested in books, but not the Bible. I rather think I have a mind, but not a heart." She smiled at Helen, an outspoken and smart girl with a reputation for unpredictable interests.

Helen laughed out loud and was immediately shushed by the librarian.

"Let's go get some hot chocolate, you and I." The two girls, Helen taller than Orie, donned raincoats over their heavy dresses and walked arm-in-arm to a nearby tea room that catered to the girls from the Seminary, talking all the way about the school and the teachers and various girls.

Once inside, warm and dry with cups of steaming hot chocolate to savor, Orie began to question Helen.

"Everyone here comes from a great deal of wealth. What does your family do?"

"Shipping, from way back, and shipbuilding before that."

Orie nodded knowingly. "Sea captains?"

"Ye-es," Helen said hesitating, sensing trouble ahead.

"As you probably know, my family works a tobacco plantation, which is tedious, hard work. We have slaves to help."

"Yes, I knew that," said Helen.

"And you approve, do you?" said Orie.

"Well, no, certainly not. But you're not the owner and so your situation is not your fault. Mother made that very clear to me before I left for school this year. She said to be nice to you."

"What if I thought I should not speak to you because your ancestral sea captains dealt in the slave trade and made hundreds of thousands of dollars transporting Africans for the slave markets?"

"That was a long time ago," Helen countered. "Now we are all abolitionists and will fight to rid the nation of slavery."

Orie began to speak and the pent-up words gained speed as they rattled out. "My mother's people are Barclays—Quaker Barclays from Philadelphia. They were financiers for the American Revolution, and my great-grandfather served the new government abroad dealing with the Europeans on behalf of America and served as the Ambassador to the Sultan of Morocco. Lots of my Philadelphia Quaker relatives are abolitionists today, but my father tells them to calm down and work something out like the British did almost thirty years ago."

Helen bristled. "Talking is not the answer. We've talked forever and there are more slaves than ever before. John Adams called slavery 'an evil of colossal magnitude.'"

As if Helen had heard nothing, Orie suggested, "Look at it from another perspective, if you will."

"Certainly. I am an open-minded person. Everyone knows that. "

"Yes, you are," Orie agreed. "Now, a cousin of mine put it this way: who takes better care of a house, the renter or the owner?"

"Are...are you comparing a house to a human being?" Helen gasped.

"It's an analogy. When one owns something, it is dear to him, but when, say, a worker is hired, he is expendable, and when he is sick or old or injured, the boss lets him go. When a man owns a worker, he takes care of him forever. Do you see what I am saying? Our slaves are dear to us; they are part of our family."

"No, you cannot buy a human being, and they don't want to be cared for, but to be free and respected." Helen trembled with emotion. "Many, many people would sacrifice their lives to save the black Africans from enslavement. It's something we must do and do soon."

"I see," said Orie. But she could not accept the fact that her words meant nothing to a girl whose company she sought and enjoyed. She had already written to her mama and papa about her pretty friend from Boston.

Helen began to breathe more evenly. "I'm sorry, Orie. I'm afraid I wasn't being nice to you."

"You were just speaking your mind, and I was too. We don't agree, but you and I don't have to agree. That's what Papa told me. But we can still be friends, can't we?"

"Yes!" said Helen resolutely. "We'll be the best friends there ever were. We'll be like an Indian girl and a settler girl. They'll never see eye-to-eye, but they were friends anyway."

Ike and Mama and John all thought the Yankees would get tired of the fight and go home. Orie was not at all sure.

CHAPTER 25

BABY DAYS AND MORE

On October 30, 1862, Orie gave birth to her first child. John was by her side at Viewmont, on furlough. They named him Henry Horton Andrews, after John's grandfather, his mother's beloved father.

Orie was entranced by her son, the very image of John and herself in the flesh. The significance of the Nativity scene depicting God's love for his people in the form of baby Jesus was not lost on her. John gave out cigars to family and friends and felt that he had arrived at an utterly satisfying stage in his life. He was a husband, a father, and a medical doctor. His tiny son gave him a sense of power and strength that melted into humble thanks for the life of this boy. John's touch was gentle and soothing to the baby, who responded with cooing to the sound of his father's voice.

Orie took her time recovering from childbirth, as there were plenty of adoring women to take care of his every need. Anna Maria checked on him in his cradle almost as often as Orie did, and the baby's aunts dressed him and bathed him, carried him around, and played with him.

Cornelia was there to fetch things for the baby and for Orie, and was content to see her mistress well and happy. The wife of

Viewmont's blacksmith, Homer, Cornelia was the mother of two children and knew how to calm a crying baby and help Orie nurse Henry. In turn, Orie took a larger interest in Cornelia's babies and asked her to bring them to the Main House on occasion. They were three and four years old, and Orie liked giving them sweets and watching them show off the manners their mama had taught them. They could also recite Bible verses in their sing-song child-ish voices, and Orie and Lottie both delighted in these occasions.

Too soon, John had to return to duty in Richmond. Many from the enormous number of sick and wounded soldiers from the Battles of Second Manassas and Antietam were still convalesc-ing at Richmond hospitals, and Chimborazo was where they were taken first. John returned renewed and refreshed and was quickly absorbed into the demands of duty. Orie's descriptions of baby Henry from week to week gave John an inner source of energy as well as deeper compassion for the young soldiers he was treat-ing, some of them only teenagers. Orie's attachment to the baby pleased John, as it added another layer to their abiding love for each other.

Life at Viewmont took on more complexity as the War contin-ued. The tobacco crop did well, which was a great relief to Ike, and taking in Soldiers who were on furlough were always welcome for shelter and food as they traveled from their camps to home and back. Some soldiers were friends or sons of relatives and lived too far away to go home. They were invited to stay as houseguests. The house was always full. The ability to feed and welcome them was an unquestioned obligation and honor.

Since Lincoln's Emancipation Proclamation had been an-nounced, some of those travelers were slaves on the run to free-dom in Washington. Many traipsed along mountain roads above the Shenandoah Valley. Word got around that the people at Viewmont were kin to Quakers in Philadelphia and not averse to helping hide and shelter them. In his role as an active militiaman, Ike was able to protect his property from raids by slave-catchers, who, he believed, were acting on the constitutional right of "return of property" for the bounty, which applied to both the US and Confederate Constitutions. His own conscience, however, made it impossible to ignore the runaways' plight.

One night when Orie had just gotten Henry back to sleep after a feeding, Ike knocked on her bedroom door and whispered that she was needed at the blacksmith's family cabin. She dressed hurriedly, picked up her medical bag, and took her lantern to the cabin, a light flickering within.

She knocked on the door, which was opened immediately by Homer, with Cornelia at his side. "Come in quick," Homer whispered as he shut the door behind her. He led her to the bedstead in the corner, to a man cowering under a quilt. "This here be Peanut. He come all the way from a Mississippi cotton plantation, where he been done wrong. He on his way to Washington, but got skairt when a farmer hollered at him to stop where he was. Peanut took off running and the farmer let loose a big ole farm dog. The dog chased him a ways and bit his leg. Peanut done fight him off with a tree branch and been lookin' for folks to help him. I found him a'layin' in the field near the smithy when I was closin' down the shop this evenin'. He done be all busted up."

Orie moved the lantern closer to the shivering form on the bed and gently lifted the quilt off him. He moaned in fright.

"Shh, you are all right. You are safe. I am a doctor and I will take care of you. Show me which leg the dog bit."

On closer inspection, she could see the right pant leg was bloody and torn. She got right to work. "Cornelia, I need some water boiled to clean him up," she said. She got scissors from her medical bag and cut away the cloth from the man's leg. Cornelia had still-warm boiled water in the kettle over the hearth. Orie handed her bandages, which Cornelia poured water over. Peanut moaned again and flinched away from Orie.

"Let's get him laid out on the kitchen table while I give him laudanum to ease the pain," Orie said. Cornelia cleared the table and helped Homer easily lift the young man onto the table where Orie could work. She gave the laudanum time to get into his bloodstream. She cleaned the wounds and stitched them up with a steady, practiced hand, while Homer held him down in a manner that both straightened and comforted him.

"I think Peanut is going to be fine," said Orie, "but he'll need to rest a few days and you'll need to feed him warm broth as soon as he's able to be held up and can swallow. He looks like he's been without nourishment for days. I'll ask Ike about clothing for him. He needs new pants and a warm shirt and a coat and hat."

"Mammy!" cried a voice from the other room.

Cornelia went in to quiet her little ones. "Hush! Don't wake up ever'body! Go back to sleep!"

Orie was ready to take her leave. "Peanut should be safe for a few days, but let him lay low. Nobody needs to know we are keeping a runaway. Peter will help get him back on his way. Cornelia, let me know if anything comes up. I'll change his bandages tomorrow and the next day. If anyone asks about tonight, tell them I was called to see about you, Cornelia. Say that Homer was worried about you."

"Yas'm, Miz Dr. Orie. We thank you for yo' help."

"You are welcome, and take good care of our patient." Orie smiled and left for the Main House, carrying her medical bag and lantern. It was cold out. The air was still and the stars were on parade across the night sky. She breathed deeply. *Thank you, Lord, for the help I can give. Thank Papa for my education. And please bless John and Henry.*

Thanksgiving without John was expected, since his furlough had been in October, but Orie had hoped he could be home for Christmas. After all, they had both stayed on duty the past Christmas. But the Battle of Fredericksburg changed many plans. On December 11, 1862, Union General Ambrose Burnside came to Fredericksburg on the post road north of Richmond with 120,000 troops, the largest concentration of troops in any Civil War battle. Union Army engineers were ordered to put up six pontoon bridges across the Rappahannock River, while Confederate sharp-shooters defended the city of Fredericksburg against them, and Confederate troops fortified defensive positions south of the city and Marye's Heights west of the city.

The infantry attack that followed the completion of the bridge was augmented by shells from two hundred and twenty artillery pieces firing from the Union-occupied side of the Rappahannock, with devastating results. By nightfall on December 11, four brigades of Union troops occupied the city, which they looted with a fury that had not been seen up to that time. Pianos were thrown out of windows and chandeliers were torn down. Drunken Union troops built fires with furniture from private homes they had smashed. General Lee was enraged, and Confederate and many Union troops were shocked at the destruction inflicted upon the city.

The battle raged for two more days. On the thirteenth, seven Union divisions had been sent in against Marye's Heights, defended by General Longstreet, one brigade at a time, for a total of fourteen individual infantry charges. The losses on both sides were terrible. There were 12,650 casualties on the Union side and 5,377 on the Confederate side.

On the fourteenth, General Burnside asked for a truce to attend to his wounded, which General Lee graciously granted. On the fifteenth, Burnside withdrew his troops. The Battle of Fredericksburg in December 1862 ended with a Confederate victory.

John and the rest of the Confederate doctors were willing to forgo Christmas to attend to the newly wounded but victorious soldiers, but John's letters to Orie were full of his loneliness for his precious wife and son. Always, he prayed that the war would end soon.

CHAPTER 26

DR. JOHN AT VIEWMONT

It was early January 1863 and John was coming home on furlough. Orie's mood grew more buoyant by the day. She thought she would jump out of her skin, she was so eager to be in the arms of her beloved John. When the day finally came and she heard the sound of horseshoes on the frozen drive up to the Main House, she threw a heavy wool cape over herself and a blanket over Henry and raced down the staircase, through the Great Hall, and out the door. Uncle Jacob followed her, as Uncle Ned welcomed John with a loud "Halloo, Mista Dr. John!"

John jumped off the horse, handed the reins to Uncle Ned, and closed the gap between himself and Orie with great strides and open arms. He kissed his wife and Henry until the baby let out a wail.

"He's cold, John. Let's get inside!"

Uncle Jacob, already back in the house, waited to open the door and give the young doctor a warm handshake and welcome. By then, the whole household was alive, with feet thundering down the stairs to greet John. Anna Maria was in the sitting room waiting for calm before making her appearance and warmly embracing her son-in-law.

After John had washed up, Martha came in from the kitchen house with hot tea, biscuits, and molasses. He ate and drank with hungry urgency and then held out his arms to hold his son. Orie took in the sight of her husband and son together with a few tears and a look of such longing that John drew her to him as well and kissed her lips as the baby watched in wonder.

All the sisters wanted to hear from John about the news from Richmond. Anna Maria stepped in and told them that John had been travelling for hours and hours and was tired. She sent the three up the stairs to rest and to give him some privacy.

"Let me know when you want Colie or Mary to take the baby," she called to them.

"Never," John whispered to Orie. "I want to be with both of you." John shut the door to their bedroom and placed Henry on the wide bed, where he could gaze upon his son.

"He's so big," he said. "He's plump and has soft hair and blue eyes, just as you wrote in your letters."

Henry smiled up at John, wriggling with pleasure at the attention of the newcomer. John picked him up and sailed around the room until the baby began to laugh, while Orie sat in her rocker clapping along with his chortles.

After a while the baby began to fuss, and Orie put him to her breast and fed him. It was John's turn to watch his wife and son in wonderment. When she finished, she burped him, changed him, and put him in his cradle for a nap.

John sat immersed in the beauty of the scene as Orie tucked their baby under the hand-stitched covers.

"Now, John, I am so very hungry for you." Orie removed her shawl and went to him, touching his face and smooth neck. He gathered her into his arms and they stayed that way a long time, not wanting to part from each other for a second or an inch. John finally slept the sleep of one no longer deprived of the sight and touch of the two beings he loved most.

When Henry's cradle began to rock and his fussing increased in volume, Orie left her bed to attend to him. The three remained in the bedroom until noon the following day.

Martha had hot coffee for them and everything else they asked for when they finally came downstairs. Anna Maria sat with them in the dining room, and soon the four sisters joined them and sipped tea while they caught up on news.

John remarked on the abundance of food on the table. Lottie said that Uncle Ike and Mama were responsible for the food, but they did not often eat that well.

"Thank, too, the Confederate sailors," said John. "The blockade battles are life and death for us and they occur on the seas and the rivers. Last month, on the Yazoo River near Vicksburg, we used the first electrically detonated underwater mine to sink the Union ironclad *USS Cairo*. We had already lost I don't know how many ships on the Yazoo in an effort to protect Vicksburg on the Mississippi. We cannot afford to lose Vicksburg and the ability to control the Mississippi after last year's loss of New Orleans. The sinking of the *Cairo* is important to us."

"Thank you, brave sailor boys," said Eddie, and the others cheered along with her.

"That's the spirit, girls," said John. "President Davis is making a speech this week in Richmond about the State of the Confederacy. I think he will have encouraging things to say. The victory in Fredericksburg saved Richmond, and at the same time showed the ruthlessness of Yankee commanders sending those troops into battle to be butchered like herds of animals. How long will decent Americans put up with that, not to mention the criminal behavior of the Yankees pillaging the unprotected city of Fredericksburg that first night after battle? They took from shops as well as every home in the city. They stole and smashed their way through basements and attics, took from or despoiled larders and pantries."

The girls looked around, imagining Yankees looting Viewmont. They put the image out of their heads. They could not bear to think of such willful destruction. Orie's mind readily brought up images of the wounded and sick Boys in both gray and blue uniforms; she knew the force of evil firsthand and knew the Lord saw and heard everything. Nevertheless, she was a witness and must force her mind to accept what was happening, even though there was great joy in her life and that was her reality at this time.

That night, Ike and Mag went to see John, and they talked about the War even after Anna Maria tried to change the subject to something more cheerful. Anna Maria gave up and led Colie, Mary, and Eddie into the dining room to roll bandages and sing hymns.

"Why, Mama? We do this every day," said Eddie.

"I know, dear heart, but the bandages are needed and too much War talk is not good for young girls."

Colie and Mollie agreed, but Eddie pouted and would not sing. She poured herself a glass of water from the pitcher on the table and returned to the sitting room, where John and Orie, Ike and Mag, and Lottie were in deep conversation about the War. She took a chair nearby and settled in, her legs crossed at the ankles. John gave her a welcoming smile and Eddie acknowledged the smile, giving Orie and Mag a look of triumph. Orie got up and sat with Eddie, putting her arm about her shoulders. Orie's cat, Matilda, found them thus and jumped up on Eddie's lap. The conversation continued.

Anna Maria left the dining room to check on Eddie and found nothing but peace and contentment. She made a mental note to thank Orie and John for including Eddie in their happiness. Anna Maria brooded on her fatherless youngest daughter. The loving attention of a mother and four sisters was not the same thing as a father's love and guidance. Eddie, eleven going on twelve, was a mystery to her mother. There seemed to be nothing that held her interest for any length of time before boredom would set in and periods of open unhappiness would ensue. Keep her close or send her more often into the world? Anna Maria didn't know. She leaned toward keeping her close.

After almost an hour rolling bandages at the dining room table, Anna Maria suggested they join the others for tea and cookies baked by Lottie. Ike, the congenial host, insisted on telling a war story that was suitable for young girls.

"Do tell, then, Ike," said his mother.

"At the Second Battle of Murfreesboro in Tennessee, the night before the battle, less than a half-mile apart, the military bands began to play. First the Union Army Band played 'Yankee Doodle' to cheers and shouts. Then the Confederate band played 'Dixie' to louder cheers and hurrahs, followed by the Yankees playing 'Hail Columbia' versus the Southerners' 'The Bonnie Blue Flag.' Imagine this on a winter's night in middle Tennessee before a battle the next day that could end up killing half of them there."

Ike had a rapt audience, the adults uneasily hoping for a happy ending.

"Someone started up the song 'Home Sweet Home,' and before the devil himself could stop it, both bands and thousands of soldiers on both sides were all singing together."

"That's lovely, Ike," said Anna Maria, and her sentiments were echoed by all in the room. "And now I think it's time to retire to bed."

Mollie handed the sleeping baby in her lap to Orie, who received him with a kiss and walked upstairs with John beside her. Bedroom doors were shut and all was soon quiet.

Ike and Mag locked down the house, blew out the lamps, and crossed the field crunchy with ice to their own cottage. Inside, Mag asked, "What happened the next day at Murfreesboro, Mr. Militiaman?"

"It was all about numbers, Mag, dear. There were thirty-eight thousand of our boys, but President Davis ordered General Braxton Bragg to send seven thousand five hundred soldiers to Vicksburg, so our forces of thirty thousand five hundred retreated after two days of fighting Union forces of forty thousand. They were not defeated, but the Union claimed it as a victory to boost morale back home after the defeat in Fredericksburg."

"That's enough for today," said Mag. She dressed quickly in her soft nightgown, put on a nightcap, and warmed up the bed with coals from the fireplace in a long-handled covered copper bed warmer. "I can't bear to think of our Boys sleeping outside in weather like this. Isn't it true the Roman soldiers had a fighting season and dead winter was not one of them?"

"Yes, dear," said Ike. "We don't seem to be as civilized as the Republican Romans, but they were surprised at times by attacks from the barbarians in France during the winter. A problem with war is that the two sides do not always fight by the same rules. Good night, Mag, dear. I love you." Shep jumped up on the bed and nestled at the foot of his master.

"I love you too, dearest Ike," said Mag, kissing him goodnight. Mag lay there awhile, not counting sheep, but thinking that there had been so many battles she couldn't begin to count them. Maybe the new year, 1863, would be kinder to the South than 1862 had been. Letters from a cousin in Philadelphia were not encouraging, however. There were some in Pennsylvania who called Southerners "treasonous" and others who wanted the brutal War against the South stopped immediately. Sleep overtook her as she pondered the dilemma, nestled beside her husband.

CHAPTER 27

ANNUS HORRIBILIS

I n January, Mag had wished for a better year than 1862, but she would be the first, with Ike, to say that 1863 was the beginning of an *annus horribilis*. Gone was the hope and expectation in the South that the two nations could become one again. People counted, saying there had been over two thousand fights and nothing was settled. By the end of January, 20 percent of the Union Army had deserted. Numbers, however, were not a problem for the Union Army, as Ike had heard that swarms of immigrants from Ireland, especially, were recruited as they stepped off boats in New York.

In January the Yankees destroyed a salt work at St. Joseph, Florida. This act reduced the South's supply of salt needed to store and transport meat. Nutrition in the South suffered. On January 11, the CSS *Alabama* sank the USS *Hatteras* off Galveston, Texas. On the same day, combined Union Navy and Army forces successfully attacked Confederate Fort Hindman in Arkansas. Even Orie, with her dispassionate and collected mind-set, could not take in the enormity of the War and its consequences, but she could see the trap closing. The busyness of her daily life allowed her to keep her sanity. She worried about everyone else—the older people, both colored and white, the children and their future, or lack thereof, and the soldiers who were putting life and limb in jeopardy to protect the South and Southerners.

Ike discussed the news he was privy to with Mag on a near-daily basis, although his assigned year as part of the Virginia Militia in Albemarle County had ended the last day of December. Knowing that Anna Maria was opposed to war talk at Viewmont, where Ike's sisters were always around, they kept the subject to themselves outside their own cottage. But Mag let some news slip one day when she and Lottie were preparing root vegetables for the soldiers to be hauled in a wagon to Charlottesville General Hospital by Uncle Ned.

"I declare, I am so undone by General Burnside. After that disgraceful slaughter and pillage at Fredericksburg in December, he led another attack against General Lee that lasted six days and did nothing but lose their own mules and horses in the mire and mud and cold," said Mag.

At first, Lottie said nothing, but she looked distracted. "I don't think I can endure this much longer. I know in my heart I'm called to missionary work in China, and these years hang heavy on my heart."

"Oh, Lottie, I've upset you. I thought you understood how much we need you at Viewmont while the War goes on."

"Yes, Mag, I've been honored to stay here and help, but the War is not ending. The Unionists will never leave us alone until we are all destroyed, and in the meantime, I should be in China rather than waiting for the Yankees to take all that we have and kill us doing it."

"Then do what you must, Lottie. We love you and need you, but if God is telling you otherwise, that's what you have to do. But wait until winter has passed."

"Oh, Mag, I do love you so. Above all, you are practical. I will surely wait until spring before I venture from Viewmont. I have it in mind to seek private tutoring, and from that income I will be able to help Viewmont and get set for missionary work."

"But how far will you have to go? Albemarle County is not safe. Be very careful about finding a position away from the battles. I am still distraught over the Battle of Fredericksburg, even though the victory was ours. Families in the countryside have been at the mercy of the Federals since the beginning, and now we know that people in a fine city lost everything they ever owned in early winter, and were left with nothing to eat or medicine for the sick. This is beyond War."

"The people of the South must survive even if it means leaving the South," said Lottie. "We won't be snuffed out."

"Merciful heavens!" responded Mag. Ike's sisters were deep thinkers as well as dramatic, but Lottie was surely thinking beyond the distance Mag was envisioning. Mag would never leave the South.

The winter was quiet on the battlefields and there were soldiers in winter encampments, but the action was going on on the waterways. In late January, the Federal gunboat *Isaac Smith* was captured and burned near Charleston, South Carolina, and two Confederate gunboats rammed and shelled two Yankee gunboats, putting them out of action, one captured and the other sunk. More good news was the South's success in driving off a US Navy fleet that had attacked Fort McAllister near Savannah. Two days later they were back, but again lost the battle and sailed away. Two days later, the Yankees destroyed another salt work near Currituck Beach in North Carolina.

Ike and his fellow militiamen were well aware that the blockade affected the citizens in Albemarle County even more than the battles nearby; the South needed supplies on a daily basis to sustain the War effort as well to keep the people supplied with things they needed beyond what they themselves produced. The hope was that England would side with them in the War, and, in fact, England did a lot to help the South. The English built ships for the Confederacy in Liverpool and sent English-flagged ships through the blockade to Mexican ports with goods to be funneled into the Confederacy. In February, the USS *Vanderbilt* seized the British merchant ship *Peterhoff,* bound for Mexico, off St. Thomas in the West Indies. British officials protested that the United States had no right to interfere with international trade. The ship was escorted to New York to await adjudication by an international court.

"What now?" Mag asked upon hearing the news.

"These things take time, so nobody knows," Ike said, "but Great Britain will probably cut back on helping us with blockade running. Other British ships trying to gain Southern ports have been sunk. The Yankees' relentless naval effort to destroy the South is lawless and winning."

Ike surmised that England did not recognize the South's independence, because that would invite intervention and England did not want to risk warfare with a much more powerful America than had been the case in the eighteenth and early nineteenth centuries. Even though Ike believed strongly that the English people preferred the South, the English government had not and probably never would recognize and officially support the independence of the South. Southerners speculated that England wanted America to be weakened by the war and would corner the cotton market with cotton from India and maybe Australia. There was also the slavery question. England had abolished slavery thirty years earlier. A very large and important door had slammed shut on the South.

By May, when the weather was warming, Orie was pregnant with her second child and her mind was on her family and her medical care of them and the slaves. After making her rounds to check on patients in the row of slave cabins, she stopped by the smithy.

"Two men from Mississippi done spent las' night with us," said Homer. "They comin' out of there so fast I wonder do dey have enough pickers in da field to plant and pick de cotton?"

Orie spoke openly. "I think they probably do, but it's a worry. Cotton's our main national revenue source, and without that money the planters will lose everything and bring us all down with them."

Orie wondered what life would be like just worrying about things like crops and workers and family and children. She had another baby on the way. And many things were in short supply. She had not had real coffee or tea since John was home in January. There were no tea or coffee plantations in Virginia; more's the pity. Since they could not buy things from Baltimore, Philadelphia, New York, or Boston, life was a struggle. When things broke and couldn't be fixed, they had to make do without.

"How's Mista Henry?" Homer asked with a smile.

"He was up with little cough last night, but better today, thank you, Homer."

"Thas' good. Cornelia, she talk 'bout 'at baby alla time. She surely do."

"She's a wonderful help to me, and Henry loves her—puts his little arms up for her when she comes in the room. Heavens, I must be going. I have lessons for Eddie and it's time to feed Henry. Cornelia is no doubt waiting for me right now."

Orie took her leave and moved swiftly back to the Main House, feeling happy with the sun on her skin and the smell of turned soil in the fields. The bright sky ruled the earth from the heavens as far as she could see, with white clouds against the blue.

At the end of the day, Orie was tired and ready for bed, with a prayer for protection for John and thanksgiving for baby Henry and her family and the whole Viewmont household.

Around midnight, Orie awoke with a start, and sat up in bed and listened. She heard a muffled barking cough. She went quickly to the cradle and put her hand on her son. She could feel his fevered hot skin and muscles that were straining and his body in an awkward position against the side of the cradle. Alarmed, she lit a candle and peered down at him writhing and coughing. She picked him up, covered him with a blanket from the cradle, and hurried out to knock on mother's and sister's bedroom doors.

"Mama! Lottie! Come quickly! The baby is sick and I need help!" She rushed him back into her room and lit more candles, while Anna Maria and Lottie came in, pulling on robes over their nightgowns in the chilly night.

Orie spread the baby out on blankets placed beneath him on a table. "Lottie, I need a kettle of hot water and clean towels. Quickly!"

Without even looking at the baby, Lottie flew out of the bedroom, down the stairs, and out to the kitchen building with the keys in her pocket.

"What is it, Orie? You are scaring us to death!" Anna Maria tried to soothe the child, but he resisted her stroking hand with an agonizing shriek and rocked himself to his knees and threw his head back.

"It's croup," said Orie, looking in horror as the baby's respiration labored and slowed; in his effort to breathe, the muscles of his neck and chest were exerted to the utmost. His glands were enlarged, his neck swollen, and the indented clavicle area showed signs of suffocation. The baby's lips took on a bluish hue, even in the faint candlelight. He was restless, frantically tossing about, well beyond human measures to comfort him.

Lottie arrived, breathless, with a steaming kettle of water and towels. Colie was with her, carrying a kerosene lantern for more light. Orie examined his nose and throat and saw thick gray material covering the back of his throat and blocking his airway. She unpacked her doctor's bag and took out a cutting instrument.

"No, Orie! It's just croup! He'll be well. Another hour and he'll perspire and the cough will loosen. I've been through this before. I've seen what happens." Anna Maria was shocked at seeing Orie draw out her cutting equipment.

"Colie, remove her from this room, please, right away. I must work quickly." She said this in such a grave tone of voice that Anna Maria stopped her pleas and let Colie guide her from the room.

Orie's medical training allowed her to focus her attention on her baby's symptoms as he grew pale all over and lapsed into apathy. She took hold of the knife and felt for the obstructing cover and mucous in order to open the windpipe below the obstructed larynx. Suddenly the baby went into convulsions from lack of oxygen, and Orie had to pull back and wait for a moment. When the muscles relaxed, Orie swiftly opened the windpipe and kept it open with a silver tube. Henry's eyes opened wide in surprise. Orie gave thanks to Jesus and God Almighty and then saw the decline begin anew. The mucus in the baby's head and throat slowly but inerrantly traveled down into the bronchial tubes and then spilled into the lungs. Orie gave the baby doses of corrosive sublimate at frequent intervals, but the lethal mucus continued its journey downward through his tiny body.

As dawn was breaking, the baby's whole system was overwhelmed by septic infection, and he took his last breath as his mother began to weep. She picked him up and held him to her breast and opened the window to the still air outside.

"Noooooooo! Nooooo!" she screamed in a voice the household had not heard since the day John had departed when they were courting. She took the baby with her under the bedcovers as he slowly lost body heat. Her mother and all her sisters gathered around the bed and understood that Henry was gone.

Outside in the rows of cabins, candles were lit and fires built. Murmurs of fear and sorrow were heard. People began to pray and sing softly. Something terrible had happened in the Main House. Homer and Cornelia clung together, knowing the candlelight was coming from Orie's room.

Ike was alerted by Uncle Jacob, and he and Mag got dressed and went over to see what they could do. They took Anna Maria back to her room and tried to settle her down with laudanum, but she was inconsolable. "Croup! That's what she said. Now the precious baby is gone. Gone." Still sobbing, she tried to explain that babies recover from croup. "They look like they're going to die. I've seen it myself more than once, and the fit can last six hours, but they come out of it. They come out of it."

Ike tried to give his mother more laudanum, but she refused to stop crying and explaining and brushed away the medicine spoon. Mag held Anna Maria's shoulders and wept with her.

Ike sent Uncle Jacob to Scottsville with Ned in a cart to order a coffin from the cabinet maker and sent word to Reverend Doll to please pray over the baby at the graveside service the next day at the family cemetery near the house. The finished tombstone read:

Henry Horton Andrews
Born October 30, 1862
Died May 12, 1863
6 mos. & 12 days
Born & died at Viewmont
Precious to the Lord and his family

May 12, 1863. It was a long and terrible day.

CHAPTER 28
CHRISTIAN FORGIVENESS

John was not granted furlough on the occasion of the death of baby Henry. The War the South believed was winnable was instead collapsing on different fronts. John and Orie suffered their mutual grief apart, and only through letters were they able to attempt to console each other. John's letters contained nothing of the War, but said that all fronts were in action and all hands on board had more to do than could be managed without difficulty.

The fall of Vicksburg was big news. Since the Confederate defenders withstood General Grant's overwhelming attacks from the water, the Union general made a convoluted attack against the land side from the west, which also failed.

On the May 19, the Siege of Vicksburg began when Grant stormed the city's entrenched defenders with a thousand troops. The city held. On the twenty-second, Grant bombarded the city with two hundred field pieces by land and two-hundred-pound shells by water. On the same day, thousands of Yankees charged the defenders with bayonets fixed. He kept ordering charges until he had amassed three thousand casualties.

Grant changed his tactics. He cut off all roads into the city, thereby cutting off all food and supplies to the Confederate defenders and the citizens of Vicksburg, and made a road to constantly run in food and ammunition to his troops from the Mississippi River. He ordered shelling of the city by day and by night. Soon, every home was damaged or destroyed, and the citizens dug caves into the muddy hillside for safety. The soldiers and citizens were reduced to eating whatever they could swallow, whether it was dead mules and horses or snakes and rats and shoe leather. Grant ordered a tunnel to be dug under the Confederate line packed with twenty-two hundred pounds of gunpowder and made a great hole, which killed few Confederate soldiers. Southerners formed a new line and repulsed the attacking Yankees. The Siege of Vicksburg lasted forty-seven days. The Yankees did not defeat the Southerners. Starvation won the battle.

At about three o'clock on the afternoon of July 3, Confederate Lieutenant General Pemberton, accompanied by Major General Bowen, left their lines and met on neutral ground with General Grant. After a two-hour talk, the men returned to their lines and the unofficial word was that the Confederate soldiers were entirely too weakened by lack of food to do anything but sacrifice themselves fruitlessly.

Rumors flew. Some said the starving Southerners were on the verge of mutiny against their officers, while others said that the soldiers were mutinous against General Pemberton for surrendering to the enemy. They would rather starve than surrender. Grant wanted unconditional surrender from the rebel Southerners, but junior officers pointed out that they did not defeat the Southerners by attacking forces, tunneled explosives, or massive artillery strikes, but by time and hunger. The "Gibraltar of the West" fell to the Yankees on July 4, 1863.

When Union General McPherson rode over the entire line of fortifications, he was amazed to learn that the builders included not one professional engineer. Union officers realized that it was the Confederate soldiers' courage that had made the fortifications invincible, not an impregnable design. Reacting also to the extreme value of their victory, Grant paroled the soldiers and allowed the officers to retain their swords and one horse cart.

Stories were told about ghastly scenes of pillage and destruction that followed the formal surrender when a division of McPherson's troops entered the city to take possession of the courthouse. To the exultant cheers of the Yankees and the deep humiliation of the Southerners, the victorious Federals hoisted the US flag to wave above the city.

Southerners believed there were not any civilized elements remaining in the enemy forces that had overwhelmed the city in sheer numbers. Soldiers reported that houses and stores alike were broken into and everything therein taken by plunderers as part of the glory of war. On Sunday, the Negroes of the city showed their contempt and hatred for the white citizens and were encouraged in this behavior by the Federal troops. Although General Grant had given permission to the Negroes brought in by the planters and those connected to the Confederate Army to stay in the city as freed men, so many of them chose to leave with their masters that the general changed the order and forbade any more Negroes from leaving. Nevertheless, many of the slaves made their escape from the chaos of Vicksburg and returned to their masters.

More rumors: Southern soldiers believed that low Federal casualty figures given by General Grant to the public were false for the sake of Northern morale. While Federal and Confederate troops shared the city for a week in the process of granting paroles, street fights broke out due to the taunting Yankees. Knots of drunk men threatened to come back on the land they fought and died on and they would be the rich owners and the Rebels begging in the streets. Southern soldiers reported that Union officers continued to talk about the restoration of the Union, while the privates talked about land grants in the South for the conquering Northern soldiers. Such talk infuriated the beaten Confederates, who believed nothing could be worse than the state of Mississippi filled up with detested Yankees.

While talk of war was kept from Orie, Southern grief and fear were in her heart. Each morning after baby Henry's death, Orie awoke with a feeling of dread and then remembered, so the shock repeated itself for days stretching into weeks. Comfort came from nowhere.

Anna Maria was isolated and aggrieved within herself. Orie saw the harm that had come between them but could do nothing to stop the widening chasm.

"Speak to her, Orie," Lottie pleaded. "She's your mother and is grieving deeply for both you and the baby."

"I cannot help her. She believes I killed my baby and there is nothing I can say to undo what's happened." Orie trembled with anger, replaying in her mind her mother's words when she saw her take a cutting knife from her medical bag.

"Orie, you have to explain to her what killed the baby. She's not a doctor like you are. She's just a grandmother who nursed her own babies through sicknesses and thought she could help."

"No! She never thought I was capable of doing anything right, and now my precious baby is gone. She never wanted me to go away to Troy to school, and then when my father died in 1853, she let me go to medical school the next year just because she knew he wished it. But she had always wanted me to follow her to the finishing school in Richmond, to become accomplished like her. I never wanted to do that. I never did that."

"Orie, you have to forgive her because you are a Christian. You know that without my telling you so."

"Yes, Lottie, I know I must forgive her, but I cannot. Not yet."

"Then go and pray about it, please, dear sister," said Lottie. "We all lost Henry, but you lost Mama too, and she lost her grandchild and her daughter on that one terrible night."

That Sunday, Orie went in the carriage with Uncle Ned, Uncle Jacob, and Mammy Jinny to hear Reverend Doll preach to the folks on the banks of the Hardware River. They all agreed the man could preach, and Orie felt herself caught up in the excitement and the singing. She felt a stirring of some hope beginning again.

"The Lord is good. He loves us and feels our pain and all will be right when we get to heaven. Hallelujah!" Reverend Doll preached.

After coming out of her room for a taste of Martha's Sunday dinner of fried chicken, vegetables, cornbread, and fruit pies, Orie crept back to rest and think. The memories came flooding back. How angry she had been when Mama forbade her to travel alone to join Uncle James Barclay and his family in the Holy Land after she graduated from medical school. She had left Viewmont in spite of her mother's pleadings. The sixty-day journey was beset with dangers for a young woman travelling unescorted, but the unafraid American girl carried a revolver along with an inbred authority to command respect and give orders. Orie became a legend both in the Holy Land and in Virginia.

When first in the Holy Land, Orie had been interested only in helping her uncle in her capacity as a medical missionary. She had her medical degree and permission from the Bedouin sheik, through Uncle James, to be in company with the tribeswomen and children and treat their sicknesses and injuries.

Although well versed in the Bible and the history of the Holy Land, Orie was not the religious adherent her mother had always been. But with her feet on Holy Land soil and breathing the air Christ Himself had breathed, Orie's feelings begin to change. She stood on the Mount of Olives and walked through the Garden of Gethsemane. She ascended the Mountain of the Transfiguration. When she visited Calvary and realized she was in the immediate spot where the Savior of Men suffered on the cross, her heart, mind, and soul no longer belonged to herself, but first to Jesus and to God his Father. She meditated on these things and had long talks with Uncle James, one of the founders of the Disciples Church and a follower who had offered himself to the church's newly formed American Christian Missionary Society.

At long last, years after denying her father's request that she be baptized before he died, Orie asked her uncle to baptize her while in the Holy Land. He did so in the Pool of Siloam, a shrine of particular importance to a Christian in the healing arts, for it was there that Jesus anointed the eyes of the blind man with a mixture of clay and spittle and told him to wash. John 9:7 says, "He washed and came out seeing."

From that time forward, Orie entered a new life that marked her as a consecrated follower of Christ. For more than a year and a half, "El Hakim" (the Doctor) ministered to the Bedouins and Turkish ladies while continuing to spend time happily visiting the scenes where the Divine Master devoted three brief years of his life, time that turned the tide of civilization.

During this time, Orie took on the study of French as the international language of the day, as well as Arabic, which the Bedouins spoke. Her ability to speak a language seldom acquired by Westerners won her great respect and affection from the Arab-speaking people and made them more amenable to her ministrations and treatments.

Orie became such a beloved figure among the Bedouins that an amorous Sheik proposed marriage to the attractive young woman as his family sat tailor-fashion on the carpets and rugs in the tent. The proposal was offered with pride and sincerity.

Orie was not silent. She produced the handy revolver and laid it on her lap, looked the Sheik in the eyes, and said to him, "I know you think you are doing me an honor, but among my people, where a man has but one wife, your suggestion would be the greatest insult a married man could offer to a woman, and if I thought you realized the affront you have offered me, I would kill you. Do not dare to ever again even think of such a thing, for if you do, I will read your mind and I will kill you."

To the surprise of the Sheik's wives, he made the most abject apologies and hastily retreated from the women's tent.

When Orie recounted her adventure to her uncle, he strenuously insisted that she discontinue her visits to the Bedouin tents, knowing the danger to his niece, with the possibility of a kidnapping and an international incident. After that, she accompanied him and his daughter, Sarah, on archaeology expeditions, which introduced her to a field of historical discovery that captivated her imagination and spirit of adventure.

She visited the outside of the Mosque of Omar, but no woman had been permitted to violate the sacred precinct of the Mosque, and few except Moslems had ever seen the inside of this most holy of the Turkish temples. An exception was her eminent uncle, who, having been appointed physician to one of the Cadi, or Holy Keepers of the Mosque, was accorded permission to enter.

On one of her excursions with her Uncle James and cousin Sarah, the Barclays' small dog happened to chase a rat and was soon lost and trapped behind stone walls. Dr. Barclay called two men and had them dig where the dog disappeared. A tunnel took them well below street level and through larger and still larger passages and tunnels. After the dog was rescued, Dr. Barclay had his workmen open the tunnel and follow it with lights toward the Mosque of Omar, also known as the Dome on the Rock, situated on the space of King Solomon's Temple. Understanding the importance of his finding, he sent a report to a group of Masons in Philadelphia, which resulted in their sending a committee to investigate the matter further. Americans were becoming actively involved in ancient Middle Eastern archaeology.

Orie, recalling the smells and exotic sounds of the ancient city, as well as the hot days and bone-chilling nights in the warm season, remembered her uncle's excitement at the discovery of the underground quarry and source of the foundation of King Solomon's Temple. She felt herself far removed from Viewmont and willingly surrendered to the blissfulness of the Holy Land in her mind. Thus, in the land of her Lord, Orie was able to forgive humanity for all the ills it had devised and wrought throughout history.

Too soon, though, the reality of Viewmont broke through her reverie. She was convinced of her own failings, but her heart was not yet soft enough to forgive. Forgiving humanity for sins throughout history was one thing; forgiving her mother was something else entirely. She would, however, give a medical explanation because of her unthinking expectation that her mother would accept the death of the baby without question.

She called for Lottie and her mother to come sit with her in her room, and they came with grieving countenances and inquiring eyes and took the chairs offered to them.

Orie started off with, "I have things to say I should have said before this and I am sorry. My heartbreak does not excuse my unwillingness to share with you the medical aspects of what happened to the baby."

Anna Maria looked up to see both Lottie and Orie looking directly at her and nodded in acknowledgment, but said nothing.

"When I said the baby had croup, I was using the shortest possible term to say that the situation was grave without going into all the ramifications of that diagnosis. Croup is also called suffocative catarrh and can simply be an inflammation of the mucous membranes of the head and throat with a flow of mucus that threatens the air flow or shuts off the air flow completely. What I had hoped to see is called a false membrane or a spasmodic laryngitis and partial swelling of the air passage, but what I saw was complete blockage by a membrane, which is diphtheritic or membranous croup. Diphtheria is another name for it."

Anna Maria gasped and Lottie held her hand.

"Yes, Mama," said Orie. "It's almost always fatal, and suffocation is a most cruel way to die. I did what I could. I opened his windpipe, and he thanked me with his eyes. After that, the disease took him unawares and he died peacefully. I thanked God I could relieve his suffering, but I could not save him. I'm also thankful mine was the last face he saw before he passed on to the embrace of Jesus."

Anna Maria stood up and the three women embraced one another sorrowfully, and then Anna Maria and Lottie returned to their separate rooms. Orie, still in a dispassionate state of mind, surveyed her feelings. She had given the professional medical explanation, as she had been trained to do, but had she forgiven her mother for the hurt she had caused that night? For doubting her daughter, the baby's mother? No, she had not achieved that Christian tenet. There was, though, hope in her heart that she could, in time, forgive her mother. She would have to be satisfied with that much. She thanked Lottie in her heart for her help. Lottie would someday be a great missionary; in Orie's mind, of that there was no doubt.

CHAPTER 29
HEAVY HEARTS

Although Orie's pregnancy began to physically slow her down through the summer, there had been very little morning sickness, so she was not as aware of her condition as she had been with Henry. With Henry, she had talked to him and prayed for him from the first weeks, and when he was born he was not a stranger. With baby number two, she avoided such natural impulses. She was in too much grief over the loss of Henry to take on another baby she could lose. As a medical doctor, she knew the odds of a successfully completed pregnancy, and worried, too, that the shock of Henry's unexpected death could have harmed her system and the baby as well. She did not consider herself a safe and warmly loving body from which to be born.

Anna Maria, so very much looking forward to the birth and believing all would be well from then on, worried about Orie's avoidance of anything to do concerning the coming baby. All she could do was urge Orie to eat more and rest more. The reminders were like jabs in the stomach to Orie. She was back supporting the war effort by rolling bandages and sewing uniforms, instructing Eddie in science studies, and checking on patients. She was busy, and the duties helped her get through the day.

When her pregnancy showed through her lighter summer dresses, the women would ask how she was feeling and what names had she picked out. These questions were not welcomed and soon they were not asked. By letter, Orie asked John what he thought about leaving Viewmont and moving to another plantation house nearby. His answer was: "Dearest, wherever you wish to live is where I too want to be. I care only for your happiness."

She spoke secretly with Ike and Mag and Lottie about the possibility of removing her family to another plantation house after the baby was born in early October.

Ike discouraged her. "Orie, you don't want to leave Viewmont with John in Richmond and a War going on." Mag agreed with Ike.

"Lottie, what do you think?" Orie asked her sister.

"I am taken aback, Orie. You love Viewmont and I cannot imagine your not being here with your family, especially with a baby coming."

Orie sighed. "I do not want this new baby to live here. There are too many sad memories, and I think I will be a better mother if I can take care of it elsewhere."

"I see," said Lottie. "Have you spoken to Mama about this?"

"No, of course not."

"Orie, I will pray about this and you must do the same. Hold my hand and we will ask the Lord what to do."

Instead, Orie stood up beside Lottie and turned to leave the bedroom. "I'm not ready to ask Him yet. Can you please pray for me, and I will pray to Him in private?"

"Of course, dearest Orie. And I will continue to pray that there will be forgiveness between you and Mama." She kissed Orie's cheek and started to open her bedroom door.

"It's not just that," Orie added. "I am constantly reminded of my shortcomings when I'm around Mama, who is always so beautiful and fully in charge of everything."

"I know, dear. I will pray and God will listen. I can promise you that."

Ike and Mag, more concerned than ever that Anna Maria and Orie be protected from news of the war, were reeling not only from the loss of Vicksburg, the South's last link to the supply line that Mississippi River had always been to the South, but also from the defeat in Gettysburg. As Ike explained it, Lee's plan was to protect Richmond by invading the North. This would take pressure off of war-ravaged Virginia and feed his troops with Pennsylvania food. The plan was approved with some concern that he was needed to defend Vicksburg at the same time. Other reasons for fighting in the North were to weaken the North's appetite for war by winning a major battle on Northern soil and to strengthen the growing peace movement there.

So to Gettysburg Lee went, but before he started moving his army northward, he came down with a "fever," which some say was a heart attack. But many agreed that Lee was not Lee in Gettysburg. And General J. E. B. Stuart, Lee's "eyes and ears," did not arrive in Gettysburg until the second day of battle, with troops exhausted from attacks by Union cavalry on the way to Gettysburg.

Also missing at Gettysburg was Stonewall Jackson, killed at Chancellorsville back in May in a major Confederate victory. At Gettysburg, the Confederates failed to take Little Round Top, with the result that the Union defenders held their high ground at the end of the day. The next day Lee called for an infantry assault with twelve thousand soldiers against the center of the Union line. This was the disastrous Pickett's Charge, which was repulsed by Union rifle and artillery fire from protected heights, resulting in great losses to the Confederate Army crossing an open field under direct fire. Lee led his army on a torturous retreat back to Virginia.

Kept from Anna Maria and Orie were the casualty figures of the Battle of Gettysburg, amounting to about fifty-one thousand killed, wounded, captured, or missing, more of them on the Confederate side. It was the bloodiest battle in the Civil War. Ike and other Virginians mourned anew Stonewall Jackson's death, believing that if he had been there, he would have taken Little Round Top and the battle would have ended in victory. As for J. E. B. Stuart, the battle at Brandy Station, Virginia, where the Yankee cavalry made the first surprise attack, lasted twelve hours and was the largest cavalry battle ever fought in the Western Hemisphere. Stuart was the victor of a very costly fight. A second surprise attack in Hanover, Pennsylvania, delayed him further, cost him more troops, and exhausted his men. The gallant Confederate cavalry commander with the plumed hat had become a target for the entire Union Army.

Ike did not disagree with the notion that the second failed attempt at victory in the North, after the defeat on September 17, 1862, at Antietam, was the turning point against the fabled invincible Southern Army. Indeed, 1863 was turning into an *annus horribilis*, with more to come. On July 4, Confederate Vice President Alexander Stephens climbed on board a gunboat at Richmond in a mission to talk to Yankee authorities about the prisoner-of-war situation. The South was holding many more prisoners than the North and could neither feed nor clothe their own soldiers. Men captured alive on the battlefield were dying in prisons. Stephens's plan would have speeded up the prisoner exchange for the benefit of both sides, but particularly for the North. Lincoln gave orders to Hampton Roads not to meet with the Vice President. Southerners were at a loss to explain such an attitude when it was Northern soldiers who were dying needlessly.

Some news was encouraging. On July 11, in New York City, antidraft rioting against the War caused the injury or deaths of a thousand people and over $1.5 million in property damage, until Union troops, who had fought at Gettysburg, put down the violence on August 16. There were also riots in Troy, Boston, New Hampshire, Ohio, and Vermont.

"Ike, dear, please tell Orie there have been protests in Troy against the draft," Mag said upon hearing the news.

"I will, Mag," Ike replied. "That news might cheer her up a bit, that people she lived and studied with are protesting the War against us."

Other news came from tiny Austinville near Wytheville, Virginia, the only source of lead for bullets in the South and close to Saltville, one of the last places to get salt for food preservation.

Union forces wanted lead and salt, not for their own needs, but to take it away from the Southerners. For salt and lead, a Federal raid brought in a thousand mounted Union troops in mid-July. When the Yankee column was discovered and Saltville alerted, the Yankees decided to attack the Virginia-Tennessee Railroad at Wytheville and then the lead mines. The South had little help to send. The whole force of fewer than three hundred old men and young boys, two small companies of soldiers, a hundred and thirty civilian employees from the railroad headquarters, and women with guns in windows greeted Colonel John Toland and his thousand troops with a hail of gunfire. Toland was killed as the Yankees took the town. The courthouse and many homes were burned and looted. When the Yankees left town, they left their wounded to be cared for by the very townspeople they had attacked. According to reports, the wounded were well taken care of.

Upon hearing all this, Mag asked Ike, "I knew the women would take good care of the wounded Yankees, but what kind of officers would leave their soldiers to the mercy of the people in the town they had just visited upon with deaths and burnings?"

"I have no answer for you, my dear," Ike replied.

On August 17, the Union Army pounded Fort Sumter in Charleston Bay with a thousand shells, and continued the next day, but the fort stood. On August 21, General Q. A. Gilmore demanded that the fort surrender or he would shell the city. The fort did not surrender. On the ninth of September, Union forces stormed Fort Sumter, and the fort still held. They used the "swamp angel," a mortar that fired two-hundred-pound shells that produced fire into the city during September. The city did not surrender.

The Battle of Chickamauga in North Georgia broke more Southern hearts. The battle took place on September 19 and 20 about twelve miles southwest of Chattanooga, Tennessee, with Union General William Rosecrans and Confederate General Braxton Bragg both struggling to gain control of the key railroad center. General Bragg and sixty thousand troops waited in the North Georgia mountains for reinforcements from General Longstreet to arrive.

Confident of numerical superiority on that day, Bragg's Confederates attacked Union forces near Chickamauga Creek. They sliced through the Union line, overran the Union headquarters, and rolled forward in a whooping and cheering wave until it broke against Snodgrass Hill. The Union Army was in full flight. Only a desperate Union stand on Snodgrass Hill held off the Confederates until the rest of the Union forces were able to escape with the aid of a reserve division and the use of a revolutionary new seven-shot repeating rifle.

Although Generals Longstreet and Nathan Bedford Forrest wanted to pursue the Yankees the following morning, Bragg's mind was on the twenty thousand Confederate casualties suffered in the battle, which included ten Confederate generals. They put Chattanooga under siege, but General Grant arrived with reinforcements and soon turned the Confederate victory into a strategic loss in the region. The constant news of battle fronts everywhere as the way of war shocked Southerners. This was beyond war—it was total destruction of a new republic gasping to breathe.

On October 1, 1863, James Barclay Andrews was born at Viewmont, named after Orie's uncle Dr. James Turner Barclay. Barclay and his family were still abroad since leaving the Holy Land. John, home on furlough, approved of the name and right away called the baby Jimmie. Anna Maria lavished her love and attention on her new grandson, thankful to her daughter for naming him after her older brother and including her branch of the Philadelphia Barclays.

"The Barclay name is internationally respected and admired, and may help him in this world, where we do not know from where our help may come," said Anna Maria.

"I named him James Barclay because of my love for my uncle, who baptized me," Orie responded, giving her mother a short glance as she put the baby in his cradle after a feeding.

"I know that, dear. I only wanted to remind you of the acceptance of the Barclay name in the North as well as Europe, and the world, for that matter. We are losing so much by the day here in Virginia, but we will never lose the respect that the Barclay name has given us."

Anna Maria was disheartened to learn that her son-in-law, John, had little knowledge of the Barclay family beyond the stories of Orie's uncle. She sought him out the next day, after he returned from riding across the property with Ike on a warm and sunny afternoon when the fecundity of the fields and woods was in the very air they breathed. Seated on rocking chairs overlooking the breadth of the rolling hills of Albemarle County, they were well aware of the preciousness of that land and the family's connections to it.

Anna Maria smiled at her son-in-law and then said sadly, "My father, Robert Barclay, died before I was born. He drowned in the Rappahannock River returning from a buying trip to Philadelphia for goods for his store. I very much want you to know the family for whom your son is named."

"And I want to hear all that you can tell me," said John. He knew that Orie's uncle was like a father to her, and had also lived at Monticello before departing for Jerusalem. He suspected there was much more to know, and also regretted that nothing about the past or dreams for the future were forthcoming from Orie. Truly, tomorrow was too distant in Orie's mind when considering the uncertainties of an infant's precarious hold on the earthly life.

"As you can imagine, John," Anna Maria continued, "when my father unexpectedly died, he left my mother a distraught young widow living at Willow Grove Estate in King and Queen County, two sons and soon-to-be three daughters. My mother's rather hasty marriage to Captain Jack Harris proved to be most fortunate in every way. My stepfather was a widowed, wealthy, childless Albemarle merchant and planter with ten plantations in the region, and Viewmont was his favorite. He cared deeply for my mother as well as for his stepchildren. Tragically, my brother Thomas died of an apparent drowning in the James River after earning a law degree at the University of Virginia. James graduated from the University of Pennsylvania medical school. He practiced his profession in Charlottesville and established a drugstore there. I was sent to a fine finishing school in Richmond."

Colie came out with a tray bearing mugs of cider for all three of them and sat in the open air, exclaiming about the view and the uncommon pleasantness of the mild day.

"What about your grandfather, Mama? Does Dr. John know about Thomas Barclay the patriot? "

"Has Orie told you about him, John?"

"Not that I remember," he said, hoping he was not putting Orie into disfavor with her family.

"From what we were told, Thomas Barclay was a great-grandson of Robert Barclay from Scotland, a descendent of Barclay, Lord of Urie. He and William Penn and others established a colony they called the Society of Friends, which is Philadelphia, the City of Brotherly Love, and practiced truth, courtesy, and honor with the Red Man. Robert Barclay was called 'the scholar of the Quaker Society,' and his writings enabled the Quakers to become a dominant factor in the early life of Pennsylvania. Robert's son David took as his bride Lady Gordon, a wealthy lady so noted for her beauty and loveliness of character that she was known in song and story as 'the White Rose of Scotland.' David inherited a large estate in Ireland, where he resided for a time after his marriage. David established Barclays Bank on Lombard Street in London, and he also purchased an estate in Jamaica, freed the slaves, and taught them trades, an example of Quaker philosophy."

John leaned back in his rocker and studied the faces of his wife's mother and sister. "I do declare that the two of you at this moment would have no argument from me that you are the descendants of a legendary female beauty." His eyes rested on their creamy, flawless skin, shining full hair, and eyes with soulful depth. "Oh, the white rose of Scotland has been the emblem of that nation since Bonnie Prince Charlie, and there is no flower more cherished than the white rose for its beauty and sharp fragrance."

Twenty-year-old Colie blushed at the compliment, and Anna Maria smiled appreciatively. "Having a charming Deep Southern gentleman in our midst is our pleasure," said Anna Maria. "But back to Thomas Barclay. His father, David, sold the estate in Ireland and settled in Philadelphia, where Thomas grew up. He married Mary Hoopes, a belle of Philadelphia, an heiress of great wealth and influence among the younger set. Thomas became a close and trusted friend of George Washington, Thomas Jefferson, and Ben Franklin. With them, he was a strong advocate in the revolutionary movement for freedom from Britain."

John thought about his son being born in George Washington's home state in a time of war against the South by the citizens of such cities as Philadelphia. How could this be?

"I like knowing that my son is a direct descendant of a trusted friend of the founders of our country," he said.

"He was not only a friend, but an active participant in the movement that led to our independence, and when our first consul to France was lost at sea, the Continental Congress named Thomas Barclay to that post. He and his wife and three young children sailed to France, and Thomas spent time in French and Dutch ports arranging shipments of blankets and supplies for Washington's troops and was also appointed a commissioner to settle America's public accounts in Europe, Barclays being bankers. After the war, Thomas negotiated treaties of friendship and commerce with Europe and the Barbary powers of Morocco, Algiers, Tunis, and Libya in North Africa."

"The Barbary pirates?" John asked.

"That was particularly difficult, but Thomas obtained for America a rare treaty with a Barbary power without promise of tribute that was ratified by Congress in 1787."

"The Emperor of Morocco became friends with my great-grandfather and trusted him," said Colie. "In the family we have a silver service from the Emperor, embossed with the coat of arms of Morocco and the words, 'To my esteemed friend Thomas Barclay, Minister of the United States of America, from the Emperor of Morocco.'"

Anna Maria added, "When the Emperor died three years later, President Washington and Secretary of State Thomas Jefferson sent Thomas back to Morocco to reaffirm the treaty with the new emperor as well as to go to Algiers to ransom Americans being held there."

Colie interrupted. "However, he never got there. At the Court of Morocco, a Spanish nobleman made an insulting remark about American women right in front of my great-grandfather. He said, 'How dare you, sir? I challenge you to a duel. You cannot insult American women without consequence.' As the one being challenged, the man chose the sword and killed Thomas Barclay as easily as if slewing a sheep." The tremor in Colie's voice showed the injury to her innocence in retelling the appalling story.

Anna Maria spoke up. "We can't be sure the duel ever took place, but the story rings true in a sense. The British consider Spanish noblemen as excessively haughty, and their view of women as mere ornaments for their husbands is well known. Your grandfather probably gave the man a stern lecture about the excellence of American women, at least, and we do know he died in Spain.

Truly, Thomas Barclay lived with the courage and love for his countrymen that God intended, but his poor children and wife suffered a terrible loss, to be sure. I, myself, was never to know my grandfather's love."

John, thinking of his brothers and son Henry, grieved anew. Since before his mother died when he was but a youth, he had not enjoyed the presence of all those he loved still living.

CHAPTER 30

BEL AIR

With all the whispers circulating around Orie's intention to leave Viewmont, it was not long before Anna Maria confronted Orie in her own way. They were alone in the back parlor sewing, and at the end of the afternoon Anna Maria commented, "It was such a pleasure to be with my daughter sewing clothing for the soldiers fighting on the South's behalf."

"Yes, Mama, it's been a productive day with lots of trousers made, and I will always remember it with pleasure too." With a solemn face she added, "I believe the time has come, though, for me to leave Viewmont, Mama, and become the mistress of my own home, now that I am married and have a family."

"Orie, dearest, my mother and I shared managing Viewmont for many years and I look forward to doing the same with you." This is true, Anna Maria thought. How can she reject this?

"You and Grandmother Sarah were only doing what you were trained to do, be the mistresses of a great plantation. But I am trained to be a medical doctor and I want to raise my family in my own home. I don't think that's unreasonable."

"It's certainly not unreasonable, but right now, in time of War, it may not be possible," said Anna Maria. I'm just postponing the leave-taking, she thought.

"Bel Air is vacant now. Reverend Timberlake passed away earlier this year, and he and his wife are buried in the family cemetery. John has spoken to one of the Timberlake daughters about taking up residence there and she was most gracious about it, saying it would ease the family's mind to have us living there, especially with the War breaking out where we least expect it. The furnishings are mostly intact, and it would not be difficult for us to move while John is home." Orie watched her mother's face alter very slightly with the impact of her words.

"I had not realized your plans were this extensive," said Anna Maria. "I knew, of course, that Reverend Timberlake had passed away, but thought some of his family would be living there. I will assume that John is in agreement with your idea and that Ike, also, is assisting you."

"Yes, Mama. Ike didn't approve of the idea at first, but he and Mag agree that it would be useful to live at Bel Air for a time, and to move there now while John is home on furlough. We will only be three miles away on the opposite side of the Hardware River and but a short distance from Mt. Ayr and Aunt Mary."

Anna Maria's thoughts tumbled in her head. Beneath the surface of Orie's detached melancholia, the young woman had organized and planned a major change for her life. Anna Maria would not lose her daughter and grandson, Jimmie, as had been the case with her son Thomas and his family, when he led them West and lost his life saving others from the cholera epidemic. She had lost other men in her family at early ages. Orie, however, was a woman. A house of her own, no matter for how long, would suit her bold daughter. Then they would be neighbors and supporters, rather than two strong personalities sharing life at Viewmont.

"Orie, dear, I think you may have come up with a thoughtful plan for yourself and your family. I don't know how much my sister Mary knows about this, but I will be happy to confide in her and help her welcome you."

"Thank you, Mama." Orie rose from her sewing chair and embraced her mother, kissing her on the cheek. She left the room to check on Jimmie. She could hardly breathe. It was out in the open. She and the baby and John would pack up and leave Viewmont. She would be the Mistress of Bel Air. Oh, to be the mistress and not just the married daughter. Oh, John, she thought, we can get through anything when the two of us are together, especially in our own home.

When John came home that afternoon after helping Ike and Peter in the fields, he stepped quietly into the bedroom, hoping to find Orie resting peacefully. She greeted him with an embrace that brought tears to his eyes.

"Oh, John, we are blessed. Mama approves of the move to Bel Air and will even see that Aunt Mary welcomes us and includes us as her extended family close by."

In the cradle, Jimmie squeezed his eyes shut, stretched, and yawned. John and Orie turned their eyes toward him, taking in his every movement and contented infant sounds. Orie scooped him up and handed him to John, his arms receptive to the weight and warmth of his son, kissing him until he fell back asleep. He sat with the baby on his lap on the rocking chair with Orie in a chair beside him, both parents taking pleasure in the infant's ease.

Like many prominent families, Orie's kith and kin lived nearby and far away, and the masters and mistresses made it their business to travel back and forth frequently to visit and to rear their children to be part of the greater family. Over at Mt. Ayr, the head of the household had been John Digges Moon, Orie's father's oldest brother, until he died almost a year ago. Mary Barclay Moon, Anna Maria's older sister, was his widow. Orie was very fond of her Aunt Mary and her nine Moon cousins, who were frequently at Mt. Ayr visiting their mother. Orie would not be alone or lonely when John was back in Richmond.

John heaved a sigh of relief. "I'm glad it's done. As much as I admire your mother, this may be the best course for us right now and you have accomplished what you set out to do. You are a remarkable woman, Orie Moon Andrews. But now I must confess my confusion over who is who in your large and complicated family. I should have asked more questions at the wedding, when so many were gathered here. But please tell me how it happened that two Barclay sisters married into the Moon family."

"It's all my stepfather's doings," Orie replied. "When John Harris married my grandmother and acquired my mother and her siblings as stepchildren, he set about playing matchmaker with his grandnieces and grandnephews. He was very pleased with the eventual marriage of Mary to his grandnephew John Digges Moon, a descendant of Colonial Virginia Governor Edward Digges of Nelson County on his mother's side. To my mother, his favorite stepchild, who was born at Viewmont after the death of her father, he bequeathed Viewmont. To his favorite grandnephew, Edward Moon, he gave no property but his business fortunes. In order to join the two, Edward had to marry Anna Maria, which he did with great willingness. Mama probably had had her eyes on him since childhood and Captain Jack knew it. The marriage was a very happy one and a well-arranged economic endeavor."

"Portraits of your father show a handsome and distinguished-looking man, but also a man with an open, earnest face. I think I would have liked him."

"Oh yes, you would have, John. It's a great sorrow for me that he died before you joined the family."

"And for me as well," said John. "As for the Moons, should I know anything in particular about them? Are they English?"

"Yes, from around Norwich. They were among the earliest colonists to arrive in Virginia, and it's recorded that Abraham Moon settled south of Norfolk. They were merchants, settling north toward Fredericksburg as well as Isle of Wight County and Suffolk. In early England, the name was spelled M-o-h-u-n. They came from Normandy in 1066 with William the Conqueror and were ship owners. After settling in Virginia, they carried on trade between Virginia and England. They showed a great deal of interest in education, which is something my father carried on. When the westward movement began in the mid-seventeen hundreds, William Moon came to Albemarle County—his wife was a sister of John Harris, and with him was his brother, Jacob Moon. The two Moon brothers patented large tracts of land lying on both sides of the Hardware River. Part of their holdings served to establish Scottsville and extended westward on the James River, and a portion of their eastern holdings became part of Fluvanna County." Orie smiled at John. "Should I stop there?"

"Yes, please," he said, shaking his head in mock dismay. "You are not just Orie Moon, but within you lies part of the mind of the genius of our country."

"You are exaggerating things, my dear. But our relatives will appreciate your knowledge on the subject of their family lineage."

"Indeed," John agreed. "Ignorance on such matters makes for hard feelings."

Within a few days, the move to Bel Air was completed with the help of Uncle Ned, who drove the family carriage bearing Anna Maria, Orie, and the baby, as well as Cornelia and a large basket from Martha and the kitchen girls filled with fried chicken, sweet potatoes, cornbread, winter squash, pickles, cider, and apple pie. John rode a horse, and Ike brought Mag and his sisters and as many things for the move that he could carry. They entered the Bel Air grounds at the main entrance, at the north façade. As they entered the house, they went directly to the back entrance to look south out over the Hardware River. In early November, the river was full and the hills rich with earthy browns, reds, and yellows. "It's a lovely view," Orie declared, inviting the others to look.

When Ike arrived with his sisters, Eddie explored the grounds. West of the Main House was a decade-old one-story guest cottage. "Orie, may I visit you and stay in the cottage? It's like a playhouse!"

"We'll see," said Orie. But Eddie was already running to see the three outbuildings on the eastern side of the house. One was the overseer's cottage, another a guest house, and the third was a pyramid-roofed smokehouse with a batten door and wooden finial at the top of the roof. "Bel Air is beautiful," Eddie shouted, after holding her breath with the excitement of it all. She found an entrance to the basement from the outside and delighted in exploring the dark and silent depths of Bel Air.

The others picked up threads of Eddie's enthusiasm. Ike murmured aloud as he examined the floors, fireplace mantels, wainscoting, baseboards, and chair rails that were designed and crafted with skill. He was particularly smitten with the delicately carved step ends of the staircase and rounded mahogany handrail.

By the noontime dinner, they were ready to sit together in the dining room and sing hymns of praise and thanksgiving for the food and shelter.

Lottie added, "I should like some real coffee someday." The others nodded in agreement.

With Ike, the resident local historian, among them, everyone asked questions about Bel Air and he smiled, smoking his pipe as Shep curled about his boots, and talked about his favorite subject: fine Virginia homes and fine Virginia people.

"Charles Wingfield Jr. built Bel Air somewhere between 1794 and 1817, basically a framed two-story Georgian farmhouse with beaded siding and one-story wings on each side and a back entrance overlooking the Hardware River. Bel Air is not as old or as large as Viewmont, but it's similar, with chimneys on the side ends of the house and a central entry and hall. The house is also categorized as Federal style because of the modillion cornice on the north and south facades. Fancy millwork, you see. As for brick, which you see so much of now, both Viewmont and Bel Air were built when native timber was the choice material, before brick replaced framed timber for the manor houses out here on the frontier." Ike left his chair and pointed out the fireplace and paneled frieze and a molded mantel shelf featuring a reeded edge with rope molding. "This makes it Federal style."

"Who was Charles Wingfield Jr.?" asked Eddie. "Was he young and handsome?"

"I suppose he was handsome when he was young. He was an ordained and licensed Presbyterian minister who was also a prominent landowner, a magistrate, and sheriff. The Reverend died in 1817. Martin Dawson bought the property in 1819."

"Was *he* young and handsome?" Eddie asked again.

"I have no idea, but I do know Dawson was cofounder of the Rivanna Navigation Company and was the company's largest stockholder. In his will in 1835, he gave the largest amount of money to the University of Virginia that had been received up to that time. Dawson's Row of dormitories at the university is part of that money. Also, he freed his slaves and gave each one two hundred dollars to start their new lives. They were to be transported to a place where slavery was not tolerated."

"Do the Yankees know about him?" asked Colie.

"They know only what they hear about by abolitionists. But truly, Nat Turner's Rebellion in 1831 scared the whites, and they passed a law that prohibited the assembly of blacks. Of course whites could teach Sunday school to Negro children and adults, as did Stonewall Jackson, and teach cooks to write down recipes and accountants to keep the books, but it was the public assembly that scared the whites," Ike explained. "For myself, I think the most interesting thing in Dawson's will was selling off his property and giving the proceeds to the constitutionally created Literary Fund of Virginia to build free public schools. He wanted three such schools, and one was to be at Bel Air. Poor children were to be allowed to attend and part of his donation was to be used to educate indigent Virginia children. The schools were to have thirty students."

Eddie and Colie agreed that Martin Dawson was a very good man.

"Eight years after Dawson's death, the Reverend Walter Timberlake purchased the estate, and he lived here until he died early this year."

Mollie spoke up. "I have to ask—was *he* young and handsome?"

"He was a fine-looking man," said Ike. Mag clapped in glee and the rest joined in.

"Reverend Timberlake came to Albemarle from Fluvanna County, where he had formed most of the Methodist churches there. He was pastor of Temple Hill Church in Albemarle County for about twenty years and was an original member of the Board of Trustees for Randolph-Macon College. He also had business inter-ests—the canal, the building of stone locks, and a courthouse in Palmyra—and did anything that needed doing, including owning and operating grist mills and running a tavern in Palmyra. He and his wife are buried in the family cemetery here at Bel Air, may they rest in peace."

The five sisters looked at each other and said as one, "Reverend Timberlake was a very good man."

The Reverend Timberlake's daughters welcomed Orie with food and goods they could hardly spare during wartime, and did so with much love for the young mother and her baby. They were happy to help out the Moon family with space for Orie and her family as well as not have to worry about an empty manor house that could harbor deserters from either side or vandals. Lottie, Colie, Mary, and Eddie came over often to help care for Jimmie and brought food from their kitchen. Aunt Mary and her visiting children often invited Orie to dine.

Soon the Mistress of Bel Air demanded to know from Ike the status of the War, which was heading into its third winter. The news was not bad. He told her that Yankee forces in Chattanooga were besieged by the Confederates and were hungry in early December. On December 5, a small Confederate steam-driven vessel sent a torpedo-like explosive into the side of a Union gun-boat, the *New Ironsides*. The ship did not sink but was damaged by a secret new and exciting weapon. President Davis visited Atlanta on December 9 and was greeted by large, cheering crowds, while President Lincoln was seen as increasingly unpopular and tyrannical. General Mead started the Bristoe Campaign in Virginia in early December, but even with a bigger army failed to successfully challenge General Lee, and he withdrew on the twenty-third.

Orie asked Ike if there was more news, and he continued his report.

Unfortunate was the second sinking of the Confederate submarine the *Hunley* in Charleston Harbor on the fifteenth, and this time the inventor, H.L. Hunley, drowned along with seven crewmen. On December 28, Confederates attempted to close the only supply line to the Union Army of Tennessee. The South lost 408 men attacking and the North lost 420 defenders of the supply line. The next day the Union supply line was still standing. During the last third of the month, the Federal forces pounded Fort Sumter with three thousand shells. The Confederate flag remained over a pile of rubble that was once a fort.

"It's all too hard to bear," Orie said.

"Hear this," Ike said. "Lincoln rewrote the draft rules in December with orders for Negroes to be drafted before white Boys. As Union Kentucky troops invaded the South, they took any military-age Negro and drafted him. Not one Kentucky white Boy was drafted after the draft rule was changed. On December ninth, a rebellion by Union Negro troops at Fort Jackson, Louisiana, was put down by the Union Army. On the other hand, we don't hear about slaves revolting against Southerners, and slaves all over the South have been taking the place of white men away from the farms fighting for the Confederate Army."

On December 7, 1863, Davis delivered his message to the Confederate Congress. He spoke of battlefield reverses, financial demands, and lack of progress on the foreign relations scene, lack of supplies and men for the Army, and sorrow that there had not been more prisoner exchanges. He spoke of the fury of the war and atrocities against the Southern people, especially against women and Negroes. His speech ended with praise for the Southern people: "The patriotism of the people has proved equal to every sacrifice demanded by their country's needs." On the last day of 1863, the *Richmond Examiner* wrote: "Today closes the gloomiest year of our struggle." As it turned out, 1864 would be worse.

CHAPTER 31

IN THE YEAR OF OUR LORD 1864

John returned to Richmond, and Orie settled in as Mistress of Bel Air. Eddie came often to play with baby Jimmie and ride her pony on the grounds when the weather was fair.

"I'm glad you live at Bel Air, Orie," Eddie said on one visit.

"And why is that?" Orie asked, smiling.

"It gives me someplace to go, where I like to go, and Viewmont is not so lively now that you and Lottie are gone."

"Any news of Lottie, dear?" Orie and Eddie were in the dining room, where Eddie was spoon-feeding the baby while Orie held him in her arms.

"Yes, Mama read her last letter to us just days ago. Lottie's happy in Valdosta. Sarah is a good student but needs theological study. The family is well respected and they treat her with kindness. They are leaders in their church and the city. And she's thankful to Dr. Broadus for the recommendation to be Sarah's tutor. Lottie says she enjoys teaching the girl and is pleased to help Viewmont with part of her salary."

"Very nice report, Eddie. Thank you. Lottie's right to be pleased with herself. Not many young women would leave home in wartime to take on a position so far away. And the young woman should have a tutor. The War has put an end to almost everything in the South, but a sixteen-year-old girl should have an education. And there could be no better teacher in the South than our Lottie. But I worry about her so far away. We don't know what battles may be near and if they have food and how safe they are. But Dr. Broadus, you may not remember, was the past pastor of Charlottesville Baptist Church and chaplain of the university and was the man who brought Lottie to Christ. He would not forget Lottie. We have to trust him to protect her."

"I'd like to go to Valdosta in Georgia," said Eddie. "I've never really been anywhere."

"No, dear, you haven't. Your father died when you were two, and then Lottie and I were away at school and then the journey to Jerusalem and now the War."

"But I'll make up for it after the War, won't I, Orie?"

"Yes, dear girl, I'm sure you will. Oops, Jimmie's had enough, Eddie. I'll clean him up and you can take Abundant Pony to the grist mill and come back with some cornmeal. Will you do that for me, please, Eddie?"

"Yes. I like to talk to Sam about things. He says I'm very well spoken for a girl not yet thirteen years old."

Orie laughed. "What were his words, exactly?"

"'Miss Eddie, I reckon you talk more 'an a chipmunk.'" Eddie giggled and put on her wrap to ride her pony to the grist mill.

"Have him sign an IOU and I'll pay him later."

"I will," Eddie shouted as she left the house, immediately wishing she had the money and could pay the Negro herself. She knew all families were struggling to have food and things they needed to keep going, whether slaves or heads of large households. Sam had a family and lived in the overseer's cottage on the grounds and looked after the property for the Timberlake family, and now Orie and John's family as well. His wife and two daughters helped in the kitchen and wherever

213

else they were needed. Everybody was short-handed and making do.

In February, John wrote Orie a letter with part of President Davis's address to the soldiers in Richmond before the spring campaign would begin. John was much taken with the speech and wanted Orie to take it to heart, but wrote that the President's tone was bittersweet and melancholy and that he had not been well of late.

> Soldiers! Assured success awaits us in our holy struggle for liberty and independence, and for the preservation of all that renders life desirable to honorable men. When that success shall be reached, to you—your country's hope and pride—under Divine Providence, will it be due. The fruits of that success will not be reaped by you alone, but your children and children's children in long generations to come, and will enjoy blessings derived from you, that will preserve your memory ever-living in their hearts.
>
> Citizen-defenders of the homes, the liberties, and the altars of the Confederacy! That the God whom we all humbly worship may shield you with his Fatherly care, and preserve you for safe return to the peaceful enjoyment of your friends and the association of those you most love, is the earnest prayer of your Commander-in-Chief. Richmond, February 9, 1864.

Orie read the speech several times and tried to picture the President speaking to all those young men and boys as they prepared to enter yet another season of battles and death against invaders who trampled the ground they marched on in great numbers and untorn blue uniforms. Orie shuddered at the harm they had already brought to the South and to people she loved.

Winter encampments in 1864 were relatively quiet because of lessons learned the previous two winters: not much progress could be made when the roads were muddy, the weather icy, and the troops sick. Keeping soldiers in the field fed was a major concern for the Confederacy. Deficient nutrition going on for the third year was exacting a heavy toll on young soldiers, some of them still growing. Sickness and death were the obvious results, which the underpopulated South could ill afford, but lack of enthusiasm on the battlefield was not evident, for the Confederate soldiers were even angrier at the Yankees for the invasion than they were hungry.

As at Viewmont, Southern farms did their best to supply food for the soldiers in addition to feeding themselves. Slaves in the South were not drafted and therefore able to continue production of foodstuffs in spite of the large numbers of white men away from home and in the Army. Women were in charge, but most women were able to continue doing what they did before the War, and it was the slaves who took on the larger responsibilities. War was a hardship for all, but starvation came later, when soldiers were completely cut off from supplies and raiders stole food from farms. In the meantime, however, the Union blockade was successful in keeping out goods coming into the South. The absence of coffee was a tiny but constant reminder of the hatred of the War and the Yankees.

John and the other doctors were kept busy with the expected cases of dysentery and typhoid fever over the winter months. When March and April did not produce prodigious battlefield casualties, John was granted furlough home to Bel Air at the end of April, his first since the birth of Jimmie in October.

The homecoming was everything Orie and John could have wished. The Southern earth was renewing itself with soon-to-be fragrant honeysuckle vines in the woodsy groves, and there were pleasant afternoons of fishing the Hardware and James for small-mouth bass, shad, and herring. Greens were prepared wilted with apple cider vinegar and served tart and fresh with spring onions. Cloaks were cast aside and sunshine warmed unwrapped necks.

The very earth softened its grip on the clay-shot soil and sweetened the air with zephyr breezes and sounds of men working in the fields, the lowing of cattle, and children at play.

John's challenges were different away from hospital beds weighed down by the suffering of the sick and wounded. There in the countryside, John considered himself a farmer and saw possibilities of agricultural success with every budding branch and sunlit patch of field. Orie, as Mistress of Bel Air, took John on tours of the estate to show him the wonders of their rural realm. The nights, afternoons, and mornings made themselves available for Orie and John to bask in each other's arms and dream of when the War would be over and life would continue, world without end.

But the lull did not last, broken furiously by Grant's crossing the Rapidan River on May 4, 1864, and placing his forces between Lee and Richmond. He invited an open battle, but Lee surprised him, aggressively attacking the larger Union Army in the Battle of the Wilderness on May 5–7, resulting in terrible casualties on both sides. It was time for John to get back to Richmond and his Boys in the hospital.

Orie and Ike kept in close touch while the battles were going on. As an Albemarle County militia member, Ike was kept fully abreast of military matters, and as a former Confederate Medical Corps surgeon, Orie felt a duty to be fully informed. The Wilderness, composed of dense thickets in Spotsylvania, resulted in a two-day bloody stalemate. The violence was accelerating with hand-to-hand fighting in the thickets as if the War must end this time around. Grant came from his Culpepper County winter camp with approximately 120,000 men.

Ike listed the details of the early-May battles in the Wilderness, with Orie resolutely listening. The names of the generals and places were familiar to her.

"Union General Getty's Sixth Corps, with the support of General Hancock, fought against Confederate General A. P. Hill. The battle raged until nightfall and exhaustion felled the soldiers. In the morning, the Federals resumed fighting and A. P. Hill's soldiers were almost overrun, when the Texas Brigade of Longstreet's corps arrived and saved the Southern Boys from disaster. Longstreet's troops were on the brink of success when General Lee's Old Workhorse was shot by a Southern soldier by mistake. During the time it took to put things right, General Hancock was able to rally his men and supervise construction of earthworks. When General Lee's soldiers assaulted Hancock's troops, they were stopped cold by crashing volleys from Hancock's dug-in soldiers. On May 7, both sides dug in and waited for an attack. Grant had suffered twenty thousand casualties in the Wilderness, but his men's spirits were high, as they felt that victory would not be denied them due to their overwhelming numbers."

"So might makes right, according to the Northern invaders," Orie murmured.

"The Union Army is an unholy alliance of abolitionists impatient with God to punish the slave-holders and Irish immigrants just off the boat, given a uniform and a gun and pushed into the slaughter," Ike said. "They have the numbers and the zeal."

"And we have so few, such precious few soldiers," Orie said.

"And underequipped, undernourished and overextended," Ike added. "They fight like Old Testament children of God, but eventually they are outnumbered, exhausted, and they fall."

Worse news came quickly. Orie was at Viewmont visiting her patients when Ike came riding up from Scottsville in a slowly measured gait as if following a funeral dirge.

"What ails you, Isaac?" Anna Maria asked when she heard him come inside.

"J. E. B. Stuart is dead," he said with a downcast stare. "He was killed at Yellow Tavern on the eleventh."

Anna Maria took a chair in the sitting room. "Sit down, son. Please."

Ike sat. "Stuart did everything he could, Mama. The Yankees were six miles from Richmond and Stuart was outnumbered. He won the Battle of Yellow Tavern and he saved Richmond, but he's gone. First Stonewall, and now J. E. B. Stuart. Lee can't do it alone. He lost his right hand when Stonewall died, and now he's lost his eyes and ears with the death of Stuart."

"How did it happen, Isaac?" Anna Maria wiped tears from her eyes. Every Southern woman was in love with the gallant young cavalry commander with the plume in his hat. Even though every Yankee in the Union Army would have given Satan a handshake for the price of killing J. E. B. Stuart, no one could touch him. It was as if a divine presence had been protecting him.

"On the tenth of May, dawn broke in a heavy fog and twenty thousand Yankees attacked though that fog. They say that General Grant could not outgeneral General Lee and so he would simply overrun him with sheer numbers. Half the Confederate rifles wouldn't fire because the powder was wet from the fog. Yankees swarmed over the breastworks, and our Boys clubbed the enemy with rifles that wouldn't fire."

"Oh, dear God," Anna Maria said, holding her hands to her heart.

"I'm sorry, Mama. I shouldn't have said that. Everyone's in mourning. General Lee says he could scarcely think of him without crying."

Ike left his mother in the sitting room with a glass of water, and left the Main House to look for Orie, who was returning from the slave cabins. He took her arm and they walked to the chairs outside, where they could talk.

"Are we in danger, Ike?" was her first question.

"Not immediately, no, but there is bad news. J. E. B. Stuart is dead. Wounded in battle on May tenth and died in Richmond on the eleventh."

"Oh, Ike. More than anyone, J. E. B. Stuart was the gallant Confederate soldier. So handsome and dashing and courageous. How could we lose with such a man fighting for us?" Tears brimmed and overflowed down her cheeks. Ike held her hand and both were silent in their grief.

"It was a strange day. Major General Philip Sheridan was gunning for Stuart, both of them cavalry commanders. Sheridan led a column of troops that stretched out over thirteen miles at times on their way to do battle. They reached the Confederate forward supply base at Beaver Dam Station that evening. They destroyed railroad cars and six locomotives of the Virginia Central Railroad and telegraph wires. They also rescued almost four hundred Yankee prisoners, captured in the Wilderness. Mind you, the Yankees had ten thousand troops and thirty-two artillery pieces. They also had rapid-firing Spencer carbines."

Orie nodded. She was thinking of John's brothers, Billie and Robert, cut down in battle on the first day. Would they all be dead soon?

"The Battle of Yellow Tavern began at noon on the tenth. Major General Stuart moved forty-five hundred of his troops to get between Sheridan and Richmond and that's where they met, just six miles north of Richmond. The Union Army had two divisions arrayed against two Southern brigades. Southern troops resisted, fighting over three hours from a low ridgeline. A countercharge from the First Virginia Cavalry pushed advancing Union troops back from the hilltop, as Stuart, mounted on horseback, shouted encouragement. As the Fifth Michigan Cavalry streamed in retreat past Stuart, a dismounted Union private, a former sharpshooter, turned and shot Stuart with his forty-four-caliber pistol from a distance of ten to thirty yards. Stuart fell, mortally wounded, and died the next day in Richmond."

"Does Mama know what happened?"

"She knows J. E. B. Stuart is dead."

"That's enough to know," Orie decided.

Life returned to its former routine, but the death of Stuart was on people's minds all over the South. Hope lost was not regained.

Men who had fought with him mourned the most. His enthusiastic love for his native state of Virginia had set him apart from even the most patriotic of Virginians in that it seemed to transcend the reality of the crushing weight of the powerful North, displaying an unlimited ruthlessness against a rural section of the country fighting for independence, at first from hostility and oppression and now for their physical survival.

More news from another battlefront came not long after Stuart's death. Ike and Mag took their carriage to Bel Air to confer with Orie. It was a warm, sunny day in late May and they sat out by the Hardware River as it rolled toward the James in full strength.

They talked about the Battle of New Market in the Shenandoah Valley that took place on May 15. "It was a Confederate victory, thanks to the cadets at Virginia Military Institute," Ike said.

Orie looked sharply at Ike. "What do you mean? Were they put into battle? Those children?"

"It appears to be so. Our defenses were failing and General Breckinridge had orders to send the cadets in if necessary. But Orie, remember, these were not children but trained military cadets. The South is their homeland. What kind of a future will they have if the South falls to the Northern conquerors? What if they never had a chance to fight? They did fight, Orie, and they turned defeat into victory."

Orie's strained countenance softened. She was thinking of baby Henry. She had a chance to save him from an agonizing death and she took it. She would always be grateful for that chance. The look of surprised relief in his eyes before he died had told her all she needed to know.

"I'm sorry, Ike. Much as we want to, we cannot put even babies into a category that is safe. A life is to be lived, no matter how short it may be."

Mag touched Orie on the shoulder in sympathy, thinking also of baby Henry, gone now a little over a year.

"The victory was necessary, Orie," said Ike. They say that General Sigel had orders from General Grant to march to Staunton with ten thousand men and artillery to destroy the Virginia Central Railroad and then move on to Lynchburg and destroy the canal complex. That way the Union would deny General Lee the Breadbasket of the South for his Army and cut off supplies for the Confederacy coming from the interior."

"I see," said Orie, remembering family visits to Uncle James's wife Julia's welcoming and gracious home in Staunton.

"The only defense in the Valley we had was a patchwork of soldiers amounting to around forty-one hundred men under the command of Major General John Cabell Breckinridge," said Ike.

"He's from the Kentucky branch of the Virginia Breckinridge family," said Mag with approval.

"Yes, I know, and he was Vice President of the United States as well as a Congressman and a Senator. And James Breckinridge of Botetourt County, the brother of this man's grandfather, served in the Virginia House of Delegates and the US House of Representatives and fought in the Revolutionary War. How dare they treat us as if we had no say in Constitutional affairs and then, when we walk away like gentlemen, they invade us militarily?" No one argued with Orie.

Ike said, "We can't help what Lincoln did, but the cadets made us proud. They marched nearly eighty-five miles north from Lexington on May eleventh to New Market, arriving on the fifteenth, often sleeping and marching in the rain. The situation was dire. General Sigel had the high ground, more soldiers, and vastly more artillery guns. Defending their intended southward movement, our soldiers' line broke after being raked by cannon and musketry fire. This was the gap the cadets filled. They closed the gap, allowing Confederate forces to regroup and push back the Union Army. But to do it, the cadets had to march across open and level ground within easy range of six gun batteries on top of Bushong Hill, and they were cut down by fierce artillery fire.

Even so, they kept going to the fence, began firing, and charged the enemy after the veterans engaged musketry fire and took advantage of a Union battery stopping to replenish its ammunition. The cadets continued pursuit of the retreating enemy until the corps was halted by order of General Breckinridge. The cadets were magnificent."

"How many casualties?" Orie asked.

Ike said, "Two hundred and fifty-seven cadets were on the field at New Market. Ten cadets were killed in battle or died later from battle wounds and forty-five were wounded."

"Thomas Garland Jefferson was a great-great-nephew of President Thomas Jefferson. He was one of the ten who were killed," Mag added. "He was seventeen years old."

"Do the Yankees know what they did? Do they care? It's as if the enemy is an alien force without knowledge of who we are and what we did to found this nation," Orie said.

"In the Bible, God wanted His people to rule themselves with His help but gave in to their demands and Saul became king. In America, we wanted to rule ourselves in obedience to God and became a country without a king. Bur Abraham Lincoln put aside our Constitution and brought war. We have a despot, a king," said Ike.

CHAPTER 32

LOTTIE COMES HOME

Come late June, Orie knew the familiar signs—she was expecting again. She was happy to be bearing a new life but frightened for the near future, not daring to think so far ahead as February. The War, it seemed, was everywhere. Even Ike and his militia friends could not keep up with all the battles and the soaring casualties. They could only say that battles had been fought on the sea, on rivers, on rural hills, in cities and woods, on mountains and rocky cliffs, in rain, broiling heat, mud, sleet, and snow, at night and at noon.

In July 1864, the summer military campaigns were roiling across the South with increasing columns of Union troops in blue and thin lines of haggard-looking men in ragged gray and butternut. Lottie continued to be away, tutoring the children of families across the South. She had taught briefly for a private family in Alabama. Then, letters were arriving from Bishopville, South Carolina, where she lived as the governess for several children in a Greek Revival mansion overlooking enormous cotton fields. After that, she lived with a family in rural northeast Farmington, Georgia, where she tutored the only child of a wealthy Baptist minister.

Ike and Mag, still subdued over the War since the death of J. E. B. Stuart in May, sat with Orie under a shade tree at Bel Air overlooking the cool waters of the Hardware River and talked about the Battle of Cold Harbor, not far from Richmond.

"I don't understand it," said Ike. "On June third at half past four in the morning, Grant ordered fifty thousand Union troops to attack dug-in Confederate troops. Within fifteen minutes, the Union attack was punished with seven thousand casualties. Since it was still early in the morning, the massacre more or less continued. After noon, Grant ordered another full-scale attack. The order was disobeyed. The battle went on for five more days before Grant asked for a two-hour truce for permission to retrieve his wounded troops. By then, few of the wounded were alive, as thousands died in the hot summer sun over a period of five days. I don't know what to think." His voice turned gruff with emotion, and the women shed unbidden tears for the dead and wounded Boys from the North.

"It's not a victory," Ike tried to explain. Mag left her chair and walked about, tears falling freely.

"No," Orie agreed, thinking of her baby boy and the child yet unborn, her mouth dry and her hands clenched.

In August, a letter came from John with news of James Jackson, son of the widow living outside Florence at Forks of Cypress. He wrote, "My friend lost an arm fighting for General Johnston in the Georgia Campaign on June 27 on Kennesaw Mountain just fifteen miles north of Atlanta. The battle was fought on the last significant high ground before the Yankees cross the Chattahoochee River into Atlanta. Please pray for him and for the troops defending Atlanta."

Orie read the letter to Mag and Ike. "What do you think about Lottie? She's in Georgia near Athens, the last we heard."

"She's not right there in the thick of it, but she should come home right away," said Ike. "The Yankees could fan out all over

Georgia while they are moving in on Atlanta. Or after," he added softly.

"If they harm my sister, heaven itself will fall on them," Orie declared, thinking of the missionary work that would be stopped before it had a chance to start.

Mag gave Ike a questioning look.

"We'll make arrangements quickly. Lottie will not be in danger," Ike assured. He remembered that Orie was still fragile from Henry's death and was now expecting again. Although the South had won a great many battles, the outlook as a whole was dismal. Sherman was there in Georgia with one hundred thousand well-equipped and well-fed men, while Johnston was commanding sixty thousand tired, hungry, and wounded soldiers. Ike knew President Davis was impatient with Johnston for avoiding pitched battles, but the lack of troops and materiel of war made it necessary. Did President Davis not understand that or appreciate Johnston's strategy to preserve the lives of his soldiers?

Ike thought it a mistake to change horses in midstream, so to speak, by making General John Bell Hood the new commander. Hood was aggressive, but he was fighting with the loss of an arm and a leg and still enduring pain from his wounds. Possibly he was not thinking clearly through the opium when he struck Sherman too late in the day at the Battle of Peachtree Creek. He lost the battle as well as twenty-five hundred soldiers. He lost another twenty-five hundred men when he attacked an entrenched artillery position within firing range of the center of Atlanta. If Atlanta fell, the whole Union Army could overwhelm Lee's defense of Richmond from the South. The courage of the Confederate officers and the Southern Boys continued to give hope to Southerners, but mistakes now would doom them.

Lottie was in danger now. Ike was sure of that. He rode his horse to Charlottesville and stopped by the Virginia militia to see about the situation in northeast Georgia. William, an old veteran friend, asked first about the state of affairs near Viewmont and Scottsville before he began to speculate about Lottie Moon.

"We don't know what Sherman will do, but likely it will be the worst thing possible," William said. "The Georgia Railroad, in Lottie's case, is still operating between Athens and Charlottesville. You need to telegraph her to come home immediately. We're surprised she didn't leave right after Stoneman's Raid on August second, when Yankee cavalry attempted to raid Athens. They came right through Flat Shoals and Watkinsville, which are near Farmington. "

"I think Farmington is very remote and tiny. It would not be worth their time," said Ike.

"Oh, the Yankees have all the time in the world to disrupt, destroy, and besiege. Get her home, Mr. Moon," William said.

Ike sent a telegraph from the militia's office and wondered if Lottie would leave her post. She was so sure of God's protection for her eventual foreign missionary work that she feared no man.

"Thanks for your help, William. I'll be glad to have Lottie home. The church is always asking for her and worrying me about how far away she is and can't I just go and bring her home."

William laughed. "I reckon that's true. People hereabouts think a lot of your family, and we'd rather she be at Viewmont than anywhere near Grant and Sherman. May God protect her now until she gets home."

Lottie was home by September and everyone breathed a sigh of relief. "Lottie, dearest, I was bereft without you," said Orie. "You will be an auntie again and I was sad that Jimmie was growing up without you. Eddie misses you terribly, and of course Mama, and Colie and Mollie. And your church people. I could go on and on." Orie hugged and kissed her sister and thought she would be completely happy if only John were there too.

Once again established at Viewmont, Lottie visited Orie at Bel Air, but was also involved in Soldier Aid Society work at Viewmont and in Scottsville and helped out with Baptist church teaching duties. She gave talks at Viewmont for the ladies and servants about her teaching posts in the Deep South and encouraged them all to think about God's plans for them after the War. She was herself planning to find a church to sponsor her missionary work, now long delayed by the invasion of the Union Army. "God expects more of us than waging War," she said repeatedly.

"Yes, Lottie, but right now we are barely surviving and the War is everywhere. Atlanta has fallen and Sherman is sowing seeds of destruction that rivals what the Romans did to Carthage," said Orie. "Did you know that the Custis Lee mansion was appropriated by the Federal government on June fifteenth for use as a military cemetery?"

"Do you mean the mansion owned by General Lee's wife, overlooking Washington, DC, from the Virginia side of the Potomac?"

"Yes, sister. It was captured by the Yankees hours after the Commonwealth of Virginia ratified an ordinance of secession."

"It's a private home. It was built by George Washington Parke Custis, an adopted grandson and ward of George Washington," Lottie wailed.

"Now that it is a designated burial ground for Union soldiers, no one from the family can ever return there," said Orie. "It's hallowed ground for the Union dead for eternity."

"I did not know they had done that," Lottie allowed. "Yes, that's worse than the Romans sowing Carthaginian land with salt so nothing would grow for a hundred years. Much worse."

"Here, hold Jimmie and tell me again how the townspeople of Athens chased away part the base-born cavalry of Major General George Stoneman," Orie said, sorry she had made Lottie so downcast.

Lottie smiled and lifted up the baby and gave him a kiss on his nose. "Well, the Athenians outnumbered the cavalry, and that's not the usual case. However, let me explain the condition of the townspeople. There were workers from the armory, to be truthful, but the rest were college professors, mechanics, newspapermen, old men, and young boys, none of whom had ever been in an army. Except probably Militia Captain Lumpkin, who had already posted two bronze howitzers in a small earthwork overlooking the Watkinsville Road, and slaves had already dug into the hillside overlooking the road."

"That would look like a rather large army, I expect, to eighty Yankees on horseback," said Orie.

"Orie, dear, the townsmen marched three miles to the position on Barber's Creek where it crosses Watkinsville Road. They marched with muskets, yes, and with canes and umbrellas."

"Oh dear, that must have been a sight," Orie agreed, eyes merry.

"The Union cavalry just stood there looking at the people, until Captain Lumpkin screamed out the command to fire the howitzers. Two or three shells hit the ridge on the other side of the creek and scattered the cavalry. They retreated and did not come back. Reporting back to Sherman was probably the hardest thing they had to do," said Lottie. "The Yankees are fallible, fearful humans. Just like us."

Orie sighed inwardly. Had Lottie not been told about the battles at Cold Harbor and the Wilderness? The terrible carnage that had resulted? No, the War she and John were living through was different from the one Lottie knew about. So be it.

Ike knew he was lucky to be home and in charge of Viewmont's fields with Peter as his trusted overseer, but everything had changed since the loss of the Mississippi River the summer before to Union control after the fall of Vicksburg. Combined with the Union naval blockade, there was little chance of successfully shipping tobacco to European markets. Also, the Confederate Congress and the Virginia Assembly had both passed resolutions asking planters to refrain from planting tobacco. This summer he and Peter were planting, cultivating, and harvesting foodstuffs badly needed by the Army in addition to tobacco as a cash crop. The Moon family was doing all right in very tight times. But each year was harsher than the one before.

A Southerner without a deeply furrowed brow was nonexistent. They would not panic. The Yankees could say what they wanted, they were in the wrong. It was appropriate, according to the US Constitution, to secede from an oppressive, despotic government, which Lincoln's presidency had long ago proven to be. They could not, would not be forced back into such a detestable union. The South would persevere.

CHAPTER 33
LEE SURRENDERS

John was home on a rare furlough for the impending birth of his and Orie's third child, which took place at Viewmont for the convenience of the Moon and Andrews families. The birth itself was uneventful, and this time Orie took pleasure in the role of new mother with her newborn son. Her firstborn, Henry, was never far from her mind, but time and prayer had replaced the memory of Henry's sudden illness and passing with images of him laughing and crawling and resting in the arms of people who loved him.

John, too, handled the new baby with ease, not looking furtively for signs of respiratory distress. "He's a redhead," he observed.

"Yes, right now, my love, but he could lose that patch of hair and end up as a brown-haired boy," Orie said, then added, "I love brown-haired boys," and kissed John on the lips. He kissed her fingers and then her cheeks before returning the baby to his mother.

"Another boy. Was that a blessing, or was it a curse from the Arab?" John smiled, rubbing the baby's back gently, feeling his strength and warmth.

"The Sheik said I would be blessed with all boys."

"All babies are blessings. As a Christian, I would like someday to have a little girl just like her mother."

"Yes, my love," said Orie, "but no time soon."

"No, no time soon." Both were silent, John thinking of the fast-falling fortunes of the beloved Confederacy and Orie thinking of feeding two babies and surviving in soon-to-be-postwar Virginia.

In the ensuing days, names were bandied about, and they finally settled on one. "William Luther Andrews," Orie declared. "From my father's side of the family."

"A fine name and his alone if we call him Luther. Welcome to the Andrews family, dear son," John said. He picked up the baby and walked downstairs to introduce the newest member of the Andrews family to everyone gathered there that day and to the household servants.

While at Viewmont, John took the time to see that Orie would have no postpartum complications and that baby Luther, too, was in good health. He spent time with Anna Maria and Ike discussing Viewmont and what to do when the seemingly inevitable collapse of the Confederacy's defense would come. He also put his shoulder to the wheel doing farm duties during the cold and ice of the Virginia winter.

Before returning to his hospital duties in Richmond, he moved his family back to Bel Air. He insisted on carrying all three family members across the threshold for the joy of reestablishing their own family home, letting Orie slide gracefully from his arms to the floor in the front entry hall. "There! The Mistress of Bel Air is receiving her two sons, I understand," he said, and, taking one and then the other from Mollie's arms, he handed the boys to Orie.

"Welcome home, dear sons. And thank God for the blessings of our family and our home," Orie said as she hugged and kissed the fidgety toddler and the newborn infant.

Orie and Mollie stored away the dinner provided for them by Martha and the kitchen girls at Viewmont, and then it was time to feed baby Luther. Orie gratefully went up to her bedroom, where she and the baby could be quiet and rest.

On March 6, the people of Scottsville were in a panic. "The Yankees are coming! Hide your food and valuables! They are taking everything! Sheridan is raiding Scottsville!"

People in Albemarle County had watched General Sheridan come into Charlottesville with ten thousand cavalrymen, Shenandoah Valley hams strapped to their saddles, and captured Confederate flags, arrogant in their defeat of the vastly outnumbered General Jubal Early in Waynesboro. Outnumbered in the Third Battle of Winchester on September 19, they were engulfed in a whirlwind of Union fury, while Sheridan rode among the infantry, shouting, "Give 'em hell" and "Kill every son of a bitch!" At Fisher's Hill, the Southerners lost a thousand men and the door to the upper Shenandoah was opened to the North.

In October, General Jubal Early led his forces to a shocking victory at Cedar Creek in a surprise attack. Rebels captured thirteen hundred prisoners and twenty cannons, and Yankees were in full retreat. Instead of pursuing the fleeing enemy, the starving Confederate soldiers raided the vacant Union camp and took food and ammunition. In the meantime, Sheridan returned, rallied the retreating soldiers, and completely reversed the Confederate's morning victory. Nine thousand soldiers were lost on both sides. The Confederates had been outnumbered two-to-one. Retreating east, Sheridan caught up with Early's forces at Waynesboro, where they entrenched themselves on a hill. Sheridan shelled them while a large force sneaked through the woods and swarmed over their entrenchments from behind. Early and his staff were lucky to escape with their lives over the Blue Ridge Mountains.

The door to the Shenandoah was then wide open to the North. The "Burning" began. Grant's order to Sheridan was to make the Shenandoah Valley a "barren waste." This foreshadowed Sherman's March to the Sea in Georgia after the Battle of Atlanta, both of which had the twofold purpose of bringing the War to the civilian population and denying any resources to the Confederacy. The

Shenandoah Valley was largely burned and the inhabitants were made refugees.

In March, Generals Sheridan and Custer found Charlottesville undefended and took possession of the keys to public buildings and the university from a committee of town and gown representatives. In turn, Sheridan and Custer promised to provide a guard against arson and looting by troops or stragglers. Then they were free to attend to their task of systematically destroying anything that might help the cause of the Confederacy. They burned grist mills, a woolen mill, a railroad bridge across the Rivanna, and another at the main depot, and exploded all military stores.

One witness likened the horrid Blue-coated destroyers to "a great blue snake." Another said Yankees kicked in his front door and grabbed his mother by the throat, demanding bread and throwing any food they could find into pillowcases. A family servant followed them about, scolding them and taking things out of their hands while they laughed at her. They smashed furniture, tore up ladies' gowns, and jabbed holes though portraits hanging on the walls. They poured flour on the floor mixed with dribbled molasses before they left.

Now galloping messengers were telling the people of Scottsville that Sheridan was on his way with ten thousand men to make more mischief and destroy the canal. Coming from the scene of destruction in Charlottesville, General Sheridan cut a loathsome figure to the people of Albemarle County as he rode his huge black stallion toward Scottsville. Before he arrived, he was busy breaking up railroad tracks, burning mills and stables, collecting food, forage, and horses, and menacing the Lynchburg garrison. Meanwhile, residents of Scottsville made themselves scarce, taking the ferry to Buckingham across flooded waters, visiting out-of-town relations, and some hiding out in the woods, especially doctors who were brutalized by the federals lest they help a wounded rebel.

The Bluecoats arrived in Scottsville at three o'clock in the afternoon to a virtually vacated town. There were exceptions. Seven-year-old Billy Beale greeted the soldiers swarming into the streets with a run to his house for a little cane with which he would defend the town. His mother had to lock him inside for the sake of safety. The Union plan was to wreck the canal and move on downriver toward Richmond. This they did. They blasted dams, burned boats, broke berm banks, and dynamited locks. Sheridan and Custer headquartered themselves at Cliffside, a private home built in 1785, and General Merritt commandeered Old Hall, built in 1830. Tents were put up for ten thousand Union soldiers on every available foot of land in Scottsville. The people endured. Memories outlasted lives.

In nearby Howardsville, Sheridan pilfered homes and stores, destroyed a mill and tannery, and made himself more infamous by stealing blooded horses and shooting their colts in the fields. The town's bank cashier stuffed the bank's money into valises, caught the last ferry across the fast-flowing flood-high James, rushed up a hill to dig a hole and bury the valises, and died of a heart attack. The raids were everyday activities for the Union forces, but the small town victims would never forget.

After the Scottsville Raid ended, the people were left with charred buildings and a smashed canal. The Union forces of ten thousand men, with some two thousand Negroes, rode southeast along the James with General Sheridan riding at the head, continuing to smash, destroy, and steal all the way to General Grant's headquarters on the James close to besieged Petersburg, south of Richmond.

With the March winds and ice having disappeared from the landscape, they marked baby Luther's second-month span of life on April 9, and John began his way back to his hospital duties in Richmond. He got no farther than Scottsville when he heard the news that General Lee had surrendered to General Grant. Amid the anguish and wailings, John turned his horse around and returned to Bel Air.

"We are safer together at Viewmont," he said, and made preparations for the move. Orie followed John's decision without complaint and suffered the fright of moving the household back across the Hardware River with two babies in tow and no one knowing what the Yankees would do next. Eighteen-month-old Jimmie crowed with delight at being back among faces, both black and white, that he had missed while away at Bel Air. More to his taste as companions were Uncle Jacob and Mammy Jinny and Cornelia and Martha as opposed to his often-sleeping little brother, for whom his interest was as fleeting as the sight of a bird landing on a haystack.

Confederate soldiers were passing through daily, needing food and shelter on their way home. Without General Lee's army, the Southern people had no hope of safety then or in the future. "The Yankees are coming," the soldiers would tell them. When Carter's Mill on the Hardware River on Viewmont's property line was burned, the household was faced with the prospect of Viewmont burning next, with no Confederate soldiers to help defend them. Anna Maria gathered up the family silver and jewelry and gave it to Lottie to bury. In a state of extreme excitement, she buried the treasure, but afterward never remembered exactly where.

Uncle Jacob packed up a mule wagon and filled it with bacon, flour, and food they could do without for several days. Clothing, too, was packed away under the straw. He drove twenty miles directly to the "de flatwoods" of Fluvanna County, east of Scottsville, where he buried the family provisions, until John came to tell him the danger had passed. Great was the delight of everyone at Viewmont when the two men and the wagonload of food returned up the long driveway, for that food was sustenance for the blacks and whites at Viewmont.

Anna Maria rewarded Uncle Jacob and Mammy Jinny for their loyalty by assigning Uncle Jacob's cabin as their home until they should both go away "to wear de white garments of de angels." Food and clothing and other necessities of life were shared among the household, as money in Virginia remained as scarce as coffee had been for years.

After Lee's surrender at Appomattox Courthouse on April 9, 1865, there were a few battles, but the war was over and Northern might had won. Lincoln had kept the Union together. General Lee told his soldiers of the Army of Northern Virginia, "Go to your homes and resume your occupations. Obey the laws and become as good citizens as you were soldiers." Men who still would have gladly fought and died for him accepted his words and went home. The fighting was finished.

CHAPTER 34

RECONSTRUCTION BEGINS

From Appomattox, Southern soldiers took trains and walked home. Some lived in Alabama and North Carolina and some were heading to the Shenandoah Valley and all points in the South. They did not know what to do other than put one foot in front of the other in the direction of what used to be home. They knocked on front doors, back doors, and kitchen doors asking for food and a place to sleep. Filled with pity, Southern women and servants took them in as best they could.

At Viewmont, Uncle Jacob or Ned would see them first and lead them to the well to wash up. Inside the house, Orie would ask a beardless soldier with a face so sad he looked haunted, "What's your name, son?"

"I's called Willy, ma'am. I'd 'preciate any food you can give me."

Orie would ask Martha to serve the soldier whatever she could. A kitchen girl would bring out cornpone and turnips, well water, and creasy greens. The soldier would eat in silence, life coming back into his bones if not his eyes.

"I'm a doctor. Is there anything I can do for you?"

"No, ma'am. I just got to get me home."

Orie prayed over each one silently. *They have suffered so much. What can I do to help them, dear Lord?* Some were too sick to keep moving, no matter how many times they said, "I got to get me home."

Anna Maria, Ike, Mag, John, Orie, and Lottie discussed the daily appearance of the ragged and starving soldiers and the dire condition of their own situation. "Our currency is worthless and we must pay the slaves or lose our property for failure to obey regulations. Taxes will come due. And there is talk that we will pay the Yankees for what the war cost them," Ike explained.

"There's not enough decency among those Yankees to go around a scrawny pitch pine in the woods," said Anna Maria. "There is no one who speaks for us."

"I worry about the field hands," said John. "There are rumors that the Yankees are urging them on to take over their masters' property and kill them as necessary and take what they want, what is 'owed' them. Fortunately, Ike and I are here and none of our field hands openly display that insolence and arrogance we see among Negroes in the towns."

"We have nothing with which to pay them, but with summer coming on we can feed them and clothe them. We'll keep them if they want to stay," said Anna Maria.

"I can treat patients here at Viewmont and make home visits, but so far, patients are not able to pay with anything but barter, and some families that were raided are entirely destitute," said John. "I may resort to moving to Florence, where the war touched them but did not grind them down as in Scottsville and neighboring farms."

"I disagree," said Anna Maria. "We can help each other when we are together."

"Mama, I helped Viewmont by living away and sending money back. Isn't that true?" Lottie objected.

"Yes, but that was when the Confederacy protected women. There is no law and no protection for women or white people anywhere now. We can't let you leave here now, Lottie." Anna Maria looked at her daughter, seeing Yankees leering at her. "Maybe ever."

Lottie's face went white.

Orie spoke up. "Things will settle down. The Yankees will tire of the ruin they left and will go home."

Wishful thinking will never end, Mag thought. Orie lived among the Yankees when she was a girl and then a young woman and was treated as one of them, but we are all hated Southerners now. The way we talk, the way we dress, the way we eat are all signs to mock us and take what little we have from us.

Nearby, Scottsville, with its former prosperity and importance as a river port on the Kanawha Canal, lay in ruins just as the canal itself, its bridges, locks, and boats burned and destroyed. But even so, Shenandoah farmers had no crops to haul to market, with seed crops burned and the labor force heading North, looking for food and work that paid real dollars. Worthless Confederate bonds and currency summed up the economic situation in Scottsville. Healthy male slaves, each one bought for more than the price of a fine townhouse, had been freed without compensation. What had constituted part of the wealth of the South had vanished like vapor.

A Presidential courier came to Scottsville and read aloud the 1863 Emancipation Proclamation to a group of terrace workers at Cliffside. Shovels and hoes were flung aside and the workers walked away. Six weeks later they came back, preferring Scottsville to hunger and homelessness in the North. Nothing was as it should be for anyone. The old barter system had come back and worked well enough. Trading goods rather than money brought the people closer together in their hardship, the formerly rich and poor alike helping one another and sharing what they could.

After Lincoln's assassination on April 14, the South was put under military rule. Virginia was designated Military District No. 1 under General John Schofield. Albemarle's commissioner was Captain William Tidball, stationed in Charlottesville. The many competent men of the county complained that County Court did not meet from May to August 1865. The lack of justice was a reminder that the loss of the war had changed everything.

John returned from a trip to Scottsville and sat on the front porch with news of the town showing a lighter side to the hardships. "If you want to read the newspaper, pay with money, no more blackberries. And at Clover's, no more peaches – think of something else."

Ike laughed. "Clover's turned down a basket of books last week worth tens of dollars, but Mag gave them peach preserves for socks for me. I needed socks like pens need ink." He lifted his pants leg and showed his new socks.

All eyes turned on the blue socks in shock. Mollie took up for her older brother. "It's still a good bargain, Ike. Nobody needs to ever see."

Mag smiled at Mollie. "That's what I keep telling him. US surplus socks do not make him a Bluebelly."

Those in the Viewmont household were able to keep body and soul together over the summer and fall and holidays. Some of the servants stayed on under Ole Miss's protection, but she was the first to admit that things had to change. One night after supper, after the three younger sisters had taken the two little boys away from the table, Anna Maria asked the others to stay seated.

"I won't go into all the reasons why, which are well known to each of you," she said. "Suffice it to say that I am not acting contrary to common sense when I report to you that I have assigned four hundred acres of land and a house to Ike and Mag. We'll take steps one at a time and see how we do. Cash is a terrible problem, but we are not alone. Nobody has money, and that also means that we can't borrow from friends and relations."

"Never a borrower be," Ike said, helping Mag up from her chair, and they all began to rise.

"Before you leave, another way to watch your wallet is to not get fined for the 'uppity' behavior of a white to a Negro," said John. "I heard it from Mary when I was there to stitch up one of her sons after an accident with a hoe." They all sat back down.

"As a doctor, I have to report to Captain Tidball in Charlottesville any killings or injuries done to a Negro by a white," John continued. "If the injury is to a white by a black, the white may be fined for arrogant behavior that provoked the action of said Negro. So I told Mary it was best to keep quiet about her son's injury and try to persuade the field hand, who was drunk at the time, to go North to freedom."

"That's all you can do," said Ike. "The Yankees have so many rules, nobody can keep them straight. But don't take that as a comfort, because what they want is to run the whites out of the South and give the vote to the Negroes. Why? They will vote for their Yankee friends, the Republicans, and all the office holders will be Republicans and the Yankees will have what they want, the South. So be shrewd and cunning like a serpent and don't step in a trap. They are watching and waiting and will take the side of the Negro against the Southern white every time. They'll have the Negro vote and are trying to disenfranchise white men at the same time."

"Do you think that will work, Ike?" Anna Maria asked. "The servants and whites have worked together, protected each other, and suffered together. There is no such bond between the Yankee and the Negro. In fact, I think there is a great disrespect for the Negro by Yankees."

"Mama, humans will take advantage of those weaker than they, and the weaker will do anything to gain power. That's biblical, Mama. We know this."

They all nodded in agreement and the discussion ended for the time.

Contrary to Anna Maria's plans, Ike sold his four hundred acres to a cousin. Then he leased woodlands and two fields from her and agreed to build a small house on the leased land. Anna

Maria was grieved, but great estates and fine farms all over the county were breaking up. Every day brought signs of deteriorating circumstances.

With further advice from relatives she trusted, Anna Maria leased out all of her property except for the house, orchards, and cemetery. Since the leaseholders had no money to pay for the leases, Anna Maria was to have her choice of revenue from one-third of the crop raised on the land. Again, money owed her could not be collected, and soon she was in debt to cousins who had income from sources other than land. The lack of money became a constant worry for Anna Maria, but she kept her person and poise intact and was ever the gracious Southern lady. Fortunately, she had enough to send Eddie and Mollie to the Baptist-related Richmond Female Institute, but suffered their absence over the holidays when she lacked the cash to pay for their transportation home and back to school. She wept at night, ashamed and angry at her penury.

Meanwhile, John was having no better luck collecting his doctor fees. Orie had always taken care of her neighbors and the servants without charge, and that did not change. Gifts were appreciated and accepted, but cash was almost impossible to come by. Time went by and the situation worsened.

By the spring of 1869, John's brother James and sister, Elizabeth, wrote to him after moving to Memphis. "Come to Florence," they wrote. "Our stepmother is still there with a house to share with you until you are settled. She will find a doctor who will take you into his practice, John, and we will be there to greet you when you arrive."

John, with Orie by his side, told the family that they had been persuaded by his family in Florence to practice medicine there in northern Alabama, where the War had not ravaged the town.

Anna Maria, chin up and cheeks blazing, agreed that the plan was necessary at that time. "I shall miss you and the two little boys with all my heart, but I see no other way."

Orie embraced her mother tenderly. "Nor I, Mama."

Later in their bedroom, when she and John were alone, Orie said, "I'm sad to see Viewmont break into pieces like this, but we can't help the situation, John. Lord knows you've tried."

"I wanted to save Viewmont for you and your mother, but we can prosper in Florence and help her in due time. Are you all right moving to Florence with the two boys?" John held Orie's hands and looked into her blue eyes.

"I'm excited, John. I know it will take time to arrange things, but we'll make our way when we get there and have our own home and plan to take back all of Viewmont for Mama."

As they lay in each other's arms that night, they were filled with hope and love for each other. The next morning, Orie whispered into John's ear, "It will be all right, dearest. The Lord looks after his sheep, and so we will care for his flock in Florence." John's heart swelled with love for Orie and his kisses blessed them both.

Lottie watched what was happening at Viewmont. She spoke to her Baptist friends in Charlottesville, and they helped her plan her course of action accordingly. She had to work. She felt alive again and was looking forward to the future. There was no money for foreign missionary work, but with a shortage of male teachers in the South, there would be positions open for her. The Lord opens doors that were shut, just as He allows doors to close. China was still there, and she would be ready when the time was right.

CHAPTER 35
MIGRATION FROM VIEWMONT

Anna Maria was in the parlor when the carriage came up the driveway and let off Lottie. She heard Uncle Jacob greet Lottie at the door and rose from her armchair to catch her daughter before she disappeared to her room upstairs. Instead, Lottie came into the parlor looking for her. Her color was high and her rustling wide skirt of brown and rose taffeta almost brought in a breeze. They embraced and kissed cheeks.

"You've hardly been home the past weeks, Lottie. We've all missed you with your coming and going."

"I've been offered a teaching position, Mama, and I accepted it." Lottie was excited and happy but knew her leave-taking would sadden her mother, and so struck a more somber note than she felt.

Anna Maria almost held her breath. *Where was the position? Probably not in ravaged Albemarle County. The curse of the War continues.*

"Sit down, dear, and tell me about it." Anna Maria was dressed for the day in an old favorite dress of royal blue striped taffeta with a lace collar and a day cap over her upswept hair. Appearances mattered to Anna Maria, and the last thing she wanted was for people to believe that their lives had changed for the worse forever. Anna Maria was attentive to her daughter and presented a

244

calm demeanor that befitted the mistress of a Virginia plantation, however defunct it may have been at the present time.

Lottie chose a chair near her mother. "It's at the Danville Female Academy in Kentucky, Mama. It's operated by the First Baptist Church and recommended as one of the best institutes in the state. I was advised to look for a position in a border state like Kentucky, which did not suffer so greatly as Virginia and Georgia and the like in the War. Fortunately, Dr. Broadus was available to give the school his approval of me. "

"Yes, he's been most helpful to you since your years at Albemarle Female Institute. I'm sorry the school did not survive the War, as well as many other institutes for young women. It's sad to see a school shuttered and closed."

"Truly, Mama. Albemarle Female Institute was the equal of the University of Virginia for women, but we were closed and the men's college was not. And there are so many women who need the education to replace the lost men. I think, however, I will like Danville, Mama. Centre College is there also, a fine college for men, and some students there are Virginians."

"That's nice, dear," said Anna Maria.

"Best of all, I'll be in the preparatory department, an academic department with training in music and foreign languages and art. They expect me to be a thoroughly knowledgeable teacher and a disciplinarian. I'm sure I can be both. And you'll appreciate this, Mama: daughters of Baptist ministers who are destitute from the War will be given free tuition. There are many young ladies from Virginia there."

"I'm sure you have chosen well. It's just that I had hoped to, well, advise you on where to go and where you have cousins and aunts and uncles."

Lottie looked at her rather sharply, but said nothing.

Anna Maria glanced down at her lace-gloved hands. *Lottie didn't want advice from me. She got this position without my even knowing she had applied for it.*

"I start in September, but I'll leave sometime in August to find a place to board and meet the pastor and principal, Mr. Duncan Selph, and the other teachers. I'll be here with you for months and I'll earn money we need by tutoring." Lottie was running words together in a rush, seeing her mother downcast. *My glorious mother is a lonely, aging widow and her home and family are breaking apart.*

"I see. Well, we may all be together for a short time before Orie and John and the children leave us for greener pastures, as they say, so we'll want to make a home they will long to return to." Anna Maria perked up, planning ahead. There was still work to be done, and she had never turned her back on anything that involved her family.

"Yes, Mama," Lottie said quietly.

And so the trek southward for the Andrews family began at the urging of John's brother and sister, who had left Florence for the time and were worried that too much time was passing and John might miss out on opportunities there. It was hoped that they could all be together in Florence when they arrived. In early fall, John drove Orie and their younger son, Luther, now four and a half years old, in a carriage to the train station in Charlottesville. There they boarded the Virginia Midland railroad train marked "Florence, Ala." Uncle Ned followed them in a carriage carrying Anna Maria, Colie, Mollie, and Eddie to wish Orie and little Luther a fond farewell. As soon as John packed the wagon, he and Jimmie would follow.

After kisses and embraces and tears from her mother and sisters, Orie and little Luther boarded the train and settled in before John left them. The conductor was solicitous of the young woman and her small son, for the journey was a long one. Orie let Luther run up and down the aisle until other passengers began to board, and then the boy had something else to do—watch the parade of people from his seat next to his mother.

An older woman from across the aisle came over and introduced herself to Orie. She held out her hand. "My name is Emma Wilson and this is my husband, Josiah Wilson. You're not alone, my dear. The War has set us on strange new paths, and with God's will, we shall find our way again."

"Thank you, Mrs. Wilson, Mr. Wilson. My name is Orie Andrews and this is my boy Luther. My husband will follow us later in a wagon with our household goods and older son. His people in Florence, Alabama, will help us make a new start."

"Far from the ruin of Albemarle County, I daresay, and Godspeed to you and your family," Mrs. Wilson said. "But I pray you'll be able to return someday. Your dear mother and precious sisters asked me and my husband to keep an eye on you and the boy, and we are honored to do just that. We're on our way to Macon, Georgia. Our daughter is married to a Methodist minister and she's expecting a baby very soon."

After all the excitement, the sound and rhythm of the train put Luther to sleep for a nap, and Orie dreamily took in her surroundings and found them good. She had not been on a train since the War ended. Now there were no trainloads of Boys in gray going into battle and no trainloads of groaning Boys returning from battle in blood-covered bandages. Oh, peace.

The train stopped in Lynchburg long enough to be considered a meal stop. Orie and Luther got off the train and followed Mr. and Mrs. Wilson to a picnic table for the four of them. Orie unpacked her lunch and the Wilsons spread theirs out on the table and shared what they had. The other passengers had brought picnic lunches or bought food from vendors, and there was pleasant chatter and children running about.

One man in particular, travelling by himself, stopped by their table and remarked on the lovely fall weather. Orie, hearing the curt, short syllables of the Northerner's speech, turned her head away from him and busied herself helping Luther find his sandwich. The man was dressed in a dark frock coat and a lighter colored waistcoat matching his trousers that were so new they lacked only receipts attached to them. His shoes were shiny and his beard was heavy.

"Are you people going to Atlanta or just a short out and about? Huh?" he asked.

Orie ignored him, thinking him rude. Mrs. Wilson, taken aback by his forwardness, did not respond. Luther stared at him.

Mr. Wilson replied, "We are going beyond Atlanta. What about you, sir?"

Orie frowned at Luther and shook her head to tell him not to stare. He stared at the Northerner anyway.

"My name is Everett Baldwin. Pleased to meetcha. I'm in investments. Be glad to talk to ya about investments while I'm handy. Good day to youse, sir, ma'am." He walked away, introducing himself to each one of the passengers before getting back on the train.

Orie said to Luther, "It's not polite to stare, son."

"Why did that man talk funny, Mama?"

"He's from the North, that's why. But it's rude to stare, so don't do it, Luther."

Mrs. Wilson shook her head and whispered, "Your boy, rude? That dreadful man should never open his mouth south of the Mason-Dixon line. You would think, after the War, he would be ashamed to *be* here. After four years of Yankees killing, burning, and stealing from us, he should know better."

"Now, Emma, the War is over and like General Lee said, we must be good citizens of this new country. The man meant no harm," Mr. Wilson said.

Orie and Emma looked at Mr. Wilson in consternation.

"Ladies, the truth is, we are bound to accept these new people." He stopped, looking distressed.

"Because?" Mrs. Wilson prompted.

"Damn it, because they have money and we do not. We will never recover without 'investments,' as the man said. We need money to repair railroad tracks, get the canal going again, plant crops, rebuild mills and schools and towns."

"Shush, Josiah, I'm sorry I got you started. It's just that dreadful, dreadful man. Let's get back on the train."

In her seat, Orie could see the investment man reading a newspaper, a large carpetbag beside him. He was a speculator and a carpetbagger. His ways were well known. He would buy up property for pennies on the dollar from people who could not pay their taxes or feed themselves. Then he would resell the property to rich Yankees who may or may not resell the property yet again. She didn't know which was worse, the absentee property owners jacking up prices or Yankees moving South and taking over businesses and farmland and cutting prices to drive others out of business. She resented his new clothes, bought from profits off bankrupt Southerners, and carefully noted the worn clothing on the Southerners. She watched the carpetbagger eat a sandwich with his mouth open as he read a newspaper. She imagined she could hear him chewing over the train's whistle and the screeching and banging about. Oh! She felt sick and had to stop looking.

It was a long train ride. They stopped in Danville, Greensboro, Charlotte, Greenville, Anderson, and Atlanta. Orie saw many speculators such as the one who spoke to them in Lynchburg. She could tell who they were just by looking at their new clothes and carpetbags.

In Atlanta, when Luther heard one man speak, he said, "Look, Mama, I'm not staring at that man."

The man turned around and stared right at Luther. "Whatchu lookin' at, boy?"

Luther shrank back toward his mother, and Orie faced the man towering over both of them. "You, sir, are a brute and I daresay I will call a police officer if you say another word to either of us."

"Who you callin' a brute?" The man's face was red and sweaty.

Orie grabbed Luther by the arm and walked up to a railroad clerk at his desk and pointed at the quickly departing man.

"Can I help you, ma'am?" the clerk asked.

"I wanted to report that man for rude behavior toward my son, but I don't think he will trouble us anymore."

"I'll alert an officer anyway, ma'am. The railroad doesn't put up with that kind of behavior."

Orie smiled at the young clerk. "Thank you very much. I appreciate your kindness and your attention."

"You're welcome, ma'am. I'm glad to be of service, I surely am." He smiled shyly and tipped his cap to her and gave Luther a big grin.

They caught up with the Wilsons, who were changing trains too. "Let's sit on that bench and get out of the crowd for a while," Emma suggested, heading for a long polished bench that looked like a church pew with space for all four of them.

Orie warned Luther, "Son, we'll be in this station for another hour, so don't wander about and get lost. There are too many people rushing about and you wouldn't be able to hear me if I called you from five feet away."

"No, ma'am, I won't." Still, he sat with his tiptoes on the floor, looking like he was about to dart down the crowded stairs looking for their train. The three adults looked at him until his feet left the floor and he settled back on the bench, sitting with his legs crossed in Indian position. "Bluebellies," he muttered.

The three adults laughed. Orie said, "Son, it's not nice to call people Bluebellies. Don't say that again."

"No, ma'am, I won't."

"Luther, I'm not speaking to you when I say this journey has opened my eyes to the perfidy of men," Emma said dramatically.

"What are you talking about, dear?" Josiah asked.

"I'm talking about the scalawag who's going to be on the train to Macon. The way he was talking to that old man made me want to scream and beat him with a broom."

"Now, now, Emma." Her husband patted her arm.

"What's a scalawag, Mama?" Luther asked, curious about Mrs. Wilson's threat to beat him with a broom.

"A very bad man, son, and what's worse, he's a traitor to the South, lying to poor people to get their land, just like the Yankees," Orie replied.

250

Emma continued, including Luther in her audience. "He wore shiny shoes and businessman's clothes, like a wolf in sheep's clothing, and told that old man he would pay his taxes for him for just half of his land near Greenville. In another year he'll have all the poor man's land, unless the old farmer can pay next year's taxes with crops raised on half the land this year."

"He trusts the scalawag because he's Southern and can't believe a fellow Southerner would cheat him," Mr. Wilson said. "The scalawag knows that and is taking advantage of him. Of course, he was probably near to starving to death himself and some Yankee paid him money to buy new clothes and talk Southerners into selling him their land for a pittance. The scalawag and the Yankee would split the money they made when they sold the old man's property at high prices up North."

"God is watching," said Emma. "He knows."

CHAPTER 36
ALABAMA ARRIVAL

John's brother James and sister, Elizabeth, met Orie and Luther at the Florence train station. "We recognized Luther right away. His red hair told us he was an Andrews," said Elizabeth. She reached out to give him a hug and kissed his cheek.

James introduced himself to Orie with a handshake, and Elizabeth with a hug. "We are mighty glad y'all are here. I'm just sorry Father is not here. His widow and our stepmother, Mrs. Winnifred Andrews, returned here after Father died in Mississippi, and we're going to her home now."

In the slow-moving carriage driven by James, Elizabeth and Orie chattered all the way from the train station to the home of Winnifred Andrews. "We are making up for lost time," said Elizabeth, who was almost breathless with her questions. "And I have another question before we get to Mama Winnifred's. How is your brother, Isaac, Orie? I so liked him when he came to visit to tell us about your wedding and to invite us. Of course, we couldn't go. What with the expense and danger there already in the first year of the War, it wasn't wise, but I pitched a fit when Father said no. I've always wanted to go to Viewmont and meet you and your sisters."

"I hope that will happen too, but we are somewhat scattered now and Viewmont is but a shadow of what it used to be before

252

the War. We're happy to be here among my husband's family, and I can hardly wait until John arrives with our older son, Jimmie. I hope you can return to Florence when we are settled in our own house here," said Orie.

"I'd like that," said Elizabeth, giving Luther a smile and a nudge with her elbow. Luther grinned and nudged her back.

When they arrived at the house on a quiet street among other well-kept houses, James jumped down and helped the ladies out of the carriage before he led the horse away. Elizabeth held Luther's hand and led Orie up the steps and into the house.

Slightly older than middle-aged, thin, and fashionably dressed, Winnifred Andrews welcomed them with tears and embraces. She and the maid Beulah pressed food and drink upon them as if the Yankees had chased them all the way to Alabama. It was quickly decided that they would stay with her until John was settled in their own place and until then, John would be the widow's man of the house.

"I'm a lonely woman these days since my husband died and the children here are grown and moved to Memphis," Mrs. Andrews said. "I have some friends here in Florence since before we moved to Mississippi, but it's not the same as having family in the house."

Orie looked around, seeing tidiness in the immaculate carpet, the polished furniture, and knickknacks on a dark mahogany shelf. Mrs. Andrews asked Orie to call her "Miz Winnifred" as opposed to "Mama Winnifred," as John and his brothers and sister had been instructed when she married their father, a widower with five children.

Orie said, "Yes ma'am, Miz Winnifred."

Elizabeth was the youngest, age five at the time. A bright child, Elizabeth remembered her mother dying. She was four years old and inconsolable. Her new mother never replaced her mama, but as a young adult, Elizabeth appreciated her stepmother's loyalty to her father and her work for the church when he was the pastor.

Before leaving Florence and returning to Memphis, Elizabeth played hide and seek with Luther, laughing as she caught him hiding behind a small boxwood in the side yard and hugging him.

"I will miss you, Luther. Even though you are my only nephew, you will always be my favorite."

"You can't say that, Auntie Elizabeth. You can't have favorites. Even I know that and I'm only four and a half years old."

"I don't care what anybody says. You are my favorite and that's that." Elizabeth pouted prettily.

Luther giggled and ran away, calling her "Bad Auntie."

"I'm tempted, but I won't call you bad nephew."

"Aunt Elizabeth is too long to say. I like Bad Auntie better."

"Listen here, Luther," Elizabeth said. "You have your mother with you, so you'll be all right, but Mama Winnifred never had children of her own and isn't used to them. You may think she's a crosspatch, but just do what she says with a 'Yes, ma'am,' and do not repeat what she tells you not to do. And mind Beulah, too. Of course, everyone loves Beulah. "

"What if I tripped by accident and broke her pretty candy dish? Huh?"

"Don't say 'huh,' Luther. That's rude. And don't run in the house in the first place. That's how things get broken. Things can't be replaced now, since the War."

"I know." He looked at her and grinned. "Can you call me Lulie? Mama and Father and Jimmie call me Lulie. Then you'll be like my big sister. Father says I'll never have a sister because of an Arab in the Holy Land."

"That makes no sense, Luth—I mean Lulie. But I'll only call you Lulie when Mama Winnifred is not within earshot. I'm sure she would insist on your Christian name."

When Elizabeth left for Memphis, Luther missed her and so did Orie. True to Elizabeth's word, Mama Winnifred didn't smile as much as on that first day, and she cried when Luther cut all the pansies in her flower garden and presented them to Orie and Beulah. The tall and slender woman with upswept gray hair and warm brown eyes took ever more frequent solitary walks and "quick lie-downs."

The day John and Jimmie arrived in Florence was a red-letter day for them all, according to Winnifred, referring to the red-lettered festival days on her church calendar. Orie was second to welcome John and Jimmie after Luther heard the wagon coming up the street and ran alongside it as neighbors came out to see and Jimmie shouted at Luther. Orie waited until John stopped the wagon in the front yard and lifted her off the ground with a big hug. Winnifred gave her strapping stepson a limp hand and a kiss on the cheek.

"Welcome back, John. We are so blessed to have you home."

"Winnifred, this is Jimmie, our oldest." John pushed Jimmie forward and whispered, "Shake her hand, son." Hearing the commotion, Beulah came out of the house, smiled a "Howdy do" at John and Jimmie and turned to look at the great wagon on the fragile grass.

When the formalities were over, Orie showed them where to unpack their things and Winnifred found Beulah in the kitchen fixing refreshments and supper warming up for later. "You be all set for the rest of the day, Miz Andrews. And yo stepson look like a handy man to me, and jus' in time."

"Yes, Doctor John will be a big help around here before they move into their own place. There won't be anything he can't do with Willie to help him," said Winnifred.

"Thas' right. Lord, the things that gonna get done!" Beulah wiped her hands on her apron and chuckled appreciatively.

When they were at last alone together, Orie said to John, "Don't ever leave me alone again."

John was taken aback by the serious look in her eyes. "Dearest, what's wrong? Everything appears to be going splendidly."

"John, I won't go into all the things that are not splendid. I only want you to know that I can abide all things when you are with me.

You have been apart from me for two months without a word. I don't want that to ever happen again."

"My dear, dear, Orie." John took her into his arms and kissed her. "Jimmie and I missed you and…"

"Hush, husband."

In due time, Orie and Luther explained to John and Jimmie the myriad rules of the small household of what not to do as well as what to do. Winnifred had John busy from early morning to night fixing, repairing, moving, making, and shoveling.

"Oh, what a blessing to have a man around the house, " Winnifred said.

"I can help, too," said Jimmie.

"No, you cannot. You're too little. You get in the way. Go help your mother."

Jimmie called her "Old Meanie" behind her back.

"John, now that you've had time to rest from that arduous journey from Virginia, you must get started with your medical practice," Winnifred said. "I want to introduce you to two of the finest doctors in town and let them help you. Dr. Higgins is my own doctor and I've spoken of you many times, and Dr. Wellborne is the oldest and most well-established doctor in the area."

"Thank you, Winnifred, if it's all right to call you that. I would appreciate the introductions and I'm anxious to start work."

"Indeed, I'm sure you are. Florence is no longer a wealthy town, but we know the value of a good medical doctor and I'm sure you'll fit right in. Your wife and I have had some words about church. I think you should go to your father's former Methodist-Episcopal church, but Orie says she wants to go the Baptist church."

"I'll speak to Orie about that. As for the introductions, tell me when, and I'll be ready. And thank you," said John. He embraced her lightly and gave her a peck on her cheek. She seemed surprised and pleased. "Dear John," she murmured.

A week later, John met with Dr. Higgins at his office on Pine Street.

"Come in, young man. Winnifred Andrews has been telling me about you for quite some time," Dr. Higgins said. "I'd like to know your medical school background and your experience, if you please. I already know that you are the son of the late Reverend Andrews and that his widow, Mrs. Winnifred Andrews, is your step-mother, a fine woman, if I may say."

That same afternoon he met with Dr. Wellborne and they worked out a plan: John would take on the doctor's selected newer patients as well as his share of the town's charity patients.

"I've been working with the charity patients for years, and now it's time to turn them over to you, and you will gain experience in so doing," Dr. Wellborne said. "When I need help with my patients, I always advise them to see Dr. Higgins or Dr. Cruikshank. That won't change. Welcome to Florence, sir."

"Thank you, sir." John straightened his chest and shook the doctor's hand firmly. He was back home in Florence, and he would make Orie and Winnifred proud.

"You may start in the morning, if it suits you, and I've got some space for you here in my office. And naturally you'll visit them at bedside. I can let you borrow medical equipment until you are able to purchase what you need."

"Thank you, sir. That's very generous of you, but I think have everything I need."

"I will see you in the morning, then?"

"Yes, sir."

"Come early and we can talk more. I have patients to see. Good day to you, sir," said Dr. Wellborne.

John hurried home, anxious to share with Orie his meetings with the doctors. He would have to have his clothes clean and ready for the morrow and a means of transportation to Dr. Wellborne's office downtown. At Orie's request, Winnifred agreed to have her man Willie take him in the carriage and for Beulah to have his shirt, coat, and pants ready to wear in the morning.

In bed that night, John confessed to Orie that life seemed to be beginning all over for him. In Memphis, he had been in his first year of practice when the call came from Billie to join the Fourth Alabama in Virginia. Now he was again starting his medical practice, but this time he was a husband and father.

"I am bursting to work, Orie, for you and the boys. I want to provide for you and take care of you. I've never been so sure of anything in my life."

"I'm glad, John. I feel unsettled still, but soon we can have our own home. Your stepmother has been very gracious to us and I'm not sure what we would have done without her. All of this will be behind us soon, and she and I will be friends and connected by your father as kin."

"Darling, you are wonderful."

Orie fell asleep that night dreaming of a house, any house, of their own, where she would not be in the way and where the house rules were her rules. Even though Winnifred claimed to be lonely, Orie could see her startle when Jimmie or Luther came into the house and slammed the door shut. Sometimes Winnifred would tell the miserable offender to "please sit down and be quiet and read or something." But more often she would look at Orie with disapproval when one of the boys yelled or ran, even outside. Or if Luther talked with his mouth open while eating.

Once Orie said in exasperation, "He's only five years old, Winnifred. He didn't mean to upset you when he said he loved Beulah better than anybody in Florence. Of course he loves you. He's just shy around you because you are so…dignified." Orie had dropped the "Miz" designation when John arrived.

"My dear, Luther is not shy. He just needs a father who is stricter with him. But I mustn't interfere." Winnifred reached for her ever-present bottle of smelling salts, breathed in, and went to her back bedroom to lie down.

"Jimmie! Luther! Get your coats on. We're going for a walk."

The two boys bounded into the parlor, saw that Mama Winnifred was not there, and automatically chased each other around and out the door without a hat or coat in the late winter chill.

CHAPTER 37

FLORENCE

The weather in northern Alabama in March both delighted and depressed Orie. Three days in a row it would be sunny and mild and new growth would push through scattered leaves on the ground, pastures, and wooded stretches. Then cold rain would settle in and the cold, damp sheets on the bed made her miss Viewmont's crackling fires and heavy woolen blankets scented with lavender.

John started his day each morning talking about his patients and what the day would bring. At night he returned tired and happy with the day's events, but worried about Orie and the boys living with his stepmother for so long. "Have you and Winnifred found a house for us yet?" he asked Orie.

"Dearest, there is nothing in good repair that we can afford. And the ones in disrepair are truly terrible. I'm afraid I should inquire about a house to rent for now. I wish Ike were here to help us. We can't move to a place and have the roof cave in and hidden damage caused by termites undermining the floors and walls."

"It's not that bad, dear. However, the long hot and humid summers can cause a problem with insects, and most of the houses have not been repaired adequately since before the War. It's important to find a house that's safe and comfortable and find it quickly. My income right now cannot justify buying a house and then have to work on it just to make it safe, when I am busy with patients."

"I understand, dear. How much rent can we pay?"

"Too little, but I have some wedding gift gold yet. We can dip into that until my doctor fees begin to add up more than they have so far. So look for something suitable and don't worry about the cost right now." John relaxed, having made his decision. He thought about his father and uncles and their foresight regarding his all-too-real need. He must never forget their generosity.

"I trust that things will work out, darling. My father left me with a belief in love and education, and Uncle James led me to Christianity in the Holy Land. You are doing the Lord's work in healing and comforting the sick."

"And I've been forever blessed to have you as my wife. Nothing compares with that."

The next day, Orie told Winnifred they needed to look for a house to rent, not buy.

"Orie, dear, you want to *rent*, not buy?"

"Eventually we'll buy a house, but at the present time, it seems that John is building his practice by taking care of people who cannot pay their bills but give him produce and things they have at home they think have value."

"I see. Heavens, I hope he gets some paying patients soon. In the meantime, I'll talk to the ladies at church and get their advice. Then we'll go out in the carriage and see the choices."

A few days later, Orie, Winnifred, and the two boys climbed into the carriage.

"Head downtown, Willie," Winnifred said. "There are several small houses for rent near the old Florence Wesleyan University campus and we'll stay away from the Tennessee River waterfront." On the way, she pointed out large houses that had been taken over by Union commanders during the War.

"I didn't realize the War came right into Florence, Winnifred. I was under the impression that most of the war was fought in Virginia," Orie said.

"That's what people think. That it was all about General Robert E. Lee and Virginia, with Gettysburg thrown in and the Siege of Vicksburg and the Burning of Atlanta and the March to the Sea. The Yankees and Confederates occupied this town about forty times, leaving the townsfolk in a near constant state of disruption and confusion." Winnifred sighed.

"That's a sore burden for the town, but the Yankees didn't burn everything to the ground as Sheridan did in the Shenandoah Valley," Orie retorted.

"No, because the Federals used the town as a base to carry the war to Alabama and points east, to Atlanta and Savannah, and west, to New Orleans and the Mississippi River. They took our houses and our food and anything else they needed."

"I appreciate the suffering here, but surely you understand the two battles at Manassas and the terrible campaigns to topple Richmond were worse." Orie fanned her red-hot face.

"Virginia did not suffer alone, is what I'm trying to point out," Winnifred said with some sharpness on her tongue.

Willie stopped in front of a small frame house in obvious disrepair near the campus.

"Oh no, that won't do," Orie said. "It's too small and John won't have time to spend fixing it up. It's too close to the public and doesn't look safe."

"Move on, Willie," Winnifred said.

"What about the university? When did it close? Will it reopen?" Orie asked.

"It closed in 1865," Winnifred said. "There was no money to repair it and hire professors and all that. I don't know what will happen. The Methodist-Episcopal Church hopes to sell it to the state. LaGrange College, established in 1830, was moved here from across the Tennessee River and renamed Florence Wesleyan

University in 1855. It was a fine college and graduates have been governors and generals and leaders in all fields."

"That is indeed a loss," Orie agreed.

On the campus, Winnifred had Willie stop in front of a Greek Revival mansion that had been the headquarters of Confederate General Nathan B. Forrest in the autumn of 1864. Winnifred explained to the boys that General Forrest had no military training, but in the course of the Civil War, he rose from the rank of private to lieutenant general. Born into the large family of a poor blacksmith, he, the oldest son, became head of the household at age seventeen when his father died of scarlet fever. General Forrest was big, strong, and energetic, and was a millionaire from his work as a planter, slave trader, and businessman by the time the War began. In addition to serving in the CSA, he supplied the Tennessee Army with a cavalry unit.

"Did he ride horses into battle himself?" Jimmie asked.

"Oh, yes," Winnifred replied. "He didn't just pay for things. People in Florence still talk about the Battle of Fort Donelson. The fort was supposed to protect the Cumberland River from becoming a highway for the invasion of the South. When the outnumbered Confederate garrison surrendered, General Forrest refused to surrender and led a thousand of his own cavalry plus others of the doomed garrison through the besieging lines. He escaped to Nashville and helped restore order to the panic-stricken city and directed the rear guard in the retreat from Nashville."

"I want to be a soldier on horseback," Lulie said, looking at a man riding a handsome dark brown horse coming their way.

"Was he ever wounded?" Orie asked.

"Several times, but he never quit fighting until his surrender in May 1865 after General Lee's surrender," Winnifred replied. "Once he was surrounded by swarming Union soldiers and he had emptied his two Colt Army revolvers. He was slashing madly with his saber when he was hit in the spine with a musket ball. He was almost knocked out of his saddle but held on, and escaped. His men couldn't believe what they were seeing. A week later, a surgeon removed the musket ball without anesthesia."

"Mercy," said Orie, understanding the peril of such a wound.

They stopped again, in front of a large brick house in a residential section, but Orie suspected the rent would be too much. They moved on.

Winnifred wanted Orie and the boys to see Sweetwater, an estate named for the creek just below the house, and Willie obliged. "This brick mansion was the home of Major John Branham, a veteran of the War of 1812," she said. "It had eight rooms and large marble mantels imported from Italy and boxwood hedges from London. Everything's torn up now, as you can see, because the house served as headquarters for Union and Confederate commanders during the war."

Orie thought about Union officers in muddy boots and smelly coats breathing the air and sleeping in the beds at Viewmont. Her family had escaped an all-too-common hardship.

"I want to live there," said Jimmie.

"Me too!" said Lulie. "We could swim in the creek."

"We could have ponies and ride trails and have pony races," said Jimmie.

"That house is not for rent," said Orie.

As Willie drove the carriage back toward town, Jimmie looked at gentlemen and ladies on the sidewalk and people in carriages. They were generally well groomed, with little outward sign of poverty. An occasional veteran with an empty sleeve or trouser leg passed by, and both Jimmie and Lulie watched them with quiet reverence.

"These people don't look like they suffered so much," Jimmie said. "Except for the soldiers."

Orie quickly defended the townspeople. "It's much to their credit that they hold their heads high and put on a fine face, but they suffered, son."

"I was right here among them before the Reverend and I moved to Mississippi for the church," Winnifred said. "Nowhere could we get salt, for instance. People tried to get it from the floors of old smokehouses. Meat goes bad without salt. People starved."

The two boys and their mother sat in silence.

"Have you had enough looking today, Orie? I'm exhausted and ready for home. I'll let you and Beulah work out something for your supper this evening. I'll just fix myself tea and toast before I go to bed." Winnifred closed her eyes.

"Of course, Winnifred. I'm sorry I kept you out so long." She motioned to Jimmie and Lulie to stay quiet.

As Orie began to meet people in Florence, especially the ladies at the Baptist church, she was invited out and regaled with stories about the town on the Tennessee River near the border of Tennessee and Mississippi.

Orie listened politely, remembering her mother's charming ways that endeared her to all. But in her mind were other thoughts. *I hate the way they carry on so, although Florence is a lovely town and the people are to be commended for their courage and endurance. But let's talk about Virginia for once!*

Orie got over her feeling that Virginia was never going to be a part of the Alabamians' conversation about the War when she realized she was pregnant again. Not here, not now, she thought. Winnifred would die. I would die. When she told John, he gave her a glowing smile and kissed her tenderly.

"John, we have to be out of Winnifred's house when the baby comes. Do you understand me?" Orie took his hands and looked into his eyes.

"You don't think Winnifred would enjoy a new baby in her home?" John looked puzzled and hurt.

"I do not, John. Nor would I enjoy a new baby in her home."

"Then we'll find a way," John said.

When John came home at night, Orie would tell him what she did that day. One day she confessed, "Ordinarilly, I thought the War was primarily in Virginia, but I was mistaken. It was here, too."

"Have you been told about the hospital at Pope's Tavern? They say a few doctors and ladies from town took care of hundreds of sick and wounded soldiers after the battles of Fort Henry on the Tennessee River and Fort Donelson twelve miles away."

"Yes, John, I've heard about Pope's Tavern at least once by every inhabitant of Florence." John looked taken aback at her implied criticism of Florence. Orie scolded herself. *Be nice, Orie. Everybody suffered in the War.* "The boys should see it, darling."

On a Sunday afternoon, John and Orie took the boys on Jackson Military Road to see the tavern-turned-hospital. "The road was built by Andrew Jackson as a shortcut from Nashville to New Orleans for the battle with the British in the War of 1812. He stayed at Pope's Tavern at that time," John explained. "In the Civil War, Pope's Tavern became a hospital for more than five hundred soldiers after battles the South fought trying to protect the Tennessee and Cumberland rivers from Yankee invasions."

"It's too little to hold that many beds," Jimmie remarked, looking up at the one-story building with a porch and dormers across the front. The boy stood his ground.

Orie and John exchanged glances. "It was probably like Charlottesville General Hospital, where your mother and I were surgeons. Hospital beds were placed all over the medical school at the University of Virginia and other buildings in town and private homes. That's how it was done, son. Florence suffered mightily in the War."

With the weeks passing, John's patients were still mostly charity cases, and he earned little more pay than he had in Albemarle County over a comparable period of time. Moving to Alabama seemed foolish and futile. And now they had to move again. So on a Sunday afternoon, he took his family out to visit Mrs. Jackson at the Forks of Cypress and seek her advice. *Maybe she had a carriage house or knew of one somewhere. Orie liked living in the country. I have to get Orie a place of her own.* Not a brooder, John was brooding.

As they drove up the rutted driveway to the Forks, Jimmie and Lulie gasped in awe at the estate, a Greek revival building surrounded on all four sides by columns with scrolled Ionic capitals. Even Orie was transfixed by the sight.

"Mama, the house looks like the picture of the Greek temple in the library back at Viewmont," said Jimmie.

"Yes, and it's breathtaking seeing it situated on the crest of the hill above everything around it. A peristyle colonnade is a rare thing to see. Eight round columns across the front. It's magnificent," said Orie.

John said not a word, listening to them talk, enchanted by a home outside Florence he had not given much thought to until that day. Indeed, he looked at the mansion with fresh eyes, seeing anew the symmetrical beauty of the great columns and the sweeping space of the verandas between the mighty columns and main house beneath the roof.

Mrs. Jackson's maid answered the door and, after telling Mrs. Jackson that Dr. John Andrews had come with his family to see her, ushered them inside.

"Come in, my dears. Oh, John, what a lovely family," Mrs. Jackson said.

John kissed her cheek and introduced her to Orie and their sons. Her white hair was in a bun and she was wearing a lavender silk taffeta dress with a cream lace collar and a dark-colored shawl over her shoulders. Although it was warm outside in the sunshine, it was cool in the house, and a fire in the fireplace would not have been out of order.

Orie recognized the style of Mrs. Jackson's dress and knew it to be at least a decade old. Of good quality and well taken care of, the dress would outlast its owner. She looked around at the interior and could almost count the years of neglect and even abuse, probably by officers of both armies who had quartered there during the War.

John asked about James, her son, saying that he had heard about the loss of an arm fighting against Sherman at Kennesaw Mountain in Georgia.

"That terrible wound kept him out of the battle for a short while, but he didn't come home to recover," Mrs. Jackson said. "He fought to the very end, commanding his brigade in North Carolina, when General Johnston surrendered. He came back to his plantation, called the Sinks, not far from here and was chosen probate judge of Lauderdale County. He's back planting cotton and works very hard, and is doing well. He's like his father—nothing stops him."

Unable to stay quiet any longer, Jimmie asked Mrs. Jackson if he could go outside on the veranda.

"I say we all sit out there for a while. It may be breezy, but there's more damp and cold inside than on the veranda, I do believe," she said.

Having studied the interior and found the furnishings faded, Orie was happy to go outside. *God's decoration is always fresh and lovely beyond imitation.*

They moved to chairs on the veranda, Jimmie dancing with glee and running from one column to the other, Lulie right behind him. Jimmie touched a column. "What's it made of? It's cold to touch. Is it marble?"

"No, Jimmie. They're all made of brick and covered with plaster," Mrs. Jackson said. "The Greeks built columns of marble, but also of brick and plaster. These are special because my husband ordered horsehair and molasses mixed in with lime to make the column fireproof and strong."

"Where did he get so much horsehair? Did he cut their hair off?" asked Lulie.

Mrs. Jackson laughed. "My husband had slews of horses and had the stable boys collect the horsehair after grooming. There was plenty for the columns."

She offered peach brandy to John and Orie, who both politely declined, and had her maid bring out a pitcher of cider for them all. Jimmy and Luther drained their cups in an instant, and Orie looked at them with a warning frown. "Only one cup. No seconds. Don't drink so fast," she whispered.

"Oh, we have plenty of cider. James keeps me stocked with cider from the Sinks. I believe our apples here in northern Alabama are about as good as the apples from Virginia. Do you reckon that's so?" she asked the boys.

"If I say this cider is the best, may I have another cup?" Jimmie grinned hopefully.

"Jimmie!" said Orie.

"Yes, Jimmie. You may have another cup, and I thank you for the compliment. We love our apples in northern Alabama," said Mrs. Jackson, charmed by the boy.

After more time treating patients and bringing home turnips and eggs, embroidered linens, and carved toys for his boys, John decided it was time to leave Florence altogether. Even though Orie insisted on going to the Baptist church, John attended the Methodist-Episcopal church with Winnifred where he had grown up, and a friend suggested buying a plot of land in Hardin County, Tennessee, where there were no other doctors. "That way, you'll get all the patients," the friend said. "The ones who can pay, those who can't, and those who don't."

That sounded fair to John. He might have to build his own house, but he thought he could do that. He wanted to try. The boys would love living in a cabin in the woods. He was sure of that. And Orie wanted to leave. But to a cabin in the woods with a baby coming? He remembered her eyes, amazed at the sight of the Forks, and her gaze at the airy height and breadth of the interior. Did she regret the move to Florence? Would she want to live in a mansion like the Forks in a year or two? After all they had been through, was he going to lose her anyway, just as he had thought when he first fell in love with her?

CHAPTER 38
HARDIN COUNTY, TENNESSEE

Having decided to leave Florence, John thought it would be better to spend his wedding gold on property he would own and on which he could build.

Hardin County was not far from Florence, on the Tennessee River bordering Alabama. It was the same county where the disastrous Battle of Shiloh had been fought, with bitter feelings among Southerners who lost the battle against superior forces and where some ten thousand soldiers had been killed, wounded, captured, or missing. While Union losses numbered thirteen thousand, this did not represent as alarming a percentage of troops as did the ten thousand Southerners.

John visited the area and all that he had heard was true: there was no doctor within twenty miles, the people were very poor, and there was no house available for him and his family. Nevertheless, the people urged him to come and that heartened him. Harder to gauge was the temperament of the people. The colored population outnumbered the whites in that small patch of Hardin County woods, and there was uneasiness among former slaves and whites as to how the situation would unfold. Neither side trusted the other in circumstances never before faced. Would his family be safe in these remote woods?

After much prayer and discussion with Orie, she said, "You would make a wonderful country doctor, John. And I could be a missionary of sorts to the people in the backwoods, and the new decade takes us further from the War. It's time to try out our wings alone, and I want my own home."

Buoyed by her trust in him, John bought a small tract of woodland facing the main highway leading west to Mississippi. He hired some Negroes living in the village nearby to cut down timber and haul it to a sawmill, where they turned it into boards. The men then hauled the wood by ox team back to the site selected for the house and began building an "up and down" rough-board dwelling. Big, burly Horace was the boss man of the small crew, and they successfully finished the house, complete with two rooms and a small hall. Broken strips covered the cracks between the undressed boards that formed the outside walls and kept out the rain and wind. The cabin looked watertight and well constructed.

"Where did you learn your building trade, Horace?" John asked. "This cabin is built to last through whatever Mother Nature throws at it. This is work well done."

"I growed up on a cotton plantation, but I leant carpentry watchin' a big fella build cabins for the new slaves," Horace replied. "He let me hep him after work in the fields and I's good at it, is what he done tole me."

Later, John looked at the work again and could not imagine Orie living there. To him, it looked more like a hunting cabin in the woods than a home for a physician and his family. It would also be the birth home of their third child, due in months. Sweat broke out on John's face, not entirely from the warming spring weather. Was he doing the right thing? Orie had never lived in the backwoods herself. This would not be like being a medical missionary with her wealthy and influential uncle in the Holy Land.

Horace suggested that glass-paned windows would bring light into the cabin. "Dat light comin' into de cabin, it make a big diff'ence, it sho'ly do," he said.

John agreed, and decided that Orie would appreciate the sense of civilized living sheltered from the creatures of the woods, but be able to look out at the natural beauty of God's woods. *Yes, she must have glass-paned windows.*

Back in Florence, he was able to buy the glass and hardware necessary to enhance the "doctor's cottage." Although the house was not yet complete, Orie was eager to be in her own home and insisted that they make their farewells and give thanks to Winnifred for all she had done as soon as possible. "I'm in a hurry, dearest," she told John. "We have so much to do." Not only was Orie unwilling to subject her husband's stepmother any longer to two boisterous boys and a squalling baby, but she was at the point where every hour under that roof brought her closer to a scream that might go on forever when finally unleashed. She wanted to be gone before that happened.

They left forthwith in the wagon John had driven with Jimmie from Viewmont to Alabama. Orie was happy to be with her beloved family on the way to their first very own house. When John apologized for the humble and rumbling old wagon, she moved closer to him on the buckboard and did not stop smiling until a wagon wheel hit a rut and she had to grab onto him to keep from flying off into the road.

"Orie! I'm so sorry," John said. "Would you rather sit in the back with the boys, where you are less likely to fall off?"

"I would not. I like sitting on the buckboard," she said, but she was no longer smiling.

She watched the road like a hawk looking for dinner and was not surprised again by a sudden lurch as they drove toward the wilds of Hardin County. The boys yelled greetings to every passerby they saw, and when John halted the horse to let the boys go behind a bush to "do their business," they hid stones in the pockets of their trousers.

Suspicious of their raucous laughter, John turned around to see them heaving stones and teasing each other when they missed. "Jimmie! Lulie! That's enough of that. Somebody might get hurt."

"Oh, let them be, John," Orie said. "You cannot know how hard they have tried to be nice and quiet boys for Winnifred. Let them shout and holler and be happy."

"Did you hear that, boys? Your mother has come to your rescue. Make all the noise you want, but don't fall out of the wagon and don't throw stones at people and dogs."

"We're catching game for our supper tonight," said Jimmie. "Aren't we, Lulie?"

"I almost hit a rabbit, but he was too quick," said Luther. "Oh, and I need to stop again to, um, find a bush to go behind."

"Me too!" called Jimmie.

John and Orie looked at each other, both shaking their heads.

"Sorry, boys," John said. "We have things to do when we get there and your mother needs to rest. We won't stop again until time to eat."

"Aww," they said in unison, but when John turned again to face them, they put a quick end to their protest.

About halfway there, John stopped at a place near a creek where the horse could rest and drink water. Orie got out a picnic basket, a large tablecloth, and a quilt to sit on. She leaned against John after they had eaten and the boys were off, looking for more stones and whatever else they might find.

"Dearest, I don't think I've ever felt so free and content in my life," she said. "You did a lot of good in Florence and I'm proud of you, but I'm so happy right now. "

"I know you are, Orie, my love, but I keep telling you, the house is not what you're used to. Don't expect too much."

"Please stop. I've always told you that as long as we are together, I ask no more." She put a stop to his attempt to say more with a lingering kiss. His attention immediately shifted from himself to his wife. Then the boys returned, John hitched the horse to the wagon, and when all were aboard, he whistled to the horse and off they went.

When John saw their house facing the road up ahead, he urged the horse on and said to his family, "We're here! The house is right up yonder." He stopped on the highway in front of the house, back in the woods just a bit. "Whoopee!" the boys shouted. They clambered out of the wagon and ran to the house.

"It's charming. And it's ours," said Orie.

John left the highway and stopped the horse in a clearing in front of the door. Orie waited until he got off the wagon and came around to help her down. Even though she was a foot and an inch taller than her tiny younger sister Lottie, Orie found her size to be a nuisance, always needing help reaching things on shelves and boarding trains, carriages, and wagons. Everything was built for man-sized men. But Lottie seemed content. Her authority came through her mind and was not diminished by her tiny, doll-like figure.

Orie stood in front of the house and planned out flowers in the yard, hedges, and a place for the boys to play close to the cabin.

"Do you like it?" John asked. "Remember, it's not yet finished."

"I love it."

John opened the door, lifted her up in his arms, and took her inside. They held hands as he walked her through the two rooms and the hall in between. The tour was over. John demonstrated the strength of the floor by walking briskly across it and pointed to the windows with a smile. Orie nodded with pleasure and declared herself the proud mistress of the cottage.

In the coming days, Orie took walks across their tract of land and envisioned what she could do as a missionary with the two to three hundred Negroes in the village about three miles away. There was no church for them in the area, and any religious instruction would have come through their former masters. Orie's family had honored the Christian obligation to spread the Gospel, and it had been easy to reach the relatively small number of slaves they had in the tobacco fields. In the Deep South, however, working in the cotton and cane fields from early dawn until dark did not allow for time off to hear about the Man of Galilee. Poor whites also lacked the opportunity to learn about Jesus.

Orie believed she was in that place at that time to stand before these people as a witness, one who had trodden the steps taken by Jesus himself in the Holy Land. She picked out a beautiful grove of oaks on level land close to their home. Here she would tell the Bible story of John 3:16: "For God so loved the world that he gave his only Son, that whoever believes in him should not perish but have eternal life."

John told Horace the carpenter of his wife's plans and Horace spent a day with Orie walking the tract and discussing what they would need to build an outdoor church meeting place. Horace had timber cut into slabs at the sawmill, which he fastened between trees with the flat side of the wood up, to serve as seats for Miz Dr. Orie's intended congregation. He helped send word to the village that on the following Sunday, a meeting would be held in the grove and "the white woman" would talk to them. On that Sunday, they came. John, Jimmie, and Lulie were with her, all of them watching the colored folk stream onto their property, with Horace and his family out front. Orie moved forward to greet them.

"Welcome! Please call me Dr. Orie," she said. "My husband is Dr. Andrews and our sons are James and Luther. I have been to the Holy Land, where Jesus, the son of God, lived and told us about God and heaven. I want to tell you all about Jesus and his stories. But first, please take a seat beneath the trees and we shall pray and we shall sing."

Nobody backed out. They found places to sit after testing to see if the slabs would hold their weight. They looked about and at each other in the grove and they smiled. A new sound rose from the space as they repeated to each other, "Mmm. Uh-huh!"

John got their attention by waving his arm. "Although it's cool in the shade of the trees, it's still a hot day," he said. "There's a well over there where I'm pointing, with a bucket and dipper. Help yourself to cool water if you feel thirsty and dizzy from the heat."

"Yas, sir. Thank you, sir," voices called out.

Orie felt dizzy, but not from the heat. She was in love. With the men, women, children, and babies. She missed her people at Viewmont, who had left after the war for work that paid dollars, except for Uncle Jacob and Mammy Jinny and several others. She would teach these people to pray and to sing. She would invite Jesus into their lives, and they would throw off the despair that burdened them.

She told them about Jesus and his birth in a manger far from home, with cows and sheep and goats sharing the humble lodging. Some of them knew the story and shouted "Amen!" She taught them the hymn "There Is a Balm in Gilead," and they got caught up in it, singing the words with such sadness that tears dropped from the faces of men and women whose hearts were still tender after lives of hopeless hard work.

Some hummed along with voices deep and rich, and some sang with clear soprano voices that made Orie's heart ache in joy. It was as if she had discovered the mystical fifth chord, the sound of heaven, and nothing more was needed to live. Not food, not water, not even sleep.

She prayed aloud for them to God, who loved every one of them since before they were born. "Praise God Almighty, oh my soul," Orie prayed. She prayed the Lord's Prayer and the people shouted "Amen, amen!" She prayed for their health and prayed for Jesus to wash away their sins and thanked the Lord for sending His Son to earth to teach the people God's holy ways.

An older woman fanned herself and told her grandson, "Fetch me a dipper of that there water 'afore I faint and miss something."

The boy took off to the well without saying a word, and Luther met him there. "Here, I'll help you," he said. He let the bucket down and cranked it back up, the water sloshing out and the rope creaking. He filled the gourd with water and handed it to the boy, who grasped it carefully. Not taking his eyes off the dipper, he said, "I sho' thank you."

Orie led them in singing "Swing Low, Sweet Chariot." The congregation sang along with hand clapping and foot tapping. Some moaned out their bliss and others swayed to the rhythm of the song. Orie understood that the words meant freedom from slavery on the plantations. Were these former slaves God's "chosen people"? She felt in her heart it could be so.

The afternoon ended and the congregation walked home slowly, humming and singing "Glory, glory halleluiah, since I laid my burden down." Orie and her family listened as their voices finally faded in the distance.

Every Sunday, the people came and Orie poured out her heart to them. Her husband and sons were always with her. Orie and John pitied the congregation for their faded and ragged clothes, especially the children's. Girls wore the skimpiest of shifts that barely reached their knees. Sometimes, though, in the heat and humidity of summer, Orie envied their cool and light frocks, but would never deviate from the long-sleeved, high-necked, full-skirted dresses that a woman such as herself was expected to wear.

Departing from Biblical text, Orie urged them to live a better life in practicality. She preached honesty, trustworthiness, and faithfulness within their families and with the outside world and pleasing God and His Son, Jesus, by such living. She also preached that men and women living together should obey the law and be married for the sake of their children. Many did so and were proud to show her their marriage papers. Their despair was becoming something that belonged to yesterday, not tomorrow.

Orie's joy got a jolt when her sister Lottie telegraphed her that their mother had died on June 21. Lottie had left her teaching post at the Caldwell Institute in Danville before school was out to care for her ailing mother. Although Lottie was bereft with sorrow, Pastor J.C. Long of the Hardware River Baptist Church proclaimed Mrs. Moon's death "a model of perfection" in that she was "calm, clear headed, joyous, and beautiful and full of faith."

At the time of her death, Anna Maria was sixty-one years old and had done all she could to give her children a good start in life. Even after suffering impoverishment caused by the War, she managed to send Mollie and Eddie to Richmond Female Institute to complete their formal education. Both young ladies did well. Mollie's essay was read at the 1867 commencement and Eddie's at the 1868 commencement. Eddie was an ambitious student, earning diplomas in mathematics, English literature, and moral philosophy. Her essay was titled "Beauty and Fashion."

According to Lottie, Anna Maria's last two years had been fraught with financial crises when she was unable to pay her taxes and had to ask her for help in return for a title to part of the land. Further upset came when both Mollie and Colie left the Baptist Church to become Roman Catholics, believed to have been accomplished by a handsome and romantic music teacher from Viewmont tutoring days. On top of all that, Anna Maria had been saddened by continued estrangement from her oldest daughter, Orie, who had objected to her mother's meddling in her child-raising.

When Orie heard about that last burden her mother had carried to her deathbed, she wept and wept. She had never meant to shut out her mother, but she had made it clear that her sons came first. How cruel she had been, and there was no recourse. Her mother was gone. She would carry this sorrow to her own deathbed.

Toward the end of the summer, the local Ku Klux Klan had heard rumors about the "white woman from the North" preaching to the former cotton field slaves and decided to pay her a midnight visit.

"It's better to silence the uppity woman now with a whipping than wait till more like her join in," the leader of the Klan declared.

"All right, then. Hit's been decided. Let's scare the tar out of them folks," the leader's sidekick spoke up.

"Y'all kin count on us!" the half dozen others in attendance agreed.

Although the confrontation never took place, due to the persuasion of the ferryman at Mangum's Landing telling the KKK that the white woman had been a Confederate surgeon from Virginia, John was convinced that continuing the religious services was too dangerous. "Orie, dear, the Klan is a danger not only to you, but to the colored folks themselves," he said.

"I confess that you are right, John," she replied. "I would never forgive myself if harm came to any of them because of me. Also, I would worry about you and the boys."

"Since our baby is due soon, we cannot pack up and leave, and you will be busy with the baby and teaching them their lessons. That is already too much for you, in my opinion."

"I won't argue with you, but I grieve nevertheless. My heart told me it was God's will to minister to the colored neighbors. Now they will think I have abandoned them."

"I have set broken legs and stitched up lacerations in the colored village, and I will pass on the word that you were shut down by the KKK. You stopped your ministry for fear of the safety of their people. There was no other way. They will understand," John said.

Orie accepted John's reasoning of the situation in her mind but not in her heart. Never a weepy child, she became a weepy woman, when there was no one to see or hear her. She was, in fact, infuriated by the situation. Unspoken between them was the notion that she was a spoiled plantation princess and simply expected to have her way, especially when she believed her will and God's were one and the same. She fretted about the baby yet to be born. Her spirits were low, and this was not a good place for a baby. The daily chores and teaching two boys who would rather be outside playing left her exhausted and anxious. In her prayers, she acknowledged herself as a sinner, unwilling to sacrifice herself and her family for tens of dozens of people who were hungry for God's Word.

Help came from an unexpected source. Horace's brother in the village offered John a guard dog puppy for his family because of the KKK threats. The puppy came from a dog Horace's white master at the cotton planation had given him after the War. "He be a Mastiff puppy, gonna grow real big and be a guard dog, but kindliest dog to chi'ren," Horace said. "My wife, Janie, she say to give that puppy to you and Miz Docta Orie."

John accepted the puppy with thanks and told him the gift would take care of any old or new doctor visits.

"I thank you, sir. I be happy about that, but we'll still bring what we can to pay you. But mostly we want you to have this here puppy," Horace said.

John hid the dog until he could show it to Orie first.

"No, John, I don't want to hold him. Not right now," she said. "I am pleased, though. We need protection from snakes and animals even more than from the KKK, although you don't know what will come of their anger and sadness. Talk to the boys. The puppy is not a pet, it's an outside guard dog, but they must treat it gently at all times. We don't want a guard dog growing up mistreated and mean."

The boys were overcome with joy over the puppy, so much so that John had to sit them down and explain the dog rules to them. "He's small now and can stay inside at night for a while, but he will live outside when he's bigger and watch for animals and people."

"Like the KKK?" asked Jimmie.

"Anyone, even people we want to see, but we want to know when someone is on our property. You can name him and take care of him, but he belongs to the family, which means me. Ask for permission before you take him off so I will know where you and the dog are."

"Yes, sir!" the boys declared. Within minutes, the two agreed to name the puppy Tige.

The baby came, delivered by a midwife who came right away at John's call. They named him Edward Moon Andrews, after Orie's beloved father.

"Another son!" John marveled. "The Arab's blessing is still in effect."

"That's just superstition. God gives us sons or daughters according to His will," Orie said.

"Of course you are right, dear," John said, believing otherwise.

Eddie was not a sickly baby, but not robust, either. His cries were not full-throated and lusty and his appetite was listless. Orie blamed herself for Eddie's lack of vitality and joy. She continued to grieve over the loss of contact with the colored folk she loved, and despaired over the things she wanted to tell them and now could not.

Edward Moon Andrews left his earthly home before he was a year old. John and Orie buried Eddie in a small hillside grave yard, not far from the cabin where he was born. He would await the Resurrection Morn alone and far from Virginia and Viewmont.

Orie had left Viewmont with a hopeful, happy heart for what lay ahead, and from Florence with the romantic excitement of living by themselves in a cabin built just for them. Now, with a baby in a lonely grave yard in the woods and her abandoned congregation living three miles away, Orie felt surrounded by sadness. John shared her unhappiness and added to it his failure to earn even a modicum of income for his family. He could do better, he assured himself. But not here.

CHAPTER 39
WATERLOO

S ometime after Eddie's burial, John moved the family to Waterloo, Alabama, on the Tennessee River about twenty miles downstream from Florence. Waterloo was not far geographically from Hardin County but a world away from the brutality of the Tennessee backwoods. They rented a house in town, where Orie and seven-year-old Lulie and almost-nine-year-old Jimmie had friends and neighbors, and the boys went to school with other children. John's patients lived nearby, not hours away on horseback. Life was more civil and less arduous and lonely, especially for Orie.

Waterloo was a river port town like Scottsville, with the advantage of nearby Florence's importance as county seat and the largest city in Lauderdale County. Unfortunately, the steamboat era had passed and also the wealth of the cotton-producing region it had once been. On the other hand, John had family friends and connections in Waterloo who welcomed the newcomers gladly.

Orie's bruised heart began to heal, away from infant Eddie's grave in the woods and away from the village of her colored congregation. Jimmie and Lulie seldom mentioned the cabin in the woods and never when their mother was with them, for fear of seeing her overcome by dark memories. Tige, however, came to the family in the Hardin County cabin and the boys remembered the cabin days with the joy of the puppy. A common sight in Waterloo was the two brothers with the large, friendly dog.

Another pregnancy. Orie wanted a new baby. Samuel Bryant was born that first year in Waterloo. John did not refer to the Arab's blessing this time, but welcomed his newborn son into their lives. Jimmie and Lulie spent most of their time staying out of the way. Orie tended to Samuel with a practiced hand and could see that this was a baby with vigor and resilience. She had things to do and she did them. Life took on a sense of normality. When he was old enough to smile and then giggle, Jimmie and Lulie performed their all-boy silliness as he stared back, enraptured.

Orie's acceptance of Waterloo was reflected in a softening of John's anxious expression. John had patients to see and he built a good reputation quickly, but the old problem of dealing with the disastrous economic fallout from the War was still there. Many of his calls came in times of emergency when his services were genuinely needed and appreciated, but not being able to get blood from a turnip was just as true in Waterloo as had been the case in Hardin County and Florence.

Left to their own devices, patients seldom went to him, preferring to meet their Maker on their own terms. Usually, wives and mothers went to his office in the front of the house begging him to go see their badly injured husband or sick child. He would always go. Payment was not so reliable, and John well understood postwar poverty. Luckily, he saw the value in remuneration for his services in the form of vegetables in season, eggs, and chickens for his growing family.

Orie never complained. Her demeanor never coarsened. She never raised her voice nor appeared less than fully dressed and completely in control. She did not put out a shingle as a physician, but readily helped out her neighbors. She attended church regularly, and only then did she wish she had a more generous amount of coins to drop in the offering plate. She hoped, mostly for John's sake, that financial security was around the next corner. It did not bother her to wear clothes that were discreetly mended or patched somewhere.

Women in Waterloo quickly learned that Orie was a physician who not only was endlessly giving of herself in times of need, but also gave help of any kind when asked. She helped them with financial and legal questions as well as personal problems and kept their conversations to herself. Word of mouth is a powerful force in a small town, and people gravitated to Orie as if she were the Biblical wise man King Solomon. Orie, for her part, accepted these responsibilities as an obligation due to her extensive education, travel, and experience growing up in a place where people had always looked to her family for help when needed. Her father, Edward Harris Moon, had been the patriarch of a prominent family, and it was expected of him to be in charge when trouble came or advice was needed not only at Viewmont, but around the neighboring area, in addition to his business dealings spread over the South to Memphis and New Orleans. He had been a busy man. Orie was busy too, and remembered that her father had taken ill, seemingly recovered, then died of a heart attack two months later at age forty-seven. Orie was thirty-seven, luckily far from that age. She would turn thirty-eight in a matter of weeks.

Her sister Lottie came to visit for a month in mid-July the second summer Orie and her family lived in Waterloo. She brought with her letters from Ike at Viewmont and a glorious letter from Mollie about her marriage to her beloved Dr. William Shepherd in Norfolk. Lottie intended to rest and enjoy herself after years of teaching and church work, all while striving to become a missionary to China. She and a colleague, Anna Safford, had left Caldwell Institute in Danville to be co-principals of the new Cartersville Female High School in Georgia the year after her mother died. Lottie was also a member of the Cartersville Baptist Church, where she taught Sunday School to young women and was Pastor R. B. Headen's indispensable associate. Most important was his strong faith in missionary work. With both a responsible job in a school and support of a Baptist church, Lottie believed she was well on her way to becoming a missionary.

The school's first year had gone well, with the student body growing from seven girls to almost one hundred. But the next year, Eddie had joined a Baptist missionary group in China and was begging Lottie to join her. Lottie and Anna Safford, both desiring to go to China, examined their contract and decided not to return on the basis of a technical requirement that the school be profitable. Although clearly successful, the school was not yet profitable, and the two co-principals took their leave. Anna answered a call to go as a Presbyterian appointee to Soochow, China. Lottie accepted a call to join the Baptist missionaries in Tengchow, China, where Eddie was stationed.

Lottie's month long visit with Orie before leaving for China placed her forever as a beloved family favorite in the view of the Andrews family. Lottie rambled around the countryside with her nephews Jimmie and Lulie, and wherever the boys were, Tige was there also. Lottie admired the dog and made the comment that the Mastiff originated as a breed in ancient Greece called a Molossian hound.

Orie asked about Molossian hounds, not having studied Greek and classical studies to the extent that Lottie had at Hollins and Albemarle Female Institute.

"Truly, it was considered a noble dog with great courage and size and used as guard dogs," Lottie replied. "I've seen pictures of a famous sculpture of Alcibiades's handsome dog. Alcibiades cut off his dog's tail, his 'principal ornament,' to give Athenians something to talk about rather than worse things he had done. Orie, dear, you have an exceptional dog, and I understand the breed to be especially protective and kind to children. He certainly watches over me. Maybe because I am tiny he thinks I am a child, too." Lottie loved being in the middle of the two boys and the Molossian hound as they went on their adventures.

Such a grand pedigree was yet another reason to brag about Tige and appreciate his many qualities, but then Orie worried about protection for Lottie in China. "At least I need to show you how to perform standard baby care and first aid procedures before you go," said Orie. "Women are the practical ones everywhere in the world. Show them how to do something that needs doing and they will listen to you on other matters."

"Yes, sister, although I hope there will be others to do those things," thinking back to when she believed she and Orie would be missionaries together. So she watched and listened to Orie talk about baby care, but like the teacher she was, talked about her students and what the year at Carterville School in Georgia had been like. When she mentioned the need to back out of her co-principal and teaching contract in Cartersville, Orie was shocked. *Was it ever permissible to cut ethical corners, even when the Lord's work was the reason?*

"How did the girls and their parents feel about your leaving the school for China?" Orie asked.

"The girls were quite excited about my adventure until they realized it meant I would not be their teacher," Lottie replied. "Then they cried their hearts out. Their parents and the townspeople were divided. Some were happy for me and proud, and others thought I was wasting my time on Chinese heathens when Southern girls needed an education." Lottie, as usual, viewed her decisions as influenced by God and by practical actions. "In the Bible, people do what they must to do God's will."

"I can see both sides, but I understand the sad students and their parents. Will you miss them?" Orie had heard of regrets and homesickness derailing more than one missionary in a foreign land. As her mother would have done, Orie was beginning to wish Lottie would stay home.

"No, Orie, I loved them dearly, and did everything I could for them, but there are other young women who can teach them, while that's not the case in China. My call is clear. It's where I must go.

Remember what Jesus said in Luke chapter ten, verse two: 'The harvest is plentiful but the laborers are few.'" Lottie tossed her hair back, and Orie knew by the look on her face that she would go to China.

Then Orie felt even more anxious for Lottie, who had never been out of the country, even though she was immensely proud of her sister. "You had better learn Chinese if you want to get along with your work there," she said.

Lottie was sitting in a rocking chair, holding Samuel and making faces at him. "Learning Chinese is my first goal. I'm good at languages, and I think that's because the Lord needs me in China and wants me to comfort and teach His children there." Samuel giggled in her arms.

"Although I loved the Holy Land and lived with Uncle James and his family, who protected me, I was happy to come home and never thought about returning," Orie said.

"Surely I will miss my home and family, but I'm answering a call I heard long ago. At one time I wished you would go with me, but you have John and the boys to look after. Now I'll have Eddie to share that life with and be there to look after her too," said Lottie.

"Ah, yes, we have always looked after Eddie. And now she's grown and looking after God's children in China." Orie shook her head in wonderment. "I have not given up on missionary work, but it will be in the South, where the Negroes are hungry for God's Word."

"We're both Christians following Jesus's command to preach the Gospel," Lottie observed. "And Eddie is in China already. I'm wondering what Mama would say." Lottie had reversed the conversation and was now questioning Orie.

"In her heart she wanted the five of us to be mistresses of great plantations in Virginia, but that era is past. I think she would approve of our decisions. She was a great Christian, after all," said Orie.

"Yes, but what about Colie and Mollie?" Lottie gave Orie a look of skepticism.

"Because they are Roman Catholic? Mama's in heaven and knows that different denominations don't matter to Christ. We all had to go in different directions anyway, and now Mama will remain the belle of them all forever," said Orie.

"You're the peacemaker now, Orie, but in a letter she wrote to me, Mama said she was wroth when you left Viewmont," Lottie said, bringing up subjects that needed airing before she left for China.

"That was my fault. I couldn't stand having her watch over my children as if I didn't have good sense. And I had a medical degree! It was humiliating. Now I'm sorry I didn't thank her for all that she did for me. Naturally, she wanted more sway with her grandchildren and I wouldn't have it. The young are cruel," said Orie.

"You worked hard for your medical degree, but Mama saw no connection between having a degree and being a proper mother. New mothers were supposed to follow their mother's guidance, and you refused to do that. It was hard on both of you," said Lottie, walking about with Sammy in her arms.

Lottie also spent time while in Waterloo writing appeals for young women to join her in China. In her letters she quoted from a lady missionary in China who reveled in the honor of being the one to tell of the Savior Jesus to people who had never heard the name of our Lord before. She also appealed to their practical side, explaining that foreign missions opened new opportunities for women in a career that "angels might almost envy." In Lottie's mind, her future as a missionary would set heaven aglow. But be that as it may, Lottie was on fire to reach China and preach the Gospel to people who had no other way to learn about the Savior. Disappointments in life had not diminished her spirit.

Orie did not envy Lottie but feared for her. The evening before Lottie left, Orie had a gift for her. It was a picture from the Holy Land of a vase of cactus leaves woven together filled with flowers from the Garden of Gethsemane close to Rachel's Tomb. It had been made by their cousin Sarah Barclay and two friends.

Uncle James Barclay had made the frame from an olive tree on the Mount of Olives. Uncle James had given the picture to Orie as a gift when they left the Holy Land.

"Oh, no!" said Lottie. "I cannot accept this gift. It's for you from Uncle James!"

"Our uncle would tell me to do this. Take it to China and show the women and children something from the Holy Land. It will keep your heart and mind centered on the Holy Land as you go about bringing the Holy Savior to them. Please do this for me."

Lottie agreed, and Orie felt a rush of purest love for her. The power and energy in Lottie's tiny body was all the more apparent against the corresponding diminishment of her own strength. She wasn't sad as much as she was thankful that her sister could still go far and accomplish much.

The next day, Orie and Lottie hugged and kissed cheeks at the train station. "You are still my little sister," said Orie. "The Chinese will think you are a doll."

Lottie smiled. "They will soon see that I am not. "

John helped her up the high steps and handed her over to the conductor, into whose hand he pressed some bills. "Take care of her, please," he said in a near whisper, while Lottie waved at Orie and her nephews.

Lottie's train took her from Florence to New York, stopping in Virginia to see the family and also in Baltimore, where she joined Anna Safford and two Presbyterian missionary men who escorted them to China. The last stop before China was San Francisco. There she received the good news that the Cartersville Women's Missionary Society would be supporting her with donations. Lottie's spirits soared.

The whole family missed Lottie's lively presence after she left. Orie remembered with remorse how little attention she paid to her younger sister growing up at Viewmont. Yes, the young can be so terribly cruel and wasteful of opportunities for happy times. *If anything happens to Lottie, I will die. I couldn't bear the loss of her. The long sea voyage, the dangers in China, the known hatred of Chinese men for "foreign devils" all scare me to death. After a woman gives birth, that youthful, joyful courage gives way to something else. I want Lottie to always be the way she is now.*

Needing more space after the birth of Sammy, the family rented a larger house in Waterloo. Although weakened by the birth and another pregnancy a year later, Orie kept up with all she had been doing when they first moved to Waterloo. She also learned things about the river port town that darkened her thoughts. The *Sultana,* a sidewheel steamboat built in Cincinnati in 1863, left Waterloo in April 1965 with a cargo hold filled with cotton, and in Vicksburg picked up twenty-three hundred passengers, most of them Union soldiers returning home from the war. The number was six times what the steamer was designed to carry. Melting snow from the north and spring rains had resulted in a flood of water rushing south to the Gulf of Mexico, and the steamboat struggled to buck the current as it headed north. The soldiers, happy to be on their way home at last, found any available spot on which to lie down and used their jackets as blankets against the chill night air.

The steamboat exploded at two o'clock in the morning, with a great sound and a fireball that blew it apart. Many of the passengers were killed outright, while hundreds held onto parts of the ship's wreckage for dear life and were rapidly carried downstream in the dark. Men burned by the explosion and with limbs blown off screamed for help in the chaos. It was said that a former Confederate soldier saved fifteen Union soldiers. The *Sultana* went down on April 27, 1865. Fifteen to nineteen hundred men were killed that night, making it the worst disaster in steamboat history.

In Orie's mind, the story kept repeating itself until the screams for help were coming not from the *Sultana's* smoking wreckage, but from the wounded, sick, and dying soldiers she had treated at Charlottesville General Hospital after the bloody Battle of Manassas.

Another story was of the Trail of Tears in the 1830s, when the US government forced the relocation of Indians from the Southern Appalachian region to west of the Mississippi River. Waterloo was the place where many Indians were shipped by steamboat to points west. Orie was told that one hundred thousand Indians of different tribes, mostly Cherokees, were forced from their homes. Fifteen thousand died on that murderous journey that took them five thousand miles across portions of nine states.

Orie bristled with anger to learn that the reason for the forced relocation was the discovery of gold in northern Georgia in 1829. Land speculators demanded that the US Congress give the states control of property owned by the tribes. Supported by President Andrew Jackson, who was a speculator himself, Congress came up with the Indian Removal Act in 1830. There were to be negotiations with the Indians for the land and transportation for the people and their household goods, including livestock and farm equipment.

But the project went terribly wrong. There was not enough government money to do what they promised, coupled with ineptitude and corruption. The result was monumental suffering of the Indians due to exhaustion, exposure, malnutrition, and disease. Orie could imagine the horror of being forced from Viewmont, herded five thousand miles across mountains and woods, and ending up with nothing to start a new life. Sometimes she felt that she was herself in exile and forced to live in hardship away from her family. Her former sense of adventure seemed to have been lost long ago.

John and the older boys knew the story but were not dismayed by it to the extent that Orie was. Another story caught John's attention. Major General James Harrison Wilson, US Army, assembled the largest cavalry force in the Western Hemisphere in Waterloo at Gravely Springs. In winter camp from mid-January to March, Wilson commanded five divisions totaling some twenty-two thousand men. He used the time for intensive military training of his troops. On March 22, 1865, Wilson's men crossed the Tennessee River to invade southern Alabama and Georgia. They burned the University of Alabama and captured Confederate President Jefferson Davis at Irwinville, Georgia, on May 10, 1865. The war ended in stages and the capture of the Confederate President was another bitter event in the downfall of the Confederate states.

When John heard the number of Union troops arrayed in Waterloo so near Florence, he thought about his two brothers who had died at the Battle of Manassas in 1861. "There were not enough soldiers to defend Florence, because the young men were off fighting or already dead," he told Orie. "So Florence was occupied and not destroyed. We never had a chance against such numbers. I never knew how outnumbered we were."

Orie comforted him with reverential silence. There was nothing to add to his words. She put baby Samuel down in his crib and stood beside John, her hand on his. "Although the South was ravaged and the death toll too high to be counted, you and I live. You were shot at on the battlefield and the bullets went through your clothes, yet you lived. You treated soldiers who were sick and dying of infectious disease, but you lived," said Orie.

"And you, a woman, worked night and day at the military hospital in Charlottesville until you collapsed from exhaustion and were near death, but you lived. You have lived through the birth of five babies and lost two of them, and you live still," said John.

They looked at each other soberly. Neither spoke. Both were thinking the same thought: *For some reason God wanted us to live. We will live in a way that pleases God, if not man. Oh my soul, praise the Lord.*

CHAPTER 40

ONE MORE TREK

Isaac Moon was born in Waterloo, the fourth son of Orie and John. Orie's pregnancy had been hard on her, and this time she failed to regain her strength after the birth. On the contrary, as physicians, she and John could see that her heart was weakened, so any exertion was unwise. Added to her failing heart was a long-standing tendency to suffer from diarrhea that had worsened. Paregoric, also known as tincture of morphine or laudanum, helped soothe the intestinal distress, but episodes had become more frequent and of longer duration. She lost weight and assumed a sickly pallor, and her very eyes looked dull. John avoided even thinking about Orie's shortness of breath and swollen ankles and feet in spite of bed rest.

While John and Orie struggled with her deteriorating health and anxiety over never-ending financial woes, a message from Ike and Mag changed everything yet again.

"Since our mother's death, and Lottie's departure to her mission in China, there is no one to live in and care for the family homestead. Mag and I have moved to Scottsville and Mollie, as you know, is the wife of Dr. Shepherd and they live in Norfolk. Would you and John consent to returning to Viewmont and providing a home for Colie?

When John read the letter to Orie, in bed with eyes barely open, he could almost swear he saw color come back into her face. "Yes, dearest, if you think you can manage it," she said. She knew she could be of no help, and instead would be a burden on her family, but oh, she wanted to go home to Virginia.

John, encouraged, studied the situation. It could be done, although there was a sniff of doomed if we do and doomed if we don't. He decided to leave as soon as possible for the now-greener fields of Virginia. The year was 1876, and they had been in Waterloo for four years. Albemarle County was slowly recovering from the war, he had been told, and it was time to return.

In April, the winter rains and cold gave way to green grass and flowering fruit trees, and John was ready with a new wagon, four mules, and a canvas top stretched over bows, placed over the wagon. He constructed a bed with springs in the rear part of the wagon body near the buckboard in front. John shipped their books, clothing, trunks, and keepsakes by railroad and gave away their furniture, with the exception of Orie's bed to rebuild in the wagon.

A large contingent of friends gathered to send them off. It was a sad farewell for them, for they would be losing a dear and valued family when the crack of the whip over the mules' heads signaled their departure. The two older boys, Jimmie and Lulie, considered the trek a "great adventure" and would tell of it for the rest of their lives. That spring and summer, Jimmie was twelve going on thirteen and Lulie was eleven. Along for the ride were three-year-old Sammy and Baby Ikey, only four months old. Also in the entourage were Orie, a bedridden invalid, and Tige, the outdoor guard dog.

What John had not expressed aloud, not even to himself, was his fear that Orie would die far from home—from Viewmont. She had never gotten over the death of Eddie, grieving for the baby all alone in that hillside graveyard near the cabin in the woods. John trusted that Orie's desire to see Viewmont again would keep her alive until they arrived there. He would ask for no more.

They headed northeast, quickly entering Tennessee from Waterloo. John set their course for twenty-five miles a day; they would go through Shelbyville and on to McMinnville at the base of the Cumberland Plateau. The first day, the mules were strong and obedient to the pull on the lines held firmly by John, as well as the crack of the whip on occasion. Jimmie and Lulie had their jobs to do, part of which was to keep an eye on Sammy. Otherwise, they watched the world pass by backward from the end of the wagon.

"Are you boys all right back there?" John would shout from time to time, keeping his eyes straight ahead, trying to avoid ruts and large stones on the road, ever mindful of Orie's condition as she lay uncomplaining on the bed behind him.

"Yes, but we don't know where we're going, only where we've been!" they would shout back. They grumbled to each other that it was too hard to hit their targets at the speed they were going in the opposite direction. Lulie threw many of his stones too quickly and finally learned to aim at large unmoving targets such as oak trees. Jimmie, older and bolder, took on spooked rabbits and wished for a large black bear before taking on birds and missing everything. Tige slept to the rhythm of the wagon ride, and when the wagon stopped, he was the first one out. He ran around sniffing madly and then joined the family at his leisure.

Orie's job was to breathe in the cool breezes of April, and with a smile on her face, she dozed off and on all day long. She had a jug of fresh spring water that John would refill from the water barrel on the outside of the wagon and cornpone to eat. She also nursed the baby, a new experience with the wagon rhythmically swaying forward in the sunshine beyond the canvas. John stopped the wagon in the afternoon and bought food for their supper at a farmhouse. The farmer invited John to make camp on his grounds, and his wife came out later with a large pail of fresh buttermilk and a pie made from dried apples, warm from the cookstove oven.

Skinny Lulie ate everything on his plate and said he'd never tasted food so good. Everyone agreed, and John noticed that Orie did not pick at her food and pretend to eat, but drank all of her buttermilk and ate a slice of pie. His heart beat a little faster. He dared not say a word.

When it was time for John to end the day with prayers before snuffing out the lantern, Orie was still awake. She added, "Thank you, Lord, for blessing this day for us." John kissed her goodnight and felt well pleased with himself. He made sure everyone had blankets for the chill night and saw the two older boys lapse into sleep as soon as they lay down next to Tige, after begging to be allowed to stay up longer to watch the night sky. John was planning the next day's route, and the next thing he knew it was daybreak.

Breakfast in the chill open air for the first time on their trek took monumental effort from John, especially, but Orie too had to rouse herself from deep sleep and tend to the baby. Jimmie and Lulie woke up astonished that they were not in their beds at home. They clambered out of the wagon and chased each other around, whooping like Indians and scaring the cows, Tige barking and chasing excitedly. Reacting to the motion and noise, Ikey rolled off the wagon and lay squalling on the ground. John rushed to him, dusted him off, comforted him, and put him in the arms of his mother. It never happened again, for Orie would not let her baby loose in the wagon until John built up the sides higher.

Orie examined her fortunately well-bundled baby while John rescued the farm animals from his boys. The farmer's wife came out with fresh eggs and more buttermilk. The boys helped their father build a fire and cook the eggs and cornpone and coffee.

"We'll get organized by and by," said John. "How are you feeling, dear?"

"The morning has had its moments, but I feel rested and the breakfast was very fine, thank you," Orie replied.

John looked at her closely. Her color and her voice were coming back. The taut gray aura she had had about her was giving way to a soft tenderness that physically embraced her baby and spread to include them all. *Nevertheless, I dare not hope.*

Camping out at night and progressing northeast by day en-thralled the three boys, and excitement grew as they approached Shelbyville. "I wish we could camp out every night and ride in the wagon all day, every day, forever," said Lulie.

"I don't think you'd like it so much in the winter," their father remarked. "Don't you agree, dear?"

"Winter will take care of itself," Orie said. "Right now, I am in heaven with my family, and my sickbed is inside a fresh-air chariot that's taking us all to Virginia. I have the songs of the birds, the rustling breezes, and the lowing of cows to soothe me. I want to be far from the sickroom. Far away."

"You don't mind the noise of the mules and the creaking of the wagon and the bumpy ride, Mama?" Jimmie asked. He had forgotten about his mother's comfort as she lay by the hour in her sickbed while he was free to move about and jump from the wagon while they were stopped.

"I mind none of it," she assured him. "You'll see. You'll be glad to be back home again. I promise."

It took about five days to get to Shelbyville. The boys were all eyes and ears as the wagon entered the town of almost two thou-sand souls. The town square was busy with men on horseback and families in carriages and wagons going to the stores and markets.

"Hey, mister, you can't find a better horse anywhere in Shelbyville," a man called out. "Buy one and tie it to your wagon and use it to ride when you need to." The man was just walking by when he noticed John looking at all the activity. He had horses to sell and thought he might have a buyer.

Jimmie and Lulie jumped from the wagon and went quickly to see the horse up close. Tige followed, although Orie called for him to stay.

"Go ahead, you can pat the horse," the man said. "She's a genu-ine Tennessee walking horse. You'd be proud to have one of these horses, I can guarantee you that much right now. What do you say, mister?" he asked John.

"I'm sorry as can be, but I can't feed another animal until I can get to where I'm going," John replied. "These mules are walking mouths to feed, but I like the looks of that horse sure enough."

"Please, please, Father!" the boys begged. Tige whined his disappointment.

"Get back in the wagon, boys. We've got to find a place to eat and sleep tonight. Your mother needs a roof over her head." They climbed slowly back into the wagon, heads down in disappointment.

"I can help you with that, mister. There's a widow lady, Miz Moffat, in a farmhouse on the limestone bluffs above Duck River who takes in travelers, feeds them too. Tell her Earl sent you. It's not far down that road yonder."

John thanked him and found the farmhouse without much trouble. Miz Moffat put them up in the first-floor room to make it easier on Orie and was a great help getting her settled. She served them and other guests from upstairs a light supper in the dining room. They stayed three days, during which time Miz Moffat did their laundry and helped bathe Orie, covered in travel dust and longing for a sponge bath with heated water and a washcloth and towels. Jimmie and Lulie brought trays of food to her in bed, and she had to confess that resting in a bed that did not rumble and bump all day was a peaceful change. John, too, rested his muscles, unused to driving mules and sitting on a hard buckboard. Jimmie, Lulie, and Sammy, accompanied by Tige, caught fish in the Duck River, which Miz Moffat cooked for all her boarders. The three boys ate with particular gusto and watched the other diners tuck into the fresh fried fish. John ate heartily, pleased with his boys.

They moved on, eager to be in Virginia. The days passed quickly as they rode through the green fields and woods of southern Tennessee. The four mules were becoming individuals and the boys had names for them: Pokey, Sleepy, Famished, and Water Hog. The boys brushed and fed them and talked to them at length. One evening Jimmie and Lulie got on the backs of Famished and Water Hog until John put a stop to it.

"They're worn out and they don't want to be ridden. Get down now," he told them.

"Aww. If you had bought that horse in Shelbyville, we wouldn't have to ride the mules," Jimmie pointed out.

John gave Jimmie a harsh look. "Boys, let's get this straight. Tennessee walking horses are expensive. We don't have enough money to feed another animal, much less buy one. I don't want to hear anything more about buying a horse."

"Yes sir," they said, each looking at the other as if the bad idea was his brother's alone.

Orie, watching John and the boys put together picnic meals, began to help out. She also leaned on John and took short walks when they stopped riding. "I'm feeling better, John. Being outdoors and away from the daily tasks of running a household and being in the sickbed has given me the chance to truly rest. I believe Nature is watching over me."

"You are indomitable, my love," said John.

McMinnville, at the base of the Cumberland Plateau, was another flower in their bouquet of travel accomplishments. John intended to stay at least overnight to rest, bathe, do laundry, and stock up on provisions. They found a small hotel in town that suited them. Orie rested on the hotel's veranda with the baby while John and the three boys and the dog did the necessary shopping. People walking by tipped their hats to Orie and said, "Mornin', ma'am," and Orie returned their greetings with a smile.

"I feel like I have rejoined the human race," she said to John when he returned.

"Well then, welcome, ma'am," he said and laughed with glee. No one could deny it. Orie was recovering.

At dinner, the boys chattered on about all the wild creatures they would see in the Cumberland Mountains, according to the old man who sold them fodder for the mules. "He's found fish and sea creatures not found anywhere else and seen bald eagles and peregrine falcons. There's caves and waterfalls and great gorges up there all the way to Kentucky," Jimmie said.

Lulie backed him up. "That man says he's explored up there all his life and that's where he likes to be."

John shook his head. "We're not staying in the Cumberland Mountains all the way to Kentucky. We're taking the shortest route over the Cumberland Plateau and will be in eastern Tennessee when we get down. It's the quickest, shortest, and safest route."

"Aww, I wanted to see the waterfalls and look for salamanders and explore real caves," said Jimmie. "Me too!" Sammy echoed.

Orie smiled to herself. It was usually the case when the boys wanted to do something that she was the one to say no. Now it was John's turn. Women seldom had the chance to see their husbands take on women's work. She watched John with approval. She wished she could show her suffragette friends at school in Troy and from medical school in Philadelphia a man who didn't wait for a woman to cook meals and care for children.

They left early in the morning of their crossing the Cumberland Plateau. Right away, the road was steep going up. It was so steep, Jimmie and Lulie had to get out to lighten the load on the mules. John instructed them to find a large rock, which he called a "Scotch-rock," and have it ready to wedge under the wheel when he signaled by shouting "Wah!" He would do this when he wanted to stop and rest the mule team and not have the wagon roll backward and crash. The two older boys did this for about an hour before Lulie, armed with a rock but with his mind somewhere else, heard his father's signal and promptly dropped the rock, which rolled down the hill. To make up for his mistake, he placed his bare foot under the wheel and let out a high-pitched scream when the wheel rolled over his toes.

Alarmed, thinking the wagon had rolled over Lulie, John and Jimmie scrambled to stop it with large rocks. John rushed to Lulie, who was not under the wheel, but lying beside the wagon holding his foot, Tige by his side.

"Ow, ow, it hurts!" said Lulie as he showed his father his bruised and bleeding toes.

"Next time, don't try to stop a wagon with your bare foot," said John, shaken with fear for his son. He picked up the boy and got out his medical bag, gently washed the toes with water from the barrel, and bandaged them. He spread out a blanket on the wagon floor and gently placed his son on it. "Let it rest. Don't be running around for a while."

Recovering from his fright, Lulie grinned and said, "My foot was a terrible Scotch-rock. I'll mind my business next time."

Orie, on her bed, heard it all. Fearing the worst as John had, she had to endure inaction; she was still too weak to help with the rescue. John came to her as quickly as he could to tell her the extent of her son's minor injuries. As they got moving again uphill to reach the Plateau, all were contemplative and quiet, shaken by the near tragedy. They reached the top that afternoon, and John stopped the mule team for a good rest along with plenty of water and fodder while they were on level ground. John, holding Sammy's little hand, Jimmie, and Tige walked about, admiring the view all the way to Alabama looking southward and Kentucky to the north. Spread before them were dense forests and underbrush, with great rock outcroppings overlooking mountains in the distance.

"I'd say we're about a thousand feet above sea level here," said John.

"It's cooler up here," Jimmie observed, running barefoot to climb on the nearest rocks and look out over the sides of the mountain plateau. John, carrying Sammy, caught up with him.

"That's far enough, son. Snakes like to sun themselves on rocks. Don't tempt them."

"Father, it's like being a hawk in the sky, we're so far up. I've never looked *down* on mountains before." Jimmie hooted and hollered at the sky, doing an Indian dance.

With that, Lulie jumped down from the wagon and limped toward his brothers and father. "Let me see, Father! I want to climb on the rocks!"

John put Sammy down, picked Lulie up onto his shoulders, and walked out on the ledge. "Jimmie, go hold Sammy's hand. Be quick!"

Jimmie stopped his dancing and picked up Sammy and ran around with him on his shoulders. Tige ran around barking.

Worn out, John hollered at his boys, "Wagon time, get moving!" Carrying Lulie, he and Jimmie and Sammy got back on the wagon, Tige following. Orie gave them all plates of cornbread and apples and fresh cups of water before John returned to the buckboard and cracked the whip above the mules' heads. Lulie tried to sit up and resume watching the scenery go past, but his toes were throbbing and he lay down on his blanket. Orie sat beside him and felt his forehead for fever. "You'll be all right in a day or two, son. You were a brave boy to try and stop the wagon from crashing downhill." She bent over and kissed his forehead. "Try to rest. Healing takes time."

Tears fell down his cheeks. His whole foot hurt and he couldn't sit up and throw rocks and see the mountains. And his mother had just told him he was a brave boy. Tears flowed afresh. He was proud and hurting at the same time. Soon he was asleep.

Orie took Lulie's place on the short bench behind the wagon's loading end looking backward.

"Heavens! There must be eight mules leading that wagon and they're going to fly right past us!" she exclaimed.

Jimmie waved at the mule driver, who shifted all the lines to his right hand and doffed his wide-brimmed hat at him and Orie. Jimmie called out, "Halloo, mister!"

They were on a level place when the large team of mules passed them, and they could see the man was hauling timber. "Oak?" Jimmie asked.

"Oh yes," said Orie, familiar with oak trees at Viewmont. "The king of trees—Jupiter's tree. Let's look for his bird, too."

"What's his bird? Who's Jupiter?"

Oh dear, thought Orie. *I never taught him the Greek myths.* "Jupiter's the Roman king of gods and goddesses, and the majestic eagle is his bird. We'll watch for one. The eagle is America's bird too."

While Jimmie scanned the sky, Orie planned what she would do when they reached Viewmont. *The library. She would teach her boys in the library at Viewmont just as her father had taught her. Those books had opened up the world and beyond to her and she would do the same for her four sons. It was not too late.*

Before it got dark and cold, John stopped the mules when he saw a level place off the road. There were rocks and lush-looking grass, and sure enough, there was water trickling down the side of a rock wall. John told Jimmie to watch for snakes and catch the water with the dipper and fill up the water barrel. With no stores or farmhouses to count on, they had packed provisions for this part of the trek. They were camping now on the top of the Cumberland Plateau. It was cold and windy that night and they were all alone on the roof of the world. That night they huddled together in sleep and heard animal cries in the distance, and some not so distant. In his sleep, Tige growled softly and whined, and his paws jerked as though he were running.

Orie was awakened by the sound of a screech owl in the predawn darkness and knew the night was coming to an end. She listened to the wind blow through the trees and thought about the harmonious celestial music that only God can hear. The Greeks believed all things had a voice, even the rocks and sand, not just the rivers and springs, and that all creatures were forever singing the praises of the Creator. She strained to listen. She fully awakened later, strangely at peace.

The next morning was cold and overcast, but alive with the cheerful chirping and tweeting of birds as they flitted from branch to branch in trees above them. John and Jimmie cooked eggs, streaked meat, cornbread, and coffee while Orie nursed the baby. Lulie, still limping, fed and watered the mules, calling them by name and warning them not to step on his bandaged toes. He practiced jumping from rock to rock, and his sore toes did whatever he asked them to.

Back on the road, the sun warmed up and Orie sat on the wagon bench beside Lulie and Jimmie, with Sammy on her lap. Looking around, they could see the new pale green of leafy hardwoods with bursts of sweet color from redbuds and fruit trees ascending the sides of mountain gorges. They were utterly alone in God's creation, except for the sight of a lone man on horseback heading west. Orie said a silent prayer, thanking God for letting her live long enough to see such beauty. She didn't dare ask for anything beyond the day. *But she wanted more.*

CHAPTER 41

ON THE GREAT ROAD

They did it in four days. They came down from the Cumberlands, passed though fertile valleys, and crossed rolling foothills. John's face was losing its red, peeling skin from so much unaccustomed exposure to the sun and was turning dark and tanned as never before, and he was noticeably more muscular about the arms and shoulders. He mingled easily with the country people and took great pleasure in showing his boys how to drive the mule wagon and pass the time with farmers.

On the other hand, Orie stayed inside the wagon and was outside mainly in the early morning and late afternoon and evening. She sought shade while preparing the midday dinner, thus preserving her creamy English complexion. She was, after all, the daughter of Anna Maria Barclay Moon. She nursed the baby and entertained Sammy with songs and games and kept a notebook on the flora and fauna she saw along the way. She also had time to think and to dream.

She had traveled to many places in the world, but nothing matched the expansiveness of the Southern countryside. The lushness of the farms and foothills, the dramatic landforms of the Cumberland Mountains, and the affection she received from the men, women, and children of the South gave her hope that the lost cause of Southern Independence was evolving into an even greater love of land and the desire to stay and prevail with dignity in spite of economic destitution.

Her mind turned to books and schools and how much they had meant to her family. Her father especially had given her an education through books and tutors at home, which was followed by her intense year at Troy Female Seminary, where she felt called to study medicine. Despite her mother's desire that she follow her lead and attend finishing school in Richmond, she graduated from the Woman's Medical College in Philadelphia. All of her brothers and sisters had grown up both loved and educated. Could she do less for her four sons? At Viewmont she would show her sons the great library and see about schools for them in Albemarle County. She dazzled herself with the possibilities of what lay ahead for her family.

They entered Virginia at the town of Bristol, where John took the family to State Street, which separated the town between Virginia and Tennessee. "Cross this street and you go from the laws of Virginia to the laws of Tennessee," John told the boys. "Look north and Virginia is on your right; look south and Virginia is on your left." He marched the boys to face north, then south.

The three older boys stamped their feet on the Virginia side and declared themselves Virginians. An older couple watched them from the shade of a bench on the Virginia side of State Street. Lulie skipped away in embarrassment after overhearing the woman say, "I declare that's a right good lookin' family. The daddy, the mama, and the baby and three young 'uns. Purty as a pitcher." He relayed those words to the others. John, Jimmie, and Lulie averted their eyes from the couple, while Orie boldly looked at them and smiled a thank you.

At Bristol, they turned onto the Bristol-Lynchburg Turnpike. Although a long way from Viewmont, they felt closer just being in Virginia. Wagon traffic picked up as they passed through the blue-grass fields and looked upon what Luther later described as "sleek

Virginia cattle on a thousand hills." The towns along the turnpike had names that John and Orie recognized: Abingdon, Marion, and Wytheville. Food to buy was more plentiful, as were places to camp for the night and even inns and residences that took in travelers.

"We're on the Wilderness Road *and* the Bristol-Lynchburg Turnpike now. Daniel Boone blazed this trail a century ago to make it easier for settlers to get to Kentucky and Tennessee," John shouted to his family in the wagon.

"I've seen pictures of Daniel Boone. Did he widen the path and make a road because he liked being in the woods all day?" Jimmie shouted back.

"I would like to do that too," said Lulie. "And wear the leather coat with fringe and the coonskin hat and leather pants." He was tired of shouting and directed his comments to his mother.

"I'm sure he liked doing that, but it was dangerous and Indians tried to kill him for coming through their lands," said Orie. "Actually, he was paid by Transylvania, a land company, to lead a group of frontiersmen to cut a swath all the way to the Cumberland Gap, so people could buy land in Kentucky."

Jimmie heard her and had ideas of his own. "Let's get out and race the mules, Lulie. We could walk to Kentucky if we want to after we get to Viewmont." He signaled for his father to halt the mules before and he and Lulie jumped off the wagon and ambled alongside, keeping a slight lead in the "race." Orie picked up Sammy, who yelled, "Me too!" to his brothers, and put him on her lap. She sang "Dixie" to him until he laughed and sang along.

When they reached Christiansburg, John pointed out the New River Trail for settlers to follow through the Alleghenies to pick up the Daniel Boone Trail to the Cumberland Gap.

"Southwest Virginia was the American frontier until Boone pushed the frontier into Kentucky and Tennessee," he said. "Now, a century later, settlers are using the Cumberland Gap as a gateway to the West, all the way to the Pacific Ocean."

The boys were tired from keeping up with the mules and went back in the wagon and stretched out on their blankets. Orie gave them all tablets on which to draw maps showing the Wilderness Road through the mountains to the Gap and across the Plains to the Pacific Ocean. They showed her pictures of trees, rivers, Indians, and cowboys, horses, cattle, buffalo, and fish on their maps. "Everything's jiggly because the wagon bumped us," Jimmie explained.

"I see," said Orie, smiling as she tried to discern fish from buffalo and cowboys from trees.

After that day, Christiansburg became a word associated with weeping boys and sad parents. Tige had been with the boys and John when they bought fodder for the mules. After the transaction, the dog was gone. They called his name; they whistled for him and frantically asked everyone in sight if they had seen their large brown dog. Whether he was taken by a dog snatcher, wandered off and got lost, or chased an animal too far away to get back, they never knew. They spent a whole day and night trying to find him, but John and Orie could look no more and got on the wagon without Tige.

Jimmie, Lulie, and Sammy refused. They begged to look some more. They couldn't bear to climb onto the wagon and leave Tige without his people and his home on the wagon. John picked up Sammy and carried him onto the wagon. The other two got on themselves, tears streaming down their faces.

"We can't leave him there. He may be tied up in a cage waiting for us to rescue him," Jimmie sobbed. Lulie thought Tige might have been hurt and was lying in a ditch somewhere, needing their help as he had always helped them. The boys were giving voice to the very things their parents were also thinking. Sammy just sobbed. The three boys shed tears that seemed would never stop. No one said an encouraging word. Later, Orie confided to John, "This is worse than if Tige had died there."

The next day they reached a level place near the Roanoke River beside a small hill thick with trees, where other wagons were already encamped. "We'll stop here. Still plenty of daylight, other families are here, and I see farmers selling produce," said John.

Orie stepped off the wagon, helped by Jimmie, and asked Lulie to hand her the baby. She looked around and said to Lulie, "I think we'll like this campground. It even has a river to fish in."

Lulie was still mute with sadness, as were Jimmie and even Sammy.

"You boys explore around, and your father and I will set up the campfire and maybe buy something fresh for supper. We'll watch Sammy."

"Yes ma'am," they said, and wandered off.

John watered and fed the mules. Orie bought lettuce, spring onions, apple cider, wheat bread, buttermilk, and eggs from a farmer's wife. One woman smiled at Sammy and offered him an apple. "This is for you, little towhead."

Sammy looked at her, puzzled. "I don't have a toe head. My toes are on the ground."

The woman laughed. She touched Sammy's fair hair and said to his mother, "He's cute as a button," and made an effort to stifle her laughter when she realized Sammy was unhappily looking at his toes and feeling his head. Orie had him help carry what she had purchased and explained what "towhead" meant. Although distracted, Orie had noticed that her coins were getting scarcer by the day and hoped John had more than she did. By the time she finished nursing Ikey, Sammy was hugging her legs in boredom. John was finished with the mules and sitting on a log near the campfire.

"Sit with me, Orie," he said. "The boys perked up some at the river. They waded in the stream and I gave them poles to fish with. I asked them to catch us some fish to fry. We'd all be the better for it with full stomachs." John patted the log and Orie joined him.

Sammy whispered in his mother's ear and she said, "Sammy wants to go back to the river." Sammy, fast losing his round baby fat as he approached his fourth birthday, nodded his head with a hopeful smile.

"I'll take him, but not for long," John said. "Jimmie and Lulie could use some time without having to watch him. Sammy's big enough to get into trouble and too little to get out of it."

John left with Sammy and came back with fish to fry and Sammy needing dry clothes, which Orie took care of immediately, the fading light bringing a chill to the air. "The boys have made friends with two other brothers about their size and went to explore a cave in that hill," he said with a chuckle. "That will keep them busy. Have another cup of cider, dear."

"I shall," Orie said. "It's quite good. Not as good as Viewmont cider, but tasty and refreshing."

When the fire was ready, John dredged the fish in cornmeal and fried it in hot fat, and the aroma made other campers look their way with whetted appetites. John and Orie went ahead and ate their portion with Sammy until they were filled with fish, skillet-fried bread, and lettuce wilted with hot grease and vinegar.

"You'd better go look for the boys, John. They're going to be eating cold fish." Orie had put on a raglan sweater to fend off the river-bottom chill.

John leaned in and gave her a kiss. "Yes, ma'am." He chuckled and walked off to the hill and asked a boy on the hill about a cave his two boys were exploring.

"Was they named Jimmie and Louie?"

"Close enough. Do you know where they are?"

"Yes sir. The Shaw boys showed 'em the hole to the cave. All four of 'em went in. I'll show you where it's at." The two walked up the steep hill holding onto trees for balance, and about halfway up the boy showed John the hole.

"Well, it looks small for a grown man to get down and crawl through. Could you go in there and get them? They're missing their supper. I'll give you a penny for your trouble."

"Yes sir, mister!" The boy took the copper Indian head penny and put it carefully in his pocket. "I'll go get me a fire torch first so I can see when I get inside."

He came back with a stout fire stick lit from a campfire and asked John to hand it to him when he got inside. He bent down on all fours and easily slipped inside the hole and took the torch. John sat down on the ground and waited. He peered through the hole and could see the torch illuminating a large expanse. He could hear echoing voices but could see no one. After a while he called through the hole, "Halloo in there!" He heard no response.

He walked back down the hill to tell Orie what the holdup was. She picked up Ikey, grabbed hold of Sammy's hand, and headed for the nearest wagon, where folks were sitting on logs around it. "What's this about a cave on that hill?" she asked. John was right behind her.

An old man with a white beard answered her. "Yes ma'am. There's a right big cave up there. But the entrance hole's too small for anybody but a young 'un. I don't mind tellin' you I ain't never been inside, but I hear tell it's big and wet and cold and dark. Boys like that cave, but no one else with any sense goes in it."

John looked worried. Orie turned to him and said, "We've got to get them out of there."

"I sent a boy in there to get them. I gave him a penny to do it and he's got a torch."

"Don't you worry none, ma'am. Them Shaw boys know their way around here."

By the time John and Orie rushed back up the hill, the boys were out of the cave, laughing and muddy and wet. When they saw their parents hurrying up the hill, dragging little Sammy, they said a hasty "Bye" to their new friends and apologized for being in the cave so long. They hadn't meant to, "But it was a whole fairyland-like place with streams and stone icicles hanging from the ceilings and wet rock formations of every shape you can think of. It's the best place we ever saw in our lives!" they exclaimed.

John and Orie began to fuss at them. "Caves are dangerous places. Folks get lost in them, lose their torch and break bones and are never found," John said.

Then Orie noticed saw that skinny Lulie was shivering in his mud-covered overalls and shirt. "You're soaking wet and freezing. Come, hurry, and let's get you out of those clothes. It's getting colder by the minute."

As fast as possible, the boys were stripped of their clothes, cleaned with water from the water barrel, dried off, and dressed in warm nightshirts. John relit the fire and warmed up the fish. The boys were hungry and ate everything they were offered. They climbed under their blankets for the night, tired but whispering to each other about the cave.

Lulie worried aloud about Tige. "I think maybe he would have gotten lost in there and never found. He would have hated that."

"Maybe God saw what was going to happen to him and saved him for something else to do," Jimmie whispered.

"Let's pray for him. Do you know a prayer?"

"Sure. Please, God, take care of Tige. Amen." Satisfied, the boys shut their eyes and were soon asleep.

Although exhausted, Orie and John did not feel like turning in yet. Their nerves were still unsettled, and although the boys were none the worse after exploring the cave, they realized the experience could have ended badly. The Shaw boys' ma and pa came over to their campsite with cups of hot coffee and apologized for the fright their sons had caused.

"It's a big cave sure enough, and if their fire torch had gone out, it could have been real bad," Mr. Shaw said. "I reckon we could have dug out that hillside to go get them, but that'd take time, and they could have froze or slipped on a rock or got really lost. No one knows how deep that cave is. The entry hole's big enough for a boy or animal, but I ain't about to go crawling in a place like that, and we told them to stay away from that cave. We been here lots. We live in Wytheville and my sister and her family live in Bedford, and we stop here on the way comin' and goin'."

When Orie and Mrs. Shaw left the conversation to tuck in their children, Mr. Shaw kept John company. "Fort Lewis is plum ahead of you. General Andrew Lewis built the fort. He was a damned good fighter in the French and Indian War and the Revolutionary War."

"Is Fort Lewis a big town?" John asked.

"Naw, it was mainly a fort that Lewis built to protect the settlers from the Indians. He built it on land owned by James Campbell. You'll see his homestead, but the fort's gone. Lewis built hisself a homestead nearby he called Richfield. After Fort Lewis you'll come into Salem. You'll see a two-story brick house place on the right with farm fields on both sides of the Great Road. Man named Johnston lives there. The mountain range that Salem butts up against is Fort Lewis Mountain. Salem people are stuck on Andrew Lewis, I'll tell you that." He laughed softly.

"I don't know the name, but I'm not from here and don't know the folks up here I should," John said.

"Well, it ain't because Andrew Lewis never did nothing. He was born in Ireland and come to Virginny with his folks when he was round about the age of your Louie. He growed up to be a surveyor like George Washington and was a officer in the French and Indian War and a general in the Revolutionary War. He ought to have a bend in the road and a mountain named after him."

"Salem sounds like a fine town," John said.

"You'll like Oldcastle in downtown. It was built to house the Roanoke Navigation Company for a canal to connect Salem with Lynchburg and Richmond before the railroads took over. Smart and up and coming people. On the east side of Salem, if you need anything, look for a brick two-story store where the merchant, William Williams lives too. "

"Thanks for your help, Mr. Shaw. We're glad to be on the Great Road with the folks heading west, while we're going east back home. "

"Well, I'm happy to oblige. Virginny's always been chock-full of good people with git up an' go, and that's the Lord's truth. Well, now, you folks have a safe trip home, and it was a pleasure to meet you and your family. If you ever stop in Wytheville, ask around for the William Shaw farm and we'll put you up. Goodnight to you, sir." The man, a son of sons of pioneer farmers, shook John's hand and made his way in the dark to his own wagon.

John joined Orie in the now quiet wagon. His evening prayer was short: "Thank you, Lord, for another day in Virginia and for the safety of our boys. And please watch over Tige."

It was in Salem the next morning that John realized his funds were exhausted, and they were still days away from Viewmont. He could not forget the time Orie came to him at Charlottesville General Hospital to lend him money for train fare so he could bring the body of his brother Robert to Florence for burial. This time Orie could not help. Neither John nor Orie had friends or family in Salem. Somehow he had to find a way to get to Viewmont.

Although nervous, with clammy hands and his stomach in knots, John kept his chin up and walked into a bank in Salem. Since the war, Southerners were almost like brothers to each other, lending a hand whenever possible, for all had suffered in the War. However, this meant that the bank cashier could tell him stories of woe that might make his situation seem to be of little account. He'd heard that hundreds of banks in the South had failed since the War began.

Nevertheless, he walked up to the cashier and saw the man was wearing the insignia of a Mason. Right away, he introduced himself to the banker and asked for a few moments in private, at which time he said, "I'm a Mason in distress," and explained his situation.

The banker promptly promised to help his fellow Mason. "How much do you need to reach your destination?" he asked, reaching for his wallet.

"I believe a loan of ten dollars will be enough, and I will leave a security of my gold watch that my father gave to my brother, who died on the battlefield at Manassas. The watch cost my father a hundred and fifty dollars," John said.

"Nonsense. I will gladly lend you the sum of ten dollars, but I refuse to take security of any kind from you. I wish you Godspeed on your journey, Dr. Andrews, and I'm glad I could be of service to you and your family. Good day to you, sir."

Dread had been stopped in its tracks. John greeted Orie with a kiss and told her of the banker's personal loan. Orie blinked back tears, feeling ashamed that she had feared John could not rescue them from the dangers of penniless travelers. The Alleghenies on the west and the Blue Ridge on the east formed walls for the magic carpet between, called the Great Road. On this ancient pathway, John drove their wagon north across the James River near Buchanan.

"O lovely world, O lovely Virginia," Orie sang in her heart to the Lord above.

CHAPTER 42

VIEWMONT REDUX

The Shenandoah Valley, like a stirring melodic Pastoral in all seasons, counts on May to bring a verdant softness and warmth to the Great Valley and a new spring's release from bitter winds and frozen ground. The lowing of cattle punctuates the peace in beauty that washes clean one's soul. Heaven seems attainable.

In such a place, the four-mule wagon team hauled the family ever closer homeward. The two older boys sang "Dixie" with great shouts at the "Hooray! Hooray!" part and "Tramp! Tramp! Tramp! The boys are marching." With spirits soaring, they asked their father to stop while they climbed down and sang "When Johnny Comes Marching Home," keeping pace with the mules. The music and marching carried them quite a way, but finally they signaled to their father to stop and let them climb back on. They both sought their blankets and rested their tired legs and lungs.

In Rockbridge County south of Lexington, Orie pointed out the site of the Red House, where Virginia Governor James McDowell was buried.

"How did it get to be red?" Lulie asked. He sat up slowly.

"Look quickly as we pass by—it's a log cabin. The Governor's father skinned the logs, which left them white, and then mixed red paint from a vein of red ochre on his land with water. Maybe he wanted to hide the house from the Indians."

Lulie looked at Jimmie and nodded. *Let's do this when we get to Viewmont.*

John let the mules rest and eat fodder at Virginia Military Institute, the "West Point of the South," while the boys climbed out of the wagon and ran up the hill to see the cannon. A cadet looking not much older than Jimmie was standing guard and shook his musket at them. The boys tumbled back down the hill like rabbits chased by a dog.

"Quite a commotion," said John.

"We weren't scared," said Jimmie, climbing into the wagon and looking back at the hilltop. "We just raced back for fun."

"Even a musket ball couldn't catch us," said Lulie, still panting from the excitement.

John smiled. "Next time, identify yourselves as Virginians before you retreat."

Neither brother had thought of that.

"That was an impressive show of speed, indeed," said Orie. "But what brings tears to my eyes is that General Stonewall Jackson was an instructor here. Your father and his two younger brothers shared the battlefield at Manassas with him. Some people still say that if Stonewall Jackson had lived, the South might have won the War. He was fearless and brilliant and full of the wrath of God as he defended Virginia from the Yankee invaders. And to top it off, Robert E. Lee is next door at Washington College. He's the President. He's over there," she said, pointing in the direction of the college's white columns in front of deep-red brick buildings at the crest of a hill.

The boys wheeled about and faced the campus of Washington College as all thoughts turned to the gentle, sad giant of a man with respect to intellect, courage, and honor. Emotion choked Orie's and John's throats. They climbed back into the wagon and John's broken voice told the mules to "Giddyup!" They were back on their way, John and Orie remembering too much sadness and the boys aware of the all-consuming love of Southerners for their heroic leader, still setting aside his life for a new generation of young Southern men, who must not despair but prevail.

Just south of Fairfield, Orie pointed out Cherry Grove, the birthplace of Governor McDowell.

"Again? I thought we just saw his birthplace," said Jimmie, lying down on his blanket.

"No, he's buried *there* and was born *here*. I want you to understand that the man was so well known for his integrity and honesty that a county was named in his honor, but after the separation of Virginia, McDowell County ended up in West Virginia. However, the McDowell family was one of the first great families to live west of the Blue Ridge. He was an educated pioneer's son, having been taught at Washington College, Yale, and Princeton. If only men had listened to him in Congress after he served as Governor. Like most Virginians, he didn't want war. He loved Virginia *and* America."

"Yes ma'am," they said. Their heads were full of the honor and courage of seemingly all Virginians.

They camped one night near where Sam Houston, the Tennessee Governor and Texas liberator, was born. In Midway, they spent the night at Aunt Betsy Steele's home, where Orie and her aunt enjoyed a reunion neither expected in this lifetime. Aunt Betsy was a distant relative, but one that Anna Maria had cherished when Edward was alive and visits were frequent, believing that kin, near and not, were the realm of the family and must be supported always. Aunt Betsy cooked food for them, gave them real beds to sleep on, washed their clothes and hung them outside in the fresh breeze. They all took baths. It had been a long time since Ikey and Sammy had been thoroughly bathed and they did some squalling, but Orie scrubbed them all the more vigorously and laughed and kissed their toes.

Practically next door was the shop of Cyrus McCormick, inventor of the reaper. Aunt Betsy took them over to see the inventor's shop, and John told his boys, "McCormick revolutionized the harvesting of wheat throughout the civilized world. A Virginian, an American, did that. Right here. Mr. McCormick lives in Chicago now, where he built a reaper factory and is a millionaire. But this shop is where he built it and tested it on Aunt Betsy's property."

The next day they were back in the wagon. They camped near Waynesboro, closing in on Albemarle County. That night the boys were thrown awake by a thundering sound and quaking earth from the arrival of a train through the great Blue Ridge Tunnel.

"What happened?!" All four offspring were alarmed and awake.

John quieted them down. "A train went through the tunnel."

The two older boys looked at him. "No train going through a tunnel ever shook the earth like this one," said Jimmie.

"It's the Blue Ridge Tunnel, the largest tunnel in the United States when it was completed in the 1850s. It took eight years and a thousand Irish immigrants and a hundred local slaves to build it. You heard it, now get back to sleep." John lay down, smiling at their awe; the boys followed his lead, but the shocking noise followed them into restless sleep.

The next morning after sunrise, the family looked down from the top of Afton Mountain at Albemarle County spread below. *This* was the Promised Land after years of war and exile.

Orie gazed at the farms and forests and hills below. John put his arm around her and stood there silently. This was the land of Orie's birth and where the two were wed and where Jimmie and Lulie were born. "Unimaginable splendor," Orie whispered.

Home at last, they were first greeted by Uncle Jacob and Mammy Jinny, who welcomed them home like long-lost children and grandchildren, then Ike and Mag came to stay and help out and visit. Mammy Jinny held Ikey and Sammy on her lap in turns and told all the boys stories of "Old Viewmont" and how rich and beautiful all the folks were in the old days. The family rested from their journey for a few days and spent time trading news with neighboring kin.

John made a visit to Scottsville to arrange for financing and purchase of necessary supplies for the farm and home and for his medical practice. He was eager to start anew yet again.

Orie was like a person captivated by unexpected joy. "Oh John, I have missed my family and Uncle Jacob and Mammy Jinny sorely. I don't think I realized how much a part of me they always were."

John remembered his brothers and was glad for Orie. "You've been brave for years living far away in Alabama and Tennessee. It's time you're back with your family."

Orie looked up at John and a kiss followed. "You are so very dear to me."

John in turn silently thanked God for the decision and the wherewithal to bring his family to Viewmont.

In a protracted mood of nostalgic gratitude, Orie told her sons of family members now gone who once walked those rooms and whose voices she could still hear in her head. She lingered long in the library. "These books were my best friends growing up. Cicero was right when he wrote about the value of literature: 'It educates the young and entertains in old age, it consoles the sorrowing and augments the joy of the joyful.'"

"Who is Cicero?" asked Lulie, gazing at the vast library of books to be read and digested.

"If you don't remember, *Plutarch's Lives* will tell you. Cicero was a fearless statesman at the end of the Roman Republic and a writer on limitless subjects."

"What do you mean, 'limitless?'" asked Jimmie, he too looking with concern at the number of volumes.

"He wrote about things such as the value of art, governorship and public speaking, old age, moral duties, court cases won, and the advantages of friendship." Orie stopped her litany of praise for Cicero, understanding the limits of patience in young boys. She was content, for the time, to simply savor the return to her favorite space, her father's library.

Their first Christmas back at Viewmont was 1876, never to be forgotten. First came hurried word that Lottie and Eddie were coming home. Concern was great because Eddie had written to Orie, John and Mollie's husband Dr. Shepherd about symptoms she was having. All three of them had told her to come home immediately.

Dr. Shepherd made the trip from Norfolk at Christmastime to be there for Eddie, such was his concern for her. He came at a time of severe grief of his own, bringing his motherless little girl Mamie, for her mother Mollie had died and was buried in October.

Orie welcomed Dr. Shepherd to Viewmont and took her little niece into her arms and cried for sweet Mollie. Later Orie told John that Mollie's choice of a husband who would come to help Eddie in the hardship of a late December journey with little bitty Mamie had been God's doing. Orie and John were at Viewmont when Lottie and Eddie arrived from Japan, on her way home. Both doctors put Eddie to bed immediately and when Dr. Shepherd got there, he insisted too that she stay in bed.

The three doctors discussed their fears and opinions. Orie said, "It may be asthma severely worsened by malnutrition and sustained exposure to wood smoke and exposure to cold. It could be tuberculosus. But it's more than physical. I think it's more than hysterical. She demands absolute quiet when that is not possible and after she was stoned outside the city gates by Chinese soldiers, she cannot stop being afraid. She cannot go back to China. The missionaries gathered in Japan on her behalf agreed to write to the Foreign Mission Board that her trip home would be permanent. They thanked her for her service and wrote that she was physically incapable of remaining in China." They all agreed that whatever was the diagnosis, the fact remained that she could not survive another winter in China. Dr. Shepherd prescribed cod liver oil and whiskey for general support and her chances of survival improved.

Colie came home for Christmas from Washington DC from her job as a counter for the Treasury Department as soon as she could get away. They sat by the fireplace in the front parlor by the hour, drinking hot coffee and cider, laughing and crying over Colie's adventures. Orie smiled at John. She was home. And life was so different from what they expected. She missed her mama and papa.

The boys' Uncle Isaac taught public school at Church Hill, five miles away, which he started doing after finding that he could not make ends meet as a managing farmer. The school year was five months long; the school day started at eight o'clock in the morning and ended at four in the afternoon. Uncle Isaac taught the curriculum with discipline, expecting his charges to show evidence of improved minds.

Agriculture they learned at Viewmont. That first summer Jimmie and Lulie dropped corn and pumpkin seeds as they followed hired Negroes working the farm under their father's direction. They wormed tobacco and spent nights with Negro farm workers after the tobacco had been cut and put astride pine poles and hung in the log barns for firing. They set snares and box traps; they hunted and fished and were at ease in God's outdoor kingdom.

Orie was their instructor when school was out. She regained her full strength while her sons studied in the halls of their Moon, Barclay, and Harris forebears. "Wash your hands, please, before taking a book off the shelf," she commanded, and kept the sight of her boys with books close to her heart.

Lulie, always thin, was considered delicate by Orie and kept home from school when the weather was inclement. To make the schoolhouse trek faster and safer for both boys, John built a trail though the ancient woods as Daniel Boone had done. The boys helped him, learning how to use tools needed to make the crooked straight and the rough places plain.

A fifth baby was born to Orie and John, the first to be born at Viewmont since Luther. Orie and John were delighted with the baby, and were especially heartened that Orie made a normal recovery, and did not repeat the almost fatal decline that had followed the birth of Ikey in Alabama. A favorite visitor was Owen Merriweather of Tennessee, a former suitor of Miss Eddie, who was there when the baby was born. Such was his interest and delight in the baby that Orie and John named him Owen Merriweather Andrews. Orie noticed that Eddie's interest in her new nephew was far less than their family friend, and thought that the absence of marriage for Eddie was God's will, indeed, as had been the end of her missionary work in China, but she continued to support the mission work through financial donations no matter how small such offerings might be.

In 1879, things changed abruptly. The heirs of Anna Maria Moon's estate decided to divide their mother's property or its proceeds among them. Orie attended family meetings and listened to what was said. Questions came up about Uncle Jacob and Mammy Jinny.

"They will always have the cabin we deeded to them after the War," said Ike. "No one can take that from them. And they have land for a garden and their daughter Rebecca is nearby to look after them. All of us visit them, and we would never allow them to suffer in penury."

All agreed that Uncle Jacob and Mammy Jinny would be all right, although they knew too that when Viewmont was removed or owned by another family, the situation would become less ideal for the elderly couple. Orie understood the economics of the times and saw that it was useless for the rest of them to think she and John could produce enough wealth at Viewmont to share with all the others and have wealth for the next generation. When the decision came to divide the proceeds of the sale of Viewmont among themselves, John was full of pity for Orie.

But Orie stood her ground. "It cannot be a different solution, dearest. We all must live, and it won't do to go further into debt after three years of working the farm. We'll take our share and do our best by it."

They bought George Harris's farm across the James River in Buckingham County about twelve miles north of the courthouse. The next year Orie gave birth to another son, whom they named Frank Moon Andrews. This time Orie and John speculated anew on the Arab's blessing.

"It's not Christian to believe in such a prophecy," said Orie.

"I agree, but how else could it happen?" John replied.

"Silly husband, my births are simply the exception to the law of averages, I would say."

"I still think—"

"Hush. We've been blessed with six beautiful boys. Leave it be."

After baby Frank's birth, Orie again fell prey to exhaustion and weakness. John moved the family to Norwood in Nelson County and rented a farm.

"This may be where we need to be," John confided to Orie. "The medical practice in Norwood looks busy and our two boys are big enough to help me farm."

"Here, I will rest and recuperate, God willing," said Orie with Christian resolve.

John hired a strong Negro woman and a girl to help nurse Orie and take care of baby Frank and little Owen while running the household. Jimmie at age seventeen and fifteen-year old Luther planted and plowed corn on the James River lowlands and cooled off in the river before feeding the mules and eating a packed lunch. They were home by sunset. Otherwise, they harvested and threshed the wheat, cut sugar cane, and made "luscious sorghum" by crushing the cane in a horse mill pulled by a mule in an endless circle.

In the fall, Jimmie did the plowing and cribbed the corn, and Lulie hauled cordwood in a wagon to Norwood Station on the

Richmond and Allegheny Railroad line for the steam engines to run on. He also hauled railroad ties to the railroad agent, adding to the family's income. John, Jimmie, and Lulie worked hard and their income accumulated.

In the spring of 1881, torrential rains caused the James River to sweep away the crops. Their work ended in unexpected failure, but on the other hand, Orie was rested and the light had come back into her eyes. New plans did not include another farming adventure. Orie was ready to go into active medical practice, and they rented Old Hall, the Beale family home in Scottsville, converting it into the first Sanatorium of Southside Albemarle.

Between the two doctors, they accepted men, women, and children as patients, Dr. John seeing the men and Orie her beloved women and children. Their patients were as "numerous as grains of sand on the riverbank," Orie's brother Ike liked to say, pleased about the success they were enjoying. Orie took a day off to see Uncle Jacob and Mammy Jinny.

"Well, my eyes be playin' tricks on this ol' woman. Miz Dr. Orie, I been missin' you and them chillen since you done lef' Viewmont. Set down in this rockin' chair and tell me how you be. Is you got another baby boy since you be gone?"

"Yes, Mammy Jinny, we have a new son we named Frank Moon Andrews, born in Buckingham County. I had a setback after baby Frank was born and we moved to Nelson County, where I had help and bedrest. Now I'm back doctoring in Scottsville with Dr. John."

Mammy Jinny gave Orie a long, hard look. "You be too old to have two babies since you come back from de Deep South. And another thing, doctoring like you doin' is too hard on a woman. Let Dr. John do the doctorin'. You git some help and take care 'a them babies, you hear me? And rest afore you be so worn out you cain't get up nohow."

"Mammy Jinny, when I was a girl I was delicate, but I'm a woman now and can handle these things."

"I reckon you be growed now and can do what you want. You always did anyways," she added with a grin.

Orie thought that she had at last won an argument with Mammy Jinny, but didn't feel triumphant. She almost wished for the old days when the old black woman would fuss at her for shutting herself in her bedroom to read and not come down for supper. She feared the old woman then, but now saw Mammy Jinny in a different light, a loving light.

The Sanatorium's success was sweet, but Orie, conscientious to a fault, became overwhelmed by the long hours and often heartbreaking work that preyed on her mind.

"Orie, darling, you have come home late every night this week seeing patients at their homes. You cannot keep this up. You are losing weight and you toss and turn in bed at night. This is not Charlottesville General full of wounded and dying soldiers." He embraced her tense and thin body, too long aware of her passive, worried stare and increasingly gaunt look.

"Dearest, I cannot leave the bedside of a child or woman in pain. I cannot do it."

"You must. It's a doctor's duty to stay well. Patients will further sicken and die. Even your patients."

Orie looked at him and did not smile at this familiar saying between them.

"What's wrong, Orie? Can you not lay aside your worries at all?"

"John, it's fall, and coming on pneumonia season and I've already lost a baby and I tried so hard to save Susannah and she died in that cabin by the creek all alone."

"You can't be everywhere and save every patient. You can only do what's possible." He embraced her tightly before letting her go as he looked into her staring eyes. He walked with her into the kitchen where her cold dinner was sitting on the table.

"I can't eat, John. I'm too tired and I'm cold." He walked her upstairs helped her into bed. She had not even asked about Frank and Owen, cared for by the daughter of the cook who had put them to bed hours before.

By December, Orie could no longer bear the rigors of doctor's work and was unable to get out of bed. She remembered Mammy Jinny's warning, which she had disregarded. This time, she was more than exhausted; she was seriously sick. She no longer thought she had to tend to one more sick patient before the prolonged rest she promised herself. She and John both noted the fever, the terrible pain in both sides, a choking cough, and difficulty breathing.

John called in a doctor from Charlottesville, who gave him the dreaded but not unexpected diagnosis: pneumonia. John's stomach wrenched and his mind was in agony.

For the next two weeks, John referred their patients to doctors elsewhere and stayed with Orie. Her body was rigid in pain and her breathing ragged, but she never complained as long as John was with her or nearby. Women came to help nurse Orie and take care of her household. John watched over Orie as he had done for Robert until death took him away.

This time Orie's pain from pleurisy and inflammation of both lungs marched on like an evil army in spite of hot water packs, mustard plasters, and medicines that should have helped her breathe and ease the coughing up of thick sputum.

Orie lay with thoughts unspoken. *Mama died when she had done all she could to help her family get a good start in life. Lottie said she died in peace. Papa died too soon and my heart was broken. But God gave me John and six sons. Like the biblical poor, there will always be sick people. Even Jesus didn't heal them all. I didn't listen to anybody. Not even John who loves me.*

When a coughing fit left Orie pain wracked and struggling to breathe, John leaned over her bed and touched her cheek. His tears splashed onto Orie's face. Orie opened her eyes and a falling tear mingled with her own tears. She remembered her baptism in the Pool of Siloam and looked heavenward, unseeing, but sensing her mama and papa and her babies Henry and Eddie.

Her vision cleared and she saw John looking down at her with such love.

"John, dearest, I want to be buried in the Presbyterian cemetery in Scottsville," she whispered. She smiled at him, her beloved.

Tears streamed again down his face. He kissed her fevered forehead and piled on another blanket warmed by the bedroom hearth to ease her body, racked with the chills of fever. Her suffering had returned swiftly after the interval of peace, words and a smile. When she ceased to fight for air and was gone, John was struck by a momentary sense of relief and he felt that God was there in that room.

Then he sobbed in the midst of family as he had not done since Robert died. But then, Orie had been there to comfort him, to hold his trembling hands and look upon him with blue eyes that brimmed with kindness for him alone. Those around him now held his hand and mourned with him, but only Orie's touch could soften his grief. He felt utterly alone.

Orie's older sons were as mute in their grief as was their father, and the younger ones shook off their sadness like a puppies after a drenching rain, but nothing was the same after that day.

Orie died on December 26, 1883, and was buried in Scottsville, in the Presbyterian cemetery. Her grave was within a few hundred feet of Stony Point, the home of William Moon I and the birthplace of his grandson Edward Harris Moon, Orie's father.

On her tombstone are the words:

Dr. Orie Russell Moon,
Wife Of Dr. John S. Andrews
B. Viewmont Alb. Co. VA, August 11 1834
D. Scottsville, VA December 26, 1883
Husband And Wife Were Physicians and Surgeons In
Confederate Army

John's only consolation at the time was that he had brought Orie back to Virginia, where she died and was buried among her people.

Orie was forty-nine years old. Her father had died two and a half weeks short of his forty-ninth birthday. John never knew Edward Harris Moon, but he asked the Lord to keep them close as they awaited the Resurrection morn.

Finis

EPILOGUE

Orianna Moon Andrews, MD, left behind a grieving husband and six sons. William Luther Andrews graduated the University of Virginia and married Mary J. Ruebush in Rockingham County, Virginia. They moved to Roanoke and became parents of eight, plus an adopted daughter. Luther was a successful businessman, a Grand Master of Masons, and a state senator. He and Mary raised their family on Kirk Avenue before they moved to land he bought from the Viewmont Land Company in 1907. This property was located on the Roanoke Country Club side of Roanoke Salem Highway, now called Melrose Avenue. The property overlooked Fairview cemetery, where he is buried along with many of his family members. His last Roanoke address was 315 Grandin Road, where he moved in 1925, when he served as a state senator. The last two years of his life were spent writing a memoir of his mother, Dr. Orianna Moon Andrews.

Luther was also the nephew of Lottie Moon, who served as a Baptist missionary to China for forty years. Lottie died of sacrificial starvation on December 24, 1912, in Kobe Harbor, Japan, on her way home to America, believing that food for her meant less food for her beloved Chinese. In 1918 the Lottie Moon Christmas

Offering became a fixed event in the Southern Baptist calendar and a holiday tradition that funded foreign missions and conveyed Miss Moon's "ideals of life commitment, sacrifice, personal holiness, and daily submission to the will of God." Lottie Moon is buried in Crewe, Virginia, along with Isaac Moon, her brother, and Margaret Jones Moon, her sister-in-law. A shrine and a large stained-glass window dedicated to Lottie Moon make the Crewe Baptist Church a destination for Baptists on pilgrimages.

Edmonia Moon was Lottie's closest relative and dearest love on earth. Once a week for thirty-one years, Eddie corresponded with Lottie, and in that way lived her life vicariously with Lottie in China, a reality that ended when the seriously ill younger sister was brought home to Viewmont on December 22, 1876 by Lottie. Edmonia was physically and emotionally unable to adjust to the grueling experience of mission work in China in the nineteenth century. Edmonia took her own life in November 1909.

Educational institutions evolve over time. Dr. John Summerfield Andrews was a graduate of Methodist-Episcopal Shelby Medical College in Nashville, Tennessee, the forerunner of Vanderbilt University Medical School. Lottie's Albemarle Female Institute in Charlottesville over the years became St. Anne's-Belfield School.

Orie's Troy Female Seminary is today the prestigious Emma Willard School, which still draws female students from across the nation and the world. In 1910, the school was relocated from a Romanesque building near the Hudson River to the heights of Mount Ida, paralleling the journey of Aeneas from the classical city of Troy to nearby Mount Ida. Its grand gray stone Gothic architecture and the setting's altitude inspire trust that the school will stand forever.

The Female Medical College of Pennsylvania in Philadelphia struggled financially since its founding by Philadelphia Quakers in 1850. In 1969, the Board of the College voted to admit male students; in 1998 it became the Drexel University College of Medicine.

Lovely Viewmont is now a private home surrounded by acres of working-farm fields on Scottsville Road in Albemarle County. Instead of slow-moving, gentle sounding horses, carriages, and mule-driven wagons, automobiles now speed past the present affluent area between Charlottesville and Scottsville.

Viewmont is more than a splendid Great House in the rolling hills of Albemarle County. It's a place of stories of people who marked their lives there. Whether they were enslaved, owned the land, inherited it, fled, or stayed, Viewmont endured.

AUTHOR'S NOTE

Orie's Story was inspired by a memoir written by her son and is categorized as historical fiction; a few names were changed to protect privacy and some events were created for the sake of dramatic interest, while adhering to the true nature of the persons involved.

BIBLIOGRAPHY

Allen, Cathrine. *The New Lottie Moon Story*. Nashville, TN: Broadman Press, 1980.

Harwell, Richard B., ed. *The Confederate Reader*. New York: Dorset Press, 1992.

Hildebrand, John R. *The Life and Times of John Brown Baldwin 1820-1873:*. Staunton, VA: Augusta Historical Society, Lots Wife Publishing, 2008. Dorset Press:

Keegan, John. *The American Civil War*. New York: Alfred A. Knope, 2009.

Keegan, John. *A History of Warfare*. New York: Vintage Books, Random House, Inc., 1994.

Lee, Heath Hardage. *Winnie Davis: Daughter of the Lost Cause*. U of Nebraska Press,2014

Moore, Virginia. *Scottsville on the James*. Charlottesville, VA: The Jarman Press, 1969.

Robertson, James I., Jr. *Stonewall Jackson*. New York: MacMillan Publishing USA. London: Prentice Hall International, 1997.

Walker, Gary C. *A General History of the Civil War: The Southern Point of View*. Roanoke, VA: A & W Enterprise, Pelican Publishing, 2008.

ACKNOWLEDGMENTS

Grateful thanks to reader and benefactor Nancy Andrews; readers and editors Barbara Baranowski, director of Christian Writers of the Roanoke Valley; Dee Bowlin, John Carroll and Mike Spillman. Jane Stuart Smith; readers: Kate Forbes; Marcia Lee Butler Holiday; Jennifer Lambert; Deka Tate; and Ken Lambert. Also thanks to Dyron Knick and Virginia Room, Roanoke Public Library staff; Evelyn Edson, Scottsville Museum; George Kegley, Historical Society of Western Virginia; Malinda Andrews; Janet Poindexter, freelance editor and writer; Georgia Turner, manager, Florence/ Lauderdale, Alabama, tourism; Mel Grimes, mayor, Waterloo, Alabama; Charlean Eanes Fisher; and Dan Smith, director of the Roanoke Regional Writers Conference held at Hollins University, January 29-30, 2017. Especially to Millard "Himself" who was beside me all the way.

ABOUT THE AUTHOR

Gail Tansill Lambert is an award-winning author and former Latin teacher with family ties to the Civil War. She has used the Moon-Andrews family history as inspiration for her historical saga, *Orie's Story*.

Lambert's travel writing has been published in *The Roanoke Times, Collinson Publishing, Senior News Blue Ridge Edition, Roanoker Magazine,* and *California Healing Retreats & Spas*.

Lambert contributed as a writer and editor for the Daughters of the American Revolution's Colonel William Preston Chapter historical project, *Notable Women West of the Blue Ridge, Volumes I and II*.

Lambert's great-grandfather, Colonel Robert Tansill, CSA, joined the Confederate cause when Lincoln sent troops to his native Virginia. Family legend states that his mother showed him the burning White House from across the Potomac River during the War of 1812 and inspired in him a passion for protecting the land he loved.